# THE DEATH

# OF FRANK SINATRA

# The Death
# of Frank Sinatra

## A NOVEL BY

## MICHAEL VENTURA

HENRY HOLT AND COMPANY

NEW YORK

THANK YOU *to Zanne Devine, George and Dixie Howard, Steve Erickson, Kit Rachlis, Dave Johnson, Naunie Batchelder, Michelle Jordan, Bob Asahina, Donna Fuhr, Sam Joseph, Robin Podolsky, John Powers, Cathy Marable, Jeff Nightbyrd, Elliot Abravanel, Roben Campbell, Harrison, Judith Kahn, Melanie Jackson, Bill Strachan, Jenna Dolan, Karen Holden . . . and the Las Vegans who shared their memories but want to remain unnamed . . . and my good friend Mike Rose, who let me use his name for a somewhat dicey character not at all like him . . . and Jodie Evans, who taught me more about her city than I could otherwise have hoped to learn.*

*Henry Holt and Company, Inc.*
Publishers since 1866
*115 West 18th Street*
*New York, New York 10011*

*Henry Holt ® is a registered trademark*
*of Henry Holt and Company, Inc.*

*Library of Congress Cataloging-in-Publication Data*

Ventura, Michael.
*The death of Frank Sinatra: a novel / Michael Ventura.*
*p.   cm.*
*1. Private investigators—Nevada—Las Vegas—Fiction.   2. City and town life—Nevada—Las Vegas—Fiction.   3. Family— Nevada—Las Vegas—Fiction.   4. Las Vegas (Nev.)—Fiction.   I. Title.*
PS3572.E5D4   1996                                    96-7603
*813'.54—dc20*                                           CIP

ISBN 0-8050-3738-1

*Henry Holt books are available for special promotions and premiums.*
*For details contact: Director, Special Markets.*

*First Edition—1996*

*Frontispiece: detail of photograph by Michael K. Nichols/Magnum.*

*Printed in the United States of America*
*All first editions are printed on acid-free paper.*∞

1   3   5   7   9   10   8   6   4   2

FOR DAVE JOHNSON

*I'm for anything that gets you through*

*the night, be it booze or religion.*

—FRANK SINATRA

# CONTENTS

THREE / *Ancestors*

# ONE

# Family

*I want harmony, oh, Mama, Mama—It is confused
and it says no. A boy has never wept, nor dashed a
thousand kim . . .*

—Dutch Schultz (real name: Arthur Flegenheimer),
his last words, in a hospital after being ambushed

•

*We only kill each other.*

—Benjamin "Bugsy" Siegel

# THE DIGNITY

# OF ISADORE FELDMAN

*T*here are no innocent bystanders in Las Vegas. Nobody comes to Vegas to be innocent. Even the kids, who may or may not be born innocent, become savvy bystanders before long— and commit more suicides here than anywhere in the world. Even the dawns aren't innocent. Desert dawns are delicate, light seems not to fall from the sky but to rise from the sands in soft and slowly swelling pastels that throw no shadows—a gauze of light, before you ever see the sun. A dawn is coming that nobody wants, not really, not in a gaudy city designed for night but so bleak in the bright day. Then comes that moment just before the neons flicker off: their buzzing, piercing brightness dulls as the sun rises and you see how light's supposed to look—and you wish for some innocence to meet it with, but all that's left of what you brought here is the wishing.

Mike Rose didn't want to see the dawn or anything else this morning. Least of all did he want to see Mr. Isadore Feldman, "Zig," that impenetrable old man. He knew where Zig was now (unless, of course, Zig lied). He knew where Mr. Sherman was too, and how to profit from him. Zig was personal, Mr. Sherman was money, and Rose knew he should go for the money. Rose was Vegas born and raised, and if the town had tried to teach him anything in his forty-two years it was, go for the money—drunk or sober, in fear or for fun, go for the money and the personal would take care of itself. Wasn't that the American way? But Rose was a slow learner. He was irresponsible. He'd been told often enough, and he had told himself, that he was taking too long to grow up. He might take longer still, he might take all morning, but he was going for Zig. *After all,* he told himself, *Mr. Sherman didn't invite me, and Zig did.*

For once Mike Rose wasn't worried about the how and why of it all. He expected all that to become clear in its own good time—and he knew, from expensive experience, that some of it would never be clear. But this particular morning all that mattered was that he probably had to kill somebody, and that others were trying to kill him; Rose would have said, and half-believed, that once people are trying to kill you, how it comes about no longer makes much difference.

Fremont Street just after dawn. 1993. It's not on any postcards. Nobody writes home about how Vegas Vic, the five-story neon cowboy who leers over downtown, waves as always with his left hand, but with his right points straight down. At dawn you wonder how far down. At this hour Sassy Sally, the neon cowgirl perched across the street atop Glitter Gulch, kicks her leg as usual, but is she inviting you to lift her skirt or booting you out of town? Here and there somebody homeless walks uncertainly in some random direction, drunk with fatigue if nothing else, after a chilly desert night spent begging between attempts at sleep in a city where sleep comes hard—a city intent on keeping you awake whether you can afford a room or not. There's an occasional cab or patrol car. The shops are closed, the casinos are open, and in the casinos you know it's dawn only by how few people are around and by the dullness in their eyes. At that hour it doesn't matter whether they're sitting at the bar or pouring the drinks, dealing or playing, everyone's eyes share the same stare, the same sense that something that's happened once too often is about to happen again. The loudspeakers play Sinatra. Bells ring on a few slot machines. The rarest thing at this hour is to see anyone talking, or holding hands.

Mike Rose didn't have to look out his window above a souvenir shop on Fremont to see all this. He knew it by whatever was left of his heart—less than should be left, he thought, but more than he could use. He'd sat in his office in the dark for hours. Not because he had seen too many movies about how private detectives are supposed to spend their time drinking alone in shabby quarters—he claimed not to believe in movies or in much of anything else, and his office was not at all shabby. No, he'd positioned himself at his desk because that room had only one door, so there was only one way a killer could approach. Rose reasoned that this gave him an edge. When they know you're waiting they maybe get too careful or too nervous or both. So he hoped.

He'd spent those dark hours with a pistol. Sometimes he rested it on his lap, where its weight was a comfort; sometimes he placed it on the desk before him and let his long fingers move slowly over the cold metal—an old .38 from the Second World War. No one ever had a license for it. It had been his mother's.

Rose wasn't familiar with pistols. His work rarely required one. He made his living by finding people who may or may not be lost, and by some of the more elementary modes of spying. Occasionally he stumbled upon the kind of crimes that society makes laws about. But when confronted with crime, most people call the police, not a private detective. "I'm just in the information business," Rose told those who tried to romanticize him (a task he liked to reserve for himself). "Not what they call 'the information superhighway,' more like the information back alley. I collect little smelly facts, that's all." But here he was with his mother's pistol.

*I think I have to kill you, Zig. It feels like I do. That's not the same thing as wanting to. Or maybe it is.*

*Or maybe Mr. Sherman and his people will kill me first. Or Mr. Lampedusa and his far more practiced people. That's a lot of killers for so early in the morning.*

He held his mother's pistol as though it might transmit some motherly message that would make things clear or right. But that had never been his mother's way.

Rose couldn't stay in the office any longer. It had been comparatively safe at night with the lights out, but in daylight a shooter on the roof across the street would have a clean shot through the wide window. That would be quick and simple: Rose wouldn't know what hit him, and would not have to kill anyone. *If I stay, it would look like murder but would actually be suicide.* He knew that was the secret of many murders. And he despised the juries and lawmakers because this was something they couldn't afford to know—it would complicate their judgments beyond endurance. *You pricks would have to live like I do, then—and live with what I live with.*

Sherman's people might take the shot from across the street, but Rose knew Zig would kill face-to-face, as he always had, and as Rose would rather be killed. *If it's going to be, let it be by an old man I've known all my life, for something personal, rather than by strangers I don't even want to know, for something that's really none of my business.*

He had found his mother's pistol shortly after she died. It was with the photographs, in a locked box of black metal, a foot deep, a foot long, a foot wide. He had wondered what such a box had been designed for, but the more he considered the box, the less he was able to imagine its makers or its purpose.

His mother had left no key. He had to break the lock. The pistol—a small revolver, snub-nosed, shiny—lay on a stack of photographs. The gleaming blue of the weapon matched the glossy blacks and whites of the photos it lay upon. That was his first impression. His second wasn't an impression at all, but a blankness: he'd looked at that first photo without seeing it—"zoned out," he would say—as he picked up the pistol. He checked it out as his father had taught him long ago. It was loaded. It was clean. He wondered if its bullets would still fire. He hefted its compact, thick, unfamiliar weight in his right hand. "Thanks, Mama," he said aloud, and continued within, *There was always a pistol behind your eyes, and here I've found it. You were always killing somebody with those eyes.* He held it, imagined her holding it, and put it back in the box.

Then the third impression struck, like a sudden dissonant chord, a terrible music that harmonized with something terrible within him, something livid and unspoken—and he had been living in that dissonance since that day. The first glossy eight-by-ten on which he'd placed the pistol, the photograph he had seen moments ago without actually seeing, was of a luscious and fleshy woman—luscious and fleshy, yet so well proportioned she seemed slim. Her legs spread to the lens. Her vulva was perfectly focused. Its every ridge and bulge shined. One long finger, with a dark pointed nail, pressed upon that lubricated mass. Her black bra had cutouts for her thick nipples and their dark aureoles. Her flesh had that mysterious quality all models long for: it photographed as touchable, you could feel the sensation of touch through your eyes. Her hair, long and dark, by some trick of lighting shined unnaturally. Her eyes sparkled under arched eyebrows, and glinted not with an invitation but a dare. These eyes never invited; they always dared—a dare that would have been naked no matter what she was or wasn't wearing. It was a challenge to all comers to measure up to her hunger.

"Hello, Mama. So *that's* what you really looked like. I always knew you were in disguise."

The woman he had known all his life had been fat, but he saw now that she'd put on her weight intentionally—the way she'd done everything—to cloak this body, this past.

He would not let himself weep. He would not give her that. But something worse than weeping began in him, down where it was impossible to hear or stop.

In the next photograph her anus was at least as vivid as her eyes, and looked almost like an eye, a dark eye with a hole instead of an iris—a black crinkled hole. Her long dark-nailed fingers spread her buttocks, that you might sink your eye or your longing or your disgust or your penis all the deeper.

Then the next photograph. And the next. A stack of twenty. He counted them, not because he cared how many there were but just to *do* something, and counting was all he could do. Twenty, then. And each added to the delirious dissonance, worse than weeping, that had shaken him since that day.

His face showed none of this, however, except that something tight in his expression became ever so slightly tighter.

When, exactly, had the photographs been taken? He was a thorough, if unusual, professional, and the question came from the professional part of him. Before her marriage, certainly, but still in the first fullness of youth. So, 1945, 1946, 1947. Where? Probably in Las Vegas. The town was so small then, they could have been taken within walking distance of his office. *You can buy this shit at your local newsstand now, but back then it would have been top secret, high dollar, Mob porn. Well, Mama, at least that keeps it in the "family."*

His mother had been conscious and sharp to the end. She knew he'd find the box. She could have destroyed it, or could have said, "Mike, there's a black metal box. You'll know it when you see it. Don't open it. Just throw it out." She knew her son, knew if he gave his word he'd keep it. She'd raised him to be that kind of man, and she'd been successful. So why had she left this inheritance?

"You're too smart for your own good," she used to tell him. They all used to tell him that, and many still did. "You think all the goddamn time," she used to say, "just like your father. It slows you up."

He remembered those words as he looked again and again at the photographs, unable to stop or help himself, and unable to stop his body from its thrust of lust, disgust, and rage.

*I may be smart, Mama, but not smart enough to know why you left me this black box.*

Since that hour he'd known less and less. And now, just after daybreak on Fremont Street, he did not quite know how to carry her pistol. He wore an expensive suit, for he'd been raised to feel that there was no point wearing a suit unless it was expensive. The gun made the jacket too bulky and lopsided when he put it in the inner pocket. Wearing it in his belt at the small of his back, where it would be fairly well concealed, felt uncomfortable—and, if he needed the weapon in a hurry, too inaccessible. It was a silly problem, it made him feel childish, and this was no morning to feel childish. He finally wedged the pistol in his belt, near his left hip, in easy reach and even comfortable but, depending on how his jacket swayed, also visible. "Problems, problems," he muttered. In movies and books people never needed to think about such things. That's why he'd stopped going to movies and reading books.

He walked to the office door, paused, took a breath, pulled the pistol from his belt with his right hand, and with one quick motion of his left he turned the knob, flung open the door, and scared the shit out of a homeless woman sitting half-asleep in the stairwell.

She stank. Her long blond hair was matted and pitiful— though once it must have hung to her waist and glowed yellow-

gold and been her pride. Her skirt and blouse had been
bought in some expensive shop far away, but were stiff with
filth and their colors had faded to an indeterminate dullness.
Her eyes were luminous, a sparkling green, but the flesh beneath them was swollen and red and dark. She stared at the
gun in the hand of Mike Rose. Then she looked into his eyes
with the secret intelligence of one who has let her mind wander
far from its original starting place. She had a good enough
body to sell herself for a good price, but her hunger-hollowed
cheeks and the state of her clothing told Rose that this option
had never occurred to her. It felt good to him to be greeted,
even in fear, by someone with inflexible principles, or inhibi-
tions, or whatever they were.

"Good morning," Rose said.

"Jesus," she said.

"How'd you get in?"

"What?"

The narrow staircase wasn't air-conditioned or ventilated.
He smelled her urine and her period and her sweat.

"How did you get in?" he repeated.

"Why don't you shoot me?" she asked softly. It was a sweet
voice, what was left of it, educated and Southern.

"Why don't you shoot yourself?" he said.

"I don't have a gun." She smiled weakly.

"Here's a hundred bucks. Buy a gun."

From his pocket he pulled a gold billfold, took out two fifties
and held them out to her. Her long, pretty, filthy fingers closed
around his bills and made a fist. His skin touched hers briefly
before he let the bills go.

"How *did* you get in?" Rose said again. "That door," he gestured downstairs, "locked behind me last night."

"A guy," she said.

"What kind of guy?"

"What time is it?"

"What do you care? What kind of guy?"

"Young guy. I'm young too."

"That's nice. What kind of a young guy?"

"In a blue suit. He was opening it. The door. Not with a key." She smiled a smile that had just remembered, just vaguely, to care about something. "Think I scared him. Me."

Rose could almost see her, too weak and tired to walk anymore that night, stepping up to the young guy in the blue suit to beg some change. He would just have jimmied the door and suddenly this smelly, skeletal apparition was right behind him with her odor of waste and her eyes bright with the incommunicable. It had been enough and more than enough to spook the young man in the blue suit, and he'd left in a nervous hurry. The scene had been something like that, Rose knew. The door had a slow spring, and before it could close she'd walked in to rest out of the chill where she wouldn't wake with a man just as filthy on top of her.

The Young Man in the Blue Suit had been one of Mr. Sherman's people, then, if he could be spooked so easily. If it had been Zig or one of Mr. Lampedusa's people, the wraith would be dead now, and perhaps Rose as well.

"Take it easy," Rose said.

She thought that was pretty funny.


Mike Rose walked up Fremont feeling unlucky, waiting for somebody else's luck to stop him. He believed that the wraith who scared off Blue Suit was as much luck as he could expect.

*The trouble with amateurs is, they don't know what they're doing, so they sometimes come up with something original. You can't predict the fuckers. Professionals are better at what they do—much—but they're easier to predict. Ultimately you're going to have to deal with a professional; ultimately an amateur is going to have to deal with you. But sometimes the fuckers get lucky, and one of the tougher lessons of this Vegas is: You can't fight luck.*

He'd left a rental car with Valet Parking at the Four Queens a couple of blocks away. His own car, a '72 white Cadillac convertible, was too well known an advertisement of his whereabouts, so he'd left it in his garage. It used to be that people who parked cars at the casinos were pros at casino life, well paid and sharp eyed, able to connect anyone with anything in a town that offered everything. The best among them didn't even give you a stub, but remembered who belonged to which vehicle and rarely missed. Now car parkers were McWorkers, mostly, paid very little—*newcomers who don't know their own score, much less anyone else's*, Rose thought. The oldtimers had known him by his first name. *The new ones hardly even know their own names.* But that was useful this morning. He wasn't likely to be recognized or remembered.

He stood a moment at the Third Street curb, looking all ways not for traffic—there wasn't any—but for a man in a blue suit. Then he crossed toward the corner entrance of the Four Queens. The doors were always open and the air system pushed a steady breeze of staleness, smoke, and disappointment into the street. Near the entrance a young man in a blue suit played a nickel slot. He was tall, thin, blond, and well groomed. He didn't look as though nickel slots were his game, but from that spot he had a view of the entire intersection at Third and Fremont. A pro would never have made eye contact, would have seen Rose before being seen and then concentrated on the slot machine, able to watch his quarry without really looking. But the man in the blue suit couldn't take his eyes off Rose. *Good, you fuck, that means you're nervous.* Rose, on the other hand, looked everywhere but at the man in the blue suit, who thought he was unobserved.

Rose was critical of the man's outfit. *It cost a few hundred, it's blue, and that's all.* But Rose admired how neatly the man concealed his weapon—and knew this meant that Blue Suit was far more familiar with guns than he. In a few steps Rose noticed all this with peripheral vision. "You see more than you look at," his father or Zig, he couldn't remember which, had taught him long ago. "You see all the way to the edges. Just concentrate on the edge instead of what's in front of you, you'll see it all real good without lookin' direct at it. That's how you become a good soldier." In those days they were raising Rose for the only life they knew, a life in the Mob.

Rose didn't need to turn his head to know that Blue Suit had left his slot machine and was following him. The smart thing would have been to go into the casino, walk right past Blue Suit, lead him on a merry chase through the maze that *is* a casino, and lose him. But Rose didn't want to lose him, couldn't bear the idea of Blue Suit hovering somewhere out there, liable to appear suddenly anywhere. *Fuck it, the next time he finds me he might have help.* Rose wanted this thing to be over with, so he continued down the street knowing Blue Suit followed. *A pro would finish me right now, two shots in the back to drop me, then step close and finish it with one to the head. But an amateur isn't gonna shoot in the open in broad daylight. Amateurs think everybody's looking at them, even when there's nobody around.*

He was talking to himself now, and he knew it for a bad sign. *If you want to find out how you're really doing on any given morning, walk down a street slowly about fifteen paces in front of a man who wants to kill you.*

*Think, think, think.* But he was only talking to himself, not thinking, and he knew that too—and knew this meant that he was more afraid than he realized. With that admission his resolve crumbled, the street seemed unusually wide, the buildings unusually tall, the pavement unusually hard, and Rose felt small and soft. "Get back in your body," his friend the Reverend Joy was always saying, and he heard that voice inside himself now. But he couldn't bring the buildings down to size, couldn't shrink the street to its proper width. His pants felt abrasive, his shoes too hot, he was sweating through his shirt, he felt trickles down his armpits, his collar scraped his neck, his heart thumped in his ears. He wanted to break and

*The Dignity of Isadore Feldman*

run but knew he must not. *Got to look normal.* A nausea of doubt unsteadied him, he doubted his very name, and knew this doubt for a greater enemy than the man who wanted to kill him. He felt stupid and alone and inadequate.

In short, it was a normal day, but with a bright, bright light upon it, the light of his death.

A walk down the block can take forever, the way a car crash can take forever. Pains spasmed in his back where muscles tensed, anticipating the entrance of bullets. Twice in his life he'd been shot, so he knew it wasn't like in the movies, you don't stagger around, all your strength escapes in an instant, you crumple, you can't feel anything, you don't know where you've been hit, don't know whether it's bad or not. It's as though somebody's turned a hot light on in your brain, so bright you can't see or think or feel. The one behind him wanted to deliver that brightness. In half a block's walk Rose had become less of a man, and he knew it and flushed with hatred of himself because of it.

He had reached the Valet Parking/Check-In entrance of the Four Queens. It didn't even occur to him to go in. He no longer had the confidence that he could lose Blue Suit in the casino. And Rose had been so deeply trained not to react to fears that he didn't even have the impulse simply to bolt through those doors.

A cabbie Rose knew was pulling out from the driveway right in front of him. Rose had to check his step to avoid being hit. *Stop, goddamnit. Talk to me. The sonofabitch won't shoot if there's a witness.*

"Hey, Sam," he said, surprised he could speak.

"Hey, Mike." The cabbie waved as he pulled into the street and sped away with his fare.

*I'm so fucking stupid. Shit. I could have said, "Wait up, Sam," just gotten in the cab, fuck the other fare, just opened the door, gotten away clean. What a fuck-up. I'm gonna die of my own stupidity. If I get nailed now, it's my own damned fault. What a lousy feeling to go out on.*

Rose was angry now, and he needed to be angry, even if only with himself. But still every step seemed to take forever, as though he could recite the Gettysburg Address while lifting a foot off the pavement and putting it back down.

A few steps past the driveway a narrow staircase slanted steeply into the parking garage. His burst of anger at himself hadn't stopped his sweat but it made him start thinking. *Okay, amateur, this is your big chance. If you get to the bottom of these stairs before I get to the top, you can plug me easy—step on that first stair, out of sight of the street, and blast away. It'll make one hell of a racket echoing through this garage, probably scare the shit out of you too, but I'll be dead and this is Vegas, nobody'll come running. But if I get to the top before you reach the bottom—that's my break.*

Rose took the first step normally. Then, out of sight of the street, he bolted to the top. Was that functionary of Mr. Sherman's scared of killing Rose? Had he ever murdered before? Was he in over his head, like Rose? These weren't questions Rose had time to ask himself, but they lived in the eagerness with which he waited now to see Blue Suit's face— for as Blue Suit turned to climb the stairs there'd be just an instant when they'd get a good look at each other.

A lot can be seen in an instant. *Poor bastard.* When Blue Suit faced Rose from the bottom of the stairs, Rose saw that he was too young to have been in a war and too uptown to know the street. He looked like some gun-freak executive with fantasies of being tough. Until that wraith had surprised Blue Suit, it hadn't occurred to him that he wasn't in a movie—that he could lose. His eyes were frightened, and he was about to learn a Vegas axiom: Scared money never wins.

He saw Rose and froze. He hadn't even reached for his gun when Rose, gripping the metal bannister, swung himself and came hurtling feet first. His heels hit Blue Suit squarely in the ribs, one on each side, and he heard the crunch of breaking bones, then felt the ribs give way under his shoes as the two men fell sprawling all over each other. "Always hit first, don't be a gentleman," he'd been taught as a boy. Rose and the amateur slammed onto the pavement, Rose on top, and more of Blue Suit's bones broke as they landed. There was the sound of tearing cloth and gasping, but Rose was only trying to breathe while Blue Suit was trying to scream.

Then something happened to Mike Rose. Blue Suit was finished and Rose knew it—not dead, but hurt too badly to hurt back. That didn't matter anymore. Rose hit him. Hit him and hit him in an ecstacy of hitting, a wild pounding rhythm, till through his fists he felt the soul of the man quail and want to leave its body.

Rose was a thin man, but he'd been taught to punch by people who knew how punishing a punch can be. Rose hit him in the face till the face broke, hit him in the chest to make its breakage worse, and Rose didn't stop hitting till he hurt his hand on the pistol still in the man's shoulder holster. "Never stop hitting a guy till he stops moving," he'd been taught as a boy, by Zig or his father, he couldn't remember, but that wasn't why he hit now. *I hate this WASP fuck. I hate this shit-ball who made me so afraid. He's never going to be the same now. No man ever is after a beating like this. He's never even going to look the same. He'll live, but he'll live different.*

Rose came to himself standing over the man and hurting everywhere. His knuckles were bloodied but, knowing how to punch, he hadn't broken his hands. Someone in a passing car gawked but didn't stop. Last night's liquor and food shot up to Rose's mouth and he caught it in cupped palms. As he shook his hands free of the stickiness and wiped them on his pants, smelling in the mess all he'd felt for the last twelve hours, a foulness enveloped him and spoke his name.

"Oh, God. Oh, fucking God."

And his soul quailed too, and he turned and moved as quickly as pain allowed up the stairs.

It hurt to run those stairs. His left leg throbbed, sudden small pains flashed in his body like bright blinking lights, and again he was afraid. Two more flights up he stopped and checked for the revolver in his belt. Somehow it was still there. He felt a silliness, an embarrassment. He had forgotten all about the gun—had been so aware of every sensation except that of the metal wedged in his belt. It seemed as though people were pointing at him, laughing at him—Zig, Pop, Mama, Alvi. He told himself, and told them, that there was good reason he hadn't tried to shoot the amateur: if he had to kill Zig this morning, and if the police found the body, and if ballistics found the same bullets in Zig and the amateur, they'd make the connection, maybe zero in on Rose. This might be true, but it wasn't why Rose hadn't used the pistol. *I don't want to kill anybody. Not Zig, not anybody. Hitting that WASP fuck was different. I was ruining him, I wasn't killing him. I don't want to kill anybody. I'm going to kill somebody.*

There were sirens now. An ambulance and a cop, probably. *This is getting messy and messy is no good—messy is for amateurs.* Which is how it struck Rose that when it came to killing, it was he who was the amateur, and he'd just seen what happens to amateurs.

He could forget about the rental in Valet Parking. With his torn clothes and his bloodied hands he looked too memorable. He had to get out of there. He knew the first cop would call for backup, and when they arrived they'd check out the parking garage. He would have to risk a witness, get a cab, get to his own very visible car—many more chances than he'd intended to take, and on top of it all he was late. *It's weird to be late to a killing. As though it's scheduled somehow. An appointment, with its own protocol.*

*The Dignity of Isadore Feldman*

And Rose saw himself suddenly not as the most important person in his own story, but as a thin and exhausted, bloodied and dirtied man, in one parking garage of many in the city, the most improbable city of all, in the middle of the great desert— a speck that called itself Mike Rose, which wasn't even his real name.

The speck knew what to do. He made his way to the far end of the parking garage, where another stairway took him to what used to be called Second Street and was now called Casino Center Boulevard. Across the street was the Check-In entrance and taxi stand of the Golden Nugget. Rose knew that if the police were thorough they'd check out the Nugget's entrance sooner or later, on the chance of getting a description. On the other hand, he knew the police schedule well, knew they were on the tag end of the night shift, and simply finding the WASP had already forced on them several hours' more paperwork than they'd bargained for. They wouldn't get home till noon now as it was, so they might not question any more people than they had to. Might even stop with the parking garage and not check out the Nugget at all. Rose decided to risk the taxi stand, buoyed by how his head had cleared at least enough for him to think like a professional again.

The cabbie wasn't happy to see a fare that looked like Mike Rose, but who ever heard of a happy cabbie?

"Arizona Charlie's," Rose said.

As they pulled out onto the street the cabbie said, "Even a joint like Arizona Charlie's is gonna frown on the condition you're in, bud."

"Not if I have a room key."

Rose didn't have a room key and didn't intend to spend five minutes in Arizona Charlie's, but if the cabbie was questioned that's where he'd say he took the fare. The man was about Rose's age, had a Chicago accent, and needed a shave. Like half the people in Las Vegas now, he probably hadn't lived there more than a few years.

"You get rolled, bud?" Only newcomers asked so many questions.

"Don't worry, I have the fare."

"Don't tell me what to worry about."

The cabbie took Second to Charleston, hung a right, and headed west. After they crossed I-15 they could have been in any midsize desert city. Before them there was no hint of the casino skyline directly behind. Miles ahead, but looking closer, the bare and jagged Madre Mountains loomed over the town. How often, in high school, had Rose driven this road with his friends to Red Rock Canyon, where the city disappeared entirely and the desert was naked and pristine? Wild donkeys, coyotes, and all manner of creatures roamed freely there still. The high school kids would drink and make love and dream. But never had he dreamed of a morning like this.

*I thought I'd never kill anybody. I thought I was different. Beating up on a guy, that's another thing—that amateur had it coming.* This stopped his thought a moment. He wasn't a man who often lied to himself, at least not so blatantly. *Okay, what I did to him after he was down—maybe nobody has that coming. Or maybe everybody does. I don't know.* Admitting this, he couldn't help admitting more, while the sharper pains throughout his body subsided into deep, troubling aches. *I was different, that's what I thought in Red Rock Canyon, that's what I thought until recently. The soldiers killed, the businessmen killed, the gamblers killed, the hoods killed. Frustrated lovers, crazy people, politicians, religious nuts, true believers, they all killed. And a lot of nice people killed too, quiet storekeepers and prim housewives, who let others kill in their name for profit or a cause and cheered them on all the way. Even kids killed now. But I was different, because in a dirty business in the dirtiest town of all, I didn't do the dirtiest*

*The Dignity of Isadore Feldman*

*thing, the thing that makes the world go round: not love, not even money; just killing.*

"Never stop hitting a guy till he stops moving." Yes, it was his father who'd taught him that. And Zig had chimed in, "Always hit first, if it looks like there's gonna be any hitting at all. Save being a gentleman for dinner with the ladies." Useful lessons for the world they'd raised him to be a part of, the Mob, the only world they knew, the only world they respected. They had been killers both, his father and Zig. Like the President of the United States, like the religious leaders, like the businessmen, like the maddened lovers, like the prim housewives, killers in a world of killers. It happened to be their profession, but to Rose that just made them more up front about the true coin of the realm than most. *They were killers in a world of killers, but I was not.* That was his pride and it had gotten him through. *Because right with the killing, right alongside it and making it possible, was the lying. Everybody who killed or let others kill in their name also lied and let others lie in their name. Lied up and down, lied about it all, lied when they said "I love you" and lied when they said "We, the people of the United States, in order to form a more perfect Union." Not me. I was different. It was all around me, I couldn't help that, but I didn't buy into it. That was me. Now there's something I can't live with and have to kill about. Because people only kill about things they can't live with. I'm signing up. After a long, long time, I am about to join the human race.*

*What a morning.*

He wasn't afraid of the actual killing. He knew how easy it was. *Nothing easier.* He wasn't even afraid of guilt. He knew all about guilt. *You don't have to kill anybody to accumulate guilt, everybody's swamped with guilt by the time they're five.* He was afraid of what his life was going to be after he lost what had made him special.

Arizona Charlie's is the kind of joint that used to be downtown and isn't anymore—an old-timey, rought-and-tumble gambling den. On the Strip these days they deal blackjack from a "boot," a plastic box that's got who knows how many decks in it; at Arizona Charlie's dealers still hold the deck in their hands, so they have to know a thing or two, and players have more of a chance. The ceilings are low, there aren't any "No Smoking" tables, and anyone with an eye for the effects can see that someone's selling speed, the drug of choice in Las Vegas, somewhere in the neighborhood. Vacationers and conventioneers rarely go to places like Arizona Charlie's. It's for locals, long-distance truckers, RV gypsies, and people driving in from Beatty and Ely who used to go downtown. At some times of the day it looks like an old folks' home—people who moved here with their children and grandchildren, old people who can't sleep and hit Arizona Charlie's instead, or who aren't comfortable at home with their families and retreat here, playing nickel slots for hours. The smoke is thick, the colors are vague, there aren't many kids underfoot, and there's nobody costumed like a knight or the Wizard of Oz or an Egyptian princess. You can sink into the pointlessness of gambling, and the pointlessness of your life, without anybody trying to convince you that you're doing anything but sinking.

That was how Mike Rose thought of it, in any case. *When sinking is all that's left, there can still be a little dignity in taking it straight.*

He gave the cabbie a fat tip, *my way of telling him to go fuck himself*. Rose, who had too much philosophy, a philosophy for almost anything, thought, *A wad of money can really be an insult if you know how to hand it over right. And it's a confusing insult, because they're glad to take the money but they don't know why this time it's making them feel small. If you stiff them they have a reason to feel righteous, but if you give*

The Dignity of Isadore Feldman

*them a good toke and you give it to them right, then all they're left with is how little they matter. Zig and my father and my mother had that move down, all Mob people do.* Rose and his brother had learned the gesture by the time they were twelve.

He buttoned his torn jacket and kept his arm over the pistol in his belt, then took the chance and walked through the rows of slots to the back entrance. It was like walking through a graveyard—the slots were the tombstones, and at nearly every one sat an old ghost in cheap rags, moving mechanically, inserting coins, pulling the handle or hitting the button, each with the same expression, an expression that was no expression at all, each gray wrinkled face a flag of disappointment, each nickel spent for a dream that didn't matter to them anymore. It would make no difference if they hit the jackpot, not anymore, but they played anyway because a long shot at the jackpot was all they'd ever known, all they'd ever been offered, and they'd try for it with their dying breath.

*It's better than watching TV.*

*A graveyard haunted by the slightly alive, who are deader than the dead, because at least the dead have been released.*

Rose stumbled over an oxygen tank.

It belonged to a skinny old man at a slot—tubes in his nose ran into the tank. Rose caught himself on the back of the chair of a fat woman who didn't even notice. The old man's tubes yanked painfully off his face, there was panic in his eyes, and he just said, "Wha? Wha?"

Rose was claiming to be sorry as he helped the man insert the tubes back into his hairy nostrils, while the man's hands fluttered and he said again, "Wha?"

A change-making lady pushed her money cart to the end of the row and said, "Sir!" Rose looked up but she wasn't addressing him. "Sir!" She seemed to have had a lot of practice projecting her voice toward the functionally deaf. "You've *got* to get that oxygen tank out of the aisle so people can pass."

Then she went on her way without seeming to notice Rose at all. There was another oxygen tank in the next aisle that he carefully stepped over, now that he was looking for them.

At least Rose didn't have to worry about witnesses here. There were a lot of people at Arizona Charlie's for this time of the morning, but there were no witnesses.

He left Arizona Charlie's by a service door in the back. It was a half-hour's walk west to his condo, where his Cadillac was parked. Zig was waiting, somewhere in the desert, and Rose felt the pull of Zig's impatience. *Punctuality is important in our circles. On the other hand, maybe the old man's impatience will work for me. Who knows?*

He thought of the man with the tubes at Arizona Charlie's, and how that man must be roughly Zig's age. And Rose laughed for the first time in what seemed a while—a giddy, throaty burst of unfamiliar sound. *Anybody wacked out enough to carry an oxygen tank into a casino at—what is it now, seven-thirty, a quarter to eight in the morning?—anybody who could be that far gone and still that determined, or compulsive, or whatever it was . . . well, he had the spark of life, didn't he? Even in that graveyard. It was okay with him to die slumped over a nickel slot, and he probably hoped he would. Better than struggling for one last breath in a smelly hospital bed surrounded by adult kids he probably hadn't really liked since they were twelve. He was doing it his way, just like that Sinatra song.* And Rose was suddenly fond of that old man for not being as helpless as he seemed.

It was a slight but steady uphill grade to his condo, and whatever he'd pulled or twisted in his left knee hurt worse and worse. He thought of long ago, when there weren't any streets where he walked now, only desert, and the Strip had been hardly visible from this vantage in daylight. When he was a boy there were only about ten casinos on the Strip, none of them more than a few stories high. The neons were bigger than the buildings back then. Between the casinos there weren't any shops and malls, just stretches of bare desert. And there wasn't an Interstate 15. The main highway was the Strip itself, U.S. 91. A half mile west of the Strip was the railroad track, then a few isolated streets west of that, mostly below Decatur. And the houses on those streets looked like what they were: little outposts of wishes on the Mojave Desert. There was a quarter mile of nothing between the Rose family's house and their neighbor, and behind their house was more nothing, nothing but the Mojave straight to the Madre Mountains. Rose was thinking of a day at about this time of year in 1963. He was walking across the desert from a friend's house, and he hurt a lot that day too.

It was the first time he'd been beat up—really beat up. They'd hit him, and then, when he was down, they'd kicked. Those kids hadn't seen that sort of thing in the movies and on TV, because Hollywood didn't film such things then. They'd done it for the same reason people always have: because they wanted to. Rose couldn't remember what "the beef," as he called it, had been about, except that the other boys had wanted him to do something and he wouldn't do it, and one thing had led to another and then he was down and they kicked. He cursed them as they kicked, and while he cursed he trembled with a fear more fundamental than he had yet felt: the knowledge that some people will do anything, and for not much reason, to their fellow creatures. He remembered still his amazement, at each kick, that they would kick him so hard while he was down.

They kicked until they grew bored with kicking, and left laughing. That was the first time Rose felt hate. A withering rage of hate in which he too felt capable of anything. He hated them not for the beating but for the laughing, and hated himself, that he could be laughed at. When he picked himself up everything hurt and his mouth was full of blood. That was the first time he spit blood, and somehow the blood coming from his mouth was more terrifying than the blood coming from the cuts on his legs and arms. He caught it on his hands and, before thinking, wiped it on his shirt.

He limped home hoping that nobody would be around when he got there, but everybody was: Mama, Pop, Zig, and his brother, Alvi. *There was nobody's arms to run to. That's not how we did it in our family. The family would back you no matter what you did, right or wrong, but you were expected to be able to take it—whatever "it" happened to be on any particular day.* When he saw three cars in the driveway he steeled himself to look like somebody who could take it. If, as an adult, he could have seen himself at that moment as a boy—the astonished fear of a boy alone among protectors who, the boy knew, had no intention of protecting him; the desperate bravery that was his only refuge from them—then Mike Rose, the man, might have thought better of himself.

The driveway door, the door they all used, opened into the kitchen and he went from the desert air, with that glistening dry freshness that was its only scent, into the gray air of Camels, Chesterfields, and Pall Malls, the incessant unfiltered smoking of the grown-ups. Alvi was in the kitchen. Alvi, like Mike, was thin and quick, with features already sculpted by intelligence, the olive skin of his people, and rich brown eyes of a deceptive depth and softness—with a blink those eyes could turn to hard gleaming stones, a capacity both boys inherited from their mother, or blaze with that particularly Sicilian gift for fierceness. Alvi was older but far more fragile, and Mike was so much his protector that even as a boy Alvi called him, in irony and self-hatred, "big brother."

That day in the kitchen they needed no words. In a glance Alvi saw how bad Mike had been beaten, and his eyes filled with tears, partly out of sympathy and partly from the knowledge that their bond would change in the next hour if Mike passed the test that he, Alvi, had failed. Both knew it would be

easier for Mike than it had been for Alvi, for Mike had Alvi's
experience to go on and Alvi had had no such clue. The older
"little brother" let Mike pass him silently, and went to his
room, ashamed of wanting Mike to fail.

Mama, Pop, and Zig were talking in what for most families
might have been a den but what the Rossellinis called their
card room. Whenever talking had to be done, the adults sat
down with their coffee and their cigarettes and played cards
and talked during their game. Gin rummy, usually; sometimes
poker. When the talk was serious, was business, they would
"shout in whispers," as Alvi used to say. Their words came
fast in hushed staccatos, raised in bursts to full-throated stage
whispers. It wasn't that the boys couldn't hear, it was that
they knew they weren't supposed to listen, and they didn't—
long before they learned why, they knew there was something
to be frightened of in those talks. *The grown-ups talked in a
code that, until we were older, we didn't quite get anyway. We
didn't know from "Mob" or "Outfit"—they hardly ever used
those words. No one ever said "Mafia," no one ever said
"Cosa Nostra"—even now you hardly hear that. But something deadly was going down—that, a kid could feel.* The
boys knew the drill. Mike was just going to have to walk up to
the grown-ups and present himself. They'd ask questions.
He'd answer. The truth, always. For telling the truth was a
matter of life and death to these people. *"Never lie to your
friends, never lie to your family." I don't know how often
Mama said that to us; thinking back, I guess it was the only
thing she believed in. I learned later that, in these circles,
once you were being lied to it meant that you were probably
going to be killed.*

Memories don't stay put. Now that he had seen those photos—seen that glowering, seducing look on his mother's face,
her youthful body—they papered the walls of every memory
of her. But the woman in that card room did not look like that.
She was fat and wore her fatness like a comfortable loose

dress, tossing its folds from posture to posture with ease. The Ava Gardner eyes of the photographs hadn't changed. If anything, the fleshy face made them more mysterious, for in this woman there was nothing of the self-defeated look of the American fat woman. Her mouth was also the same, luscious and sensuous, playful and pitiless, as though enjoying some private pleasure surrounded by her bulging cheeks.

With her were Pop and Zig—"the dago and the Jew, the two-headed monster," his mother called them. *Pop was one of those Tony Bennett kind of Sicilians, small, compact, "built like a fire hydrant," Mama used to say.* He had hard features but tentative eyes. *He was what we call "a stand-up guy," that was clear, and yet, he was never sure. I know now that he was never sure, because I've seen his look in my mirror, and on the face of my brother.* It was the look of a man who could be trusted to act as though he was sure, whether he was sure or not. *I know now that meant he was doomed to be small-time, doomed to be used. There was something in the whole setup that he never accepted all the way, though he acted like he did. I know now that Mama disliked this in him, and I know now that that was the uneasiness between them that me and my brother always feared.* She stood with her husband, but not because she respected him; she stood with him because she respected herself. *To Mama, a vow was a vow. After you made it, it was too late to do anything but live it out.*

Zig, also small and powerful, was absolutely sure—every gesture, every look was sure. His gray eyes went from warm to cold like jump cuts in a movie. His friendliness seemed genuine, and perhaps was, but even in midsentence it might disappear, and what took its place was impenetrable. He would do anything to fulfill a loyalty or a duty, and Zig's "anything" took in a lot. He looked like a butcher and he was, but the butcher he looked like was a guy in a deli and the butcher he was was a guy who could do to people what people do to chickens and cows—except that butchers don't look quite so eerily intelligent, as a rule. Rose never understood why Zig didn't rise in the rackets. Intelligence is prized in that world, for it is even more rare and crucial there than in most worlds. The only conclusion Mike could draw was that Zig didn't want to rise. He had found his vocation, his niche, and liked being a hit man better than being a boss.

In their rough way, those three in the card room shared the class, the style of the peasants who had imitated aristocrats for centuries and now, in this town, could walk easily among them. *A style I've been trying to live up to all my life.*

Never had Rose tried harder to live up to it than that moment when he presented himself to them as a beaten boy.

Mama took a long drag on her Camel and spoke the first word blowing smoke: "So?"

"They kicked me, Mama. I was down and they kicked me." His boy's voice felt very small and high.

"Who?"

He said nothing.

"Did you hear me? *Who?*"

He said nothing.

"Goddamnit, WHO?"

He flinched and everything in him wanted to say, "Paulo and those Mormon kids," but he said nothing.

"When I ask you a question I expect an *answer*."

"Your *mother* expects an *answer*," Pop said, and his hard hand shot out.

The boy took the slap without flinching, as was expected of him. He felt blood run in his mouth again but swallowed it down.

"There's more where that came from," his mother said.

Zig watched with clinical interest, as though watching a mechanic make a minor adjustment on an engine.

Mama said, "I'm only gonna ask one more time."

The three looked at him for several seconds as they smoked.

The boy held himself in with a strength that was less corrupted, less full of doubt, than it would ever be again.

"Now I'm asking again. Watch me ask again. Watch close. *Who?*"

The boy could not speak now even if he wanted to. A horrified silence filled his mouth like a gag.

All three adults smiled at the same time.

"My kid don't rat," Pop said.

"Course he don't," Zig said.

When Alvi had been subjected to the same treatment and had "flipped," as his mother later said, her withering contempt had lasted days. She'd made Alvi so sure that she wanted an answer that finally he'd gone against all her previous teachings and told her, and it was never the same between them after that. It was the most drastic, fearsome change Mike had yet seen between two people, and he'd had an overwhelming horror of the same thing happening to him. Now that he'd passed the test he wanted to weep with release, but he knew that weeping would cancel out everything, and with more will than he had yet exerted in his life he kept back the tears.

"Come 'ere," Mama said to the boy, "lemme see the damage."

They took off his bloodstained shirt, took off his torn pants, poked and prodded him. They had a medical knowledge of the injuries inflicted by beatings. His father could tape a cut so perfectly that it healed without a scar. "Healing hands," Mike's friend the Reverend Joy would have called them.

As they tended his cuts and bruises, Zig said, "This is a guy who can take a beating. He's a stand-up guy, this kid."

It was the best thing they knew to say about anyone. The boy glowed.

"Your first real beating," Pop said with pride. "That's something."

*I beamed under that approval, but at the same time, deep down, I was going a little nuts. They liked that I'd got beat up. No A I ever brought home from school—and until then all I got was A's—had brought this kind of approval. That's when Zig and Pop started giving me those lessons, like, "If you're ganged up on, you pick just one guy, don't try to fight them all, grab one guy and try to fucking DAMAGE him, no matter how the other guys are hitting you—they'll think twice about ganging up on you again. Nobody wants to be that one guy."* In their eyes he had entered their world—so much so that he half expected them to offer him a cigarette. At one and the same time, the boy felt a pride he'd never known and a fear he'd never guessed at. As with many of his breed, that alloy of pride and fear would become the signature of his life.

"Is this gonna happen a *lot?*" the boy asked.

The grown-ups laughed as gently as they ever laughed.

"Maybe," his father said. His father often began a sentence with "maybe," no matter what the answer was going to be—which was how he got his Mob name, Eddie Maybe. But this time "maybe" was his entire answer.

Mama got Mike a clean shirt and trousers and put them on him. It was the first time since he was four years old that he hadn't had to dress himself.

"There," she said, "you don't look too much the worse for wear."

"Naw, he looks great," Zig said, "looks like a man, don't he, Eddie?"

"Maybe. Sure he does. A real little man."

"Now you gotta revenge," Mama said.

"You gotta make it right," Zig said.

"You find those guys one at a time—" Pop said.

And Zig finished his sentence, "—and wail on them. Beat the shit out of them."

"Make it right," Mama said.

The boy was shocked. Alvi, having failed the first phase of the test, had not been asked to proceed to its next phase, so Mike hadn't any idea that this too was expected.

"I'll make it right," the high small voice said.

The project would take the next several weeks, and would finish Michael Rossellini's standing in school. From being a teacher's pet he became a problem child, and his A's were a thing of the past. This annoyed his parents, but not greatly.

Now they'd spent enough time on him for one afternoon and, lighting fresh cigarettes, they turned back to their cards. But the boy couldn't leave, couldn't move. He stood and watched, and for once they didn't seem to mind.

"This is an interrupted hand now," Eddie Maybe said. "I don't like playing from an interrupted hand, it's bad luck."

"Nickel stakes and he's talkin' about bad luck," Mama said.

"Maybe—but you know how luck kinda spreads, Rosie, from one thing to another, good luck and bad. Never fuck with luck."

"You're a case, Eddie," Rosie said.

"A new hand, Rosie."

"Rosie," Zig said, "deal a new hand, what the hell?"

"You too?" she said. Her porn-girl's eyes flashed in her matron's face. "You shouldn't spook Zig, Ed, you know he's gotta go somewheres."

Even when very young, the brothers knew that their mother was the only one of "the wives," as they were called, who was allowed to talk business. It made them proud.

"Yeah, I gotta go somewheres, Rosie, so don't screw aroun' with my luck. Deal a new hand."

Mike would learn years later that "gotta go somewheres" meant that Zig had a "commission," a job to do. In his case, that meant a hit. But even then the boy felt something twisted in the phrase.

"Where you going, Uncle Zig?" The kid wanted to be one of the grown-ups.

"Where'm I going!" Zig laughed. Eddie and Rosie laughed too. "Don't worry 'bout where I'm going."

"*Somebody's* gotta worry about it," Eddie Maybe said, "but not your Uncle Zig."

The other two laughed uneasily and looked at Pop as though he'd said something wrong. Those looks stopped any further questions the boy might have had.

"Okay," Mama said, "a new hand." She crushed her half-smoked cigarette, scooped the cards expertly, and dealt again. "Mikey, whatsamatta, what're you standin' aroun' for, you got a load in your pants?"

*It was Mama's stock line when she wanted us out of her sight. I didn't want to get out of sight. I felt like a very small person standing before a very large door that had always been closed to me but now, finally, opened just a crack. I couldn't have said so then, but for a second I'd seen these three as they saw each other. For just a second it had been clear. And I felt, behind that door, a great darkness—a darkness that beckoned me to enter. A darkness that was alive somehow, and that marked you with a touch of class—more than a touch. And marked you too with a dangerous purpose and an inescapable obligation. I didn't know till much later that half the world watched movies about such people and tried to imitate their walks, their looks, their style, but somehow, standing there, "with a load in my pants," that day I knew why. Mama, Pop, Zig—their world made absolute sense to them. More sense to Mama and Zig than to Pop, and it was a sense that Mama and Zig welcomed and that Pop was nervous about, but it did make a kind of sense and they lived by that. Died by that. It was an acceptance of something other people tried to reject but secretly admired, even longed for. Call it the darkness on the other side of that door. Call it "noir," like the college kids do. Call it what you want. If someone has it and you don't, you stand aside for them, almost every time.*

The boy went back to the room he shared with his brother.

Alvi lay on his bed, on his belly, facing the wall. Mike said nothing to him. He sat on his bed and looked out the windows, his mind a blank now, overwhelmed, his body aching, his clothes smelling of fresh laundry. The windows faced west and south. South he could see (it seemed so far away now) the backyard he'd recently walked from, where he'd been beaten, nearly a mile off. West, there was nothing but the Mojave Desert and the Madre Mountains. And the day was so bright the light itself was brittle with brightness—a brightness so bright you can't see through it sometimes, the way you can't see in the dark.

Rose remembered all this as he walked slowly and painfully. The two sources of pain—his wounds and his memories—bled into each other. Each made the other somehow more bearable, almost as though his life meant something.

He walked among the ugly sprawl of tract houses and condos, angular behind their pastel-tinted cinderblock walls that sported logos like "Rainbow Estates" (in a desert with precious little rain) and "Spring Meadows" (the nearest meadow was about three hundred miles away). In memory he saw the desert as it used to be in this valley, and felt both urban sprawl and ancient desert to be equally unforgiving. He wanted a cigarette bad. He had smoked his last sometime last night. Maybe Zig would have one. "Can I bum a smoke before I shoot you, Zig?" he said aloud, and laughed. Zig would have laughed too. It was his kind of humor.

Mike Rose was surprised that he wasn't afraid. He was merely brutally tired. "The life energy," as Reverend Joy would call it, had left him. Every step made it worse and only the pain in his knee seemed to keep him awake.

The uniform in the guard box at his condo complex looked at him strangely as he walked through the gate, but the man was Old Vegas and said nothing. Rose thought, *Another wit-*

*ness*. He just noted this professionally, however. Somehow the memories of his childhood made it matter less, whether anyone knew, or what would happen if they did.

He couldn't go up to his place and change. His brother, Alvi, was there. Alvi was between crack-ups. Alvi's real life now was his crack-ups, and everything else was an easing off from the last and a building up to the next. He was in the build-up stage now, it was coming on fast, and Rose couldn't let him be involved in this in any way. Alvi still could not stand up to a grilling, and for the best of reasons: unlike Rose, Alvi had rejected every injunction to be tough, rejected them utterly and without compromise and with an insistence that Rose could only call integrity. Alvi made it a point of honor not to bear life, life being what it was. Rose imagined Alvi sleeping the sleep of whatever psychiatric drugs were in fashion this year, a sleep with no dreams, no remembrance, when Alvi's face was again the face of a boy. It pleased Rose to know that Alvi had slept through these last hours and might sleep through the hours to come.

If Rose died this morning, Alvi would be alone. Rose let himself think that thought fully, for a moment, then made himself stop thinking it.

He opened his garage door and sat in his car, his '72 Caddy, a white convertible. It was plenty big enough to go to sleep in, but he didn't lie down. Just started the engine, backed slowly out of the garage, and drove the narrow curves of the complex, driveways not built for anything as wide and long as a car like his, and he remembered to pull his jacket over his mother's pistol as he went past the guard.

A professional reflex, nothing more.

When things weren't so sophisticated, when only the Mob could do what corporations do now, when crime was against the law and not built into the law, there used to be a place up toward the test site, about fifty miles northwest, off U.S. 95.

Before you got to a tiny spot called Cactus Springs, up a dirt road that is still surprisingly well kept, up that dirt road a few miles, a road on which anything that moved could be spotted from the rocky crags in plenty of time, past where the road turned out of sight of the highway, there used to be a place, a kind of small resort. There, people could hide when they were hot, people could be questioned when they were abducted, and what was left of them could be disposed of in the wasteland beyond. Anything at all could go on, quietly and at leisure. That kind of place. Each Outfit had one—New York, Chicago, Kansas City, Cleveland, New Orleans. They were from another time, before the police had fleets of helicopters, before directional laser mikes could bug a place from a mile away on a clear line of sight, and before Nevada became so populated, back when everyone functional from senators on down was in somebody's pocket and proud of it. Now those little "resorts" weren't practical anymore. Nor were they needed. Vegas was big now, a million people and counting, and the bigger a city gets the more you can get away with right in the middle of town. So those little resorts are deserted now, and forgotten.

At least that was what Mike Rose had assumed when Zig left his message. He was surprised that the dirt road seemed so well tended.

Up a grade and down, and behind a small mountain that was no more than an enormous jagged rock sticking up from the desert, there it was: a warehouse-type building, a few bungalows, and a villa. Just one car. Zig's brand-new Olds. He bought a new one every year, and had ever since he'd embarked on his chosen profession. *I'll have to do something about that car, if I'm still alive when this is over. Wouldn't want it seen from the air.*

He parked his Caddy next to Zig's Olds. He half expected to find Zig in the Olds's front seat in a mess of blood and brain, having made himself his last "commission." But the Olds was clean. *He's waiting for me in one of those rooms. Watching me, probably, right now. Unless he's fallen asleep. Zig's old, after all. Even Zig, at his age, falls asleep now and then without intending to. What'll I do if he's asleep? Wake him up? It would be cruel to do that, and cowardly not to. Some choice. Be awake, Zig. Wait up for me, like a parent.*

He thought he'd check the bungalows, then the villa, then the low, large one-story building with the garage doors. Then he said aloud, "The warehouse for last? That means that's where I think Zig is. The warehouse for first, then."

He got out of the car. The drive had rested his left knee, but made it stiff. He flexed it a little, and that hurt. He checked the pistol, put it back in his belt. He felt observed now, but not in immediate danger. "Outfit guys aren't marksmen," Zig had told him once. "Outfit guys kill close up." Keeping it personal was part of Zig's signature, and he wasn't going to change now, on what he might be thinking of as his last hit. And it struck Rose that Zig, now eighty-ish, probably hadn't killed in years. Was this a sentimental journey, then, for the old man?

*It's too late or too early to be scared, or to wonder much. That's for before and after. Anyway, I'm no fucking Hamlet. I always thought Hamlet was a wimp. He wouldn't have lasted an afternoon in Vegas.*

Autumn is lovely in the desert. The air is soft. The light isn't always so hard. The sun hasn't that terrible weight, that capacity of exerting pressure and bearing down on you. These buildings housed irradicable sins. Not many miles away, atomic explosions had lit the land—from above, then from underground. Experiments for murder the Mob would have thought impractical, because what could be more unprofitable than atomic war? In this desert horrors had been contemplated and achieved, small and large, high and low, by criminals, scientists, generals, and politicians. The desert retained no memory of any of it, the way it did not retain water or blood. What a perfect place for human beings, a place where you could do anything yet leave no mark—except upon yourself.

Rose took his time walking to the warehouse. One of its large, barn-like doors was ajar enough for him to step through. Inside, through the high narrow windows, the desert lit the building with an even, almost shadowless light. In one corner there were a couple of old movie cameras, a bed, and some props. *So they made porn films here too, back when porn was still fairly primitive. Snuff films too, probably. This might be where my mother had those pictures taken. No way of knowing. Oh yes, there is. I could ask Zig. He might know. There he is, sitting on that crate.*

Zig had his back to Rose, sitting on a crate catty-corner from the porn set. *Your back to me, Zig—isn't that a little theatrical? On the other hand, you could be sitting with a gun in your lap.*

"Like the song says, Mikey"—Zig was speaking softly but the building had fine acoustics—"there's no one in the place except you and me. Have any trouble finding it?"

"I was out here a couple of times when I was a kid. I remembered."

"You're still a kid."

Zig turned around as Rose walked toward him. *Yes, there's a gun in your lap. Looks about as old as Mama's.*

Rose stopped about ten paces from Zig.

"Jesus, Mikey, you're a mess. What happened to your clothing?"

"You're not my only problem, Zig. Sorry I'm not well groomed enough for this meeting."

"So am I. These things should be done with style. You at least could've shaved."

"I need answers more than a shave."

"Answers are overrated, kid. Believe me."

"I believe you. I need them anyway."

The old man sat erect, contained. His alert, square face was closely shaved, his thin gray hair neatly combed. His clothes were the best and perfectly pressed—gray slacks, a silk shirt open at the collar, gleaming shoes. Instead of getting flabby with age he'd gotten thinner. The backs of his small hands were hairy. A bright, expensive ring shined on his pinky. His face had no color, and his eyes had grown colorless too in a strange way—no longer the gray of living eyes, but the gray of eyes in a photograph. He was left-handed, and held the pistol in that hand, casually, with no air of threat, but with total familiarity, the way a pro golfer holds a club or a baseball player a bat. There was still that air of absoluteness about him. *I wonder at what age he found it, or was he simply born with it. There's no trace on him of what he paid for it.*

"In the Outfit," Zig said, "when a guy messes up—or say he can't handle things anymore, and he's gonna crack, and cracking ain't allowed—when that happens, your friends kill you. If possible, your best friend. Me, I call that civilized."

"So do I," Mike Rose said.

"Course, anything can get messy. Undignified. Say this guy, he has things he should say—but, he don't wanna say them. Then he has to be made to say them. It's unpleasant work."

"Sounds unpleasant."

"Now, there are always specialists in that work who enjoy it. Get off on it, as you kids say. They like messy things, they like torture. Everybody has their function—God is a genius at that. Even some fuckin' maniac, he has a function, a place in life, if he can find it. The Outfit gives some-a those guys a place in life. I call *that* civilized. You?"

"I get a little impatient with those people, Zig."

"Well, you're young still. Anyway, I never enjoyed that action."

"You're all heart."

"Is this a time for sarcasm? Sarcasm's for kids. I'm tryin' to talk to you like a man."

"I appreciate that."

"You should. Anyway. Messy, I never enjoyed. I would always try to call in a specialist, if messy—"

"Torture—"

"—was required. Sometimes there was none around. Then I would have to do the duty. I was a professional. I did what was necessary. I didn't shirk. It left a bad taste, but whataya gonna do?" Then with a sudden weariness he said, "We're dead, kid."

"We were born dead, Zig."

"I should have studied Kabbalah, like my father wanted for me to. I'd know better some of the crap you come out with. For a dago, Mikey, you'd make a good Jew. But that we're dead—that's not philosophy. That's what some people out there want, and they get what they want."

"Not always."

"Christ, I wish you looked decent this morning. It's unpleasant to look at you, Mikey. No offense."

Rose smiled. "None taken." Unlike most people, who look younger when they smile, smiling always made Mike Rose look older.

"So whataya think?" Zig said in a total change of tone. Now his voice was sitting on a bar stool and had all the time in the world. "Do *you* think Kennedy was a Mob hit? The CIA? Do *you* think Oswald acted alone?"

Rose smiled again, and looked even older. This was, he realized, their last conversation, and neither was eager for it to end.

Rose said, "I grew up in Vegas, Zig. I know a setup when I see one. Three shots sound like three shots. When a hundred people say they heard a lotta bullets whizzing over their heads from two, three directions—and when some of those people are combat vets—they probably heard what they heard. No reason for them to invent that."

"No reason whatever."

"We've talked about this a couple of times in the past, Zig, remember."

"I do remember, Mikey. And what did I tell you? Let's see if *you* remember." His voice was no longer casual.

"You told me Kennedy was killed by marksmen, and Outfit guys aren't marksmen. Outfit guys kill up close."

"Real close. We gotta. We gotta be *sure*. I mean, Benny Siegel was hit by rifles, but the shooters stood at the window about five yards away from him. That's as far away as Mob guys get."

"Let's hear it for intimacy. What's the point, Zig?"

"What's the point of anything, Mikey? I'm trying to tell you something."

"So tell me."

"Impatience again. Grow up. I'm an old, old man. Lemme take my time."

Very softly Rose said, "Take all the time you need, Zig."

Zig's hand caressed the pistol on his thigh. "I will, Mikey, I will."

Rose's pistol was still in his belt, *but unless he shoots me in the head I'll have time to shoot him too. He knows that. Maybe that's the deal. Both of us.* The tightness in his body eased. Zig saw that unmistakable sign of Rose's willingness.

Zig continued, "So, Outfit guys weren't the shooters—in Dallas. We were approached. *I* was approached. I laughed. 'You arrange where I can hit him in a hotel room, when he's with one of those broads of his, that would be a maybe.'"

"Who approached you?"

"A middleman who thought he was a somebody, but he had middleman written all over him. *You* know what happens to middlemen in deals like that: they get very accident prone. This guy, he had his accident real quick."

"Who was he?"

"Whata you care? You gonna call the *New York Times*? Anyway, they were gonna have to do their own hit, that was clear. So I said, 'Why don't you give me the *real* commission.' You know what that was, Mikey?"

"I can guess."

"You was always a smart kid. Smartest kid I ever knew. You and Alvi. We were proud of you."

"Thanks."

"Proud of your *brains*, I mean."

"I know what you mean."

"So, like you guess, the *real* commission—lemme put it this way: Kennedy was hit just before Thanksgiving? Well, those shooters never got no Christmas presents. They were pretty good shots, but they weren't smart like you. *They were the connection.* They were the only ones who could rip the whole thing open. Just one name: the guy that hired them. That woulda led to all the other names. He had to go, that suck-face middleman, and the guys who knew his name had to go."

"You knew the name."

"No, I had another middleman. It's a great country for middlemen."

"And for accidents."

"Anyway, those shooters, they *had* to go. It's hard to imagine anybody being dumb enough not to know that, but like I said, they weren't Outfit guys. An Outfit guy is always looking to see where he fits in the deal. These assholes thought they were making history or something."

"They forgot that history is just another deal."

"They couldn't forget what they never knew, kid. Anyway, I hit the shooters. There were three crews, I hit two of them. Six guys: shooter, spotter, guard—three a crew. Six. It made your father very nervous."

"He disappeared around then."

"He sure did."

"He didn't get any Christmas presents either, Zig. We waited for him on Christmas. Mama had been saying he was away on business for a few weeks. She stopped saying that on Christmas. Me and Alvi weren't dummies, even at that age. We weren't going to believe that shit on Christmas."

"What'd you get your father that year?"

"A present. Forget it."

Zig sighed from a far place inside him. "Your father."

Rose let his eyes drift over to the porn set. *It ought to be in a museum—The Museum of Unnatural History. Those old cameras on the tripods. That bed probably has stains all over it. Stains upon stains. So my father partnered up with Zig for those hits. So what? It wouldn't have been the first time. And something soured and he didn't make it home. Am I supposed to be shocked, Zig? Because it was about some fucking politician named Kennedy? You've gotta believe that some people are more important than others to be shocked at that.*

"Look at me when I talk, kid."

Rose looked at him.

"Answers are overrated."

"You said that, Zig."

"Answers don't answer a goddamn thing. You get an answer, and you're still right back where you started. Big fucking deal."

"You're getting philosophical, Zig."

"I apologize." Then the sigh again. "Your father. I liked that man. Very much, I liked him. He had your mother and I didn't, but that was just how it was. Your mother would never sleep with a Jew anyway. Even me. I knew that would never change. Your generation, it's different, but ours—she wasn't prejudiced, you understand. And she . . . loved me." It was Zig's opportunity to look away.

"We figured that out a long time ago, Zig," Mike Rose said softly and kindly.

"Women . . . they're disgusting. Only *she* was not. She was the only one who knew the score."

*You don't know about the photographs, do you, Zig? Lucky you.*

"So what's the score, Zig?"

"Don't be stupid. Anyway, she'd never sleep with a Jew. She wasn't prejudiced. And she was no more a good Catholic than I am a good Jew. It's just that . . . there are lines you cross, and there are lines you don't, and with everybody it's different, and that was a line she couldn't cross. It wasn't prejudice."

*It was her way of keeping your balls in the palm of her hand. Killing you is one thing, Zig, but telling you something like that is another. I'll pass.*

Zig's eyes were fixed now on the porn paraphernalia at the other end of the building.

"Your mother . . ."

*Or do you know about the photographs?*

Now Zig looked at Rose again.

"Your father. What was it with him? What made him so fucking nervous? He was a stand-up guy, don't get me wrong, but he was a *nervous* stand-up guy. And that made other people nervous. People who don't tolerate to be nervous very well."

"People like you?"

"People I had to tell the truth to. We tell the truth in our business, kid. To each other. We keep secrets, we bob and weave, we play angles, but when it comes down to it we tell the truth—to each other—or we're dead. The guys who last are the guys who don't get nervous and who tell the truth to their friends."

"My father didn't last."

"What did he think that made him so nervous those weeks? What was he feeling? What? What was he going to do? I mean, what . . . did . . . he . . . give . . . a SHIT who was President of the fucking United States? Didn't he know better than that? Didn't he know the score, hadn't he been playing the game, the *real* game, for years and years? And what did Eddie Maybe . . . what did Eddie Maybe care?"

"It got to him, huh?"

"Scared him. They were shooting off fucking *atom bombs*, just over that hill *right there*—that didn't scare him. He'd whacked guys he didn't even know just because Benny or Moony or somebody told him to. Doing it is enough. Doing something is *enough*. Do you understand me, you little shit?"

"What I do is enough."

"Sure it is."

"At least, it used to be."

"Before *what?*" Zig was interested in this new data.

"Before recently."

"Then you're getting soft," Zig said softly.

"I was always soft."

"That's true. In a hard kinda way. Like your old man. Ah, Mikey . . . I always liked talking to you, kid."

"Thanks, Zig." Rose knew this was a great compliment.

"I never talked to many people."

"How could you?"

"Right. How could I? Remember all our talks, about history, about politics? I read. That always surprised you. I'm the kinda Jew who reads. Like Meyer Lansky. He read all the time. I didn't have his brains, but I could read. And you're the kinda wop who reads. Like Joe Bonanno. He even wrote a book. And Charlie Lucky."

"Lucky Luciano *read?*"

"You know how Charlie Lucky died?"

"A heart attack. In Italy."

"A heart attack, in Italy, on the way to an airport, where he was gonna meet this guy, and they were gonna rewrite this guy's movie script about Charlie Lucky's life."

"No shit?"

"No shit."

Mike Rose had been standing a long time. His knee throbbed. But there was no sitting down, and no stepping back from this moment. Zig wanted to die where he'd often killed—in this building. Because of course that was what went on here, besides pornography: questionings and killings, out of sight of the bungalows and in out of the desert sun and the chilly night.

*But why are you talking so much? You're making the whole thing ridiculous.*

"You're a loose end, kid," Zig said finally. "Like me. I'm a loose end, now. Things have been stirred up lately. You know how, you know why, you know who stirred it up. No need to think about that now. Nobody's fault. Couldn't be helped. At first I was aggravated about it, but not anymore. Now I'm just tired. Tired is a way of going soft too, Mikey. Don't get too tired. Don't be like your father. One week he was a man, and the next week he was too tired to be a man anymore."

"What made him tired, Zig?"

"I was tellin' you. It got to be too fucking much. 'Too mucking fuch,' as he used to say. Too mucking fuch. For him. It was like he'd been sleepwalking all his life, and *boom*, he was awake. Who the hell asked him to wake up? Kennedy? Nobody. God, your mother . . . she loved that bum. When I say 'bum'—"

"It's a figure of speech."

"A figure of speech. Right. She loved him. I don't know. 'Member she'd tell him, 'It's 'cause you look like Frank Sinatra'? To tease him."

"He looked like Tony Bennett."

"That was the tease. You and your brother look like Frank Sinatra, kinda. That's the tease."

"It's just 'cause we're thin. So was Mama's father and brothers. We take after the Veneticos, not the Rossellinis. But it used to bug Pop."

"When she was dancing at the Flamingo, when Benny opened it, she had a thing with Sinatra. A little thing, a weekend or something. Or at least she *said* she did. You knew that. Drove your father nuts when she'd say that. And that's why she said it. 'He looks like Frank Sinatra, my husband. That's why I married him.'"

Rose added, "'Frank Sinatra was not a disappointment.' That was also something she used to say. But all the times he played Vegas, while Pop was alive and after he . . . 'went away on business,' she never went to see Sinatra's shows."

"'Cause Eddie Maybe woulda killed her. Even from the grave, he woulda killed her. And she *liked* him for that, respected that, *expected* that. I mean, Eddie was nervous but he was no mouse. Rosie would not have married a mouse. Anyway, she loved him. 'He looks like Frank Sinatra.' That was her answer. That's how stupid answers are."

"You got a cigarette, Zig?"

Zig reached into his shirt pocket with the hand that wasn't touching the gun, and flipped the pack to Rose. Chesterfields. Rose lit one, inhaled deeply, and started to toss the pack back, but Zig said, "Keep it. I'm tired of them."

"Where's Eddie's grave, Zig?"

"Out there somewhere." He nodded toward the desert. "Not a grave, really."

"Really?"

"I gotta laugh."

"I hope it's funny."

"Don't get sentimental, don't be a schmuck. Who cares, when a guy is dead? You're not *that* soft. You're not a fool."

"So what's so funny?"

"With the new development going on—the new goddamn 'family Vegas'—people wonder why they don't dig up no bodies. All this construction these last years, all over the desert, and no bodies. They don't dig 'em up 'cause we didn't bury 'em. You strip them down, take them way out there off some little road, dump 'em naked. With the coyotes and the foxes and the insects and the birds, how long do you think they stay there? In a few days, there's a piece of 'em here, a piece of 'em there, a piece five miles off. Everything gets scattered in places where only the animals hide, where *nobody* goes. Sometimes you cut off the head and bury it deep. If you're being thorough. And if it's important. Usually . . . who gives a shit?"

Rose didn't want to be surprised, but he was. He didn't see, really, what was so shocking about that information, but it shocked him. *What does this old man want of me, that he's telling me all this? I should just shoot him now. God knows he deserves it. But it's gotta be his way. And his way, I don't know why, is words. It looks like he means to say all the words he's never said. Okay, old man. Okay.*

"Your father," Zig was saying, "he was nervous. Worse than nervous. Spooked. One horny, lying Irish fuck, son of a gangster just like you, what did it matter that the fuck was a president? *We* got him elected, for Christ's sake. You know how close that election was? Without Chicago he would have lost Illinois, and without Illinois he would have lost the whole sideshow. And you *know* who gave him Chicago? Sam Giancana and Jimmy Hoffa. They talk about Guatemala, they talk about Mexico, they should have been in *Chicago* in 1960. Free elections, my ass."

How many times had Zig been in this building, demanding that somebody talk? How many times had he hit them, cut them, burned them, torn them, all too literally, limb from limb? How many times had he ripped off ears, fingers, testicles, penises, breasts? All for talk. Talk, talk, talk. And how many had talked, not for life, which they had given up hope of when they entered this building, but for quicker death? But how many of them had talked as much as Zig was talking now? Very few. And so he talked and talked and had to talk. It was the unforgivable sin in his world, the one sin he had not committed: talking. So now the old man sinned, and sinned on, and couldn't stop his sinning. As Rose looked at Zig's helplessness, he thought of how the FBI reported Mob informers giving them thousands of hours of testimony—one informer, thousands of hours each. He had never believed it. He believed it now. And Lucky Luciano died on his way to rewrite a script about his life—a life that could not be rewritten. At least Zig wasn't attempting that. Zig was torturing himself and talking. And the cameras and stained bedding at the other end of the room—and the gleaming photographs in his mother's black box—were a silent chorus of agreement with the old man's incontinent defecation of talk.

Zig was saying, "He'd come to *this* town, Kennedy, the city *we* created, he came here with that fucking Sinatra and that fucking WASP Lawford, and we'd line up the broads to suck his dick, suck it in the steamroom, suck it in the bedroom, *suck it under the table during the floor show*, for Christ's sake, Sinatra singing while some broad is sucking that guy, that guy—he was just like us, he and his old man and his brother, *they* had guys whacked. If his own guys couldn't do it, he or some flunky would ask us, direct, indirect, who gave a damn? Before the election, after, who gave a damn? *What* was there for your father to be so fucking nervous about? 'This is history, Zig,' he said to me, 'we're fucking with history.' So what *isn't* history? And who gives a shit? And what did *he* know from history, Eddie Maybe? He never read a book in his fucked life. I don't know, Mikey, your father, he started thinking like a broad, like Marilyn Monroe or somebody. We bought mayors, we bought cops, judges, senators, governors, every kind of prick who eventually becomes president, we bought 'em, we always have, we always will, isn't *that* history? Your fucking father."

*My father died in this room. I know that now. Zig killed him. Mama had known, and they'd stayed tight friends anyway. I have some answers. Big fucking deal. They change nothing. Zig was right. I have something else too. A kind of helplessness. He's begging me to kill him. All his other friends are dead, I'm the only friend he has left. He'd killed his friend, killed many friends, and he is begging to be killed by one. To be executed by a stranger horrifies him. Zig's afraid of something, after all. I wish I was angry. That would be nice.*

"Fuck," Zig said, "I feel like a melting suppository."

*I don't have the stomach for thousands of hours of testimony. Let's get this over with.*

"So, Zig, the guys had to know how far Pop had gone with his nervousness?"

"Right."

"They couldn't just kill him. They had to *do* him."

"Right. Smart kid."

"*You* had to do him. Right here."

"Right here."

*That was thirty years ago, plus a few weeks. You look at faded dark stains on a concrete floor along the far wall in a building that has garage doors, and you think oil slicks. You don't think blood. Some of their screams must still be clinging to the walls. About fifty miles down the road there's a city that squats ugly in the day and glitters pretty at night, and millions of people a year fly to it, drive to it, take trains to it. And they come from all the other cities, and most of those cities have big rooms just like this one. And you took a plane to other cities in other countries and there were more rooms like this, above ground, below ground, with uniformed thugs, thugs without uniforms, what was the difference?* Rose felt like he was standing in the dead center of the world.

*I could refuse. I could walk away. He could put that gun to his head and forgive himself. But he's his own stranger, isn't he? It would be just as horrifying. He needs for a friend to do it. Hi, friend.*

"There used to be a meat hook there, kid. I wonder who took it down. I wonder why. That would be an answer, wouldn't it? Fuck it. You beat a guy silly. Some guys, that's all it takes. They spill everything, you kill 'em easy, you don't even dirty your suit. Be back in town for breakfast. Some guys, they're tougher; or maybe they don't *know* anything— but you gotta find out. No loose ends. You smash their ankles. You smash their kneecaps. Some of us enjoy doin' that, some don't, and some, like me, it don't matter. Then that hook that used to be there, that meat hook . . . if they haven't spilled by then, you pick 'em up and slam them down on that meat hook, so it goes right up their asshole. *That's* when your suit got dirty, and your shoes. Some of my 'colleagues,' I guess you'd call them, that's when they get really angry—*angry* at this schmuck for bleeding on them, for shitting on them, for making them work in a pool of piss and shit and blood. I guess they have a beef. 'Unsanitary working conditions.' Jesus Christ. But I always thought that was funny, that's when I'd laugh, at these colleagues getting angry at a guy we're killing 'cause he's bleeding on us—but they would really get angry, and I would *really* laugh. And then . . . the guy's got a meat hook all the way up his ass, he *knows* he ain't goin' nowhere now, but maybe he's still not talking, maybe he's that tough . . . or *maybe he's got nothing to know*, he'd talk if he could but *he hasn't a clue.* But—"

"You gotta find out," Rose said.

"I gotta find out. So now you do things to their teeth, their ears, their eyes, their balls, their cock. If what's left of them is still blubbering 'I don't know'—because by then the vocal chords are all gone with the screaming, there's no more screaming, there's just this kind of gurgly whisper—well, then, you believe the sonofabitch. If he doesn't know by then, he *really* doesn't know. You pop him between the eyes and it's over.

"I told the boys, when they gave me the commission, I said, 'He's only nervous, that's how this guy is, he ain't gonna go to the G or the *New York Times* or anybody.' They looked at me funny. The look that means, 'Shut up, or it could be you.' The only time anybody in the Outfit ever gave me that look. The *only* time. I resented that. And I resented your *father* for making me look bad. But as it turned out, he hadn't ratted, he'd never rat. But it took a long time, it took a lot of . . . treatment . . . to be sure. It was a long time before my colleagues were satisfied, let's say. Some things, kid, take a damn long time."

*There wasn't any more time now. Not for me, not for him. There were still questions I wanted to ask, especially about Mama, but Zig was right, there wasn't much point in answers, there wasn't much point in solving this kind of mystery. No answer could be satisfying enough. No answer could make up for knowing the question.*

*The only answer was not to know the question.*

Rose slowly pulled his mother's pistol from his belt, held it at his side.

"You did that to my *father?*"

"I did that to my friend."

Zig slowly raised his pistol and leveled it at Rose. Maybe Zig would kill him yet, out of an old reflex not to leave witnesses.

"Mikey, you know why you're here."

"Why, Zig? Tell me." Rose's voice too was now a gurgly whisper.

"That wasn't a question. You *know* why."

"Tell me. Talk me to death."

"You little bastard, you know."

Rose still held the pistol at his side.

"Mikey, I've done . . . questionable things."

"It's a little late to start questioning them, ain't it, Zig?"

"It's never too late to fuck up."

"You're breaking my heart."

And he was. That was the aching in Rose. The thing he had always called his heart was breaking.

"You gotta do it, Mikey. You're the only one. The only one who can make it count. You can't not do it. I need it, Mikey. I need it from you."

"You don't deserve it from me. Just *because* from me it will count. You don't deserve that of me, Zig."

"If you don't do it, you little prick, I'll kill you where you stand."

"That's not gonna work, Zig. If I do it just to save my ass, it don't count anymore. Funny life, ain't it?"

*"Mikey."*

"Did my father beg to die?"

"Yes. He begged."

"But even then you didn't do it."

"Not till we were sure. And even then . . . not for a while. We had to be more than sure. The stakes were high."

"The stakes are high now. They've never been higher."

Rose stared with fascination at something he had never seen: Zig Feldman's face melting like a candle in fear. *I am the first person in his experience—with the exception of my mother, I guess—whom Zig can't bring himself to kill. But he can't leave this building either. Can't bear to live after all he's finally said. Can't even kill himself, 'cause that wouldn't count, not in his book. Maybe staying in the building till he died of thirst would count a little. He's disciplined enough for that. But if that's the only option, it wouldn't count enough.*

"You're not gonna get it from me, Zig," Rose said. "Kill me, if you're gonna kill me."

Rose stepped closer to the old man. Only two steps away now. He looked down the barrel of Zig's weapon. It was an automatic. Zig's hand was shaking. That alone could set it off.

"What are you *made* of?" Zig said.

"Broken pieces. Maybe if you pull the trigger they'll come together one last time."

They looked into each other's eyes. Neither was sure what he saw, or what the other saw. And that uncertainty was the last unbearable thing.

Except that there is no last unbearable thing.

Zig dropped the automatic. It went off when it hit the floor. The sound was enormous, echoing as the screams of years ago had echoed, as the bombs over the mountain had echoed, but all those echoes of past and present were the only scream that Zig would scream, except soundlessly, with his mouth closed, his lips trembling, his eyes . . .

Rose met Zig's eyes. The explosion in the old man's eyes was louder, and echoed farther, than the discharge of his gun. *I don't owe the man, but I owe what is in his eyes.*

Then Zig's eyes fell. His hairy hands shook. His knees shook. His old lips trembled. His color drained. His soul was leaving him, but he wasn't going to die of that. He lifted his eyes to the younger man again. They weren't really eyes anymore.

Rose turned from him, and felt with the flesh of his back what his turning had done to Zig's eyes. His mother's pistol weighed in his hand. It seemed to stop him and force him to turn back toward Zig. He watched as though from a distance while his own arm raised and pointed the weapon at the old man. Zig's eyes that were no longer eyes looked at Rose with something that was no longer sight. Rose gazed deep into them, and his arm was his own again, and his hand, and his finger, as he pulled the trigger. *I fired, the recoil shook my bones, chilled my spine, lit my eyes. I fired and in my chest the broken pieces of my heart sought each other and a sweetness filled my mouth, a bloody honey. I fired and understood everything, understood nothing. I fired and knew that God was watching, watching from the farthest and the nearest place of all, and I wasn't alone for the first time in forever. I fired again, that the watching would continue, but the chambers were empty. I fired again, kept pulling the trigger, but there was only the cold sound of metal upon metal, nothing upon nothing. Then only my trembling.*

Rose fired every bullet into Zig's groin. Zig was screaming, *but I didn't hear it as screaming, I heard it as a kind of melody.* And the knees of Mike Rose weakened, and he crumpled, lay on his back. Rose listened to Zig screaming while staring at the featureless ceiling. Lying there, he slowly became as much himself as he could again. And had a thought that he could identify, with some comfort, as his own. He thought that all Zig's life Zig had wished for his last moments to be dignified. *Poor Zig, with your murderous dignity. You can't be dignified with six bullets in your groin. They don't kill you right away, either.*

Zig was undignified for quite a while before he died.

*H*e did to Zig's body what Zig had done to his father's.
Stripped it. Dragged it into the desert.

Zig's nakedness was hard for Rose to take. Ripped and
bloody around the groin, but also softer and spongier than
he'd expected. The way the flesh sank so deeply wherever he
clutched it, and the skin so gentle and womanly in the places
without hair. And the blood got all over Mike Rose. On his
hands and pants and cuffs. The stuff of Zig's intestines stuck
to his shoes. Zig hadn't said what they did with the clothes.
Rose buried them in the desert. The pistol too. Left Zig's car
in the building. Wiped his prints.

As Rose performed these acts a phrase said itself to him at
irregular intervals: "thousands of hours of testimony."

*Before, it was only the world I had to live in. Now I'm part
of what makes the world what it is.*

He sat at the wheel of his car with no idea where to go. His
knee ached terribly. The fact that there were people back in
the city who still wanted to kill him was a distant thought that

seemed to apply to someone else. The urge to survive, which had propelled him through every experience of his life, seemed distant as well, like a sentence spoken in a language he no longer understood. He only knew he had to get away from this place, or he'd begin listening for the small sounds of the beings who even now, he knew, were nibbling at Zig.

He drove back down the well-kept dirt road. With a dim professional reflex he wondered who kept it, and who put the fix in to keep it kept, and was it an old order automatically renewed by some minor Mob functionary who'd inherited a list of fixes from another minor Mob functionary; or was it something more conscious and current? He forgot the questions as he asked them.

*I know a good place to go. I'll go to church.*

He took a long drag from one of Zig's cigarettes as he hit the turn on the highway where the city came into view. The unfiltered Chesterfield was a harsh taste from another time. Sinatra's brand. Why did he know that? It was one of the games the grown-ups had played. "What's Dean Martin smoke?" Rosie would say. "Viceroys," Zig would say. "Kools," Eddie Maybe would counter. "Fifty says Dino smokes Viceroys." "A hundred says it's Kools." "What's Marilyn Monroe smoke?" "She don't." "I saw her smoking at the Sands." "She don't carry, she bums." "For fifty?" "For a hundred." And then they'd laugh their smoky, confident laughter that Mike and his brother so loved to hear.

*I'll go to church, that's what.* What had the chamber of commerce called Las Vegas? "A city of churches and schools."

The city spread out before him in its valley. They don't make postcards of the view from the northwest. It was as though a concrete fungus was feeding on the desert, spreading west, east, and north, a growth with shiny scabs. It filled the valley to the base of the mountains on the east, where the Mormons' six spikelike spires shone over their massive temple. Soon the fungus would reach the mountains to the west. The angular, oddly shaped casinos on the Strip were tiny in the distance. The farthest, the black wedge of the Luxor pyramid, was the only form that had an identity from miles away, the true identity of its shape: the builders, after all, had modeled it after the world's largest tomb. Even in miniature from many miles away it said, "Death."

*I should leave now. I should have left a long time ago. But I can't. I don't. In a few hours, under a purple sky, it'll all light up and throb in all its colors and all its nakedness and shamelessness. It'll sing and cry and strip for strangers, one big dancing hooker of a town, leading everybody on with the neon in her eyes, playing for stakes so high—your immortal soul—that no bookie'll give odds.*

*I loved shooting you, Zig. I loved it, Mama. You knew I would. I never felt anything like it. It's the only time I ever had God watching me. I recommend it to all seekers after truth—which is my profession, after all.*

"Facts aren't necessarily the truth," the Reverend Joy had told him often. *Gotta get to church.*

He did not think of Mr. Sherman, and he did not think of Mr. Lampedusa. Nor of Mrs. Sherman. Nor even of Alvi, who had woken suddenly from the far place of a Thorazine sleep, had been frightened, and wondered where his brother had gone.

The first time Mike Rose had seen Gino "The Gentleman" Lampedusa, Rose was still Michael Rossellini and Gino was not yet "The Gentleman." In those days he was called "The Touch." He was thin faced, efficient, vicious, and trusted. He was easy to trust because his eyes hid nothing. So the first time he came to the house, ringing the bell on the kitchen door, and an eight-year-old Michael Rossellini opened it for him, the boy was frightened. The eyes of "The Touch" did not hide their discomfort in the presence of children, nor their disapproval that a man with his mission should be met at the door by a boy. The child felt somehow, and automatically, wrong. The man didn't even address him, but called out sharply, "Eddie Maybe!"—as though he had every right to take such a liberty in another's house.

The boy was shocked at this rudeness. He lived among Sicilians who never entered another's house without a gift—a box of pastries, a bottle of wine—no matter what the errand. The Jews he knew had the same custom. Except for Mormons at school, into whose homes he was never invited, he had no experience of others. The cut of Gino's clothes, the look of his eye, and something purposeful in his posture marked him as Sicilian and Mob, but he had no white bakery box or bottle in his hand, nothing for their home but his force and impatience. When Eddie came into the kitchen his eyes shined with obedience.

"Gino, come in, come in. This is my kid Mikey."

The Touch didn't even look at the boy.

"Where can we talk?"

"Mikey, go outside, or go to your room, somethin'."

The men went into the card room. The boy stayed in the kitchen, very still, and did what he was forbidden to do: tried to listen. But all he heard was The Touch's harsh low tones, punctuated by his father's "Yeah, Gino," and "Sure, Gino," and, "It'll be done, absolutely." Before they were through the boy went outside. After the cool, acrid air of the house, the Mojave's dense heat was a cleansing shock. The boy's feelings, for which he had no words, coagulated into a sulk. He wanted to defy his father and that disturbing man. The man's sleek black Lincoln in the driveway was empty. The boy knew the hierarchy of this world, knew that if the man had no driver he was still in the lower echelons. This made him resent the man's intimidations all the more. He sat himself painfully on the sun-hot metal of the Lincoln's fender—an act of disrespect he could get away with. When The Touch came out he recognized the gesture, but his eyes flashed not with malice but with regard—something they had never shown Mike's father. It was one of those thousand moments when the boy decided he would never be like his father.

Gino Lampedusa had learned manners since. It was said that Frank Costello himself had given the lecture, and that practically overnight The Touch had become The Gentleman, exaggerating the proprieties with carefully calibrated, insulting gradations that did the work of intimidation far more effectively than his old rudeness.

Gino the Gent was in his sixties now, powerful and feared. And what he wanted to find out about Mike Rose was what others had once wanted to find out about his father: was he a loose end? In this sense Rose had become his father after all.

Mr. Sherman had a more corporate way of putting it. For him, Rose was "an interruption in the loop." Rose had heard him say it, and had enjoyed the phrase.

"You don't look like a detective, you look like a mobster."

"I'm a victim of style abuse. Blame it on my role models."

"Are you trying to be humorous?"

"Mr. Sherman, pay me enough and I'll undergo fashion therapy. Surely they must have that. Then I'll look like what you think I should, and we can resume business."

"We have no business," Mr. Sherman said.

Mike Rose did not like WASPs. It was a fundamental, unforgiving bigotry. He would make the occasional exception for a White Anglo-Saxon Protestant woman, but the men got on his nerves. They never seemed to realize that they too were an ethnicity. The upper-status ones dressed alike, walked alike, spoke alike, and had the same repertoire of facial expressions; the lower in status did too, but they had more variety—cowboys, working stiffs, whatever. But both upper and lower seemed to have no awareness that they were as noticeable, distinct, and predictable, in their manner, as Sicilians, Jews, or Mexicans. Just because even if you were Japanese you had to dress like a WASP to do big business, didn't mean WASP wasn't an ethnicity.

Mr. Sherman was a prime example of the type. Tall, stiff, expensively cut but dull clothing, and eyes that said, "I reject imagination as a matter of principle." He was white, but he could never have been mistaken for an equally white Irishman, Frenchman, or Pole. Mike Rose and Mr. Sherman loathed each other at first sight—and to Rose the mystery was not Mr. Sherman's technological variation on crime, but how and why he had ever married Mrs. Sherman, who was nothing if not imaginative. But this was a failing Rose was aware of: his inability to figure how or why WASP men chose their women, and vice versa. ("There *are* some WASP guys I like," Rose had once said to Zig. "I like some Texans. And I like some Southerners." "They're different," Zig had said. "They even die different. Know why? The colored. They got the influence of the colored.")

Mr. Sherman had insisted that he and Mike Rose had no business. That was a WASP's way of saying that you're nothing. Rose would have resented this in any case, but especially because in Mr. Sherman's case it was a lie.

They were in a high suite at the Mirage, facing south. The city glittered below, the cold blue of Caesar's and the colder red of the Rio reflected on the window pane, while a couple of miles south a bright, thick beam shot straight up from the top of the Luxor pyramid—they said that airplanes circling over Los Angeles three hundred miles away could see it clearly. *Like a shining highway of souls departing the tomb.*

"Mr. Sherman, I didn't invite myself into this action, my invitation was engraved by your wife."

"You're just her messenger boy—"

*Don't push your luck, you WASP fuck.*

"—and I want to deal with her," Mr. Sherman finished.

"She seems to think you'll do her bodily harm."

"She has nothing to fear, Mr. Rose."

"Well, that makes her very special."

"I'm not going to fence with you, Mr. Rose, and I am *not* going to do business with you. Tell Claire that."

"I figure everybody's entitled to one mistake per deal, and you're making yours. Here's how it is: I represent her, you want to deal, you deal with me. You harm a hair on her chinny-chin-chin, and you have to face me. Think you're up to it?"

"You're leaving, Mr. Rose."

*I can't tell if he has guts or if he's just too used to getting his own way. This failure of perception is making me really uncomfortable.*

"I said, Mr. Rose, that you're leaving."

There were two younger WASPs in the next room. One wore a blue suit.

"The nice way's nice, but the hard way is more interesting. See you around, Mr. Sherman."

"That's not likely."

Rose let him have the last word and left. The Mirage was more a mall than a casino or a hotel, and as Rose walked past the desk in the lobby he paused to watch the sharks swimming in the enormous tank that ran the length of the wall behind Check-In. *And they say that Steve Wynn, the builder of this joint, doesn't have a sense of humor.*

The Mr. Shermans of the world—and the Steve Wynns, for that matter—were very dangerous in a not very interesting sort of way, and they brought out in Rose a side of himself that he didn't trust: the wise-cracking character who was taking too long to grow up.

Now, ripped, bloody, in pain, smelling of wastes that Zig had dripped upon him and of his own fatigue, Mike Rose drove into the city without a thought of Mr. Lampedusa or Mr. Sherman, or with any concern for what he viewed now as mere technicalities: the "why" of why they wanted to kill him, and how it had all come about.

*It's the only time I ever felt that God was watching me. Is that in your father's Kabbalah, Zig?*


He took U.S. 95 into downtown and got off on Stewart. There were quicker ways to where he was going, but Stewart was the old way, the way he had long gone from his old apartment, just off what was now a Stewart Avenue slum, or from his office, two blocks south on Fremont. Like many who'd lived in Vegas for decades, he was confused at times by the greedy growth of the last few years, and he would find himself lost in his own city. They tended to take the old ways, the old Vegans, partly out of reflex and partly as a way to keep hold of a world they were losing.

Red lights are longer in Vegas than in most places, much longer, and Rose idled at the light at Stewart and Las Vegas Boulevard for what seemed an endless time. But he was past impatience. He lit another of Zig's cigarettes, looked up, and there was that wraith.

It was only four or five blocks from this traffic light to his office. How long had it been since he'd given her the hundred? How had she spent the last—was it six, was it seven or more, hours? She wasn't crossing the street, she wasn't looking at anything in particular; she was merely standing, staring vaguely north. She had a slightly arched way of standing that seemed like swaying—but that was the breeze rippling her skirt. She actually stood quite still, and she started when he beeped his horn twice. She looked around. When he beeped again she looked at him. It took her a moment to recognize him. The light changed to green, but he didn't accelerate. Instead he motioned her toward his car. The vehicle behind him honked, and the vehicle behind that. Rose said, "Get in." She couldn't quite comprehend, and he leaned over and opened the door on the passenger side. She got in gracefully, and her grace surprised him. He hit the gas before she'd closed the door but that didn't faze her. The door closed on its own with the acceleration.

He had become accustomed to how, when you were "in a situation," as Zig would have put it, you kept running into people of that situation. *"Synchronicity," the Reverend Joy calls it, as though that explains it.* Whatever it was, it was a fact of life, and a professional had to be on guard for it. It made the world a combat zone in which no matter where you went somehow you were always behind enemy lines. There was something in the nature of things that wouldn't let you hide or keep a secret.

*I'm thinking again, Mama. You didn't think, you figured. That's very different. Whenever you wanted to make me uncomfortable you'd turn those porn girl's eyes on me—I didn't know what they were then, but I felt the charge—and you'd say, "So what are you, The Thinker? Go sit on the toilet, that's a good place to think."*

The wraith was staring at him. *If you weren't so skeletal you'd be beautiful—and if your long, golden hair weren't so dirty, and if you didn't stink.*

"You smell now," she said. "You didn't before. You're like me now. Do you want your money back?"

"Didn't you buy a gun yet?"

"I don't buy."

"So what are you going to do with the money?"

"I'm saving it for graduation," she said.

"You look pretty graduated to me."

She tried to smile girlishly, but she was so pale, with her skin pulled so tight on the bones of her face, she looked more like a girl who'd died smiling.

Just west of Pecos Road they passed the bleak, fenced building with the sign that read: City of Las Vegas Detention and Enforcement.

"Is that where you're taking me?" she said.

"Then why would I drive past it?"

"To get me to talk."

"And what would I want you to talk about?"

She smiled her dead-girl smile again and kept her eyes on him.

He said, "Detention and Enforcement's a place for fuck-ups. Grifters, muggers. I've never known a *real* criminal to spend an afternoon there."

"Where are we going?"

"What do you care?"

She didn't, so she said again, "You smell too now."

They passed trailer parks, mobile homes, a cinderblock house with old red gas pumps in the yard and three horses standing at the fence watching traffic. "Horses," the girl said. And everywhere, swatches of desert recently flattened for construction, houses and apartments half built, work crews intent on the task of making an unlivable place livable. *Is God watching them as He watched me? He's watching this girl, that's for sure. She feels His eyes on her all the time. She can't stand it, and can't live without it. I've just learned what that means. It's all I want to feel again. No matter who I have to kill. But I wouldn't feel it if I shot this girl. Or strangled her. That's good to know. You only feel it with particular people, then. How wise of God. This constant demand of His, that we choose and choose, and choose carefully. Zig and Pop followed orders. That's not choosing carefully. How unwise of them. You can lose your soul that way, I'll bet. This girl is trying to get rid of hers, and clutching it at the same time. A familiar feeling. Must be why we're so easy with each other. Maybe I'll marry her. Maybe that's why I'm taking her to church.*

"Will you marry me?" he said.

"Not yet."

*You didn't come clean all the way, Zig. Didn't mention how taking Pop out left Mama for you. Couldn't 'fess that, not even to yourself. You liked to think better of yourself, and who can blame you for that?*

*Mama and Pop. Me and Alvi hid in the spaces between them. Pop couldn't find us there, and Mama never tried—she seemed to think a certain amount of hiding was good training. How wise of her.*

Almost at the end of Stewart, where it dead-ended into the rising mountains, Rose turned left onto Hollywood Boulevard. This surprised the girl. *How old is she? Twenty-four? Thirty?* If she thought he might do her harm, she was accepting it almost graciously. But "thinking" for her wasn't like thinking for him. It was clear that she lived within one inescapable thought that, for her, took in everything. Her eyes were fixed on the spikelike spires of the Mormon temple that loomed above the rooftops several streets away. They looked to her like six syringes, sticking the points of their needles straight into the sky. He was catching her thought, or she his, for he was realizing what the place had always looked like to him, though he'd never been conscious of it before: less like a church than a device, a sharp-pointed trap, for the impalement of some huge creature that might pass there. *God, no doubt.*

Before the city had gotten too big and the corporations moved in, its affairs had been divided comfortably between the Mormons and the Mob—and the Pentagon, exploding its bombs on the horizon. Each pretended to ignore the others while each profited from and used the others. *Another perfect marriage.* Now things were more complicated, more hidden. *But that's the way with marriages. Maybe I will marry her.*

Still three streets from the Mormon temple, or device, or whatever it was, Rose pulled into the driveway of a building that was neither a home nor a church, but had elements of both. *A condo convent.* Built in the abrasive style of the New Vegas, angular and bright and conceptually lopsided: long, narrow windows on walls that weren't high enough to create a sense of proportion; rooms jutting in half-circles from a structure that was otherwise sharp angles. Like most of the new developments, the condo convent repeated one anomaly of design over and over, cramming as many buildings on the lot as could be gotten away with until with repetition the structures made a kind of insistent sense. The sign over the driveway, bare in the sun but lit at night by pink spots, read: Church of Religious Discovery.

When Rose stopped the car the girl seemed reluctant to get out.

"Don't worry," he said, "they don't sacrifice virgins."

"What a shame."

She opened the door and just stood—that odd way she had of standing, not as though she was swaying but as though she was about to.

"They'll help you," he said.

"Help me with what?"

"You can get some food. Clean up. Rest a few days."

"Do they pray?"

"I suppose they do."

"Do you?"

"Do I look it?"

The Strip and downtown lay about eight miles behind them, small and hazy in the valley. He was looking at the town, not at her, when he said, "Do you?"

"Do I have to go in?"

"You don't have to do anything."

"Are you going in?"

He nodded yes.

"Alright, then."

They walked together up the steps, and though they weren't holding hands they had the air of holding hands. *I owe you, kid*, he justified himself to her silently, *you were lucky for me this morning, maybe saved my life.* "I owe you" is a big deal among Sicilians—though the Reverend Joy says owing is dan *gerous to the people you owe, because their karma gets mixed up with yours, and that may not be good for them. Of course, the Reverend could be full of shit.*

He pressed the doorbell and it rang with deep, resonant chimes. The Reverend Joy opened the door herself.

"Are you as full of shit as the rest of us?" Rose said by way of greeting.

She didn't smile.

In bare feet—long and exquisitely shaped feet, with toenails painted silver—she stood a head taller than Rose, stood with the proud yet inviting carriage of the showgirl she'd once been. Vegas showgirls don't dance. They step slowly and purposefully, bare-breasted and bare-legged, balancing a towering headdress of bright plumage. The Reverend Joy, now sixty, had left the life but hadn't lost the style. Her hair had always been a gleaming ash, silken and long, and turning silver had not changed it much. She had the high cheekbones and strong nose that keep facial flesh from sagging, and though she reveled in wrinkles that the desert sun deepened almost to scars, her face had not so much aged as merely changed the nature of its beauty. Her mouth was aristocratic and wide, her eyes, a rare neon shade of violet. She had learned when very young to project her beauty like a force, a field of energy that even the mighty approached tentatively. This sense of force had not aged at all. She was the only human being, besides his brother, whom Rose trusted completely, and though she did not trust Rose, she loved him. "You are *almost* the man of my dreams," she would tease, "if only you weren't so chicken-livered." He had rarely seen fear in those violet eyes, but that's what he saw now.

"Michael, what have you done?"

"What have I *what?*"

"Oh, God, Michael."

"That's what we're here about: God. And," he nodded toward the girl, "something to eat." He saw their rank smells register on Reverend Joy. "And a bath might be nice. Separate baths, of course."

*Damnit, Joy, God was watching me. Why did it have to be then? Why not once ever before?*

The girl was gawking. Whatever she had expected, it was not the Reverend Joy. She, the girl, had been proud of her apparition-like impression; now, confronted with this very different, far stronger apparition, she felt invisible. She could not move.

"I thought I'd never refuse you," Joy said to Rose.

"Are you going to refuse me now?"

"No. But soon, perhaps." She looked at the girl and her eyes softened. "Please come in."

But the girl couldn't move.

Joy wore something that might have been pajama bottoms if they weren't so silken and bright, white and billowy. And Joy's white T-shirt showed very clearly that she had but one breast—a breast that, though sagging, retained a suggestion of its original fullness. Its small nipple pressed against the cotton. Joy and the girl locked eyes and took each other in. There was respect in Joy's eyes. The girl softened when she saw that.

"I'm not going to marry him yet," the girl said.

"Smart kid," said Joy.

They smiled at one another, as though a secret was being passed between them that excluded Rose utterly.

"This is . . ." Rose began an introduction, then stopped. "Whoever this is."

"Michael only brings people here on condition that he doesn't know their names," Joy said kindly.

"Smart kid," said the girl.

"That's Michael," Joy said. "*Please*—please come in."

"Virginia," said the girl. "Me."

Joy extended her hand and the girl who called herself Virginia took it, and the two went inside. Rose looked back at the city before he followed them in. For a couple of decades, from his birth through his adolescence, it had been a place where adventurous people, or people hoping to be adventurous, came for a few days to attempt to live the lives they saw in movies. Gambling was merely a vehicle for that. The Mob understood this instinctively and supplied the proper setting and the necessary distance from "real life." They were paid for this service through the gambling, but Bugsy, cruel, doomed Bugsy, understood the real impulse when he set the style. Now the infectious surreality of the city fed on itself, people caught it like a virus and carried it across the land. Rose could not have said this, but felt possessed by how all their lives seemed mere expressions of the city.

*The insects and birds are feeding on Zig even now. At twilight the coyotes will begin. At least we can die like other people. At least the creatures still want to eat us.*

He followed the women inside.

The Church of Religious Discovery had a gentle, vague decor. Deep rugs and colored cushions instead of furniture. Crystals everywhere, of every shape and size, glinting with reflected light. The walls were painted such soft pastels, it seemed you might put your hand through them. Polished logs beamed the ceilings. Women, most of them quite young, sat meditating in a large chapel-like room. Others walked silently on bare feet with an air of purpose. There was a feeling of protection. Rose liked to tease Reverend Joy, saying it looked like a New Age idea of a harem. "Are you the resident eunuch?" Joy teased back. The tease wasn't cruel because she'd been stroking his cock at the time.

He was remembering that moment when Joy came back into the room.

"Have you handed her over to one of your minions?"

"She's being fed. Then she'll be bathed. Are you hungry?"

He didn't remember the last time he'd eaten, but he wasn't hungry. In any case, the food Reverend Joy served was macrobiotic, or some kind of "biotic," and didn't taste like food to Rose. "I could use a cup of strong coffee with about five sugars and some cream."

"That's how your mother used to drink it."

"That's how I used to drink it too."

"You know I don't keep sugar here."

"According to your religion you're not even supposed to keep coffee."

"It's not a religion, Michael."

"Sorry. It says so on the sign."

She looked him up and down—his torn, stained clothing, the bruises on his hands.

"Michael, what have you *done?*"

"Gino the Gent's your patron here, isn't he?"

They had never spoken about this directly.

"He thinks he is."

"Will anybody call and tell him I'm here?"

"I'm the only one who could."

"And Mr. Sherman hasn't the connections or the imagination to find out."

"Who's he?"

"A remarkably uninteresting man. The trouble with my work is that usually the people who hire me are squares."

"That was usually the trouble with my work."

"In my profession I can be a snob, in your profession you couldn't."

"That was part of its charm."

"I'm not going to tell you much, Reverend. At least, I don't think I am. Why do you look so . . . sad?"

"Your aura is black, with flashing bright lights."

"Gimme a break."

"Even the walls don't want you here."

"Joy—"

"And a shadow, a host of shadows, is following you. I never thought I'd be afraid to touch you. I am."

Reverend Joy looked her age, though a magnificent version of it. Now her fear made her look old as well. Rose had only seen this happen at rare times in bed, and then had pretended to himself not to see it. She was nearly nineteen years older than he. He had been born the year she'd first stepped naked in front of people. Joy wasn't her real name. It was her show-girl's, then her stripper's, then her prostitute's name—her "getting naked" name, Rose called it. But she'd used it so long it had become more real to her than her "Christian name," as the old usage had it, a name Rose had never known, never asked to know. In Las Vegas many left those names behind.

Rose suddenly wanted to cry. Joy shifted to the "eye," as she called it, that could see, or that she imagined could see, auras, and "saw" that his aura brightened with the urge to cry. She reached and touched his cheek and "saw" his accompanying shadows flinch. Of course she was old enough—just—to be his mother; that was something they never even joked about, or mentioned in any way. But Joy had never felt maternal about much of anything. In her religious circles she was a leader, not a mother. So to feel maternal toward Rose now depressed her deeply. Her fingers on his face felt old to both of them.

"I'll give you a bath, Michael." And she took him by the hand like a child.

"Hey, Mike," his mother had said, "you gotta come to the joint tonight, I got this dancer with one tit."

"Was she born that way?"

"Naw, she had cancer or something. One tit and one scar."

"You running a freak show down there, Mama?"

"You're a man. Almost." He was sixteen. "Are you telling me you don't wanna see her?"

He hated his mother's frankness about such things; at the same time, it was the world they lived in, and to be anything but frank about it was not possible. It was what he'd been born into. There were always some Jews in the Sicilian Mob, and there were always one or two Sicilians in the Jewish Mob, and Eddie Rossellini had been a soldier in Bugsy Siegel's outfit in the days when the Mob built the Flamingo, the first casino on the Strip. Rosie Venetico danced as "Rosie Vee" in the chorus. By the time the boys were born, Eddie was overseeing various strip joints and brothels for his bosses. Eddie was good with the employees, as stern or good-natured as he had to be, but he had no head for business and leaned more and more on his wife, who did. Gradually the unusual arrangement was accepted by the bosses, and Rosie Vee was "in," at least as far as strip joints and brothels were concerned.

*In the old days everybody was weird, so a kid had to think that was normal. The mothers of your friends were hookers, strippers, showgirls. The fathers were dealers—card dealers, not drug dealers—or musicians, or hoods. That was one tier. The next tier were doormen, cooks, waitresses, maids, porters, guys who parked cars. There was an older, more legit Vegas too, the country club set who profited off it all but felt superior; they didn't mix with the likes of Eddie Maybe and Rosie Vee. And the likes of Eddie Maybe and Rosie Vee had children, just like anybody, and that's who we were. And since Mama and Pop not only felt no shame about who they were, but felt that anybody who wasn't "in" was an idiot or less, they were frank.*

"Yeah, Mama, I'll come down."

"You do that. I want a male opinion I can trust."

"Hey, if they give her money they like her, if they don't they don't. You don't need my opinion."

"But I want it."

*Being sixteen didn't matter, the cops who came into our joints were on the payroll.*

So Rose went to the Golden Garter that night, near Fremont and South Main, and went in the back way. The "dressing room" for the girls was just the back hallway, fitted with mirrors, lights, hooks, and shelves. Handbags and street shoes were lined against the wall. In those days nobody dreamed of stealing anything in such a place; people got their hands cut off for that. That was where he first saw Joy. She was taking off something he'd never seen: a prosthesis. *I gawked at the twisted scar mass on the right and the rosy round globe beside it, and it was like one of those photos of an ancient ruined statue on the art class wall. She was in her midthirties but had the gift or curse of looking ten years younger. "If I'd've looked my age I'd've gotten out of the life sooner," she told me once. I stood stock-still, staring.*

"Well, boy?" she said, half smiling. The "boy" cut him.

"Excuse me."

"Not a chance." And she laughed and let him pass. There were other women in the hall, dressing and undressing between shifts, but he didn't remember them. He sat at the runway where the new dancers debuted.

*Mama brought me a beer and one of the waitresses lit my cigarette. Several girls danced before Joy came on. This kind of dancing, if you can call it that, some dance with their crotches, some their legs, some their asses, some their tits, some only their eyes. They bend and twist, shove their body parts at you, pull away, hump themselves on the pole, put their fingers in their mouths, then touch their fingers to their assholes, emphasizing crotches or breasts or legs or butts, whatever they feel best showing off, and if you like them you put bills between their breasts, in their G-strings, in their mouths, between their toes, whatever body part they offer you, and I'm still always surprised at how soft their skin is, and at how many kinds of softness your fingers can brush lightly in a night, bill after bill. Of course in those days they didn't take bills from me. They danced hard for me and for Alvi because Mama smiled when they did, and it paid to make Mama smile.*

*And then Joy came on—though I didn't know her name yet. But when her gleaming ash hair caught the color of a blue*

*The Ministry of Reverend Joy*

*spot, so that it was like she had a neon halo—I recognized her: I'd seen her, she'd been a star showgirl at the Trop—the Tropicana. But she'd had both tits then.*

*That night at the Garter she towered over the other women, at least six-four in heels, and when she stood right in front of you on the runway your eyes came up to her shins and you looked up from that perspective at that wild height of beauty crashing down on you, and it made you nuts. She wore a billowy white top when she began, and looked like she had two great tits, but when she lifted it off there was a prosthesis like no other, sequined and glittering and with a glass eye where the nipple should be. I heard myself screaming with some of the other guys, not cheering but screaming, like girls did at Elvis. There were us screamers and there were some guys who looked a little sick, who wanted to tear their eyes away but couldn't. And then she unbuckled the prosthesis and twirled it around while she pumped her hips, and threw the thing to Mama, who laughed when she caught it, not the mechanical laugh she used on everybody, but a fat laugh from her fat belly. Then Joy didn't so much dance with her body as with the force of her beauty, until she knelt before you and shoved the scar in your face and then the tit, the scar then the tit, and above both would be her gleaming mad smile.*

*I absolutely had to have her. And so I learned the finality of some kinds of wanting.*

"You made great money dancing," he said to her years later, "so why'd you hook too? Greedy?"

"Do you have to be a detective about *everything?*"

"Yes," he said, stroking her scar.

"I like men . . . in bed . . . as much as I like women. But women are better for relationships. *But* . . . I wanted men too. *But* . . . men always humiliate you. One way or another, men always humiliate you. If I was going to be humiliated anyway, I wanted to be paid for it."

"You're crazy."

"I was. I really was."

"I don't humiliate you."

"How do you know?"

Sometime that same year, a year of questions, he said, "You never take money from me."

"You were a boy when we started. You're still a boy."

"What if I surprise you and grow up all of a sudden?"

"I'm not worried." And later that night she added, "If you grow up right you still won't be a *man*. You'll be something like a woman. And if you don't . . ."

So he had other women and so did she, but every few weeks or months or years, depending, they'd find each other and still need each other. And in between—they'd just talk sometimes, check in. Her becoming the Reverend Joy didn't change things between them, except that she said even more things he didn't understand, or didn't want to.

*The only answer is not to know the question. Once you know the question, you're fucked.*

*I started to learn the question that time at the Golden Garter, before Joy, when Pop was still alive. Me and Alvi practically lived in the joint. I was nine, or eleven, something like that. There was this fleshy tall lady whose name for getting naked was The Alabama Slammer, and I was gawking at her one night, and she got a big kick out of it, and when she finished her number she came right to me and scruffed my hair, and I didn't know where to look or what to do, and she laughed and rubbed her big sweaty perfumed breasts into my little face, and held me to her, and I squirmed to get away but the squirming just made me feel every part of her, and she tickled my crotch, laughing throaty and playful and all-powerful all the while, but when her fingers and her hard painted fingernails, pink nails, felt I'd stiffened down there*

*into a hard-on as small around as a short pencil, her laugh-*
*ter became a sticky inescapable cascade of coos, as though*
*her breasts were laughing, as though her thighs were laugh-*
*ing, her breasts that she held my face up to and her thighs*
*that vibrated against my chest, and the hard bone just above*
*her G-string poking me. For as she laughed she held me*
*tighter, not playful anymore but with desire, and I felt her de-*
*sire and I didn't know what it was, only knew its force, and*
*then she let me go and I was standing alone, watching her*
*bare ass walk away.*

*Pop had watched. Through Alabama's coos I heard his*
*laugh as though far off. "Go, baby, give 'im a taste! Right in*
*his face! Make a man of 'im!" And Mama, she laughed too,*
*but not really, she just made the sounds while her eyes, her*
*Rosie Vee eyes, had that glint, that glint that always said, "I*
*know something you don't know." I'll bet after she died she*
*looked at God that way. And when the girls saw Pop and*
*Mama get a kick out of it, they all got into the act sooner or*
*later, with me and with Alvi, and The Alabama Slammer*
*came back for more after that, and took me into the corners,*
*and did me how she wanted, her big mouth all over my little*
*thing. And I loved it and I hated it, and I came back for more*
*and I ran away from it, and it was like we kids were every-*
*body's good luck charms that they had to rub against, like*
*somehow we made everything alright. And I can see now how*
*they'd feel that. And nobody ever wanted us to grow up.*

"What kind of trouble are you in?" she said.

"It's not very interesting. Just fatal."

"I hate these shadows around you."

"Lay off the psychic shit, will you?"

"It's as though your come would be black."

"Joy, have you ever felt that God is watching?"

She liked to undress him slowly, almost ceremonially, liked
to begin their lovemaking while he was naked and she was still

clothed. Sometimes she stripped him above the waist first, sometimes below; if he wore a hat, sometimes she saved it for last, or slapped his face and let it fall with the slap. If this was maternal, neither noticed nor admitted. But this day she didn't want to touch his clothing, especially his blood- and shit-encrusted shoes, but she did.

"I'm going to destroy these things," she said. "Burn them."

"It's okay with me. But you'll be destroying evidence. That's a crime."

The word made her smile, her first real smile since she'd seen him at the door.

From several vials she poured different colored oils into the swirling waters of the hot tub. The colors blended into a bright blue. The waters opened his pores gently, as though with many small and precise fingers.

"Breathe," she said.

He closed his eyes and breathed deeply and slowly. The breathing brought up tears. He didn't fight them, but sobbed silently, softly, embraced by the water's heat. *There isn't anything to cry about. This is just exhaustion. Everybody in this game sat at the table 'cause they wanted to play, and everybody knew the odds. Nothing to cry about.* When that had finished he opened his eyes.

"You getting in?"

"Not into *that* water. After it's drained, and I fill it again, I'll get in."

"At least take your clothes off."

Now she had to remind herself to breathe. She never hid from herself how crucial it was for her to be thought beautiful by men, by everyone. For many years to be beautiful and to be alive were the same for her—one was not imaginable without the other. That she'd always understood this did not mitigate how it had ruled her life. To become older had in part meant a challenge, not to imitate the beauty of youth—she'd been too beautiful, when young, to hope for that—but to find a new beauty that carried the same air of command. This search led, to her enormous surprise, to the spirituality that now was her life, or the structure of her life. But still there was her Michael. Her mixed-up Michael, who tried so hard not to be a criminal despite his attraction and aptitude for crime—as she aged he fed her with what she still needed. She didn't need it from everyone anymore, but she needed it from him: his adoration of her beauty. Her breast sagged, the flesh of her belly and abdomen hung in small folds, her thighs were crinkled, her ass hung loose, her neck was deeply creased, there were liver spots on the backs of her hands—and her Michael saw this clearly, even minutely, as beautiful. She called this his "integrity." His powerlessness before her beauty—the presence of it still so strong, long after the physicality had deteriorated—was still sometimes all that mattered to her. And she knew that sometimes it was all that mattered to him. Neither called this love, but then they didn't call anything love. It still thrilled her to become naked in front of him. That was all that mattered. And if this trouble of his proved fatal—would that finally break a heart that had never allowed itself to break, or would it somehow free her? That thought was in her mood rather than her mind, as she pulled off her T-shirt and let her billowy silken pants drop from her waist, while her wrinkled body fed on his eyes.

From the Golden Garter as a boy, to the bars he frequented now, to the billboards on every taxicab and above so many Vegas streets, Rose had seen naked beautiful women almost every day of his life. Their perfection was only a sameness to him. But Joy's scar compelled him, and now her aged body compelled him as he watched her. The slow destruction of her beauty worked upon him as the only release he knew, and he found it more gently beautiful than harsh perfection. As she disrobed before him he drank her in. *Why isn't God watching me now? Has my come turned black, as Joy said?*

She drained the water and filled the tub again. She said, "That girl told me you proposed to her."

"Well, *you'd* never marry me."

"It's stupid to say reckless things to someone in her condition."

"What other things *are* there to say to someone in her condition?"

"I hate it when you let yourself be stupid." She looked at him strangely. "I suppose I was irresponsible . . . when I took you, when you were a boy."

"What were you supposed to be responsible to?"

"I'm not sure."

"Let's not start talking like squares, Joy."

"They're not wrong about everything, Michael."

She poured oils into the new water, slid in beside him, and they held each other. Across twenty-five years each had composed a map of the other's body, like a geologist's map, every detail of the topography, every layer beneath, what areas activated in what mood, in what moon, in what season, each knew the way to the other's obsessions, and each knew that all that matters in sex are obsessions, and that everything else is a compromise, and neither compromised with the other. That was why they didn't spend much time together. The shadows Joy saw, or thought she saw, clung to him now, clung to him as she did. She was afraid, but she knew how to be afraid, how to let her fear excite her, excite him, making love with the most unwilling part of her, letting that part be violated, watching its violation from other parts of herself, always a voyeur of herself, as she was when she'd danced. When he came his jism was the substance of shadow; to both it felt black. She drank it down. Each felt that what he'd done had passed into her, and she didn't need to know the details anymore, it was enough to feel what they were made of.

"It's alright, Michael."

"I don't think so."

"It's alright if you go all the way through to its other side."

"I don't know what that means, Joy."

"Then you'd better find out."

She let the water drain again, then rinsed with new water, and they sat there, thigh to thigh, hand in hand, letting themselves dry. His forty-two-year-old body, still fairly young, bulging a little in the belly, sunken a little in the chest, but the legs strong, hairy, shapely, and the large varicose vein that bulged upon the length of his cock like a scar. "Too much violent masturbating," she'd tease, and it was true. And her sixty-year-old thighs, the flesh hanging and finely lined, the veins in relief on her long feet. They sat in that rich stillness of people who had never wasted time with one another.

"Has God ever watched you?"

"It's happened," she said. Sometimes with you, she added to herself, hurt that he'd not felt that with her, and concealing, as always, how he hurt her. "It's happened," she said again.

"And then what?"

"The first time, God surprises you. And then . . . God waits for you."

*I want to kill again. Badly. I want to understand everything and nothing again. But I don't want to want it. Is God waiting there, or somewhere else? Or do I have to be killed now, to feel that again?*

"If you go toward where God is waiting," she said, "it will be alright . . . whatever it is."

*I don't want to understand her, but what's "wanting" got to do with anything.*

"I didn't think we had God in Vegas. Only Mormons."

"You don't read the scriptures. God likes deserts."

These words were strange to him. He'd never talked about God before. The sense of understanding without understanding disoriented him.

It was twilight. In the city in the valley, neon met the coming night. High clouds passed above and caught the city's colors, glowing faintly red, faintly blue, faintly green—glowing clouds that could be seen a hundred miles away. Everybody would be impatient in the city. Its night demanded something of you, and you felt it even if you rejected the demand. Mr. Sherman and Mr. Lampedusa would be impatient. Mrs. Sherman and Alvi too. Wondering where he was and what his next move would be. He wondered too. The Reverend Joy had ministered unto him, and he could no longer put off taking some sort of action.

Suddenly the girl stood over them. She was breathless—apparently she'd run from room to room in the unfamiliar buildling, searching for them. She wore a white terry cloth robe, she'd been washed and scented and fed, her hair had been cleaned and combed and was as full and golden as Rose had imagined it would be. But her eyes had not changed.

"I'm ready," she said.

One of Joy's minions, as Rose called the people of the Church of Religious Discovery, came in after her, a young brunette dancer he recognized from a club called Cheetah's. She said, as though posing a delicate question, "Virginia?"

Virginia looked from Joy to Rose, from Rose to Joy, as though tracing with her eyes the sexual bond between them.

"I'll go with her," she said to them, "but I'm ready."

When they left, Joy looked at Rose severely.

"You're right," he said. "I was stupid."

They didn't speak of Virginia again until a while later, in Joy's personal quarters. Then, as though they'd been discussing her all along, Joy said, "How did you meet her?"

Rose told her.

"So you owe her. And if you owe her, I owe her."

"You once said something about karma and owing—"

*The Ministry of Reverend Joy*

"Some of your karma gets stuck to some of theirs. And vice versa. Life is sticky."

"Did you throw out the cigarettes that were in my shirt?"

"I had them burn everything."

*Not having Zig's cigarettes is almost as depressing as that girl. I wanted to finish that pack. He gave it to me, damnit. They were a gift.*

# THE TOENAILS

# OF ALVI ROSSELLINI

*I don't wear blue jeans, I don't wear shorts, I don't wear sweatpants, I don't wear canvas shoes. Alvi makes fun of me about it. He says I look like an old movie—"or a grown-up, which is worse." If I'm home relaxing I wear robes, "like an old-fashioned pederast," Alvi says, "or Clifton Webb—which is worse. What the fuck are you trying to live up to? I spend half my life in mental wards, but you're the one wearing costumes wherever you go. If you die before me I'm going to have them bury you naked. You ain't gonna die wearing a costume for God."*

Mike Rose walked out of the Reverend Joy's barefoot in her yellow silk robe. It was a radiant, tender yellow, the silk molded to his body, faintly scented with Joy's smell. His unshaven face and his hairy calves were incongruous, but not the strangely radiant brown of his eyes. Mike Rose had a strong face and a set, tough mouth, but his eyes could have belonged to someone else entirely, some man who had looked on a world very different from the neon and desert of Mike Rose. He didn't know this about himself, didn't know his eyes gave so much away.

They were his brother's eyes, too—though, unlike Rose, Alvi was aware of their quality. But they weren't the eyes of Eddie Maybe or Rosie Vee. There was no way for even Alvi to know whether some combination of their parents had produced a new strain, or if some ancestor far back, some priest perhaps, had looked at Sicily with the same immediacy and tenderness. Wherever they came from, the eyes went well with Joy's robe.

The brake and gas pedals felt unfamiliar to his bare feet, and the insubstantiality of the robe made him feel as if he were driving naked. When young he had often dreamed of driving through the city naked, and on into the desert, and on and on. He'd woken from those dreams fully rested and strangely happy. *Whatever happened to those dreams? I could do that now, drive off like that. No, I'm low on gas. I never had to stop for gas in the dreams.* The evening chill woke him, and the slick satin caught the chill and sheathed him in it. His head cleared and he could think again—though he wondered how much good it would do him.

Turning right onto Stewart Avenue, he saw how the city sparkled in the valley, each single light precise and strident. The white beam of the Luxor pyramid shot straight up, and the blue-green of the MGM, the bright red of the Rio, the ice blue of Caesar's, the gold hue of the Mirage, the glare of the Strip and the dimmer pulse of downtown, and all the tiny lights of homes that spread into the Mojave, the neon language of his world, said to him and to all in an electric voice that was high-tension indeed: "You can have what you want. You *can* have what you want. You must have what you want. You *must* have what you want. What do you want? *What* do you want? Just say. Just admit. It will be yours."

The Devil had once offered something similar to Jesus, and people had been hunting him in deserts ever since.

The city at night never failed Rose, always excited him, awakening something within that he could not escape and would not forgive. Bitter, happy, absolutely in his element, he drove fast toward the lights.

The guard in the booth at the entrance of his condo complex was Old Vegas and very good at not showing surprise.

"Nice night, Mr. Rose."

"Nice night, Mr. Fitzgerald."

"Some, uh, *gentlemen* are waiting for you."

The guard had taken a risk and hadn't enjoyed it.

"Thank you, Mr. Fitzgerald."

"Don't *mention* it."

"I won't."

His condo, like all the others in the complex, was a two-story affair in a three-story building. The first story was a two-car garage. You climbed a stairway to the front door above the garage. A good plan for a view. Lights were on in every window, which meant Alvi was home. Since he was a boy, when alone in a house Alvi turned on all the lights. Alvi was what the Outfit called "a civilian," and in Vegas the rule still held that noncombatant family members were left in peace. Alvi's mental history was widely known, which in this case worked for him in two ways: Lampedusa would know that Rose could not trust Alvi with crucial information, and he would also know that the more hysterical, or in pain, Alvi became, the more likely he would be to spout fantasies and incomprehensible ramblings. Also, the years of breakdowns and mental hospitals made Alvi useless to the police or the FBI—it would be child's play to discredit him as a court witness. Alvi knew this and flaunted it. One of the few things he did not fear was the Outfit. Everybody knew that Rose would sooner or later go to

*The Toenails of Alvi Rossellini*

wherever Alvi was, so there was no need to kidnap Alvi. Just wait, and Rose would show. As he was doing now.

There were three of them, sitting in a Lincoln Towncar parked in front of Rose's garage. *Three, eh? I'm flattered.* As Rose pulled up they got out of the car. While his brights were on he could see them but they couldn't see him. Two young soldiers, dangerous and unpredictable, insofar as Outfit people are ever unpredictable, because they'd be eager to prove themselves. The other was a man in his fifties whom Rose knew well, Salvatore "Weeps" or "The Weeper" Carlisi. He was beefy and pasta-fat, with disinterested eyes. In no matter what situation, he looked bored. He was a trusted lieutenant now. The tag came from his younger days as an enforcer and debt collector: "They see Sallie coming and they break down and cry." All three were immaculately dressed, Carlisi conservatively, the younger men in dark jackets over black shirts; one sported a lavender tie, the other's was turquoise. These events have their own decorum, and Rose enjoyed how meticulously the men performed the choreography: moving just so, taking their places, standing just so far apart, their expressions showing exactly the proper level of impassive menace. It is now impossible to know how much Hollywood learned from the Mob and how much the Mob learned from Hollywood, after sixty years of mutually slavish imitation, but Rose always enjoyed the show.

*Now I'm going to cut the lights and step out of the car, and how I look is gonna surprise you, and that worries me just a little, because you people are not very adaptable to surprise.*

When Rose opened the car door and stepped into their view, even Sallie Carlisi couldn't maintain his impassive pose. His face didn't change much, but it changed enough, while the young men simply gaped. It was Rose who looked impassive, making his unshaven face all the more incongruous perched upon Joy's delicate robe. He waited for them to speak.

"Uh, Mr. Carlisi, uh," Lavender Tie said, "you didn't tell us he was a fag."

"I didn't know." The Weeper smiled slightly.

"Not even a very pretty fag," Turquoise Tie said, and added hastily, "Mr. Carlisi."

They had spoken without permission, a serious breach of etiquette in this situation, and as they realized this they looked at The Weeper nervously.

"Did we catch you at a bad time, Mikey?"

"Is there a good time?"

"Looks like you been havin' one."

"You know me, Sallie. Nothing but laughs."

"Listen, faggot creep, you don't talk to Mr. Carlisi like that, you—"

Rose cut off Lavender Tie while still fixing his eyes on Sallie: "When you get old enough to ask me a question, kid, I'll answer it. Until then do what you're told. Sallie, these boys aren't terribly well trained."

"They got time to learn. That's more time than you got, Mikey."

"What's the message, Sallie? And why do you need these babies to help you deliver it?"

"'Cause I don't wanna get my suit dirty."

The fear in Rose swelled his bladder and he clenched hard against peeing. He had one card and only one, and he played it.

"Nobody's suit's gonna get dirty tonight, Sallie."

"Oh? Tell me why."

"Because some clowns—" And for the first time he looked directly at the younger men. "Was it you two? They lost track of me for the better part of a day. That's a long time in our line. I could have taken out quite an insurance policy in that time. So nobody's gonna get dirty or dead because, Sallie, you're gonna tell Gino the Gent that he can't afford the chance. He thinks I'm smart and so do you, Sallie—something

87          *The Toenails of Alvi Rossellini*

you two boys wouldn't understand—so you know I may have such good insurance that even if you stuck me on a meat hook and I told you all about it, it wouldn't do any good, my insurance would kick in and Gino's ass would be on a spike too."

"Complicated isn't good, Mikey. Complicated is just confusing. Nobody likes to be confused, Mikey."

Rose hadn't lied, which was important to him, and he hadn't told the truth, which was also important to him. And what was most important was that he was standing alone with nothing against a lot of something. That was the pride of his life.

Still, he knew what was coming next, and feared it.

"This can't go on forever," Sallie said.

"No, Sallie, it can't."

"Hurt him," Carlisi said to the underlings. "A little, but enough."

The younger men finally had something to do, and they did it harshly, expertly, under Carlisi's knowing eyes. They yanked off the yellow robe, then they hurt Rose more than a little, concentrating on his bladder, his kidneys, his stomach. No one could have held his urine during that, and Rose didn't. When they saw he was peeing they hit him harder. Rose couldn't help but grunt with the blows, but he made no other sound, and this unnerved them a bit, and they hit him more. Finally he lay beneath them in his own piss. They rubbed his face in it. He turned to look up at them with everything in him that knew how to hate.

"You can take it, Mikey," Carlisi said. "I'll give you that."

"I wonder if the stains'll come out," Lavender said, fingering the robe. Lying on the pavement, it had soaked up some of Mike's urine.

"Take it to the dry cleaners, they'll tell you," said Turquoise.

"Yeah, I think I'll do that," Lavender said. And to Rose, "If the stains come out, asshole, I'm gonna screw a girl who's wearing this robe."

"Yeah," Rose managed to hiss, "but you'll be thinking of me."

Carlisi actually laughed. Lavender kicked Rose in the groin. He lay naked on the pavement clutching his testicles as they walked away, got into their car, and drove off.

He hadn't tried to defend himself. In these situations, it's bad form—especially as it does no good. He had played a nothing hand very well and they knew it, and that was going to have to do. He felt lucky Carlisi was there. Sallie had the authority to go against a direct order if he thought there was good reason. If it had been only the younger men, Rose would be dying instead of hurting.

He lay naked, trembling on the pavement, until the pain eased enough for him to move. A car passed on the driveway while he lay there; the driver pretended not to see him. Before he could lift his head, he heard footsteps not far off. The walker stopped suddenly, and the footsteps faded in the direction they'd come from. *I don't blame them. It's not their action.*

He stood slowly. His long soak at the Church of Religious Discovery had helped his knee and his bruises, but Carlisi's boys knew how to bruise on the inside. Penetrating, radiating pains forced a thin stream of pale vomit through his clenched lips. When he stood, his bladder let go again. His urine was rusty with blood. *That's normal. Don't worry about that. When you get hit like they hit, it's fucking normal.* Sweat broke out all over his body, smelled of fear, and made him colder.

Holding the bannister with both hands, he climbed the staircase and rang the bell.

Alvi opened the door.

"Go on," said Alvi, "give me a line for *this*."

"I just can't seem to keep my clothes on lately."

"Not bad."

Rose collapsed in his brother's arms and blubbered, "Alvi, Alvi . . . Alvi, Alvi . . . what the fuck is it? *What?*"

Alvi blubbered back, "I don't *know*, Mike," and held his younger "big brother" tightly and whispered fiercely, "I depend on *you*, Mikey."

Alvi's feet were bare and his toenails were painted silver. ("It just makes me sleep better," he'd explained to his brother, "*I* don't know why.") He wore jeans that were faded but immaculately clean and pressed to a sharp crease. Like his brother, he always wore T-shirts underneath his shirts, no matter how hot the weather, and usually his shirts were starched white with long sleeves carefully rolled to just below his elbows. His hair had already gone gray—he presumed this was from all the electric- and insulin-shock treatments—but his face looked surprisingly young, almost an adolescent's. Like his brother, he had the odd trait of seeming older when he smiled, but even then he didn't look his age. The gray, carefully combed hair; the youthful olive skin; his thinness; and the way he had of not looking directly at anyone except his brother—when he spoke he would look over your left shoulder, as though watching someone behind you—all combined into an impression of a perpetual stranger, intentionally and defiantly letting you know that you and he were not in the same room, not really, and that if you denied this you were a fool. The only person Alvi permitted himself to be in the same room with was his brother.

Now he lay the naked Rose on the couch.

"Shut off the goddamn TV, will you, Alvi?"

"It's not really on."

"Yes, it is."

"Just the picture."

Cary Grant seemed vastly amused with himself as he said something quickly to Rosalind Russell.

"It's a puppet show, Mike. I'm the only person I know who's not a puppet."

"Fuck you. Turn it off."

"Yeah, what do *you* need movies for, you try to make *everything* a movie."

"I know you're pissed at me. Please."

"I just like seeing you helpless. I like you getting to know what it feels like." But Alvi's eyes were tearful and frightened. "How about I run you a bath?"

"Everybody's bathing me lately. But shut off those fucking idiots first."


Rose soaked in the tub. Alvi sat on the lid of the toilet. The water was as hot as Rose could stand, and the bathroom was steamy with it, the mirror fogged over.

"You want a cigarette?" Alvi said.

"Very much."

Alvi lit one and held it to Rose's lips. Rose reached for it, but Alvi pulled it away. "I'll hold it. You touch it, it'll just get soaked." Alvi held the cigarette to his brother's mouth while Mike took two deep drags, then kept it there for several moments longer.

"You want me to smoke it or eat it?"

"Oh. Sorry." He puffed shallowly on the cigarette himself. "You're not gonna tell me a damn thing about this, are you?"

"Zig told me . . . once . . . that answers are overrated. I used to think he was wrong."

"You hear from Zig today? I can't find him anywhere."

Zig was the only other person Alvi ever sought out.

"Why were you looking for him?"

"Trying to find you."

Again Rose hadn't lied and hadn't answered. Alvi, who usually spotted this ruse, was too shaken by his brother's state to notice.

"So where the hell were you?" Alvi said.

"I was at church."

"Jesus."

"Not exactly."

"Don't call that tax scam a church, man. That's sacrilege."

"When I left they were at evening meditation. Looked pretty churchy to me."

"Joy recruits hookers for Gino the Gent."

"She *saves* hookers."

"She gives hookers and dancers a place to crack up. Or die, if they got AIDS."

"Right."

"And she recruits their replacements."

"She never turned out anybody *I* brought there."

"That's her favor to you."

"Is it? Maybe. Alvi—"

"If you can't admit it, you can't admit it. But you don't lie, Mikey. *Everybody* knows that tough Mike Rose don't lie."

"That's right, I don't lie."

"Not admitting something isn't the same as lying, right? Right. It's worse."

"Aren't you supposed to be taking care of me right now?"

"No. You're supposed to be taking care of me."

The truth of this made a heavy silence between them.

"Alvi, why don't you go watch your talking silent pictures?"

"She recruits hookers for Gino the Gent. Homeless girls who think they're finding safe haven—so instead of the street, they wind up in a brothel, if they've got the looks, except for *your* charity cases. And she's an old woman—"

"Sixty's not old—"

"—and you still touch her privates. You're a sick fuck, brother."

"I *feel* like a sick fuck."

Rose had to pee again. He lay in the tub and let it happen. A rusty stream came from between his legs and stained the water.

"Jesus, Mikey. Oh, Jesus."

Rose saw with what effort his brother resisted the need to bolt from the bathroom.

"So you hid out with her?" Alvi said.

"Who said I was hiding?"

"And she won't sell you out?"

"Never." *But Sallie knew exactly when I'd show here.*

"That makes her and me . . . and Zig. Who else is on your side?"

"Give me another drag."

Alvi held the cigarette to his brother's lips again, then doused it in the reddish bathwater. The ashes floated down, leaving gray trails.

"What did you do that for?" Rose said.

"Are you kidding?" Alvi said.

"Alvi, why don't you go paint your toenails?"

"I'll paint them right here."

"You keep that stuff in the medicine chest now?"

"It's a tranquilizer, isn't it?"


Alvi sat on the toilet lid with his bare feet propped on the sink, painting the nails of his toes with small fastidious strokes. It was the third time he'd done it that day, so the silvery layers were thick. While Alvi tended his toenails, Rose drained the tub as he lay in it, and filled it again. The sound and steam of the water also filled the silence between the brothers and soothed both men.

*I am going to get things straight in my head right now. Now that Zig is . . . taken care of . . . the animals are taking care of him right now. . . . What are you going to think, Alvi, if you ever find out? I've broken our unspoken pact and joined the cannibals? Will you feel like the last human being alive?*

*Got to get things straight in my head. Now. Except that with the Zig part over, the rest of it doesn't seem to have much to do with me, not personally. But I'm going to get it straight in my head anyway, as a professional exercise.*

*The problem of Mr. Lampedusa: Alvi says something in Zig's bar that spooks Zig. Doesn't even realize he's done it.*

*Nobody's ever seen Zig spooked before. Lampedusa gets wind of this—probably from one of Zig's waitresses, who probably gets a little stipend from Lampedusa to keep an eye on things there. Lampedusa puts two and two together and gets really spooked. Lampedusa thinks I'm a loose end too. Seems like ancient history, what Zig knows, but you can't be sure, they could be planning a hit on this president too, they could be always ready to hit any president who might upset the apple cart. Zig gets word they're spooked and knows he's finished. Starts inviting me to kill him. He has his reasons, lots of reasons—I don't think he told me all the reasons. Anyway, I do it. Meanwhile, Lampedusa is worried because he can't find Zig, can't find me. Sends his best boy. I throw Sallie a curve. Sallie has to get instructions before he can do anything final. Nothing will happen tonight. They've got too much figuring to do, and none of these geniuses figure very fast. Alvi can paint his toenails in peace, for tonight.*

*Solution to problem: none. Dance with the developments. Spin the wheel. See if the little silver ball lands on the black or the red, and hope it leaves you with enough chips to bet again.*

*Second problem, separate problem: the problem of Mr. Sherman, unpredictable WASP fuck. Second problem unrelated to the first—I hope. Except that Mama used to say there is no such thing as a coincidence. And I've learned that when things become "a situation," everything in the situation relates to everything else—if not at first, then damned soon. Rose's theory of relativity. Every good cop knows it too, if you can find a good cop. Crazy Virginia, even, is now part of the situation—another one of the last human beings.*

*So, Mrs. Sherman picks my name out of the phone book— she says. When I was a kid the Vegas phone book was the size of a pamphlet, now it's five inches thick. But she picks my ad: "Mike Rose—Private Information." After a lot of foreplay, she asks me to keep a computer disk her husband wants very much. He sends that amateur Blue Shit, Blue Suit, and, after what happened to that sap, Sherman and his people are scared, I bet. In their world that guy probably passed for tough. They're looking for me by now, but nobody who could point them to me will talk to them, they'll think the WASPs are FBI. Anyway, people tend to think I'm Mobbed up, so they don't answer questions about me from foreigners.*

*On the other hand . . . here is where the fucking situation connects Problem One with Problem Two, wake up and smell the whiskey, Mr. Rose:*

*If Gino the Gent hears I'm being looked for by WASP strangers who might be FBI, then his nervousness about me goes up. Very high up. Outfit guys are cunning but not that bright—the days of Meyer Lansky and Charlie Lucky are over—so if Gino gets nervous he might do something he wouldn't otherwise do, something rash, and that's bad for me, and bad for my brother.*

*Solution: Kill Mr. and Mrs. Sherman.*

*A possibility.*

*And I felt God watching me.*

*And, yes: Joy recruits new talent for Gino's joints. I always knew it and now I admit it. Happy, Alvi?*

*Look at you, Alvi, painting your toenails—and with little cotton wads between your dainty toes, because you saw Marilyn Monroe or somebody do it in a movie. One of your "silent" movies. "In the rec rooms at the hospitals," you said, "they've got the TV on all the time, everybody's on tranqs and everybody smells and stares at beautiful puppets who talk nothing but nonsense. I can't tell you what a victory it is to watch those people, their mouths moving, and I can make them shut up, they're saying nothing. That's not crazy, Mikey."*

*God watches you all the time, doesn't he, Alvi? He's gotta keep track of one of the last human beings.*

*You do your little dance for him, with your white hair and your silver toes. You know God's watching—even if you don't know you know. And you look at everyone around you, never in their eyes, you look just over their shoulders, 'cause God is standing behind them watching you.*

*You still look me in the eye. That's how I know I'm the only one who can still hurt you. Because you haven't given up on me, like I have on myself.*

*So why did God choose today to watch? Why that moment? What kind of a God is that?*

Their parents explained the difference between the brothers this way: Alvi was the way he was because he was born on a night that snow fell; Mike was the way he was because he was born on the dawn of a bomb test. All families invent and cling to their metaphors, and life supplies metaphors so extravagantly that it is only a matter of picking and choosing.

What Rosie and Eddie didn't say was that Rosie, who feared so little, feared snow.

Snow is rare in Las Vegas. Years may go by without any at all, and many years without more than a trace. But on a night in 1949 snow fell gently, for two hours, almost an inch. Rosie felt the pains, but did not want to take the short drive to the hospital through the snow. She sat at the window facing west, in the room already decorated for the baby, the room the brothers would share. She sat watching the snow settle on the desert, and Eddie could not make her move. Perspiration lined her forehead, her clammy hands held her belly, and she would not look at or answer her husband when he said, "Rosie, we gotta go."

Snow fell gently on the desert, and if Eddie Maybe had been alone even he, whose coarseness was rarely satisfied by any but the coarsest imitations of beauty, would have been moved by the delicate settling of snow upon this harshest of ground. But all he could say was, "Rosie, we got to go," and all she could answer was, "When the snow stops," and all he could say was, "It could go on all night," and all she could answer was, "Don't say that."

It did stop soon, and they did get to the hospital in time, but driving there she told him, "Go slow, real slow," and as they passed long swathes of desert with the occasional lighted house, in what was still only a small Mojave town, where no tall building had yet been built, and where the neon of the Flamingo, the Thunderbird, and El Cortez were all that shined on what would be the Strip, neons that couldn't be seen through the low clouds of snow, Rosie and Eddie could have been anywhere, nowhere, and Eddie lost his last defense against her fear, and felt sure she and the baby would die. When they did not, and as dawn came he held his son in his arms, the relief Eddie felt was not because of the boy but because the snow would be melted by the time Rosie woke and looked out the window.

Later that day they felt what all couples feel with a first-born, a kind of giddy confusion, and neither ever spoke of that night again, except to laugh that Alvi was "strange," as they said, because it snowed in Las Vegas the night he was born.

From those same windows that faced west, they watched the mushroom clouds rise above the Madre Mountains. With some bombs the house would rattle, with some it wouldn't. Always the cat wouldn't let itself be touched, for hours, after a blast, and across the road the two horses in their neighbor's pen would not eat. But everyone was excited, everyone was expectant, and although at first the blasts weren't announced, everyone usually knew: the day before, the military would order the airport not to let small planes fly over certain areas, and phones would ring across town, eager people alerting each other to be up at dawn to watch. The afternoon Rosie's labor pains began the phones had been ringing all day, and the Rossellinis requested a hospital room facing west. It was well known that they were "connected," as they used to say, and they got what they requested. Rosie and Eddie were very happy that evening, and into the morning. It seemed to them a good omen, a festive way to celebrate, flowers and drinks and cigars and friends in the hospital room at dawn, the baby in her arms, the nurses and doctors sharing the family's champagne—it was as though Rosie willed the birth to come in time so she could watch the great cloud rise with the infant and little Alvi, not quite two, in a highchair by the bed. The infant Michael would have no memory of it, of course, but the bomb was the first event he witnessed.

Later there were clouds he did remember. Family and friends driving to Angel's Peak to see not merely the heights of the cloud, but the entire roiling column of smoke and dust. They would sit, bundled up against the chill, with their backs to the site, waiting for the flash. It usually came just after first light. To the east the desert glowed with pastel tints, and many miles off in the valley the lights of the houses and the neon sheen of the new casinos were somehow comforting in their tininess, and comforting too in how you could go so far away and still see home. "Which one's our light, Mommy?" "That one right there," she would say, and their father would say, "See that sign blinking on and off? The string of lights near it that comes toward us? And then the string of lights off that? Oh, I'd say about the twentieth light—can you count them?— that's probably ours." And the little boys would try to follow the lights and count, until suddenly their shadows would be cast before them more starkly than ever they had seen, as though the shadows were being burnt into the ground. All would turn as one, and the shock wave would come through their feet and shake them, so thrilling, and then the cloud, the greatest and hugest thing that they had ever seen or ever would see, would grow like something alive, something incredibly hungry and happy to be alive, a being all glinting eyes, all shifting and dancing body, rising, rising, impossible that anything could rise so high, so fast, so hungrily. The concussion of the wind would hit then, press their clothing against their bodies, sting their eyes, blow their hair.

And then the great tower of cloud would lean in the direction of the wind and slowly come apart.

In high school, after the tests went underground, Alvi did an extra-credit paper about the bomb picnics and discovered a queer thing: everybody remembered different colors. He remembered bomb clouds that were mostly white, his brother remembered they were mostly red, and others said green, or brown, or even yellow—and people who remembered several colors in the clouds didn't remember the same colors. His teacher gave Alvi an A for this discovery, but when Alvi asked what it meant, his teacher adopted a tone Alvi had learned to ignore, a tone that said, "I don't really know, but this explanation will do."

Their mother wasn't sixty-five when she died of thyroid cancer—probably from the blasts, they knew by then. But if that fact bothered her she never said so. And the boys could never quite connect what they learned later—about Hiroshima, about cancer, about the end of the world—with those dawn-light bomb picnics that were the most thrilling and happiest memories of their childhood.

*Kill Mr. and Mrs. Sherman. That's pretty simple. But get the money she owes me first. That's even simpler.*

*See how responsible I am now? See how grown up I've become, Zig?*

Every couple of years during their childhood there would be a sprinkling of snow—always at night. Sometimes it would fall while they were asleep and be gone by the time they woke. Seeing it in the paper—even a slight snow was front-page news—or hearing someone speak of it the next day made them sad not to have seen the snow, like remembering vaguely that one has had a marvelous, healing dream, but not remembering the dream itself. Gradually they realized their mother's fear of snow by how she behaved the day after: it was the only time they ever saw her fat, arrogant strength uncertain. She would lash out about small things as though half asleep. Once, after a night of snow, she sat by the window as though waiting for it to snow again. She said nothing for hours. It was strange to have her home after nine at night—she usually went to the club to supervise "my girls," as she called them. The boys made coffee together, in the percolator. They had never done it, but had watched it being done so many times; now they helped each other do it, and added the right number of sugars—four—and milk, and Alvi brought it to her in a cup and saucer, with Mike behind him carrying a folded napkin. When she saw them standing there, so proud of their gift, her face softened to an expression they had never seen, as though she might cry, and for moments the three looked at one another and were strangely happy. Their father came home later, and as soon as he stepped through the door, she was instantly her usual self, and the gentleness that had descended on them vanished.

Many years later it occurred to Mike and Alvi—separately—that their mother came from Cleveland, where snow falls all winter.

"Are your toes dry, Alvi?"

"Shiny and dry."

"You may not like Joy—"

"I hate her."

"—but you guys got the same taste in toenail polish. Same exact color. But she's got nicer feet."

"I like my feet."

"Could you get me a drink?"

"Bushmills or Absolut?"

"Bushmills."

"One cube or straight?"

"Straight. No. One cube."

Alvi brought the amber liquid in a small bar glass, and the first sip woke Mike and brought all the pieces of him that had seemed to separate and float in the ambiance of the bath closer together.

"Why were you looking for Zig?" Mike asked.

"I wanted to tell him I was sorry."

"Sorry for what?"

"For whatever I said the other day that upset him."

"He wouldn't hold it against you."

"I kind of wanted to know what it was. I mean, I was talking and suddenly he got weird."

"Probably just reminded him of something. You never know with old people."

"I guess Zig *is* old. I guess he's real old."

Mike finished his drink and stood up in the tub. The standing made him a little woozy and brought the aches back, but they were dimmer now. He could handle them. He stood naked and shaved at the sink.

"You going out?" Alvi asked, like a little boy.

"Yeah, I got some business. You gonna be alright?"

"Could I go with you?"

"Not tonight. We'll go out tomorrow night. Sinatra's playing the D.I. I was thinking of going, if you want. Then we can watch Steve Wynn blow up the Dunes."

"Man, everything's changing. It's like all the things that shouldn't change are changing, and all the things that should change aren't."

Mike looked into his own eyes as he shaved. For the first time in his life he noticed how soft and tender they were, and it irked him, because they looked like the eyes of someone else.

"I miss the old house, Mikey. You ever miss it?"

"No."

"Maybe we could drive past it tomorrow?"

"If you want to."

"You know who's living there now?"

"I don't think about it."

"I do. I dream about it a lot. It's where my dreams happen."

"Could you lay out some clothes for me?"

"Sure, Mikey. How dressy?"

"The usual."

When Rose had finished shaving he went into his bedroom and looked at what Alvi had laid out expertly on his bed. A dark suit, white shirt, gold cuff links placed by the cuffs. Sheer black socks beside a pair of very fine, very soft, brown shoes. A red-and-black striped tie, and beside it a tie clasp with a small diamond centered in it. His wallet and billfold, the only things that Reverend Joy hadn't burned, were in the glove compartment of his car. He dressed carefully as Alvi watched. When he looked at himself in the mirror and combed his hair, for the first time all day he recognized himself. Except for those stranger's eyes.

"The women'll fall all over you, Mikey."

"What do I want with women who can't stand up?"

Alvi laughed shyly. It had been a long time since he had even attempted to be with a woman.

"How do you think I am, Mikey? How am I behaving?"

"You're doing good, Alvi."

"I sound alright to you?"

"You sound fine."

"I feel safe here."

"Good."

"It's okay having me here?"

"Hey," was all Rose said. His brother smiled. And Rose made the classic Sicilian gesture between men, a light slap on Alvi's cheek, a gesture that carried gently the same message as the island's implacable proverb, "My brother and I against my cousin, my cousin and I against the world." Alvi beamed, as though all day he had been waiting for just that.

"I worry about you out there, Mikey. Did you get beat up by anybody interesting?"

"It's just business, kid. A bad day at the office. I'll be okay."

"You're an asshole, Mikey."

"I know, Alvi."

Alvi walked him to the door.

"You got everything you need, Alvi?"

"Everything, yeah."

"There's food enough?"

"Everything. You do look great, Mikey. Just like Frank Sinatra."

"Don't start."

"You're only about four decades behind the times. For a Sicilian, that's pretty good."

"Alvi?"

"I just worry about you, tough guy. I worry about the stupid things you think are important."

"Well, now I've got you to take care of me again and tell me what's *really* important."

"And I will too." Alvi's eyes teared, "You come to the door fucking *naked* and collapse, and pee blood in the tub, and I'm supposed to act like it didn't *happen?* Is that what you expect? And *I'm* the crazy one in the family?"

"*I* never said you were crazy."

"No. You never did," Alvi admitted. "You're not finally getting Mobbed up after all this time, are you?"

"Is *that* what you're worrying about? No."

"You're an asshole, you really are."

"We agree."

Rose looked at the plaque Alvi had put up yesterday on the living room wall. Burned into the wood was the Mormon slogan, in captial letters, FAMILIES ARE FOREVER.

"You really gonna be a Mormon on me, Alvi?"

"It's the only way to save us, Mikey." Then, "Don't fuck up out there, eh? I need you."

*The Toenails of Alvi Rossellini*

"Paint your toenails again, take your medication, watch your silent movies, and remember that's *my* town out there—"

"That's nobody's town—"

"—and I can take care of myself."

"You've changed, Mikey. That's all I'm gonna say."

"That's not all you're gonna say and you know it."

"It's all I'm gonna say right now. Go on, get outa here, before you make me mad and I won't let you have the keys to the car. I'll ground you. And I won't let you have any more cigarettes."

"Speaking of which . . ."

"Hold on."

Alvi went into the kitchen and came back with a pack of Kools.

"Menthols now?" Rose said. "And you call *me* an asshole?"

# THE BROOMSTICK

# OF EDDIE MAYBE

*T*he town felt no different with the thought of murder. Rose imagined that surely some places would. Surely, in some far-off village or city, if a man went purposely toward murder the walls would know, and it would be ever so slightly harder to open doors, and there would be a faint sticky resistance on the pavement where you stepped, and every stop sign would jar you. *That's silly. The history of everything says so.* He was headed down Sahara toward a right turn onto Paradise Road, but he had no dread of seeing *Paradise* hanging over the intersection, no more than the gangsters who'd named it years ago. This was *their* paradise after all, and murder merely one of its rituals, and not the darkest one.

No, here something buzzed in the neons and approved.

He drove past Palace Station. *What a silly name for a casino. What does a palace have to do with a station? Big looming ugly thing for small-time cheapos. That's what this "family casino" shit is, a con man's phrase for cut-rate suckers—suckers with no pride, who bring their kids to watch them be suckers, so the kids can learn to lose like Mom and Dad.* The road arched over Interstate 15, bright with cars and trucks. *They got a religion that says God is watching* that? Then the glaring enormity of Circus Circus on his right, and the unfinished concrete tower of Vegas World looming to his left. The tower was by far the tallest thing anyone had ever built in a desert. The rough, absorbant gray of its mass seemed not to shine in the spotlights but to devour their brightness— the only structure on the Strip that dulled, rather than radiated, light.

*The way I stank after handling Zig, I've spent hours in tubs and I can still smell it.*

He waited a long time at the light where Sahara crossed Las Vegas Boulevard, the Strip. *Suckers to the right, low-lifes to the left.* North of Sahara Avenue the world darkened, the Strip ended, and those who walked in that direction were not tourists, not suckers, but people with darker concerns and seamier intents. *A few blocks that-a-way street walkers on their break sip coffee at the counter of White Horse Drugs. You won't find them in the phone book, with its pages and pages of "escorts," and its ads for the "ranches," which are really brothels. White Horse Drugs is where they end up, Joy, your recruits, after the smack and coke of Gino's joints have taken their prices down.* And across the street, the Sahara— and atop its tower the only prominent clock in The City Without Clocks displayed the hour and the temperature: 11:30, 58°.

*Will I kill again before morning? What a question. How many people ask that question on any given night?*

The city had more clocks these days, but Rose had a less sure sense of time. How long had it had been since he had driven these streets early in the morning, with what was to come as unimaginable as it was inescapable?

*Action. Stay in the action. Doesn't matter what that action is, as long as it's really yours. The thing is, is that a philosophy, as Zig would say, or is that what I'm stuck with because*

*I grew up here? Vegas. Stay in the action. And stick close to your people. What else is there?*

*Running unexpectedly into God. That's what the fuck else there is.*

*If you can't find your action, you end up like Alvi—standing in the parking lot of the mental hospital, in those new clothes I'd bought him, watching me drive up, looking somehow like a hitchhiker the way he held that small bag of whatever he saw fit to take home. Toenail polish, probably. His scared smile, his bright eyes, his white hair. Joy's hair silver; Alvi's, white; Zig's, gray—I'm the only one whose hair's still dark. Silly. I feel older than all of them. Alvi, about to try it on the outside one more time. Doesn't it boil down just to, Alvi could never find his action.*

"Hey, big brother," Alvi had said to Rose as he got into the white car at the hospital.

"Hey, Alvi." Rose had squeezed his shoulder.

"How's the action?" Alvi said.

Rose had wondered if Alvi really wanted to know. He'd been two years in the mental wards this time, and the Vegas he'd left wasn't the Vegas he was coming back to.

There was no way to ease Alvi into it. Look in any direction and the town had changed. They drove streets that hadn't existed when Alvi had his last breakdown—wall after wall of pastel-tinted cinderblocks, and behind each wall the roofs all slanted the same way. A different color wall, a different slant to the rooftops. Another color, another slant. Then a mall. All for the people who'd come by the thousands to work in the huge new casinos, and the thousands who'd come to service those thousands, and the thousands more who'd come to escape whatever was going on beyond the edges of the desert. About a thousand a week, for the last several years.

It had been early morning. The jagged Madres to the west were dull orange in the light, spotted and lined with sharp shadows—boulders and ridges. They looked impassively down upon the metastasizing city, knowing one day it would be desert again. In the time it would take to say so, one jet and then another ascended steeply in the distance. *Suckers heading back to America. They come to the desert neon to "try their luck," try to be other people, and leave in disappointment because that's not the way luck works.*

The Excalibur had still been under construction when Alvi had gone in. The MGM and the Luxor were blueprints. In the hospital Alvi had seen the new city on TV, and now he felt as though he were driving into the TV—virtual reality, indeed.

"Where we going?" Alvi said.

"Where do you think?" Rose smiled.

Alvi smiled back, a smile that looked a little embarrassed at itself, as though what right had he to smile?

"So how do I look, Mike?"

"You look good, Alvi."

"I feel good. I do. I'm good, Mike. I got good plans this time."

They drove east on Tropicana toward the Strip. When they hit the I-15 overpass Alvi marveled at its new entrances and exits, built for the new traffic. Where Tropicana crossed Las Vegas Boulevard, the great golden lion's head of the new MGM, with its open maw into which people walked, glared past them at Merlin—Merlin, who stood with arms spread, a wand in his hand, perched on a balcony high on the Excalibur. His robe and magician's cap glittered with lights. The impassive, know-it-all heads of Easter Island stared down too from in front of the Tropicana. And down the street to their right the Sphinx herself—part beast and part woman, her face more Vegas showgirl than Egyptian queen—reclined before the black Luxor pyramid. As with any good showgirl, you couldn't read her expression. She was staring across the street at a church before which a golden Jesus, robust and thickly haired, stood with arms spread wide as if about to embrace something that only He could see.

Alvi blinked from one to the other as they idled at the long light. Rose wished he'd driven another way.

*Are you thinking, Alvi, that at the end of the world the MGM lion and the Luxor's Sphinx will bound toward one another, to play or fight or fuck, and Merlin up there—whose arms are spread just like Jesus'!—will swoop down the air toward the Savior, while the Easter Island heads rise from the ground supported by their enormous bodies, hidden beneath the sands till the freedom of Judgment Day?*

"This is pretty neat," was Alvi's comment.

"Glad you like it," said Mike Rose, "we did it just for you. Barely got it finished in time for you to get out. The whole town was worried, but we made it."

Alvi beamed. The Luxor had opened not two weeks before. They'd hoped to avoid crowds by scheduling the official opening for four in the morning, but even at that hour more than two hundred thousand had jammed the streets—more people than voted in Nevada during the last presidential election.

The light changed, and they continued east on Tropicana toward Paradise Road, each of them looking north as they crossed Las Vegas Boulevard—looking toward the Dunes sign.

*Pop used to joke that the Dunes sign looked like an erection going up and down all night. Mama said it was supposed to be a flower, growing and wilting. Then they'd laugh in that way that kids don't understand and are suspicious of. To us kids the Dunes sign wasn't anything but itself: the prettiest neon on the Strip. Just a pillar with a sort of minaret on top, all in reds, golds, and blues. The red and golden lights would rise glittering up the pillar, the gold letters DUNES would flash at the top against a background of blue, flash off, and the reds and golds would sink down to the street, over and over. Kids like that sort of thing.*

*Steve Wynn's gonna blow it up in a few days, but whenever
we look down the Strip, whenever we think of it, we'll see that
Dunes sign. Some people calling themselves a "historical com-
mittee" tried to save it as some kind of monument, but the
town thought that was a joke.*

"Glad I got out in time to see it blow," Alvi said. "It's like
a funeral I had to be at." Then, a little worried, "I can go,
can't I?"

"Neither one of us is strong enough to stay away."

"You worried about me, big brother?"

"You worried about *me?*"

"I always worry about you, Mikey. You're crazy."

When married people look at each other as Alvi and Mike
did then, they look like brother and sister; when brothers look
at each other the same way, they look married.

At Paradise Road they turned left, then quickly right into
the parking lot of Zig's On Paradise.

It was, especially for Las Vegas, a discreet bar and restaurant. The Z on Zig's neon flickered a little, and had for years.
Zig, like many old people, rarely slept, so he rarely left his es-
tablishment. It was open twenty-four hours, and Zig was almost always there. He lived in a small one-bedroom apartment
within walking distance, rarely drove his car, and had apparently lost interest in anything but his bar and his memories.
He had done his last "commission" a decade ago, when nearing the age of seventy. He was still capable, he felt, but had de-
veloped an aversion to travel and an even greater aversion to
breaking in young "soldiers." "Do whatever Zig says and
watch everything he does," was a typical instruction an underboss would give a new "colleague." But Zig grew more and
more bored with men in their twenties, and more and more resentful of their obvious discomfort around him. In effect, he
retired to the bar that the Outfit had helped him buy long ago.
Some men he respected were still alive, still bosses, but he
didn't know the new ones well; some he didn't know at all, and

they didn't know him except as a legend, a man who had worked for legends—Benny, Moony, Lucky, Meyer, Costello, Moretti, Anastasia, Genovese. The sons of Eddie Maybe and Rosie Vee were the only people Zig counted as friends after Rosie died. She had been dead more than two years—her death had triggered Alvi's last breakdown—and Zig had grown quieter since, and moved more slowly. But every gesture was still deliberate, absolute. He enjoyed the details of running a little place, and served honest drinks and good food to people he would just as soon have killed.

Whether by intent or habit, Zig's place was very like those intimate Mob restaurants of the New York of his youth. It was always dark, lit with an unspecific reddish light. There were no windows. There were candles in the booths twenty-four hours a day. The bar was brighter only because of the profusion of neon beer signs that glowed above the mirror. There was a jukebox and some slot machines against the wall. Zig had made one concession to the New Vegas, however: video poker games inset into what had been a fine polished-wood bar.

Walking in from the desert sun, Alvi and Rose stood for a moment while their eyes adjusted to the dimness—a moment that hadn't changed for what seemed all their lives. *We'd go to Zig's On Paradise, the whole family, when Alvi and I were kids. Pop in a beautifully tailored suit—tailors do well on the Mob—looking more like Tony Bennett than ever. Mama looking like a mom, and nothing like the photographs she left me, except for her eyes. And me and Alvi, just kids like any kids. And Zig would come out from behind the bar and kiss my mother's cheek and shake hands with my father—shake hands even if they'd seen each other only a few hours ago. That was a nice thing about that generation, at least with the Sicilians and the Jews, how they'd always touch when they met, shaking hands or squeezing arms or patting each other's cheeks. There'd be Frank Sinatra or Judy Garland or Duke*

*Ellington on the jukebox. The grown-ups would talk. Me and Alvi would play the pinball and the nickel slots. Zig would serve us at the bar, where he ate—we were the only ones he ever did that for, dinner at the bar. The grown-ups would drink Seven-and-Sevens, and me and Alvi would drink Virgin Marys. And we'd all watch Ed Sullivan on the black-and-white TV over the bar—Zig didn't get a color set till 1970—and that was Sunday night.*

Alvi and Rose were always boys as their eyes adjusted to the dimness of Zig's bar, then they grew into the present till they could see—Zig standing before them, smiling at Alvi.

"How's the action, Uncle Zig?" Alvi said.

"Good. Always good when I see you boys standing together."

Zig shook Alvi's hand and patted his cheek and fruffed his hair. Alvi's hospital was only a half hour away, but Zig would never have thought of walking into a mental hospital and Alvi would not have expected or wanted him to.

"So how do I look?" Alvi asked Zig.

"What happened to your front teeth?"

"I think I left them in some shrink's arm." They all laughed. Alvi fished in his shirt pocket for his bridge, and placed it in his mouth. "Better?"

"It's good."

Zig shook Mike Rose's hand. Zig had unforgiving hands. Even in age they transmitted a shocking strength.

"Come sit," Zig said, "I got food."

Mike had told Zig when to expect them, and there were two steaming plates of linguini and red clam sauce on the bar. *Nothing says "Vegas" like primo linguini and clam sauce at eight-thirty in the morning. Or even better: three in the morning.*

"You boys want wine, some beer?"

*I liked being called a boy at my age—at least from Zig. It made me feel I had some chances left. Two or three or four days ago.*

"A beer, Zig," Alvi said. "A . . . a . . . what kinda beer should I have?"

"Should you be having any?" Mike said.

"Listen to *him*," Zig mocked, "he must think he's your big brother, Alvi. He must think he fucking knows what's good for somebody else."

Rose ignored Zig. "Are you allowed to drink, kid?"

Alvi looked at no one when he said, "You know how many pills I take, Mikey? I take a pill not to get depressed. I take a pill not to get bipolar."

"What the hell is that?" Zig said.

"It's one of those vicious little words they keep in books," Alvi said, "and if you're bad they sic it on you, and it bites you and it doesn't let go unless you take their pills. And the depression and bipolar pills together, they make my hands shake a little, Mikey, so I take a pill for that too. And all these pills together blur my vision a little, or it's an insulin sensitivity, or some goddamn thing, and for *that* they got no pills left. You know what I'm saying?"

"Doesn't sound like you should have a drink."

"It sounds like I wanna beer. A simple working man's beer. You gonna tell Zig not to give it to me?"

"What good would that do?" Zig said. "It's your action."

"That's exactly right," Alvi said.

*Those were the rules, and they'd always been the rules: you don't get in the way of anybody else's action—not among your own people.*

"But what *kinda* beer?" Alvi said.

Zig poured Alvi a Coors, out of the conviction that Coors wasn't really a beer anyway.

"Fuck it," Rose said, "give me a Bushmills."

"One cube?" Zig said.

"One cube."

Zig poured himself a vodka.

They clinked glasses.

"Welcome home, Alvi," Mike said.

Their plates and glasses rested on glowing video poker screens.

"So, Zig," Alvi said, tapping his screen, "what'd you do?"

"What you see."

"You musta pissed Mike off."

"I piss Mike off regularly."

"Didn't piss me off," Mike said, "just made me sick."

"Mike's gettin' old, Alvi. Soon he'll be older than me, he's gettin' so fussy."

"I just don't like TV light shining up through my whiskey."

"Here comes the lecture," Zig said.

"Video poker has ruined every fucking bar in this town. And it fucks up how women look. They make themselves up—"

"Listen to this, Alvi," Zig said, "your brother's made a study."

"—in front of mirrors, they make themselves up. Mirrors where light comes at them from the sides and from on top. They sit at a bar now and TV light shines up at them from under their faces. They'd not made up for that. Makes them look like ghouls."

"You're right, Zig," Alvi said, "he's made a study. You know, Mikey, you're really crazy."

"Yeah, you keep saying that."

"Mike ain't crazy," Zig said, "he just thinks too much."

*Zig knew so much about death, but not enough to know that for forty-two years he had watched his own death grow and come toward him, had educated it, spoken to it, eaten with it, loved it, yes, and called it by a human name, and had never known.*

*Zig had always been a kind of discipline for me, an exercise in perspective. Nobody could tell, just meeting Zig, who he was, what he'd done, that he wouldn't think anything of sticking an ice pick in your eye. Maybe because he'd killed fewer so-called "innocent people" than a B-17 pilot over*

*Dresden or a B-52 pilot over the Mekong Delta. Lots fewer. That didn't make Zig right, but it made for perspective.*

"Watch out, Mikey," Zig said, "it's *thinkin'* that makes you old."

They were quiet while they ate. The wall at the end of the bar was crowded with framed photographs. A wedding picture of their parents was among many. A photo of all of them, and some strangers, in the desert—it must have been an A-bomb picnic, those were the only kind of picnics they'd had. Zig and their father together, grinning, arms around each other. And many celebrities. Zig and Frank Sinatra, signed. Zig and Sammy Davis, signed. Zig and Marilyn Monroe, unsigned. Zig and Jerry Lewis, signed. All the big shots from the old days. Alvi stared at the wedding picture. It was posed so they'd look like statuettes on top of a wedding cake. This was the beautiful Rosie, the dancer at Benny's Flamingo, the body that had exposed itself in so many ways, covered for the wedding in layer upon layer of fragile white lace, and the eyes for once revealing nothing but what she thought happiness should look like. And young Eddie, so boyish, so bright eyed, standing beside his prize. There were millions of photographs just like it, on millions of walls, mantels, bureaus, and millions of sons and daughters who at some moment or other looked at those photographs as Alvi was looking now, wondering who those people were, and what that moment felt like, and how that moment changed into what would happen later.

"You miss them, Mikey?"

"I guess. *Those* two I never knew."

"Yeah, you did. We did. Those two very people."

"Maybe you did, Alvi. I didn't."

"Then I feel sorry for you."

It was making Zig uncomfortable.

"You guys want another drink?" Zig said.

"And look at you, Zig, with all those big shots," Alvi said. "You were a handsome guy."

"I'm still a handsome guy." He put fresh drinks in front of them and changed the subject. "Everybody's bitching about the Dunes getting blown up, like it's a tragedy. They say it's a landmark. A *land*mark! It's a fucking sign with a casino stuck to it. Some landmark."

Mike said, "*You're* a landmark."

Alvi said, "The old Mormon fort, that's a landmark." More than a hundred years old, it was the founding building of the city and the first on the Strip.

Zig snorted, "Buncha religious nuts build a fort, and that's a landmark?"

"Mormons ain't nuts. I'm a Mormon. What's the score?" That was said by Dee, the waitress who'd just come on duty. Zig's waitresses dressed Old Vegas style: heels, net stockings, and something like a one-piece bathing suit with sequins and lace and cleavage. The rest of the town had changed so much that she looked incongruous even to Mike, but the bar was Zig's time capsule and he required the look.

"You don't look real Mormon to me, Dee," Mike said.

"Every see me take a drink? Have coffee? Smoke? No. I'm LDS." Mormons often referred to themselves as LDS, for Latter Day Saints. "Ever since I quit the chorus."

"I'm gonna be a Mormon," Alvi said.

"You're gonna be a *what?*" Rose said.

That Zig's surprise was visible was a surprise in itself. He didn't have to say anything.

Dee softened. "I'm glad for you, Alvi. Really I am."

"I told you, Mikey, I got good plans this time. Our whole family's gonna be in Heaven, Mikey. Zig too, I think."

Dee smiled and walked off.

"You know," Alvi went on, "when one person becomes a Mormon you save the whole family. Or something like that."

*Remembering, I see Zig's eyes as very bright right then, but I can't be sure they really were. They probably weren't. He couldn't know what was about to be said.*

"So . . ." Zig paused as though trying to use exactly the proper words. "You're gonna look into the . . . genealogy and all that. You're gonna dig up the old shit. That's what Mormons do, right?"

"Oh, yeah. It's a big project. I'm gonna get right on it. Take instruction, everything. Gonna find out everything, Mom, Pop, ancestors, the whole bit."

It didn't seem to Rose a mentally healthy way for Alvi to spend his time.

"I'm gonna get our family into Heaven, Mikey."

"That's how they say it works," Rose said. "If you follow it all the way, with Mormons the whole family stays together in Heaven forever—the ancestors, the descendants, everyone. You can convert dead people. It's quite a religion."

"Convert dead guys?" Zig said. "That's rich."

"I'm gonna be a detective, Mikey, like you, but a religious detective. Find out about the ancestors, find out about all that stuff we didn't know, Mama, Pop, all that stuff they'd never talk about, and bless it all, and the truth shall make us free, free and right for the Heaven thing, all of us in Heaven, where we fucking *belong*."

"They let you out of the hospital for this shit? This *way?*"

Rose was sorry to say it even as he said it, but he couldn't stop the words.

Yet they didn't seem to faze Alvi.

"My doctor was a Mormon," Alvi said slyly. "But I'm good, Mikey. You said so. Zig said so."

"I said so. Zig said so. Alvi, Mormon's a WASP thing. You're weird, but you ain't no WASP."

"Everybody's everything, Mikey."

"Another fucking philosopher," Zig said.

"'Make it right,' Mama used to say. Gotta make it right."

"Make what right?" Zig said.

"I *understand* what now," Alvi said. "This is how. Heaven is how."

*Zig pasted a smile on his face. I had never seen Zig smile phony before, so I knew by then that he was pretty upset. And Mama and Pop, Frank and Marilyn and Sammy, all smiled at us from the wall as though we were making them very happy, doing something they'd waited a long time for.*

Alvi spoke as though from a far-off place. "Mama said, 'Your father knew what was coming. He called me from the road. When he was away "on business." He knew what was coming.'"

Zig had no expression now.

"Drop it, Alvi," Rose said. "There's no goddamn point."

"She musta told you that too, Mikey."

"No. She never told me much of anything, brother."

"Well, *I'm* tellin' ya. I don't *know* if I can find out what she meant. I probably can't. But then, Mikey . . . then . . . then you bless the *mystery*, and . . . you see, Mike? It's the mystery, and from there: Heaven."

With bright eyes he looked from Mike to Zig to Mike again. "He knew what was coming, Mikey. Tell him, Zig."

Zig said, "You tell *me*, Alvi. When you can tell me, I'll tell Mike."

Alvi looked away from Zig, away from Mike—looked around as though for help, until his eyes fixed on the photo of his parents on the wall.

Mike said as tenderly as he could, "I'm sorry, kid—it sounds like a lotta mental hospital jive to me."

"Yeah? Well, it's not."

"It's still good to have you back, Alvi."

"Yeah?"

"It's good to have him back, right, Zig?"

Zig said hollowly, "It's good."

"Yeah?"

Alvi looked at them again.

"Yeah," Rose said.

"I *want* it to be good."

"It's good."

"Your food's gettin' cold," Zig said.

*In a funny way that was the sweetest thing Zig ever said. He loved Alvi. Me, I just tried to change the goddamn subject.*

"Sinatra's playing at the D.I. in a few days. I was thinking we could go."

"Are you kidding?" Alvi said. "Is he still alive?"

"If he were dead he'd be playing the Imperial." The Imperial was a low-rent casino built of cinderblock, wedged up next to the Flamingo, across the street from Caesar's Palace. Its continuing show was called "Legends," where celebrity lookalikes impersonated many of the people on Zig's wall.

"Frank had a drink right there," Zig said.

"Right where?" Dee said, walking by.

"Right where Mike's sitting."

"There wasn't no video poker here when Frank had that drink."

"Enough already with the video poker, hey, Mike?" Then intently to Alvi, "Alvi, this isn't a thing you should do, looking back. Looking back is not what we do."

*How do you spend your life behind a bar with photographs of a man you'd slammed down on a meat hook?*

*Was that about penance? Was that about honesty? Was it a kind of waiting, waiting for someone—for us—to know?*

"But we got to, Zig," Alvi said almost dreamily, "gotta look back, 'cause, I mean . . . there's nothing to look *forward* to. Nothing but God, Zig. And we can't imagine God." Zig's lips tightened but he had no time to respond because Alvi said immediately to his brother, "Shit, Mike, you were named after Frank."

"Except that my name is Michael."

"Your middle name. I wonder if that counts with the Mormon thing. I mean, I wonder if Frank is a kind of a relative.

Michael Francis Rossellini. Mama always said you were named Francis in honor of Francis Albert Sinatra."

"Is his middle name really Albert?" Rose said. "Poor sonofabitch."

Zig said, "Is Mike gonna be counted as a Rossellini even though he changed his name to Rose?"

"Yeah, Zig," Mike said, "I think 'the Mormon thing' will cover that."

"You shoulda kept Rossellini," Zig said. "Rose sounds Jewish."

"If I'd kept Rossellini, my clients might think they were hiring a hit man."

Zig gave Rose a look. For a lot of people that look had been the last thing they'd seen in this world.

Changing the subject had done no good. The tension hadn't left them. All three were upset. Alvi had left the hospital with this gift of salvation for his brother; within he had glowed with the dream that finally, finally he had something to contribute to his family. Sicilians can never be at peace with themselves until they can feel that, somehow, they have contributed substantially to their family—and for them this includes the dead as well as the living. So Alvi hurt desperately as he felt his brother's rising suspicion. He hurt so, that he didn't notice how Zig was perspiring.

"Mikey . . ." Alvi said, like a plea.

*I've heard and thought more about God in these last two or three or four days than I ever have in my life. And what has it amounted to? I killed a man, and now I'm probably gonna kill a woman.*

*God has made me one dangerous motherfucker.*

*God made Dee dangerous, and she didn't even know it. When did she make that call? It had to be her. Gino the Gent must have said something like, "I wanna know if Zig ever starts to lose it, even a little," and had one of his people come*

*in to Zig's On Paradise to eat once a month or so, and leave a*
*hundred-dollar bill under the napkin for a tip. Something like*
*that. The pay phones were in the washrooms. She must have*
*made that call before noon.*

"Now *look*," Zig said, and Alvi flinched. Zig had never spoken to them in that tone of voice. People who had heard that
tone of voice from him were usually about to die. "We don't
look backward. We don't look forward. God is something you
study in a book, a book called the Kabbalah. You leave the
book alone, He leaves you alone, you leave Him alone, everything's okay. What do dago Sicilians know about God anyway?"

"That's what I *mean*, Zig, Mikey—Mormons *know*."

"Brother, they're WASPs, and all WASPs know is how to go
to the fucking moon, and a lot of goddamn good that's done
them."

"What about *computers?*" Alvi said, angry now—and Alvi
rarely allowed himself anger. *I liked that, Alvi getting angry*
*for a change. I felt good all of a sudden.*

"I'm sure you've noticed how everybody's *behaving* so well,
now that we have computers," Rose said. "And how people *be-*
*have* is the only fucking standard."

"How people behave," Zig chimed in. "The rest is conversation."

"Computers," Alvi insisted, "are important."

"They're a long way from God, baby."

"So are we, Mikey. So are *we*. I'm a Mormon." He laughed
suddenly. "I'm a moon-going, computer-loving, pill-taking,
linguini-eating *Mormon*. You don't like it? Too bad."

"You're a gonif," Zig said gently.

*For some reason that I'll never understand, we were all*
*happy for a second. And then that second passed.*

"So what's your next step?" Zig asked Alvi quietly.

"There are records, there's all kinda stuff. I gotta study. I gotta take instruction. And I gotta figure out what Mama meant. About Papa. And—everything." He laughed again. "I got my whole life ahead of me, except backwards."

"You finished with your food?" Zig said.

Their plates were empty.

"Yeah, Zig," said Alvi, puzzled.

"You want more?"

"No, thanks. It was great. I'm stuffed. I haven't eaten good in two years, 'cept sometimes Mikey would bring takeout from here. But you know takeout, it's not the same, you know?"

And just as suddenly as he'd laughed, Alvi wept small incoherent sobs.

Rose put his arm around his brother's shoulder. "I'm glad you're out, Alvi. You know I am. Zig's glad. It's just . . . a little late to get religion, but . . . you do what you want."

"No," Zig said.

"Come on, Zig," Mike said.

"What are we, kid, a buncha assholes? Are we people who don't know what's going on? Are we people who don't know what we've done? It's everywhere, it began a long time ago, and once it begins, and you're in it, you know you are not like these fucking squares who don't know who they are, but like *us*, who know, who have the *dignity* of knowing, of not pretending we don't know. Once it begins . . ."

Zig looked suddenly shocked. He could not believe that he had spoken that way. But he had heard his own words, and heard the sound of his voice, which had spoken more clearly than his words—and Zig knew that Mike had heard, and that the walls had heard.

"It's catchy, Alvi," Mike said. "Zig's talking like you now. I'll be next. Then Dee, then the customers, then it'll spread around till fucking Steve Wynn's talking like you pretty soon. No wonder they keep you locked up."

Alvi felt the intention of his brother's comfort, smiled weakly, and said, "You're crazy, Mikey."

"You kids sure . . . you don't want more food. It's fresh. I had them make it just for you."

"No, Zig, thanks," Rose said. "How about boxing it up, we'll have it for lunch too."

"But what Alvi said about takeout—"

"That's because in the hospital we had to eat it out of the containers. In the apartment, we'll eat it off Mama's best dishes. It'll be great, how's that?"

Rose kept expecting Zig's face to be again as he'd always known it, but it had shifted into a place of terribly certain uncertainty. *Clearly Alvi wasn't going to be out of the hospital long and his research would come to nothing—he didn't have it together enough to dig up anything real. It wasn't that. It was just that somehow he'd lanced something in Zig, a swelling that had been growing slowly in that one-bedroom apartment night after night, and now the substance in the swelling was seeping out like pus and couldn't be stopped. Thousands of hours of testimony. Not guilt. Hatred. Throwing God's world back in His face. For thousands of hours.*

Zig brought them the carefully folded, carefully wrapped takeout boxes. Linguini and red clam sauce.

"You're gonna heat it up, right?" The look hadn't left him.

"Sure, Zig," Rose said.

"Want some garlic bread?" It would never quite leave him again.

"Sure."

Dee—with her pretty, long showgirl's legs, in net stockings and high heels; Dee—with the bright smile of her relieved, converted conscience; Dee—with plenty of change for a phone call to Gino the Gent; Dee came to them when she saw them get up to leave.

"I'm really glad for you, Alvi. It sure is good to see you too."

*She would never see Alvi again. Alvi would never see Zig again, nor Zig Alvi. Alvi, Zig, and I would never shake hands again, or pat each other's cheeks. And nobody had a clue.*

*The Broomstick of Eddie Maybe*

"Alvi, Alvi," Zig said fondly. And then with deep resignation, "You do what you gotta do—if that's your action, kid, that's your action. Everybody just does what they gotta. God too. That's all we have in common with Him. I told my father that once, a long, long time ago."

"Gee, Zig," Dee said.

"Uh, thanks, Zig," Alvi said.

"You gonna be in later, Mikey?" Zig said. "I gotta talk to you. Business."

"Business?"

"Drop in."

"Sure, Zig."

"Take it easy, Alvi."

"You too, Uncle Zig."

"And you're not gonna eat the linguini cold? You're gonna heat it up and eat it off the plates?"

Rose tried to smile. "You know, Zig, for a Jew you'd make a good dago."

"The worst thing about Jews is the food, kid. It's you wops got the good food."

*And he patted my cheek with his hard hand.*

*Willie Moretti ran the New Jersey Mob in the old days. They say he helped Sinatra get his start. When the syphilis got to him his mind started to go and so did his mouth. He couldn't help himself. He was a respected man, but his colleagues had to do something about his mouth. For all I know, Zig was one of the shooters.*

*The day I first got beat up, when Mama grilled me and Pop and Zig were so proud, and then they said I had to "make it right," I think it kind of broke Alvi's heart. I think that can happen. You can be only about eleven years old, but everything breaks in your heart and kind of starts to drift apart and you can never catch up to the pieces. It wasn't just that I'd done something he couldn't do—because he knew damn well I couldn't've done it unless I'd seen what he'd gone through first. It was that now I was part of them. And that meant he was all alone. That was the look he had that day, when he finally turned his face from the wall and he looked at me sitting stunned and scared on the bed. It had always been him and me, different from them. But now I was going to be something like them, and he was all alone. And I always wanted to prove he was wrong, that he wasn't all alone, that I wouldn't leave him for anything, no matter what. But there are ways you can't help leaving people. You leave them by just the way you are. So I was always leaving him, though I never left him.*

*That day, we didn't know what to do. But after a while Pop came in with his broomstick.*

"So, hey, you guys, who's got the Spaulding?" Spauldings were pink rubber balls, about the size of tennis balls, and they had tremendous bounce. They bounced higher than any other kind of balls.

Their father always asked, but he always knew the answer: Alvi kept track of the Spauldings.

"I got one, Pop," Alvi said.

"So what are you waitin' for, Christmas?"

Alvi smiled, got the ball, and Eddie Maybe and his sons went into the desert behind the house, with Eddie saying what he always said when he got out that broomstick.

"In the city"—and when he said "city" he always meant New York—"all we needed for good times was a broomstick and a Spaulding. 'Go play in traffic,' the grown-ups would tell the kids. Joking, right? They always said that. I can't say that here, 'cause you wouldn't know what the fuck I was talkin' about. They got no traffic here, you never seen traffic. But that's what we'd do, we played stickball in traffic. The stick was a broomstick just like this, and the ball was a Spaulding." He pronounced it "spaul-DEEN." "And you could hit a Spaulding so far, that the field was the whole block. You had your team strung out from one corner to the other, not one outfield but *three* outfields, one behind the other, 'cause you hit a Spaulding so far. And if there were cars coming you didn't give a shit, you ran the bases anyway, *that* was the game, we played in *traffic*, and not one of us ever got hit by a car. And that's stickball, and you'll never be a New Yorker unless you can play stickball—and you guys know you're dago wop New Yorkers at heart. Not this fuckin' Foreign Legion outpost. The Big Apple. The real thing. My kids are New Yorkers just like their old man."

*That was our big thing, to be New Yorkers one day. And to this day neither one of us has ever been there.*

*So, since we didn't have a team, and there wasn't any traffic, we played how many times you could hit a Spaulding in a row. Because it's tough to hit a Spaulding with a broomstick. It's a SMALL ball, and it's a thin stick.*

Two would get out in the desert, and the one who was hitting would stand just back of the house, facing the Madres, toss the Spaulding up with his left hand, get quick into a batting stance as the ball went up, and try to hit it as it came down.

Even a small boy can hit a Spaulding a long, long way, so the two who were catching would have to run hard in the desert trying to shield their eyes from the sun and catch the Spaulding on the fly—because if you caught it on the fly, which was almost impossible jumping over sage and yucca, tripping over mounds and snake holes, but if you caught it on the fly then the hitter's turn was over, all his hits in a row were canceled and he was out.

*It was the three of us. It was our favorite thing. We never played it again after Pop disappeared. I don't think I ever saw another Spaulding after that.*

That day they played a long time. Alvi was still bigger than Mike, so he could hit farther. On one of his turns that day he hit fifteen in a row, got happier with each shot, and Eddie

Maybe yelled to the sky, "This kid's a New *Yawk*-a, a real New *Yawk*-a!" And for a little while the alone look left Alvi's eyes.

*Even young as I was I saw what Pop was doing.*

When they were too tired to play anymore they played a little more anyway, until finally the game ended the way it always ended, with Alvi saying, "Hit it with everything you got, Pop. Hit it *way* out there. Lose the ball." And Mike chimed in, "Lose the ball, Pop." And as their father tossed the Spaulding in the air and swung, both were yelling, "Lose the ball, Pop, lose the ball!" *And our father connected and that ball sailed out farther than we could ever run.*

*Killing makes me think too much.*

*Like my father.*

The effects of the bath were wearing off and the pains of the beating radiated again through his abdomen and crotch. Rose was exhausted, but the idea of sleep made his nerves shiver on the edge of panic. He was able to admit the reason for this: that the man he was when last he'd slept had not killed, and until he slept again he would keep some unbroken connection with that man; but how far from himself would he be when he awoke after his next sleep with that connection broken?

As he turned into the parking lot of Zig's On Paradise he saw the same black Lincoln Towncar that had been parked in front of his garage earlier in the evening.

He parked beside their car. Their windows rolled down as he stepped out and closed his door. Sallie wasn't with them. Turquoise and Lavender were on their own, Turquoise behind the wheel, Lavender at the passenger window where Rose stood.

"Jesus," Lavender said, "you shouldn't even be standing."

"You get used to pain as you get older, kid. That's something you have to look forward to, if you live long enough."

"Hey, man, what are you the loose end of, anyway?"

"Sure you want to know?" Rose said. "'Cause then you'll be a loose end too."

"That's pretty good," Lavender said. "Sallie said you got brains."

"If I *really* had brains I wouldn't have to talk to a putz like you."

"Why get personal?" Lavender said, genuinely offended. "None of this is personal. You got brains, you oughta know that."

"It's *all* personal. That's something else you'll learn."

"If I live long enough?"

"If." *Maybe I'm about to overplay my hand, but what the hell?* "So you guys don't know where Zig is either, eh? Must be important, for two sports like you to sit around waiting for him."

"I already took your pretty robe to the cleaners. You sure looked cute in it. For a fag."

"I look cute all the time. Ask anybody."

Lavender pressed a button and the tinted window started to close in Mike's face. Then the window stopped, and went back down. Lavender had finally thought of the right question: "Say, what are *you* doing here?"

"Wondering about Zig, same as you. He's a friend of mine." Again, Rose hadn't lied and hadn't told the truth. But not lying was becoming more and more difficult.

"Watch yourself, Brains. You're not better than *anybody*."

"True enough."

Rose turned his back on Lavender and went into Zig's On Paradise.

The place was buzzing. The booths were full. Most of the bar stools were taken. It was nearly midnight and their rush had started. By the time this crowd left, the place would start filling up with dancers from the various shows, here for their dinner. Dancers can't eat before a performance.

Dee was behind the bar, looking frantic.

"Mike, where's Zig? You seen him? He doesn't answer at home. This isn't like him."

"Lots of people looking for Zig, Dee. I'd be very interested if you heard from him." Her eyes couldn't meet his. Sallie or Gino had no doubt told her to call as soon as Zig appeared. She didn't like the chain of events she'd willy-nilly become a part of. But in Las Vegas there were a lot of people that Dee, and almost anybody, could not say no to. Mike Rose was respected by those who knew the score because he was one of the few who'd said it and made it stick.

"So, what's the score?" Dee said, as she always said, making herself meet his eyes again.

"Nothing-nothing, baby."

She laughed nervously. "I wish Zig was here. It's not that he really *does* anything, I mean, except pour drinks, but the joint runs smoother when he's around, and it don't when he's not. Bushmills with one cube?"

"Club soda with no cubes. The stomach is kinda jumpy tonight."

"Oh yeah? And Mike? A lady's looking for you."

"And I'm looking for a lady."

"Where the hell is she? She was right here." Dee pointed to a bar stool. An unfinished drink and a pack of Virginia Slims were on the video poker screen in front of the empty stool.

At that moment Mrs. Sherman came from the direction of the ladies room. Her face tensed into an inquisitive smile when she saw Rose. Again Rose could not imagine her with Mr. Sherman. She was so very thin, so very blond, and her nervous, resentful intelligence played upon her face with such precise gradations of approval and disapproval at everything she saw. She must have been a constant irritant to Mr. Sherman's forced and posed stolidity. Rose felt his body wonder what the static electricity of her energy would be like in bed—as though his body didn't know or couldn't believe that he intended to kill her.

It had to be done tonight, because Dee would report this too to Sallie and Gino—they would want to know *anything* out of the ordinary now, regarding Zig and his circle. Rose couldn't afford to have them draw the wrong conclusions.

*Bullshit. I just need to do it again. Feel it again. Get God's attention again.*

*Before He gets mine.*

She smiled at him, as though she was glad to see him. *Maybe she really is. Maybe nobody ever knows what their death looks like, or who's carrying it.* She was such a strange mix of pretty and ugly. Pretty in the clarity of her eyes and the sensuality of her mouth, ugly with the big beak nose and the skull-like thinness of her face—as thin as homeless, crazy Virginia, but as though by choice, to make some defiant point of her own by just walking into a room. Yes, that was how she walked, making her point with every step, and Rose liked it more than he wanted to.

"Everybody said you come in here sooner or later." *So I'm right, you have been asking questions. I knew you'd be here if you'd asked any questions.* "They should have said later."

"Why didn't you call?" he said. "I've got a machine."

"I know too much about electronics to trust telephones anymore, for anything important. Hello."

"Hello."

She sat on her bar stool, and Rose stood wedged between her and the man on the next stool. She was so thin that this wasn't difficult. *She doesn't know that my mother, my father, my brother, and Zig, are watching us from those photographs on the wall.*

"Frank Sinatra once sat on the very stool you're sitting on."

"Who's he?" she laughed. Her expression registered exactly her measurement of the man.

"He sings love songs."

"What a waste of time."

"That's his picture, near the cash register."

"*Exactly* where his picture belongs. I *know* who he is."

"Of course you do."

"What was he doing here?"

"Slumming, same as you. Except that he came from this kind of world, and I doubt you do."

"You doubt correctly."

She reached for the Virginia Slims. Rose pulled out his lighter and as he lit her cigarette he said, "I thought you disapproved of smoking."

"I disapprove of many things I do. But these"—she gestured with the cigarette—"I thought I was long past *these*. It's this town. It's as though all the colored lights and all the billboards of busty ladies are pointed straight *at* one, and one needs"—she held up the cigarette—"a smoke screen."

After a moment she said again, "It's this town."

"Mrs. Sherman—" he started quietly.

But she interrupted even more quietly, saying, "Mr. Rose . . ."

"Yes?"

"I hope there's a certain . . . leeway . . . in your behavior. Because," and she brought her mouth up to his ear and whispered, "I think there's somebody we have to kill."

"Funny, I was just thinking the same thing."

# Strangers

We both had a kind of instant undstanding.
It was something that never left us.

—Charles "Lucky" Luciano,
of his first meeting with Meyer Lansky

•

What is organized crime? Your answer will be,
"When people sit down to talk of committing an
illegal act." But what about the acts that should
be illegal? Licenses . . . banks . . . tax shelters. I
could go on and on. If the rich didn't use the poor
for their selfish interest, organized crime could
never exist.

—Meyer Lansky

•

He often spoke to me of the musical sounds he'd
heard in his head since childhood. He trusted
these sounds, which he suspected were perhaps
from another dimension. He felt the music was a
power from a source he didn't understand.

—Shirley MacLaine, of Frank Sinatra

*W*hat's that look in your eyes?" Mrs. Sherman said.

"I'm not sure," said Rose. "Do you find it charming?"

"You wouldn't like me naked. Naked I'm like a pair of scissors."

Rose was discovering much about the word *kill*: that when said by people prepared to do it, bodies quickened and something alien occupied the eyes—a person became both more and less, as when taking a drug, and what happened next was all a matter of whether you welcomed the more or regretted the less. Mrs. Sherman was voracious for the more; Mike Rose was nauseated with the less; but neither could stop themselves, and that was what she named "desire" in his eyes.

And her eyes—*jet black, like an Indian's. Weird, with that blond hair. They give nothing. No sign. She's a world unto herself. I like her.*

"Who is it we're killing, lady?"

"You've met my husband?"

"Couldn't figure him as *your* husband."

"Not insightful that way, huh?"

She crushed her cigarette in the black glass ashtray. She had long skinny fingers with clear hard polish on the nails, but her nails weren't filed to a point. Blunt tips, like a man's.

She was a wonderfully ugly woman. Her hair—what she called "California yellow"—looked false, because she moved and talked like someone with dark hair. Her skinny, agitated blond body seemed somehow dark haired too. In fact, she hated her blondness, hated being "a blond," it felt like a trick played upon her dark nature; but she relished hating it, and this was part of the air of resentment and irony that steamed off her gestures and glinted in her eyes. She knew how disturbing it looked, that genetic fluke of black eyes and the blondest hair, and she liked to disturb. She wouldn't have dyed her hated hair for anything.

Mike Rose ran the fingers of his right hand across the back of her left hand. She allowed this. His forefinger tapped her wedding ring, the point of its large glittery stone.

"That's a lot of marriage."

"Sometimes marriage is a career move."

"You must have had a lot to trade."

"I made him crazy. He decided to marry that. He got what he asked for."

"He must have something I didn't notice."

"He used to. He's had great success in his endeavors. It's made him rigid and frightened."

"It can do that."

"And tedious."

"It can do *that*. So now you've decided on divorce."

"Divorce is banal. I like better the idea of being a widow."

"That'll cost you twenty thousand more."

"Isn't that a little steep?"

"It's about midrange—for a pro. Course, there are bars in this town, in any town, where you could get some amateur to do it for fifty bucks, except that they might decide it's easier to kill *you* for the fifty. Not a service you want to go cheap on, believe me."

"I imagine not. Still. But . . ." Her eyes flashed and she gave a brief harsh laugh. "Agreed."

"This computer disk you and he are fighting about—if he dies it's all yours?"

"All mine."

"Power and money. Boring. And a lie."

"Excuse me?"

"I don't think I will. And I don't feel like explaining myself. It's not in my job description."

He looked at her hard, and she let him look. He was looking to see if she knew what she was asking of murder. She did not. She was simply and terribly having a good time. At last, she wasn't a supporting player in somebody else's movie. *She thinks she's the producer, the director, the star.* It had not occurred to her, not seriously, that anything horrible could happen to her flesh in this venture, much less to her mind. (Her soul didn't come into consideration. She didn't believe that anyone had such a thing.) *I am going to do you a great service, lady. I am going to teach you that life is not a movie. You're going to find that out just before you die.*

She saw this in his eyes, and he let her see it, but because she'd never seen anything like it before, she let herself think that his feelings were something like her own. And now she felt he *would* like her naked, and that he sensed her talents in bed. She decided to like him, in the ironic and half-contemptuous way she reserved for liking what she liked best. She liked the classy cut of his clothes, she liked the fatigue in his face, she liked the deep-brown eyes that in their tenderness were so at odds with the tough set of his mouth. She hadn't expected to enlist an intelligent man in this project—it was her training and her conceit that truly intelligent men did not live on his level of the world. She also liked how he surprised her, and she was still too full of herself to realize how dangerous his intelligence could be for her. At this moment she liked how, when she took another cigarette from her pack, with a seamless gesture he reached for his lighter and lit her up. She'd come of age in a generation when that didn't happen often. He was right, she thought she was in a movie, and he was helping her think that by his look, his suit, his cigarette lighter.

"You owe me money," he said, "I had a lot of expenses on your account today." He told her what happened with Blue Suit. She liked that too. And she liked how much money he was charging her. "Three grand worth of suit, shoes, shirt, cuff links, the works." She made noises of protestation, but that was a formality. It made her feel powerful to give him the money. She liked the feeling of buying such a man.

They were touching now as a matter of course. Wedged between her bar stool and the next, he felt her leg first brush against his, then rest against it—and felt the messages passing through the cloth of her dress and his pants, the flesh of each giving up its initial resistance to the other. Somehow, without intention, they'd become intimates—far more intimate than either had wanted. The word "kill" can do that too, often faster and more unavoidably than the word "love."

They were smoking. They were looking closely at each other's mouth and eyes. They were making decisions: when to get the disk, and how to bait Mr. Sherman into a situation in which he could be killed. Their voices were soft in the loud bar, they spoke close to each other's ears, like lovers. Her ideas for trapping her husband were naïve—products of overheated fantasy and zero experience—but Rose listened, nodded, neither lied nor told the truth about his thinking, which was: he intended to kill her before her plan could take shape. Before dawn, in fact. His heart beat fast. The pain radiating through his body throbbed to the rhythm of its beat. Zig's On

Paradise bustled all around them, but its action seemed distant. Then the chorus girls and chorus boys began to fill the place for their late supper.

They wore their street clothes, which always were nondescript, as though to compensate for the near nakedness of the dazzling costumes they'd worn all night. But though all were frazzled and tired after performing two shows, still they moved like dancers, especially when together. They moved in concert and in counterpoint without thinking about it, without knowing it, and their bodies transmitted a muscular sensuality that others couldn't help but feel. As they sat at tables and squeezed themselves into small spaces at the bar, bantering and gossiping—"Well, I couldn't *help* it, I stubbed my *toe.*" "Union rules say we're supposed to change into *dry* costumes, was yours *dry*, the second show mine was *sopping.*" "Complain and you're gone, girlfriend." "You two don't have a relationship, you have a weather report, partly cloudy today, maybe sunny tomorrow, storm clouds coming." "If that singer misses her cue *one* more time." "You'd think the audience would notice." "They're all from Iowa and Japan, what do they know about noticing." "*I'm* from Iowa." "Well, you're not from *Japan*, are you, honey?" "*I* don't remember *where* I'm from" and the laughter and the sighs and the orders for drinks and food—they shimmered with the satisfactions and disappointments of people doing what they'd set out to do, people whose young fantasies had become painfully and proudly real.

Mike Rose liked them enormously. It was his favorite time of night in his favorite place. Not till several of them said in several ways, "Hey, Dee, where's Zig?" and "*You* don't know how much is on my tab, Dee, Zig does," did Rose remember that this time had changed forever.

Mrs. Sherman was bristling. "Who *are* they? Is it a college thing?" Zig's was near the UNLV campus. "Aren't they up past their bedtimes?"

"Dancers."

"I can't hear myself think."

*Considering what we're thinking, that may not be such a bad thing.*

Dee leaned suddenly across the bar. "Mike, *where's* Zig, this place is nuts tonight."

*Sure, Zig would have known Dee would make that call— after he'd calmed down a little. It would have to be Dee, the pure one, the one who didn't used to be so pure, the one who got along best with Zig, his favorite employee. That's the way things are done and he would have known. A special eye had to be kept on him. A loss of composure, in a man like Zig, was like a screaming nervous breakdown in anybody else.*

Dee would have been uneasy after that call, not because she'd guess its outcome, but just because she'd gone behind Zig's back. She'd have been a little jittery, and off her banter. Nothing like that could pass by Zig. And he would have been especially nice to her the rest of the day. That's how it's done too. Too late to kill her—she'd already made the call. No point in revenge because she'd done nothing very wrong by the standards of his world. Best too that no one suspect he knew, so he'd have time to make his move. And, for him, the only move left was Rose. So later that day he called him.

Zig said, "Mikey, can you talk?" "Yeah, Zig, Alvi's asleep, he's exhausted, didn't sleep last night, excited about getting out." And Zig said, "I got a job for you." "What kind of job?" And Zig said, "Our kind of job. Call it a commission. My kind, your kind, of job." "We do different work, Zig." And Zig said, "Not so different, Mikey. A matter of degree." "A matter of disagree. Let's not get confused here, Zig." And Zig said, "I got a job for you. I'm too old. I need you. Nobody but you." "You never needed anybody in your life, Zig." And Zig said, "I needed your father. He got dead on me. I needed your mother. Now she's dead on me. Now I need you." "Is it my turn to get dead on you?" And Zig said, "That's up to you." "Are you alright, Zig?" And Zig said, "Don't start asking me that. Don't. It's time for you to grow up, I think. I think that." "I don't know what you're talking about." And Zig said, "That's the point, kid. But you will." And Zig hung up. *I kept listening to the dial tone, feeling a fear I did not want to understand.*

*I guess the vultures get to eat the eyes. They get there first, and the eyes are what's most exposed. I never did close them, like they do in the movies. The coyotes must usually get the intestines, but those bullets opened Zig up pretty good, so maybe the vultures got lucky this time and got the intestines too, and what was left of the bladder, and all that. So the coyotes would have gotten what? The fleshy thighs, the arms, and digging into the chest cavity. I guess it's the insects that get the brains.*

"This place is always nuts at this time of night, Dee."

"Do creeps like that come in always?"

Dee pointed to three skinheads with their girls, all wearing rings and studs in their noses, cheeks, lips. No one could have been more out of place at Zig's On Paradise. Zig would never have let them in the door. The rings sticking from their lips, the studs protruding from their nostrils and pale cheeks, caught in Rose's stomach. They were young, strong, obscene, and loud. One rarely saw their particular mode in Las Vegas. *They like being ugly. They're throwing it in our faces. They're letting us know that ugly is all we've left for them to be. But I hate them for giving in to it.*

Dee said, "If Zig were here he'd throw them out. I don't know how."

"Want me to?"

"Naw, I don't know. Naw. But thanks, Mike."

*She certainly doesn't know Zig's dead. Doesn't suspect her part in it. And if she knew she'd cry and say, "They made me do it, what choice did I have?" Isn't that what people always say? Isn't that what makes the world go round?*

Mrs. Sherman smiled. "If she'd said yes, you'd have just thrown those people out? They don't look very throwable."

At the Golden Garter he'd had years to watch the bouncers, his father, and even his mother eject the unwanted.

"It's not so difficult," Rose said. "Spot the leader—that's the quieter one there, the one who's sitting so he can see the whole room, they're all playing to him—and take him down, fast. They're off their turf, they'd leave noisily but easily."

"You're a brave man."

"Brave only works if you know what you're doing. It's not a substitute for anything."

"Do you think I know what I'm doing?"

"No. That's why you're paying me."

Something crossed her face.

"What?" he said.

"*What* what?"

"What's on your mind?"

"Oh. That." She smiled—an engaging smile, rare for her. She enjoyed the level of attention he gave her. She wasn't used to it. Again she had no idea how dangerous not being used to things could be. "I was thinking, if I could find this place, so could my husband."

"I knew you'd be here. You'd ask around, and you look weird enough to be talked to by the people who'd know. He doesn't."

"I think I'll take that as a compliment."

"You might as well."

"Hadn't we better go get the disk?"

*I don't really want to. I like us here. To leave sets everything in motion. I've been stalling.*

"Let's go, then," he said.

He put a ten on the bar.

"That's a stiff tip for your club soda. Showing off?"

"If I were showing off, it would have been a fifty."

She laughed. "It's this town, isn't it?"

They made their way toward the exit as three showgirls came in. Taller than the dancers, more full bodied, the showgirls walked as they would for the rest of their lives, long after they left the business or the town: an erect, short-stepping prance, as though balancing a towering feather headdress above their spike-heeled nakedness, with the gaze of a beauty that pretended not to see what it was looking at. The dancers were alert, the showgirls languid. The dancers were jittery, the showgirls tired. The dancers chattered, the showgirls hardly spoke. The dancers seemed dancers every moment, the showgirls seemed detached from what they did. They towered over Rose and Mrs. Sherman. She'd bristled at the energy of the dancers; she receded before the polished beauty of the showgirls. She'd stared at the dancers with all her cultivated arrogance, but she looked away from the showgirls, pretending to see neither them nor the way Rose drank them in. He liked the dancers better, but felt more kinship with the showgirls. Once, before cancer took her breast, Joy had been the most beautiful showgirl in the world. He thought of Joy as he followed Mrs. Sherman into the cool night air. He and Mrs. Sherman walked as people do when they know that later they will be naked together—that had been decided, without words, during their talk of killing. Their bodies had taken that for granted, and they would merely follow their bodies. *I guess I'll kill you then. You'll almost like it, at first.* But for a few steps Joy walked beside them, bodiless, voiceless, looking as she did when very young, naked but for her glitter, the long, full, ash-blond hair reflecting neon, the great pink feathers swaying above her head as she walked and stared past all she saw. *"Michael, when you sleep with someone, their karma is part of your body for six months. When you kill, their karma is yours forever." When did she say that? No wonder she was so scared to touch me today.*

"We'll take my car," Rose said.

The Lincoln was still parked beside his Cadillac. He knew Lavender and Turquoise watched through the tinted glass. They were getting a good look at Mrs. Sherman. *Probably calling Gino right now on their cellular, describing her, asking should they wait for Zig or follow me, hoping I lead them to Zig. Gino will be puzzled about Mrs. Sherman. And if anybody finds her body tomorrow, and it gets in the papers, he'll be more puzzled. He'll be sure, then, she's not FBI—nobody kills a fed—and he'll waste some more time wondering who she really is. The more time he wastes, the better for me.*

*Mrs. Sherman sure seems cheerful about killing her husband.*

*Those two in the car, and me, and Mrs. Sherman—a parking lot full of killers.*

He headed west on Tropicana Avenue toward the Strip.

"This is quite a car," Mrs. Sherman said. "I feel like I'm in an old movie."

"The oldest one there is."

He was watching the rear view as much as the street ahead. *There's the Lincoln. Gino or Sallie must have told them to stick close, that if they try to be subtle I'll spot them anyway and lose them. That's respect. And don't think I don't appreciate it, boys.*

They crossed Koval. On their left was the smallish San Remo and the bright, blazing Tropicana. On their right, the massive blue block of the new MGM. *It opens New Year's Eve. They're paying Barbra Streisand eight million bucks to sing lies about her love life all night. They wouldn't pay her eight cents to sing the truth.*

"This town," Mrs. Sherman said. "It's two in the morning in the middle of the desert, and we're in a traffic jam."

"I'll give you this town in a nutshell, Mrs. Sherman. This blue monster on the right is going to be the biggest hotel in the world. But it's not gonna be a union shop. Of course, they don't want the unions to picket their opening, so what does the hotel do? They buy the sidewalk. That way, nobody can picket. Even the sidewalks are for sale around here."

"And what's more, people buy them."

"You understand perfectly."

He took a right at the corner and headed north on the Strip. Mrs. Sherman took in the Easter Island heads of the Trop, the Merlin atop the Excal, the Sphinx of the Luxor, with a mix of fascination and disgust not unlike his own.

"Human history has come here to die," she said.

"Or to win the jackpot. There's not much in between to do around here."

*It's just possible that she couldn't handle what she's planning in a city that was real to her. Let's give her the benefit of the doubt. Doubt may be all that we have left. The last of the saving graces.*

*I used to think that killers couldn't afford philosophy. But maybe that's all we can afford. After all, it comes so cheap.*

In the traffic the Lincoln was already three cars behind.

*Sallie, those boys of yours aren't very good. You know why? They didn't grow up in the slums, like you and Gino, or even in Vegas like me—they grew up in the suburbs, where all the wops moved when the colored started to take over the slums, and the suburbs don't teach the skills of our world. That's the slow death of the Mob.*

*Who are all these goddamned people in these cars? Where do they come from? And what satisfaction can they possibly get driving bumper-to-bumper in the middle of the desert at two in the morning? They drive bumper-to-bumper wherever they live to go to work every day, and then they take a vacation and drive bumper-to-bumper to gawk at neon. Say what you want about Mrs. Sherman, she wouldn't settle for what these assholes are settling for.*

*Look at her, that red dress hiked up on those skinny thighs. And the way she's slipped her heels off her bony feet. She wants to put her hand on my leg, I know she does. Or maybe I want to put my hand on hers.*

He reached and put his hand on her knee, then lifted her dress higher till his hand held her midthigh.

"That's a liberty, Mr. Rose."

"That's what makes it so nice."

She lay a hand on his and squeezed it, and returning the favor he squeezed her thigh hard, and they rode that way slowly in traffic. *Her leg's so skinny, but her flesh is so taut, she's a high-tension wire.* She lay her head back on the seat and spread her legs slightly and pressed her bare feet into the Cadillac's carpet. *We're both so hot. Why can't that be enough for us? What does it need the rest of this shit for?*

They drove past the soon-to-be-gone, falling-apart, thirty-five-dollar-a-night motels, where when you check in they ask, "Have you been here before?" *That's their way of telling you that your room is a toilet and your neighbors aren't likely to be nice people, they're not here for a convention, they're here looking for petty crimes to commit, and you're petty enough for their definition of crime. Those places will be gone soon, torn down for more malls and theme parks, and that'll hurt me—I've gotten a lot of business from those sleazebags.* Then the Alladin, *that jinxed joint.* Then Bally's, the lavender neon of the building, the bright pink sign. *Used to be the MGM. I remember the night it burned, and all those people died, more people than ever died in this town in one night or one week, and the flames rose hundreds of feet into the sky, you could feel the heat a quarter mile away, and Alvi stood beside me crying. I didn't cry. I put my arm around Alvi, and watched the flames.*

*Gotta make my move soon.*

The light at Flamingo Road was long. Many people crossed the street. Crossing from Bally's to the Barbary Coast, with the Flamingo's neon blazing beyond it. And crossing from the Barbary to Caesar's Palace. But nobody crossed anymore to the Dunes. It was fenced off, on the southwest corner, empty, dark.

*They'll blow it up tomorrow night. It's already exploding in my head, along with everything else. God, I'm gonna hate to see it go down. God, I hate this town. You got to hate something that gets you to feel emotions about anything as chintzy and useless as a casino. Alvi says I love it, but he's only known me all my life, what does he know? And her thigh feels so good. And my hand feels so good to her, I know that. Why can't that be enough for us? The Lincoln's four or five cars behind us now. And here's this low-life tapping at the window, wants to hand us one of those leaflets advertising "escorts" and "private dancers" and "ranches," ads for whores, he thinks we need one even though he sees a broad in the car. She's just staring at him.*

"What does he want?"

*And he sees my hand on her thigh and still waves that leaflet with the pouty, topless doomed one on the cover. And there's the green light. Gotta make my move.*

He gunned the Caddy across Flamingo Road, hugging the right curb, shooting past the Barbary Shore. The cars behind didn't pull out as fast, and one was a van that the Lincoln couldn't see past. *That van's my luck.*

*The Flamingo isn't anything anymore like what Bugsy built, but he'd love that neon over the entrance now, like a great pink-feathered crown atop a showgirl's head, and all the feathers gold tipped, and all of it pulsing with light. Look at her staring at it, look at the light reflecting on her shiny red dress. She thinks she's so damn smart—"Human history's come here to die"—and she hasn't got a clue.*

*I kind of like her for the clue she doesn't have.*

"Hold on!"

Mrs. Sherman didn't expect the sudden surge on the gas, then the slam on the brake while Rose spun the wheel right and the Caddy's rear end slid in a controlled skid and he heard brakes screech behind as he gunned it again. *Christ, I'd've been a good wheel man.* He'd made an expert right-angle turn into the driveway of the Flamingo, pedestrians careened out of his way as he sped down the long narrow alley toward the parking garage, bouncing hard over two speed bumps. *If we're lucky that van blocked those boys from seeing what went down. If we're really lucky they rear-ended the van when it hit its brakes, they're catching hell from Sallie on the cellular, and they're exchanging license numbers and insurance companies with the squares.* He swerved at the parking garage and took the driveway that went to its left, came out on Audrie, hung another left, a right on Albert, a left on Koval, never taking his right hand off her thigh.

"I'm impressed, Rose, but what *are* you doing?"

"We had a tail. Nobody you have to worry about. Another dilemma entirely."

"I'm the one who's paying for your time at the moment."

"That's why I lost them. They might have insisted on delays that would waste your money, or your husband's money, or whatever you're paying me with."

He took a right on Sands, continued where it fed into Twain, then slowed to normal as he turned left and north on Maryland Parkway.

"Who were they?"

"There's a kind of etiquette in this town—or there used to be. You don't ask questions about any action that doesn't involve you."

"If they're following you they're following me."

"They don't care about you."

"How flattering. Was it the Lincoln in the parking lot?"

"*Very* good. You'd be a pretty good partner, Mrs. Sherman."

He meant it, for a moment, and she basked in it, for a moment, and smiled a smile as close to girlish as she ever would again.

She hadn't expected to respect him. It was a new and queer sensation for her. The "kill" word had opened her in strange ways, to herself as well as to him—opened her into conflicting sensations, sensations she wouldn't have thought could exist together. They passed through her in waves like bands of different colors on a neon sign. Excitement of the kill, desire for him, fear of herself—of finally exerting herself in this way that had no exits and no turning back—and fear of the games he was playing, games she knew she only partly understood. If the word had occurred to her, she would have had to admit she was happy—a happiness she'd never guessed at: thrilled to be thrust beyond what she'd known or trained for or even wanted, beyond not only the rules she'd been taught but the rules she'd taught herself. And she wasn't alone in this newness. She was with him.

She didn't trust him, but she trusted what he knew. And trusted that he wanted her. She didn't care why. The force of his desire was enough, for now. Her husband had dimmed for her long ago. Her hatred of herself, of her husband, and of their world had become the medium in which she lived. She'd learned to make her hatreds work for her. And now here was this man who'd made his hatred of himself and his world work for him. She understood that much. And it was enough to wordlessly understand that, and feel his hand on her thigh, and sink in the plush seat of the big car, and press her bare feet into the carpet, and cruise down this dark quiet street with their dark purpose, this street of a city that lived as she did, by its own rules. She wouldn't have said so, it wouldn't have occurred to her in these terms, but like many who let go in Las Vegas, she felt she'd come home.

Driving north on Maryland Parkway in the wee hours there's little to be seen. The malls and department stores, all dark, are much like anywhere else. Cars are rare. And the brightness of the casinos, many blocks away, masks the intensity of the desert stars. It's the same city, but on this street, as on few others, it wears a different mask. Mike Rose and Mrs. Sherman relaxed in that difference.

"I assume you're a good gambler," she said, to say something and to hear him say something. There were no hard edges on his baritone voice. The rhythms of his speech were sharp, but the quietness of his tones softened that, and he had an intimate way of directing his words, as though he'd known one a long time. Not like her voice—crisp, pointed.

"You said something?"

"You a good gambler?"

"'Cause I live in Vegas?"

"'Cause you still have your hand on my thigh."

"You need a head for numbers to ace blackjack or craps. I don't have that. You have to sit in one place for a long time and tolerate dull company to be a good poker player, and I can't do either. I enjoy roulette, though."

"You would. But isn't that a sucker's game?"

"That's me, a sucker from way back."

"That's not true and that's not charming."

"A sucker is anybody who gets some secret or not-so-secret satisfaction from losing. That makes us both suckers."

"What am I losing?"

"The only words for it are religious, and they don't work anymore."

"I think I'm getting tired of being your straight man."

"So talk."

"Let me explain what's on the disk. It's—"

"Don't even try. I don't have that kind of mind."

"And you don't care. That's alright, I don't either, anymore. It's just a poker chip to me. God, did you hear that? This town infects one's metaphors. I'm an educated woman, damnit. Or I used to be. Not that it does one much good."

"You've got an educated thigh, I'll say that."

"Hmm. The disk—I really *do* want to explain it. I want to show off."

"You've done a pretty good job of that all along."

"Haven't I? Now about the disk—"

"Look, I don't care. What's on the disk, how much money you can make off it, or whether it's some new something or other that may or may not change civilization as we know it— I don't give a shit. What interests me is where I fit in the deal. The part of the action you're paying me for, that's all that interests me. That, and your thigh. The rest sounds like the garbage you WASPs always run around bothering everybody about. WASPs are always coming up with something that makes things bigger, better, faster—and everything gets worse."

"You really *are* a snob."

"Want me to take my hand off your thigh?"

"I'll kill you if you do."

She enjoyed saying that very much.

Several days ago, when he'd seen her for the first time, he'd been running late. She was standing in front of the street door to his office on Fremont, and the sun brought out the deep yellow of her long hair. She was tapping her feet and cracking her knuckles. Her clothes were the best kind of expensive—texture complemented color, various yellowish beiges that made her hair seem even lovelier; slacks and blouse that didn't call attention to themselves, not really—yet just standing there she made everybody else on the street look uncouth. But they were the clothes of a calmer, more contained person. They were a lie on her. He could see that before they exchanged a word. She'd never been calm a day in her life. She did her nervous ticks in patterns, foot-tapping, knuckle-cracking, shifting weight from one hip to the other, then taking small steps like a jittery horse at the gate. *That's what gamblers call a "tell."* She would be like this anytime anything forced her to stand still.

"Mrs. Sherman? I'm Mike Rose."

"You're twenty minutes late, Mr. Rose."

He wasn't prepared for the black stones she used for eyes. They made his impression, standing next to her, entirely different from what it had been from just a few yards away. Nor was he prepared for how skinny she really was. Her clothes were carefully tailored to soften her extreme thinness. There were nights she liked to shock with her appearance, and afternoons when she didn't.

As he unlocked the street door he smiled as well as he could manage—she was a prospective client, after all—and said, "It's a city without clocks, as I'm sure you've heard. There's a . . . laxity, you might call it, about time, kind of built in. That's why I chose such atmospheric business quarters." He gestured to the crowded sidewalk, and down Fremont toward the Four Queens, the Golden Nugget, Binion's, Sassy Sally, Vegas Vic, Glitter Gulch, the Golden Garter, the Plaza, all of it, and added, "Good for watching people."

"If one happens to like people."

"I'm trying to say I'm sorry."

"Then say it."

"I'm sorry."

*Interesting combination. She's nervous but she's not insecure. It's not the nervousness of fear, then; it just looks that way. I suppose that makes people underestimate her.*

When they were seated in his office he lit a cigarette, his first of the morning, and Mrs. Sherman said, "Do you have to do that?"

"I'm just full of mistakes this morning, aren't I, Mrs. Sherman?"

He went to put it out, but she said, "That is not necessary. It *is* your office."

He showed his surprise.

"What?" she said.

"I was just deciding, Mrs. Sherman, to take you at your word and continue my smoke."

That, in turn, surprised her.

"What?" he said, smiling only a little.

"I didn't expect—" She stopped, then began again, "I didn't expect this meeting to be quite so . . . exacting."

*Her fidgeting stopped. Once she's actually within a situation, she can control her nerves. Very interesting.*

"What would you like me to help you with, Mrs. Sherman?"

"I want information, not help."

"And now that we have *that* straight—"

*She can't take her eyes off the cigarette. For someone with her insides it must have been major to quit—especially to quit and not gain weight. She didn't quit for her health, I'd bet a grand on that. I'd guess she hated having to ask people if they minded, and having so many say they did. Yes, she'd hate having to go through that umpteen times a day, and her hate would show, and she couldn't afford that.*

"Maybe this is a mistake," she said.

"It usually is."

"What do you mean?"

"It's usually a good idea to leave people like me out of your personal life, if this is a personal matter. People like me usually dig up things that most people would be better off not knowing."

It was movie patter, though it happened to be true, and he indulged in it because it gave clients a reference point and let them assume an attitude. Most of them came without one, and needed one badly.

"Do you tell all your clients that?"

"Some version of it."

"And that lets *you* off the hook?"

"A hook that can be got off so easily isn't a hook."

She liked that, and he liked her for liking it.

"Mr. Rose, I wish I had come to you with something interesting, but I haven't. It won't seem interesting to someone like you. It'll seem common and silly and a little cheap—because it is. A woman checking up on her husband. And I suppose all women checking up on their husbands have to do a little dance to get themselves to speak of it, as I have."

"Some do, some don't. I like the ones that do better."

"Why?"

"It all means more to them."

She liked that too.

"But perhaps you don't take domestic cases, like Jim Rockford?"

"If I didn't take domestic cases, I'd starve."

"My husband is a kind of genius, Mr. Rose. Do you meet many geniuses?"

"I've met some." *I wonder if Meyer Lansky or Elvis Presley count as geniuses in your book, lady.* "I understand that they're pains in the ass."

"That seems to be their right. My husband's a computer genius."

"The world seems full of them these days."

She took an envelope out of her purse and put it on the desk. "That contains his photograph and itinerary. He's coming here for—"

"The Nerd Convention, we call it."

"It's an odd sensation to defend him—I don't think I ever have before, I'm not that kind of wife—but whatever else he is, he is not a nerd. If he was, I wouldn't need your services, would I?"

"We might have different definitions of the word." *A nerd is anyone who lives mostly in his head. I'm kind of a nerd. I suspect you are too.* "Actually, I was going to look in on that convention anyway."

"You don't seem the type," she said a little too quickly.

Rose put out his cigarette. She watched him do it.

"Electronics and computers are making my profession obsolete—at least, that's what the guys who *sell* them are claiming, and a lot of suckers are believing them. Thought I'd take a peek, see if there's any truth to the sell."

"I would have thought that they're giving you the tools to be even more dangerous."

"Maybe. Though 'dangerous' isn't how—"

"We keep stumbling over each other's words, Mr. Rose."

She smiled again. She shouldn't have. And she suddenly knew it. She was overplaying, engaging Rose in too much conversation. The usual client is embarrassed, nervous, and angry, all three. They came to him either because something had pushed them over the edge or they were scared something would. They came to him because something had made them feel powerless and they wanted to hire a little power.

*They usually think they're a better sort of people than I am, and they're probably right.*

Most of his clients had romantic problems or were trying to find somebody who didn't want to be found—somebody who'd come to Vegas to get lost, which is a mark of ignorance, Vegas is hard to disappear in. It's too small, too obvious, there are too few places to hide. The average client engaged Rose in as little conversation as possible. They felt they were doing something vaguely illicit by hiring him.

*The more square they are, the faster they want our meeting to be over with. Only the ones who are really worried make this much conversation—the ones who have not only problems but trouble. And Mrs. Sherman is smart enough to savvy she's tipped her hand.*

*She ought to fold. Cancel the assignment and try again with someone else, someone with whom she'll watch herself more carefully, someone who can't see into her act. If she doesn't fold it means she can't, she's pressed.*

"So you'll take the . . . the assignment? The case?"

"The case." *We're sticklers for words, Mrs. Sherman and I.*

He told her his fee. *They're usually shocked, but she's not—and I hiked the price a bit for her, to give her a good excuse to pull out, but she hasn't. She must really be planning some mischief.*

"That's acceptable," she said of the fee.

*Might as well tip my hand too. I have nothing better to do.*

"You look like a complicated person, Mrs. Sherman."

"That can't be very hard to deduce. For you."

"A problem like this, a marital problem—simpler people go to someone like me. More complicated people, they tend either to handle it themselves or get some sort of therapeutic help."

"Well, perhaps," she said slowly, "I'm a complicated person trying to do what a simpler person would do, in order that I may become simpler."

"You have high hopes, lady."

She gave that the look it deserved, and gave him her private number in San Diego, explaining that she and her husband had different phone lines. She had flown into Vegas for this meeting, she said; she was flying back that afternoon. *Of course, just because you gave me a San Diego number doesn't mean your phone rings in San Diego. With call forwarding it could ring anywhere.*

After she left he sat smoking a cigarette and idly folding and unfolding the check she'd left him—a retainer much larger than anybody honest would have considered.

*She'll either put a stop on the check and never see me again, or she'll be back within the hour and tell me something like the truth.*

She didn't knock, just opened the door and walked in, graceful, relaxed, dropping her act for the first time in a long time. He liked the set of her mouth and the flash of her eyes when she wasn't feeling caged. She sat down and crossed her legs and smiled.

"Everything I've said to you, as I think you realize, has been . . . obfuscation."

"Bullshit?"

"If you prefer."

"Good. It was boring. And that seemed out of character for you."

"Thank you."

"So now that you've decided, almost against your better judgment, that I'm exactly what you're looking for—"

She put the computer disk on his desk.

"I need you to hold this for me. The people who want it—my husband, actually, and his associates—are going to want it very badly. Things could become difficult."

"Important things generally do."

"Most people believe my lies. Including myself, now and again. Why didn't you?"

"I don't lie. That takes some fancy dancing sometimes, but I don't lie, Mrs. Sherman, at least not consciously. Make a discipline of that, and it gets pretty easy to spot lies in others."

"Not even for business purposes, you don't lie?"

"Not even."

"That must make life . . . interesting."

"Exactly."

*What a look.*

"It's not a *moral* stance then, is it? No. Not at all." She grinned. "It's—"

"An experiment."

"Ah. I'll buy *that* dream, sweetheart."

They sat quietly a few moments, never taking their eyes off each other.

"I'll tell you what, Mr. Rose. I won't lie either. Not to you."

"Why?"

" 'Why' is a question I've given up on, Mr. Rose."

*And now we're parking in an alley, bent on murder. She's looking at me with just a quiver of alarm. She has no idea where we are or why. Driving north on Maryland, after you* cross Sahara, even the malls and shops are gone, and it's just little houses, some of them nice, some of them dinky, back from when Vegas was a little town, more than three wars ago, a little town of five thousand or so, most of the guys building Hoover Dam or working the railroad, with a few rough dens on Fremont, and the families lived in these houses in this part of town, but the sidewalks weren't paved then, and there was no great glow from the Strip and downtown to dim the stars, and at this hour of the night, or the morning, or whatever it is, all the lights in these little homes were off then as they are now, but the doors weren't locked because nobody was worried about killers like us driving by. She's worried. This neighborhood's too dark and quiet for her. She's too proud to ask where we're going, and maybe too scared of the answer. No. She's having too much fun to be really scared, for now. And she's all confused about her thigh.

So am I.

When we crossed Fremont she almost asked, because about a mile to the left was my office and Glitter Gulch, but we just cruised down another dark street.

I could have killed her there and met God and taken on her karma forever like I did Zig's and like he did Pop's and so many others. Zig died bursting like a boil from the pressure of congealed karmas he was too small to hold. That's what Joy would say, anyway. Is there ever any forgiveness if Joy is right? I could have just pulled over and—she's so thin— snapped her neck, no blood, dumped her on the street, gone on. It occurred to me, but I let it go. It might have been her thigh, it might have been how much I like her, I hate her but I like her, and . . . I want to see how the night's going to play, how the least innocent dawn of my life is going to come— maybe I'll let her stick around for that. Inside and out my body hurts, hurts bad, and all that seems to be keeping me awake is desire for her.

*And now we're parking in the alley, and she's looking at
me, and she's damned if she'll say, "What are we doing here?"
I like her for that.*

He took her in the back way. He still had the key, still had
privileges. They'd sold the Golden Garter years ago, he and
Alvi, and it had gotten them the condo and a well-stuffed safe-
deposit box (Rossellinis did not believe in banks), but they still
had privileges. So he pulled the key out in the alley and
opened the featureless metal door, opened it upon the stink of
sweat and smoke and alcohol and perfume, and the heavy
rhythms of disco, and the bright lights of the hallway, which
was still much as it was when he first saw Joy undressing there,
underthings and street clothes hanging from hooks, walking
shoes in pairs against the walls, a young woman undressing,
another dressing, the glare of the makeup lights, cosmetics on
narrow shelves by the mirrors, and, where the mirrors faced
each other from opposite walls, their images multiplied
smaller and smaller, disappearing into what now might be
called virtual something or other. Mrs. Sherman walked behind him, careful not to step upon the things on the floor,
careful not to brush against what hung from the hooks, careful not to touch in any way the women dressing and undressing in the narrow corridor, and careful, most of all, to avoid
eye contact with her reflection as it passed through the various
mirrors. But she could not help seeing herself for instants—
the hall seemed so long and there were so many mirrors—seeing her yellow hair, which gleamed so in the harsh light; seeing
her black spike heels, with spaces for her long bony toes; seeing the long, tight, red dress with the slit up the thigh accent-
ing her thinness, very expensive, very sluttish, which was why
she'd chosen it, to wear for him, for the town. Mrs. Sherman
felt startled, disoriented, even tricked, and something worse:
insubstantial, beside these fleshy girls with their huge, too-

perfect breasts that seemed to have a life of their own, a life the girls merely carried. Mrs. Sherman tried to remember the last time she'd been in a room with naked women. Not since she'd sculpted her thinness. She felt tested and consciously called upon herself to meet the test, and fixed her eyes upon Mike Rose's back, the certainty with which he walked, the fine cut of his suit. She hated and loved him, just for a moment, but it changed everything. She had dared herself often, but it had been a very long time since a *man* had forced her beyond her boundaries, and he'd done it with such seeming effortlessness. She laughed to herself with the words: "I'll make you pay."

Rose, for his part, felt her presence behind him intensely. *Why did I bring her among all these witnesses? Guess it doesn't much matter, after the witnesses at Zig's. A fucking lot of witnesses, though. The night is crowded with witnesses. Now I'll have to leave her out in the desert with Zig. Zig whose parts are already being carried to God in the mouths of coyotes.*

Mirrors lined the walls. The ceiling was a mirror. Mrs. Sherman was relieved there was no mirror at her feet. The music was deafening and anonymous and androgynous, piercing voices male or female, she didn't see how anyone could tell, singing something mechanical and repetitive about touching and love. She hadn't the impression so much of women everywhere as of breasts everywhere, and legs, and asses, body parts loosely organized around faces and G-strings, net stockings and bras, body parts in motion between high heels and purple and green and lavender hair. There were three runways of women dancing, or whatever it was they were doing—body parts gyrating, swiveling, bouncing, a sexual calisthenics for men who were somehow obscenely clothed, for their clothing made their faces seem especially naked as they gazed, dazed, at whatever body part caught their eye or was shoved in their face. She wondered if her clothing made her face as naked as the men's, and she wanted to rip off her dress to de-emphasize her face. She told herself again that she would make him pay for this. She told herself too that she must master this place somehow, make her mark upon it, or else she would never be able to leave, not really.

Then she caught him looking at her, smiling.

"I didn't realize we were on a date," she said. "Do you take all your 'thighs' here?"

"I grew up here. My family used to own this joint."

"I'm bourgeois enough to be impressed by that."

"I know."

It was difficult to talk above the music—at least, to talk as they'd become used to talking.

He said, "We're here strictly on business, Mrs. Sherman."

"My business?"

"Naturally." And he added, "You're standing in a historical place. The first topless joint in Las Vegas."

"Will this be on the test? Will there be a quiz?"

"There—"

"Always is. See, I'm learning your style. I can hear the punch line coming."

"Obviously we're—"

"Meant for each other? That's too easy. How about, we like the same flavor of doom?"

"Too educated. How about just, I can't take my eyes off you."

"Too true."

He couldn't tell what she was feeling for him, but the intensity of the feeling, whatever it was, made him want to kiss her very much. For that matter, he didn't know his own feelings. Joy had danced on that runway. His mother had stood where they were standing—watching, laughing when Joy had revealed her scar to the shock of Mike and the other men. Rose had never brought a woman here before, in all these years. He felt the bond forming with this woman, and it confused him—while another part of him, incurably moral, was shocked at how the thought of killing her made her more desirable.

He took her arm and walked her half the length of the runway bar. Waitresses and dancers flashed recognition at him. They didn't look like women who respected many men, so Mrs. Sherman was impressed by their respect for him. She didn't know that most people on this level of Vegas knew that though he wasn't a gangster, gangsters treated him with the familiarity of one of their own, so they stepped aside for Rose as they did for the Mob.

Rose stopped behind two stools, one empty and one occupied by a large young man, beefy, preppy, and radiating the anger of self-pitying loneliness. A dancer was standing with her arm around him. She stroked his cheek with her free hand—a gesture that excited and clearly confused the large young man. His eyes were hungry, hers routinely cheerful until she noticed Rose.

"Mike!"

"Trixie. It *is* 'Trixie' still?"

"I'm thinking of changing it again." Her face moved close to the young man's. "Do you like 'Trixie' or 'Maggie' better? Think about it, will ya?"

"Excuse me," Rose said to the man.

"What? We're busy."

"I'd like for this lady," he motioned to Mrs. Sherman, "to sit on that stool—the very one you're sitting on."

"There's, uh, other stools."

"That's not the point, though, is it?"

"Stop showing off," Mrs. Sherman said. "We know you're tough."

Rose ignored her and said to the man, "If you're gracious about this, I'll purchase a table dance for you from Tricky Maggie here."

"I like that," the girl said, "but it's too long."

"If you're *not* gracious," Rose said to the man, "I'll have them throw you out."

"He's got that kind of juice, sugar," the girl said confidentially to the young man.

"Well, why don't *you* throw me out?"

"Because I've got nothing against you, and they'll be a lot nicer about it than I would."

The young man wasn't quick with words. He tried to say something, but sputtered. Rose gave the girl a fifty-dollar bill.

"Dance for the man."

"For me, first," Mrs. Sherman said.

"Can you wait?" Rose said to Mrs. Sherman.

"Certainly not."

"Can *you* wait?" he said to the young man.

The beefy preppy person was angry and confused. But he had the sense to be frightened. Something radiated off these people, something that would be merciless toward him, something he knew he could not match.

"Why . . . why don't you just give *me* the fifty, and I'll just go?"

"Because I'd rather give it to her."

Rose was smiling. The girl was smiling, so that even her breasts seemed to be smiling, and with pink powder upon them they smiled with an eerie glow under the dark blueish lights. Mrs. Sherman was smiling too, and her smile was the worst of all, because now she wanted to see something happen to the young man.

"Okay," he said. "Okay."

He stood up and walked to another stool.

"What's a table dance?" Mrs. Sherman laughed.

"She's cherry, Mike," the girl said. "Oh, boy."

The booths against the wall were deep and small, there were high dividers between each booth, and small tables in front of them through which shining metal poles ran from floor to ceiling. Rose sat at the bar, on the stool from which the young man had retreated, and the girl led Mrs. Sherman by the hand and sat her in the nearest booth. Rose and Mrs. Sherman lit cigarettes at the same time, and at the same time lifted their drinks to their lips. Women, naked but for some net and string, danced on the bar behind Rose and in the mirror behind Mrs. Sherman, and upside down in the ceiling, where she couldn't help glancing though it made her dizzy as her own face hovered above her as exposed as a breast.

The music thudded. The girl began to move.

*No matter how far you go or how hard you try, your obsessions get there ahead of you and wait in ambush. You've disciplined yourself, you don't do that shit anymore, don't need it anymore—and the secret shameful places in you touched by those obsessions, they're not hungry anymore, and even if they are you're not going to feed them anymore, you'll let them die of hunger, die of thirst, parts of you that are better off dead.*

*But they never really die, they never even sleep. They just wait. Parts of you are always waiting; much of what you are is just their waiting. Until, through no fault of your own, through nothing you set up, something or someone comes to awaken those parts you thought were dead—as though all the while, and secret from yourself, you've been calling out, begging for something to come and quicken the deadness in you, come and waken the corpses within that you've been dragging around. We gauge our maturity by the dead weight within us.*

*Maybe what wakens the dead is that you kill someone. For some people it's shoes or boys or leather. It never makes any sense, never even looks very real. Or sometimes it's something as easy and somehow scary as one woman brushing her breasts against the cheeks of another. So no woman can really get to me unless she's got some dyke in her. And it's being pulled out of this woman now, yanked straight out of her eyes, eyes wet and black and scared now, and fierce with being scared.*

Mrs. Sherman sat rigid, and the girl who couldn't decide what to call herself, the girl whose breasts and face seemed to live different lives, the face harsh and playful, the breasts so bountiful and serious, that girl saying in a whisper that cut through the din of mechanical rhythm, "Don't *move*, sugar, I'll do the movin', I'll move like ya always wanted to, I'll drive you crazy like the boys, skin is skin, baby—*man*, you got weird eyes, let's peel this dress a little, gotta spread your legs like the boys to do this right, nice cloth, *I* see those panties, Mike's in for a treat . . ." the girl's staccato patter so removed from her body's undulations, as with hands as practiced and firm as a gynecologist's she spread Mrs. Sherman's knees, and bent and swayed her breasts so that they brushed the inner thighs, touching where Rose's fingers had clutched, and then the girl raised herself slowly while pumping to the rhythm, and now her breasts brushed Mrs. Sherman's cheeks again, cheeks still hot from the first touch, and the girl stepped slowly but pulsing to the music, stepped upon the low table in front of Mrs. Sherman, and clung to the shining pole that went through the table, and turned, and her ass shined in Mrs. Sherman's eyes as she swiveled it around Mrs. Sherman's face. Mrs. Sherman's face and thighs tingled, her skin felt like the battleground of two assaults, one from without, one from within. In the last hour two people of different sexes had breached a boundary in her, touched longings she'd disciplined herself to do without for a very long time. The wetness she'd felt for that hour, the waves of inner heat, the shortness of breath—they were as new as they had been the first times, long ago. She thought wordlessly that perhaps this is what she'd been saving herself for, preparing herself for, and she had only reached this place through the decision to kill her husband, a decision that made her happy in a way she'd never guessed possible. It wasn't that she wanted to sleep with this girl. She didn't. But as the girl was saying again and again, "Skin is skin, skin is skin," and it was as though the girl was preparing her, like a lady in waiting, for the man, and she wanted the man more and more now, his eyes were fixed upon her, his eyes were filled with something she had never seen in a man's eyes. She didn't know what it was but it fed a hunger in her. Again she thought that she would make him pay for this journey—it was an item of faith with her that a man must pay for any feeling he inspired in her—and for the first time Mrs. Sherman thought that she must kill Mike Rose. She had a small pistol in her purse. She could kill him easily. The girl brushed her ass against Mrs. Sherman's cheek. She wanted to bite it, but she would save her bites for him. It had been a long time since she'd remembered how much she liked to bite. That other man, the large young man, he was watching too. She suddenly wondered if Rose had thought of killing her. There seemed no reason for him to. He wouldn't do it for her husband, she knew that—and she believed him about how he didn't lie. "But yes," she thought, "look at him, he thinks he's going to kill me. He doesn't know himself as well as he thinks. He can't kill me. He loves me—a little but enough. But I can kill him. I'm going to. I love him, a little, and a little is a lot, and I can't let him do that to me, can't let him make me love him." Her skin tingled all over her body. The girl now pressed the soft flesh of her thigh first gently, then firmly, into Mrs. Sherman's crotch, Mrs. Sherman's panties were soaked, and she felt her fluids slick against the girl's thigh as it moved to the music, and the girl was a little dizzy with victory, but Mrs. Sherman didn't begrudge that, not now, and just as she was wishing that the girl would dance forever, that this was a way to remain forever, caressed by so many lusts, with his eyes upon her and the girl's flesh teasing her and her own flesh teasing her, just as she was wishing this, the music ended.

"Give her another fifty. I've had a religious experience."

•

They were sitting at the bar, Rose and Mrs. Sherman, and another girl was gyrating for them. It wasn't really dancing that these girls did—they were nothing like the performers eating at Zig's, they had neither the infectious energy of those dancers nor the shining arrogance of those showgirls. With few exceptions, their faces were rougher, more dissipated, and deeply tired—fatigued as much with disgust as with effort. Sooner or later it was impossible for most of these girls to resist the impression that their true mirrors were not on the walls and the ceilings, but in the despair and self-loathing on the faces of the men who stared their bodies into nothingness.

"What happens to these girls?" Mrs. Sherman spoke as though the girl, who was swaying her breasts from her face to Mike's, couldn't hear.

"What happens to anybody? They get tougher, harder, drier. Some crack up, some hook, some leave. Some get religion, some get killed, a few get rich. They get older. They get fat. They wonder what their lives were all about. Just like librarians."

"Just like truckers," Mrs. Sherman said.

"Just like computer experts."

"Just like killers."

"Are you guys married?" the girl said, bending so her nipple touched the tip of Mrs. Sherman's large wedding stone.

"Partners in crime," said Rose.

"That's what I said," laughed the girl. "Do I get a fifty too?"

"What'll you do for it?" Rose said.

"Anything—within reason."

"Within reason won't work. You get a twenty."

"I thought," Mrs. Sherman said, "that we were getting my disk tonight. Not that I'm not having a *divine* time."

"I'm all business, lady. You're sitting on your disk."

"You're kidding!"

"That's why I pushed that kid off these stools. Think I go around doing that kind of thing just to impress clients?"

"No, I thought you were doing it to impress yourself."

"I told you I grew up in this joint. You're sitting on my old hiding place from when I was a kid. Nobody, not even my brother, knows about it."

*And after I kill you tonight nobody will know about it again. But, I tell you, I'm getting a little exhausted with this "kill" word. It was giving me juice, now it's starting to drain me. It's weird how a word can change its meaning all through the day.*

Some other girl now was waving her ass in their faces. The music seemed to have gotten louder. *Some big convention must be in town for this joint to be this crowded this late.* A wave of middle-aged guys in modest suits came in. *They've all got wedding rings. They'll love that kid who touched the ring with her nipple.*

"I like this place, I've decided," Mrs. Sherman said.

"It grows on you."

"So how do we get my disk without being too obvious?"

"Like this."

Her dress was hanging off her thigh at the slit. He parted it some more, exposing her leg, and then, as the girl had done, put his hand on her knee and spread her legs.

"Is this your idea of not being obvious?" she said.

"Sex—"

"Don't say it, don't say it, I know what you're going to say: sex is the least obvious thing in a joint like this."

"Very good again."

"I'm catching you, like an infection."

And his hand went down her leg as the girl shimmied breasts in her face, then his hand went under the stool, unlatched the compartment he'd built there long ago, the disk fell into his hand, he pressed the compartment till he felt it click shut, pressed the disk along her thigh as though drawing a line, and placed it in her lap. She grabbed it and put it in her purse. He lit a cigarette and she took it from him. He lit another for himself. Mrs. Sherman had asked Rose to keep the disk because she'd had no confidence in her ability to conceal it from her husband; that was before she'd hit upon the simpler plan of murder.

Now, with the music and the nakedness and the disk in her handbag and Rose's hand resting again on her thigh and her bare leg hanging from the stool and her bony foot in spikes tapping the rhythm, she was thinking that anything was possible, anything at all.

She said, "Did you go to school? College, I mean."

"This is my school. What did you major in?"

"Science. Computers."

"Why?"

"Computers are ruthless. I liked them for that."

"Weren't you a little young to understand that in college?"

"Too young to understand, not too young to feel."

Another girl had started her gyrations before them. They were a very popular couple. The men in modest suits had filled the bar stools and booths all around them, because the girls were putting on the best shows for them. To the men in modest suits, Rose and Mrs. Sherman were as exotic as, in some ways more exotic than, the girls, and were watched almost as avidly. The couple had been putting twenties in the dancers' G-strings, and between their breasts, and between their toes, and in their mouths. Twenties are a very large tip—dollars are common, fives are considered generous. But the men in modest suits didn't know this, and tried to follow the example of the exotic couple. Nights like this happen rarely, and the girls of the Golden Garter were on a feeding frenzy. There were a dozen table dances going on at once, and all the girls wanted to work that runway, and the music throbbed, and it all seemed to revolve around the long yellow hair and the jet-black eyes and the skinniness of Mrs. Sherman. And Mrs. Sherman gloated on it, thrived on it. She was the center of all their energy, she was making her mark on the place as she'd promised herself. In many ways it was the happiest night of her life, and Rose sensed this without knowing why. *A good day to die, then. For it's sad to live past your happiest day.*

"Look," she was saying, "how the girls run their hands over their bodies, what does that remind you of? It's like they're in a shower, it's the same gestures, the same I use to wash my body."

"I'd like to see that."

"You very well may. Give me a fifty, I like her. I'm going to teach her something. I think I've discovered a knack for this sort of thing."

At Zig's On Paradise she'd paid Rose's expenses in cash— three thousand dollars, in hundreds and fifties. She'd explained how easy it was to hack into a credit card computer and find out where the purchases were, so she was "doing this trip" on cash. She'd liked it when he told her he'd never had a credit card or a bank account—"It's not how I was raised"—and had never bought anything except with cash. "How do you pay your taxes?" she'd asked. "With a money order," he'd said. Now he was dropping half of what she'd paid him at the Golden Garter, and that felt appropriate. He didn't have to look at the men in modest suits to see how this affected them. Their sense of obscenity was excited more by how he and Mrs. Sherman were spending money than by the nakedness. Rose gave her the fifty.

As the girl once again bent her breasts into the woman's face, Mrs. Sherman said, "I want to stick this fifty in your crack. I'm surprised I haven't seen anyone do that."

"What, honey?"

"Your crack, *honey*. Turn around. Bend over. Good, honey. Now, like you did before, spread your cheeks with those long pink fingernails. That's right. What a sweet behind you have! How prettily molded." To Rose she said, "Mine's so bony, you'll see." And to the girl, "And now I slide the bill into your crack, like so. Now, *flex*. And stand up."

They could feel the heat rise from the men in modest suits. The girl seemed very pleased. Rose wondered whether she'd still be pleased about it if she lived to be an old woman.

"You thought of that all by yourself, did you?"

"I want you," Mrs. Sherman said. "In my crack. All over. Mike, I'm going crazy."

"Let's go."

They were both trembling.

As they walked out, arm in arm and hip to hip, she said, "They must have to shave their pubic hair a *lot*, to keep that . . . area . . . smooth. That would drive me crazy. If they let it go for even a couple of days, it would get bristly, itchy. Shaving that often, it's almost like being a man."

"Wait, why are we going out the front door, sugar, your car's in back?"

"The hotels'll be full with this convention, sugar. There's no point trying to find a room, sugar. We can't go to my place, my brother's there." *And he doesn't need to see me kill you.* "And we can't go wherever you're staying, 'cause I don't know where it is, and I don't want to know."

"Why, sugar?"

"Because if I get caught and tortured I don't want to be able to say where it is."

"That's noble of you."

"No, just Sicilian. I don't want my torturers, if I should ever have torturers, to be satisfied. That would *really* bother me."

"Are you really Sicilian?"

"Very really."

"So we're going to your office?"

"Good girl."

"Somebody may be waiting for us."

"We'll kill them."

She laughed.

He hadn't lied, but the truth had just changed.

*Okay, God. If somebody tries to kill me or her, between now and dawn, I won't do anything to avoid it. Hear me? Is that a prayer, or what? And if we live, I'll take that as a sign of Your approval. Fair?*

Fremont Street was empty but for the neons. The air was chill. He put his arm around her, and they walked in sync, body to body, like people in love.

*It is terrible to be happy when happy changes nothing.*

"Happy?" she said.

"Yeah."

"It's like a new pair of shoes. It's pretty but it pinches."

"You're drunk."

"A little."

Her face, especially around the mouth, was ten years younger now—free of tension, not pursed in irony or defiance. And it needed something to do.

"Kiss me," she said.

*Kill us now, God, if You're gonna.*

It was the kind of kiss into which people disappear and are sometimes never found again. The kind of kiss into which cities and countries and whole civilizations vanish. Her science and his Sicily disappeared. Parts of them would never come back. If they lived, they'd have no choice but to call that moment "love."

"I didn't know about that," she said, more tenderly than he thought she could speak.

"I did once, but I'd forgot."

"I won't forget."

"I don't think I will now either."

*Oh, Christ. I'm in love for five minutes and I've told my first lie in years.*

A cab went by, then a patrol car. They walked past the open casino doors of Sassy Sally's and Binion's. All Rose's professional instincts told him to notice who played slots close to the exits, but he disciplined himself to his promise and prayer, kept his eyes only on the woman who was, for these moments, his woman. *Let them follow, let them come, if they're in there—let them kill, before we do.*

Only when they crossed Third did he look across the street toward the Four Queens and down that block, where he'd ruined Blue Suit twenty-three hours ago.

*It's amazing I'm still awake. It's her. She's a walking amphetamine.*

They crossed Fremont and stood in front of the door to his building.

"How romantic! It's where we met!"

"But when we met the lock wasn't broken," Rose said.

Mrs. Sherman took a small pistol from her handbag.

"Would you like this?"

He took it from her silently, thinking of his promise. *I'm going to let them kill us, baby, if they're up there. You won't mind, not really.*

He felt strangely at peace as he climbed the stairs. In fact, they were the most peaceful moments of his life. So Rose was disappointed when they found no one waiting. His promise to God remained untested.

"They've made a mess of your well-appointed digs," she said.

There was no reason to turn on a light. The neon of the street was enough to see by. Anything that could be broken had been. All the drawers were open, their contents everywhere.

"Your husband and his people are both thorough and ineffectual."

"That's a pretty good description of them once they get ten feet away from their keyboards."

"Fucking amateurs, thinking that the disk would be here. A pro wouldn't even have bothered."

*The Skinniness of Mrs. Sherman*

"Amateurs are the death of culture," she said breezily.

The black metal box lay overturned on the desk. Two photographs of Rosie Vee were torn in half, the rest were scattered on the desktop. He watched as she picked them up and held them to the light, one by one.

"These are great," Mrs. Sherman said, "but I wouldn't have thought you'd need them."

"Don't you like my mother?"

"Oh, boy."

The harsh and dissonant music that had played deep in him, incessantly, since he'd first seen the photographs—it played in his eyes now. The woman met those eyes with her own, freakishly black. She shook her yellow hair. He was hers now and she knew it. She saw the killing thing in his eyes now too, and knew it for what it was, knew it had been hiding there, aimed at her, all along. She took him in, how well-dressed he was, and how naked of face, and desire struck her, a hot wave from within, and she was thankful for it, and thankful that he could see it. She slipped the dress from her shoulders and it seemed to whisper against her skin as it fell. The bones of her ribs, her hips, her kneecaps, invited impalement. Her breasts were small, with pointy little nipples. It might have been a pitiful body, but for the strange sheen of her skin, her exquisite lace panties, her spike heels, and her hatred. It was a body molded by hatred, and, naked, it exposed and expressed the hatred, which had become the sheath around her core. Yet still it—the hatred—invited, and dared, like Rosie Vee's eyes in the photographs. He wondered what had made Mrs. Sherman hate so deeply, but no explanation would have satisfied either of them. "All things can be justified," his brother had once said, "which doesn't help matters any." Hatred was how she felt herself to be *most* herself. But she was exposing that self to him as a gift, her gift of love.

"I told you," she said, "I'm not much naked."

"Not much. Just everything."

"Ooooooo."

"Look." He gestured toward the large window. Their reflections lived in the glass as transparencies. They looked like two ghosts, one naked and one clothed. *We're already dead.*

"At least I don't look like your mother."

He went to her and tentatively put his hands on her as she stood very still. He ran his palms, not his fingers, over her shoulders, her rib cage, her hips, and found the sharpness of her bones sheathed in a silken softness of skin, so soft it softened him—it broke his heart. She saw the breaking in his eyes. A tenderness welled in her that her hatred could not bear.

"Are you going to hurt me?" she asked softly.

"Yes."

"I couldn't stand it if you didn't."

"I know."

And he went about it, the hurting. And she went to a place she'd never been, a place she'd always known was there, a place she'd despaired of ever finding, as with terrible kindness he hurt her and hurt her, and she felt truly naked for the first time in her life.

And the closer he took her to the center of that place, the more she had to give up her hatred. She didn't want to, but she did.

*I've never inflicted pain on a lover, never wanted to, but I'm doing it and doing it, hurting.*

She was wracked with coming and weeping. Coming for the first time in years, weeping for the first time since childhood. From a far place she smiled and said, "You're still so well dressed."

"Are you still strong enough?"

"I'll be strong enough."

She hurt him as much as she had the strength for, then hurt him more with a new strength. When he was naked, she saw the bruises of the beatings he'd taken in the last twenty-four hours and hurt him in those places, truly hurt him. He felt

*The Skinniness of Mrs. Sherman*

each nauseating pain as a kind of forgiveness, coming from her, and he wept now, *I am forgiven, I am forgiven not by God or the world—which have forsaken the right to forgive, forsaken that right by their awfulness—but by you. I cannot kill you now, though I know that now you do not want to live past tonight, do not want to leave what you are in this moment for what you'll become tomorrow, but I cannot kill you. You've forgiven me everything else, forgiven me for being alive— "Excuse me for living," my father used to say to my mother— but can you forgive me for loving you? No. You never will. Don't stop then. Kill me if you want to.* She picked up broken things and cut him, and laying him down on the floor, mounted him, wildly, with a wave of strength that amazed her, she'd never felt so strong, and hurting him even more she drove the killing thing from his eyes, and she grieved to see it go, and grieved to feel it go in herself. She would not kill him. "Oh I don't know where I *am!*" she screamed as she came and came again, and he came deep in her and knew his jism was neon white.

She lay down on top of him and clung to him. "I don't know where I am" were the last words he heard her say while she still loved him.

# THE SLEEP OF A CLAIRE

# AND A MIKE

*P*eople who've drawn blood from each other sleep deep into their wounds. And whatever's been stirred by the wounding, and whatever's released through the wounds, and whatever passes from wound to wound, tests such people in a realm of sleep so subterranean that even dreams can't plumb that far. For this place within, the darkest of all, is deeper by far than dreams. In such a sleep, the substance of one's darkness itself moves and changes form. And so the sleeper changes. And, because it causes no dreams, nothing memorable remains from these subterranean shifts. Nothing but change.

People who sleep stained with the drying blood of one another—blood drawn not in lust for pleasure but blood lost for expiation and release—they sometimes sleep so deeply that they do not rise, as dreamers do, into wakefulness as we know it. They cannot rise that high from their descent. They wake instead, for a while at least, into a differently charged world, a world with the properties of neon, where furniture and walls and faces and mirrors assume, for them, neon's glow.

It is easier for such people to wake in Vegas than elsewhere, for there is so much neon in Las Vegas that life will not feel as strange to them as it would anywhere else.

Mrs. Claire Sherman and Mr. Mike Rose fell into this deepest of sleeps, a sleep very close to death. To use Mike Rose's recent terminology, God watched them while they slept, though neither would remember. They fell asleep with Claire Sherman's angularity atop the smooth planes of Mike Rose's flesh, breath to breath, blood to blood, wound to wound, and their skin registered each glowing or darkening shift in the subterranean substance of the other.

She rejected. He accepted. She rejected the exchange of personality with him—that exchange so essential to love. He accepted all that had happened and all he had become in these last days. It is as though, while sleeping, each had been dipped into their elemental nature, and each would awaken sticky and dripping with that substance as with blood.

And of all this nothing could be seen but their two bodies on the floor, barely moving, breathing in concert.

# THE SUGGESTION

# OF MR. LAMPEDUSA

*M*rs. Sherman woke first. She could have no comprehension of the exhaustion of Mike Rose. She thought for moments that he was dead. This made her happy. She'd had the strength to kill him, after all—had loved him enough for that. When she determined that he was alive, she could hardly bear her defeat, nor forgive him for it. For she had no illusion that the kind of closeness they'd felt could withstand the day, much less the attrition of daily life, any daily life, even a killer's daily life. She said softly, "Vampire love—can't stand the light."

She had not made him pay, and would not, she knew now. A man like this pays in his own way, on his own terms. As she did. In this sense she had met, finally, a man. Had loved, finally, a man. She was aware that something had happened in the depths of sleep that she did not understand, some rejection, but she *had* loved him—this, she knew—and now loved him no longer. For several hours he'd been the love of her life. She sensed that some lives only last several hours, no matter how long they seem.

She had cut him with her sharp, glittering ring. Cut him

across the ribs. Now, for the first time since it had been placed on her finger, she took off the ring. It was a struggle, but she finally got it off. She placed it on his forehead. "Uneducated boob. Beautiful man. Welcome to your third eye."

She felt where he'd hurt her and that, at least, was real and good, and she thanked him for the tender cruelty he'd inflicted upon her flesh. She had not been tender with his. She could kill him now. Put her small pistol to his head and fire. The thought excited her, and she sat on her haunches naked beside him and contemplated it. Not while he was asleep, she decided. It wouldn't be the same, wouldn't be love. It wouldn't be his tender brown eyes, looking at her, accepting her, as she had never been accepted, willing to take anything from her, anything whatsoever, as they each had been for a time. It wouldn't be his grunts and moans and whimpers and tears as she'd hurt him and hurt him. No, she was not going to be able to make him pay—and this was as far as she was ever to go with love. She comprehended that much. The knowledge that she'd lived the most intimate hours of her life the night before, that knowledge struck her, then left her, and she became less. She put on her dress, looked for the small pistol and put it back in her purse. Picked up her spike heels and clutched them in one hand. Barefoot, she picked her way through the broken things on the floor, opened and closed the door as quietly as she could (her last act of love), and went, a neon person now, out into the neon world, a killer at last, utterly confident, regretting nothing, and barely remembering the uncharted violent beauty of a few hours before. Her defeat was total, all the more so because it felt so much like victory as she hit the sunlit street with such energetic, skinny certainty.

His personality scattered in his sleep. It happened every night. In a person as fragmented as Rose, the pieces drift apart in sleep and never come together again with quite the same relation to each other. Almost, but not quite. Sometimes some piece would not come back to his waking state for days or even longer, but would stay in the realm of sleep, to be dragged through his waking hours as a kind of numbness, a sense of strange weight to be pulled here and there, a vague knowledge that some part or parts that were present yesterday or a week ago were for the time being not participating.

Every morning—or noon, or early evening, whenever he happened to wake—he rose with the sensation of falling. Of falling up, not down. Woke surprised. And, every time, there was a moment when he didn't know who he was, or where. It passed so quickly, and he was so accustomed to it, that he hardly noticed. Except now and again he would go, still naked, to the liquor shelf, pour a shot of whiskey and sip it slowly down. It steadied him. Joy had said once that "the night people," as she called them, had an unconfessed terror of sleep. He thought of that sometimes when he needed "the wake-up drink," as he called it, but he never admitted to himself that during sleep was when he found life most unbearable—nor that this was why he fought sleep, never slept until he was too exhausted not to, or until he'd had a few drinks, too many drinks, and could approach the bed without fear, a fear he took for granted the way he took for granted never sleeping in total darkness.

The scattering of his psyche in sleep—this was Mike Rose at his most elemental, the center of him, a center that never cohered. Waking, he'd force it to cohere with his attention to style, to his clothing, to his code. And this had taken *all* his attention, and giving it his attention was the only cohesion he knew or could imagine. But now when he woke on his back on the floor of his office, amid its debris, naked and in pain and alone and afraid, he didn't care about cohesion anymore.

He woke with a feeling of having fallen upward, through the hardwood floor. *God watched me in my sleep. God has always watched me in my sleep, I know that now. That's why I've always fought sleep so hard. So why only in my sleep, and when I killed, did God watch?* His body was in greater pain than he had ever known. He felt stiff everywhere he'd been hurt, and he'd been hurt everywhere. Yet the pain seemed distant, almost as though it were someone else's. With difficulty he raised his hand to the strange pressure on his forehead. His fingers felt her wedding ring, and he picked it off his forehead as delicately as though it were a flower, and held it before his eyes. *I wonder what kind of monster she's busy turning into.*

His ribs stung. He ran his fingertips over them, remembered what she'd done with the ring. *The cuts are deep enough to leave scars, now they've gone unattended so long. I probably left scars on her too. Good. We'll have to remember now, especially when we don't want to.*

*Hmm. Frank Costello. What are you doing in my mind?*

He had suddenly thought of when Vito Genovese had tried to assassinate Frank Costello. The shooter had fired up close, shot Costello in the head. The bullet got Costello behind the left ear, traveled under his scalp, around the back of his skull, then came out behind his other ear. In a few hours Costello left the hospital under his own power with nothing worse than a headache. The bullet left no aftereffects.

*Why did I think of that?*

Rose got to his feet. It took considerable effort. He had to hold on to the desk to stand up. On the floor were spots of blood. On the desk were photographs of his mother. His eyes rested on the one with a carrot up her ass, and she looking over her shoulder with a large friendly smile. *How long has it been since I haven't really cared whether I lived or died? I suppose since I saw the photographs. The only logical reason to keep going is to keep Alvi company—but I'm not really doing much of that, am I? I suppose it's pride. Some point to prove. I can't remember what the point is just now, but I sure the fuck must need to prove it.*

He reached the phone, sat back down on the floor, dialed his own number. It rang several times, which made him frightened. *Where are you, little brother?*

A woman's voice answered, saying with a slightly Southern lilt, "Hello?"

"Who's this?"

"Virginia. Me."

"Now what?"

"We love you."

"Who's we?"

There was a rustling sound and the voice changed.

"Hey, Mikey."

"Sorry, Alvi."

"I'm not good, Mikey."

"I'm sorry, Alvi."

"I'm not good. I was good, but I'm not. I like your friend, though. She's great. But she's not good either, you know?"

"Yeah, I know."

"Can I be best man?"

"Shit."

"Are you good?"

"No."

"You okay?"

"Sure."

"You lyin' to *me* now, Mikey?"

"A little. But I'm in one piece. More or less. Nobody's tried to kill me for about twenty-four hours. That I know of."

"Then come home."

Mike Rose had no idea how much, in the impenetrable depths of that sleep, he had accepted. He did not think in those terms. But he knew that the action had left him behind. Somewhere during the day—it was now late afternoon—Mr. and Mrs. Sherman, Gino Lampedusa and Sallie Carlisi, and God knew who else had gone on without him. He could have been killed easily. He hadn't been. This meant that on some level he had become irrelevant, which bothered him far more than the danger.

*The thing about your action is, it better be your action, not someone else's. That's how people disappear in this world, they get caught up in all kinda action that ain't theirs. I went to sleep ahead of the action, and woke up not even knowing where the action is.*

*Which makes me the loosest end of all. So I probably don't have a chance.*

*The only chance left is to behave like a man who hasn't got one.*

It felt strange being naked in his office. *It's a first.* He daubed himself clean and shaved in the small bathroom. Cleaned the cuts. Everything hurt worse than it had the day before. A certain level of pain was becoming the medium in which he moved. *Amazing, what you can get used to.* And as with Mrs. Sherman, there was something neon about the world for him this day. *I feel like I'm on drugs.*

He did something he found distasteful: put on the same garments he'd worn the night before. *Makes me feel like a hooker. They always put the same clothes on after a fuck.*

As he cleaned, shaved, and dressed he tried to summarize his dilemmas.

*The Gino and Sallie thing . . . they've either bought my bluff about insurance or not. If they did, they'll make some move to test me, see if they can depend on me. If they didn't, I'll be dead by tomorrow morning. Alvi too maybe. Or worse than dead. Lock him up in a straitjacket ward and throw away the key. Sorry, kid. It's not that I don't care anymore. It's that sooner or later your heritage catches up to you, and you either survive that or you don't. And it's your heritage as much as mine, though we've tried to run from it in opposite directions.*

*The Mr. and Mrs. Sherman thing . . . I just don't fucking know. Out of my control, out of my comprehension even.*

*The God-is-waiting thing, the kill thing . . . I need to find another gun. And I know where the right gun is. Then I think I may just kill whoever shows up. Except her.*

*If God started it, let God finish it.*

*Oh yeah, and the Alvi-Virginia thing . . . ha, ha, ha, ha, ha, ha, ha-ha-ha-ha-ha-ha-ha . . .*

He was laughing hard enough not to hear the footsteps on the stairs.

The door swung open and they walked in, two WASPs with guns in their hands, and whatever they expected to see, it wasn't Mike Rose laughing alone.

It had been so long since he'd laughed that he almost couldn't stop. This made the WASPs nervous. They thought their guns should be enough to stop an unarmed man from laughing.

The female had an unspecific but polished beauty, except for her angry eyes. She held her gun with a little too much assurance, as though she were demonstrating how a gun should be held. She was dressed in expensive sporting clothes—the canvas shoes, the sweatpants, the jersey, all top of the line, all brightly colored. She had a large handbag slung over her shoulder. She was in her late twenties and had the kind of face Rose found most alien: sharp, smart features with perfect, bright teeth, but an expression that seemed to carry no history that he could see. *So many of them are like that, these afflu-ent WASPs. They walk around as though the past just kind of evaporates behind them.*

The male was a bit like Blue Suit, but in sporting clothes. Each had a fashionable weapon, a "nine," as they say these days. The male's had a silencer.

He'd stopped laughing as he took them in, but the feeling of laughter hadn't stopped inside him.

*I'm kind of interested in living long enough to find out why I don't care, and to see if there's anything left that I do care about.*

"You two young people look like you expect a lot out of life."

"We don't intend to give you many chances," the female said.

"I don't see why you should give me even one."

"We want the disk, and we want to know where Mrs. Sher-man is."

"Tell you the truth, I don't think I'm working for her any-more. I think I got fired. I'm not sure."

"That's not good enough."

"You the geniuses who tore up my office? Of course you are."

"Mr. Rose—" the woman began.

"Your whole plan was that you'd wave those guns at me and I'd be scared. I'm not, so you don't have a plan. And I wouldn't give you the information even if I knew it, which I don't anymore. You're prepared to commit misdemeanors to-day but you're not really prepared to commit a felony, not this morning, not a capital offense. That's something you're still working yourself up to. Keep plugging. You'll get there. By as soon as tomorrow you may be ready to kill me."

"Are you crazy?"

"No. Maybe. For some reason having guns pointed at me brings out the best in me. So do it."

"Do what?"

"Shoot. I'm not giving you what you want, so shoot. Your

friend yesterday thought he was ready to gun me down in cold blood, as they say, but he wasn't, not quite. You're even less ready than him."

The male and the female exchanged looks of confusion.

"What if we just beat the shit out of you?" the male said.

"I'm getting used to it. I'd probably like it."

"Look," the male said, "we're serious."

"You're hopeless. If a man is measured by his adversaries, I'm sinking more in my own estimation every day. No, don't say anything. I'll explain again. The whole point of those things in your hands is to shoot people. And if you're not willing to do that, then holding those things doesn't much matter, you get my point? This is kind of funny, really. Various people want me dead, or at least out of the way, for various reasons, but they're uncertain enough and the reasons keep fluctuating enough so that nobody's quite willing to kill me. Not yet. It's confusing for them, and confusing for me, so don't feel bad about being confused. You're probably too young to remember Jimmy Durante, but as he used to say, 'Everybody's gettin' into the ac'!' That's how he said it: ac'. Get it? People point guns at me, I do stand-up. That's because I'm a stand-up guy. That's an Outfit joke."

"You're not much of a comedian," the male said.

"I'm not much of a detective either, these days. That's okay, though, you're not much of a shooter."

"Walter was our friend," the male said.

"Who the fuck is Walter? Oh. The guy in the blue suit? See, I *am* a detective, I figure stuff *fast*. He wasn't much of a shooter either, by the way. You said 'was'? Did he die?"

"Do you care?" the female said.

"In a funny way, I do. I know God wasn't watching me then. It'll fuck up my emerging theology if I killed him without knowing it."

"What?" the female said.

"Did your Walter die?"

"Not yet. But he might."

"Bet he won't."

"How do you know?"

"It's a theological hunch. That's something Jimmy Durante *didn't* used to say. Are you guys through?"

"You think you're so cool," the female said.

"No, I just think you're out of your depth. Now get out of here, before I practice my theology on you. Shit, you don't know what I'm talking about. Get out of here anyway. And if you see Mrs. Sherman, before you kill her—if you've reached that stage by then—tell her I love her. Tell her I love her anyway."

"We should kill him," the male said.

"Excellent," Rose said, "do it. Like the guy said in the movie, you'd probably be doing me a favor."

"He thinks he's *so* cool," the female said. "He thinks he doesn't care."

"I don't care? I don't *care?* I don't care about what *you* care about. I don't care? I *care* . . . I care *about* . . ."

He was staring at them with a face they'd never seen.

"I care. I don't . . . know about what . . . yet. Don't . . . know anymore. But it's *there.* I almost wish it wasn't. Gotta, gotta . . . find out . . . I'm a detective, right? I oughta be able at least to find out . . . WHAT I CARE *ABOUT.*"

The change was so quick, the face so stark, that when he shouted the last word the woman almost shot him.

Rose saw the move, saw her stop herself.

"There's hope for you yet, lady. You almost did a human thing."

Rose took one step toward her.

The male's pistol went off.

With its silencer, it made the sound of a suppressed cough.

"Jesus, Edward," the woman said.

Rose stood still. He couldn't tell whether he'd been hit or not. *Sometimes you don't feel it till you move. I don't want to move.* He slowly turned his head toward the Edward person.

That man stood with a shocked face and trembling hand watching where his bullet had gone into Rose's desk. He had fired from fear when Rose moved, without knowing he was firing.

Rose laughed.

"Shut up," the woman said.

"I just don't care if you *kill* me. That is not not caring."

"What?" the woman said.

"I can't explain everything." *I give it a good try, though.*

"I said shut up." The woman was standing with her gun at her side now.

"You need a reason to do things," Rose said.

"What are you *talking* about?"

"You silly-ass WASPs hardly ever do anything without a reason or an order. And you're always second-guessing your reasons and your orders are always vague. You don't know why you're here anymore. You've never known why you're anywhere. Get the fuck out of here. 'Cause if I get theological on you, you'll be dead."

"Shut *up.*"

"In fact, if I ever see either of you again, I'm going to kill you. And I don't need a reason or an order."

*Who's gonna show up next? Elves?*

*It feels incredibly satisfying to tell people you're gonna kill them when you mean it. But that was too easy. Does anybody in this situation know what they're doing? I sure don't. We're all bouncing off each other like billiard balls, waiting to land in a pocket, any pocket will do. I hope Gino and Sallie are a little more definite. Somebody's got to make a move. The kind of move there's no coming back from. Or we could go on like this forever. Just like real life.*

Mike Rose resisted the impulse to drive to Joy's. *Very likely she called Gino after I left and told him where I was going. Very likely that's why Sallie's timing was so good yesterday—waiting for me when I arrived. Not a betrayal, not exactly. Not in our world. "Reality therapy," she might call it. I had filled her with black jism. The darkness she felt in me maybe acted upon her, too strong to resist. An exchange of personality: love. It wasn't a betrayal, not exactly, it was more a part of the exchange. And what did I take from Mrs. Sherman? It feels like neon. The woman has neon in her blood.*

*Crime reveals everything.*


*Mama always said I was a thinker. "You think too much, it slows you up." No, Mama, it makes me go too fast inside.*

*Mrs. Sherman loved your pictures, Mama. The thing I can't live with is, so do I.*

*And Pop—I wouldn't have had these last days if you hadn't died when and why and how you did. Don't think I'm not grateful.*


*Theology is a bitch. Time to go home.*


Yesterday he had seen twenty silver toenails. Now there were ten more.

*What's different about her? Aside from the fact that she's sitting on my couch . . . next to my brother . . . and he's painted her toenails.*

The difference was a sense of purpose. The cascade of freshly washed golden hair almost to her waist, the bright powder-blue billowy silken bottoms, the tightish white blouse. *Her breasts have fallen but they're still sweet.* Her eyes now green, now gray—the skeletal one who called herself Virginia—*I don't believe for a second that's her name, but Joy isn't Joy's, Zig isn't Zig's, and Rose isn't mine—*she sat with Alvi as though she'd been looking for him a long time.

"Welcome, Virginia, to the home of the Rossellinis."

"This ain't the Rossellinis' home," Alvi said, "you know where the Rossellinis' home is."

"Welcome to the encampment of the Rossellinis."

"So if I marry him I'm Mrs. Rossellini, and if I marry you I'm Mrs. Rose?"

"She's got some choice, hey, Alvi?"

*Alvi's looking over my shoulder, not into my eyes. Oh my God.*

"Alvi?"

Alvi met his eyes.

"Sallie Carlisi called," Alvi said.

*Great. The move is being made. I don't have to make it.*

"And?" Rose said.

"Wanted to know where you were. I told him I didn't know, but I thought we were going to Sinatra tonight."

"Good."

"'Good' is what Sallie said too. I always liked Sallie."

"Yeah, he's a real likeable sort of guy, that was always my impression."

"You know what I mean."

"A Sally is a guy?" Virginia said.

"A Virginia is a virgin?"

"Vestal," she whispered.

"You know what that is, Alvi?"

"I'm not real good, Mikey."

"Vestals," Virginia said, "tended the sacred fires of the sacred goddess in the sacred temple, and bared their sacred flesh for sacred men."

"Too deep for me."

"Nothing is. For anyone."

"Isn't she great, Mikey? But she's not good either."

"You know, when Alvi says that, it's not a value judgment."

Virginia loved that. She let forth a laugh as golden as her hair.

"We're gonna be a helluva family, Alvi."

"You gonna marry her?"

"One of us should. Do you care which, Virginia?"

"I can't tell the difference anymore. Are you twins?"

It was Alvi's turn to laugh.

*I'm sorry, Joy, I'm not being responsible. Or maybe I'm being really responsible.*

She said, "Do you have silver toenails?"

"I'm seriously considering it. Nothing would surprise me these days, Beautiful."

"Am I beautiful?"

"Very. Isn't she, Alvi?"

"She's great. And beautiful."

Her eyes got wet. *Once everything's gone too far, there's nothing left to do but push it farther.*

She said, "I used the gun money—"

"What gun money?" Alvi said.

"—for a cab. Her Holiness told me where you live. I don't think I like her."

"I hate her," Alvi said.

"Then I hate her," Virginia said.

*Alvi looks straight into Virginia's eyes. I haven't seen him do that to anyone but me and Zig in a long time.*

"What gun money?" Alvi said again.

"That's how we met. I gave her money for a gun."

"That's how we met." Virginia smiled.

"She used it for a cab instead."

"Mikey . . ."

"I know, kid."

"Stop calling me kid. I'm older than you."

"He'd call God kid." Virginia laughed.

"Look, Beautiful—I know you hate Joy now, but I want you to go back there for a few days."

"Then I won't marry you, I'll marry Alvi."

Alvi smiled. Then darkened. "Why can't she stay here, Mikey?"

"'Cause we're getting phone calls from Sallie Carlisi."

Alvi took it in, and smiled.

"I'm in it too, now?" Alvi asked.

"You always were, kid."

"That's good. It's time."

"That's the truth."

"And the truth shall make ye free," Alvi said.

"The truth shall make you crazy," Mike said.

"Same thing?" said Virginia, bright-eyed.

Alvi smiled. "Isn't she great?"


"Joy?"

"Michael, Michael. I've been thinking of nothing but Michael."

"Look—"

"I lost your customer."

"No, you didn't, you gave her away. I want you to take her back for a while. I don't want her caught in any crossfires."

"She's already been caught in more than we can guess at."

"You know what Sallie's boys might do if they got carried away. We've got enough on our heads."

"Yes. We do. Alright."

"Come pick her up yourself."

"Of course. Still love me?"

"When any of us has a choice about who we love, and how, you'll tell me, right?"

"You'll be the first to know."

Without saying good-bye they hung up at the same moment.

Rose had made the call from his bedroom, with the door closed. From his window he could see his city. It was dusk, and the neons glowed. The orange-red of the Rio, the ice blue of Caesar's Palace, the gold of the Mirage, gleamed amid the pulsating shine of the Strip. In the distance the white beam of the Luxor shot into the sky. And Rose felt the satisfaction he always did when the dark came on and the lights came up. For the darkness was a kind of light too—as though the desert light had not been turned down, but turned up somehow, into another spectrum where light took on the hue we call dark.

He took his time putting on fresh clothes. They looked much like the clothes he'd taken off, but they felt stronger in their freshness, and they helped Rose feel stronger.

Before he put on the jacket he went to the closet, reached to its topmost shelf, and took down an old cardboard box. He opened it carefully, though care wasn't needed. His father's shoulder holster, with its .45 automatic: There had been several among his father's things. He'd found them when cleaning out the old house after his mother died. He'd kept one. *Thought I was keeping it for sentimental reasons. Should have known better. Who did you kill with this thing, Pop?* He checked out the pistol. There were several clips, and he put one in the pistol and one in his pocket. *If it had been only sentiment, I wouldn't have kept the clips, would I?* The holster was a nice cross-draw shoulder rig, and fit well. When he put the jacket on it didn't show a bulge that he could spot. *You were a pro, Pop. A nervous pro, maybe, but a pro.*

Rose went into the living room. Virginia and Alvi were glum with the prospect of parting. Rose wished he could hear how they spoke when alone.

"Better get dressed, Alvi."

"You'll be beautiful too," Virginia said.

"I wish you could come," Alvi said to her.

"Not a good idea," Rose said.

"I know."

"I know too," Virginia said. "Bang, bang—big deal. You think *that's* danger? You're little boys."

Alvi looked at her but she wouldn't look at him. He didn't know what to say, so he went to get dressed. From his bedroom came the voice of Frank Sinatra. A song about autumn leaves. It was a voice of tender grief, a voice of longing, a voice committed, for the length of the song, more to longing than to love.

"I love Alvi," Virginia said. "Are you jealous?"

"What do you think?"

Rose lit a cigarette. She asked for one and smoked it awkwardly. She coughed. Now Sinatra was singing about how he was drinking again. The lyrics were sad but his voice was not. He seemed glad his woman had gone, glad he could drink again, glad she'd given him reason enough. There was always a she at the heart of the songs, and she was always just arriving or had just left, and she was always an excuse. *An excuse to feel, an excuse to sing. What's my excuse?*

Alvi walked in dressed much like Mike.

"Even with your gray hair, you look so much like your brother!"

Alvi looked the part now—looked the heritage. The well-cut suit changed his posture, changed even the set of his face. With these clothes, his expression betrayed an arrogance, a note of almost cheerful, careless menace, as though he couldn't help himself, as though the style he'd avoided all his life was his for the taking, and required no more than the proper costume.

"Feel like a Mormon now, Alvi?"

"Feel like I'm dressed for Halloween."

"Every day is Halloween in this town, kid."

"Yeah, Mama used to say that."

"Aren't you gonna wear shoes?"

"But he looks so beautiful without them," Virginia said.

"I hate to," Alvi said.

"Alvi . . ."

"Okay, okay."

The doorbell rang.

"There's your ride, Virginia," Rose said. *Or Joy called Sallie again, and it's him with a semiautomatic. What do you say, God?*

But Rose didn't hesitate to open the door.

"Hello, Joy."

Joy never went out into the Vegas night without dressing like the showgirl she'd once been. Even at sixty: the pale dress of fine cloth and indeterminate color, a color somewhere in the spectrum of her ash silver hair, the lined face radiating not so much beauty as a memory of beauty—beauty, and terrible experience. No one could look at her without wondering, "*Who in the world is that?*" Sometimes people even asked for her autograph, just because she looked as she did. "Were you a movie star?" they'd ask. "Of course," she'd laugh, and sign *Marilyn Monroe* or *Dorothy Malone* or *Norma Desmond*, whatever star name struck her.

"Hello, Michael. Alvi."

Michael smiled, Alvi glared. Alvi and Virginia were looking at Joy's feet, those long, aristocratic, perfectly formed feet in heels that left space for the toes.

Thirty silver toenails in one room.

"I'm gonna get some shoes," Alvi said.

"Hello, Virginia."

"Hello, miss."

Sinatra started singing about how he wanted all or nothing at all.

"She calls you Michael," Virginia said.

"She always has."

"What do you think of me really?" The shift was total. No longer a gamin, no longer speaking from a secret place. Suddenly a sharp, intelligent woman, speaking directly and deserving of straight answers.

"Where did *you* come from?" Rose said to the new Virginia.

"I'm always here. Watching and waiting. What else am I supposed to do?"

"You could try taking care of yourself."

"I've tried that. I did it well enough but things happened and I lost interest."

"I know the feeling," Rose said.

"Virginia?" Joy said.

"Is that my name? I suppose it is. Might as well be. It's no more ridiculous than 'Joy.' Mike—Michael—whatever *your* name is: do I have to go with her?"

Joy said, "You don't *have to* do anything."

"As long as we understand each other," the new Virginia said.

"When was the last time," Joy said, "that somebody understood you?"

"He's putting on his shoes."

"Michael—" Joy started to say.

"You two like me better when I seem helpless," Virginia said. "Everybody does."

Rose shrugged at Joy, who smiled back.

Sinatra was singing that half a love never appealed to him.

"I like that song," Virginia said. "You people all care about each other so much. That's a gift. Who gave it to you?"

"We gave it to each other," Joy said. "It's all we have, really. And we may be losing it."

"You may lose each other—most people do," Virginia said. "But you won't lose the caring about each other. You're all too tough for that. I wish I was you."

"We care about you," Rose said.

"You do," Virginia said, "you really do. It's so sweet and pointless, but you do. I don't want to go with you, your Holiness."

"Then don't."

"But I don't want to go back to the street yet. There's love afoot, after all. Don't want to get lost. That's too easy to do."

"It is, isn't it?" Joy said.

"And they don't want me to stay here. They've got trouble. They think I'm too sweet and silly to understand. But everybody's in danger, isn't that true, your Holiness?"

"If you call me that again I'm going to slap you silly."

"Thank you. That's respect. That's better."

"I respected you from the first."

"That's true. You did. Wish I could say the same. Hello, Alvi. *Nice* shoes."

"What's wrong, Virginia?" Alvi said.

"Nothing's wrong with your *shoes*, Alvi." The new Virginia laughed.

Rose said, "Alvi, could you take her out to Joy's car?"

"First," Virginia said, "I need to say good-bye to myself."

She got up and went into the bathroom.

Alvi watched her leave the room, and for the first time in a long time he looked his age. He said, "It would be nice not to understand when somebody says 'I need to say good-bye to myself,' wouldn't it?"

Joy said, "Now you sound like your brother."

Virginia returned to the room without the confidence with which she'd left.

"Take me out to the car, please, Alvi. The grown-ups want to be alone."

Sinatra was singing about leftover dreams.

"Did you ever meet him, Michael? Sinatra?"

"Could have a couple of times, with 'the boys.' Avoided it."

"Why?"

"Something about Mama. Didn't want to get that close, I guess."

"When I had two breasts and wore feathers, he had a crush on me for a whole week."

"Didn't everybody?" And, with a darker voice, "You never told me."

"He kept coming to the show, coming backstage, asking me out. I wouldn't go. Just orneriness. Wanted to make him beg. *Wanted* to go—he's the most charming man I ever met. Ever. Which surprised me, really. I didn't expect that."

"Mama used to say, 'That Frank Sinatra, he was not a disappointment.'"

"She was right. Finally he got Johnny Roselli to give a dinner. Showgirls did *not* refuse invitations to Johnny's dinners. Johnny sat me next to Frank. I kept refusing him and finally he said, like a little boy, Don't you know I could have any girl in the show! I said, Frank, so I could have any man on the *planet*. I watched his blue eyes closely then. There was anger, there was jealousy, there was disappointment, and then, so quickly, respect. And he laughed. And he had me. And now look at *your* face: anger, jealousy, disappointment. And now, respect. You've been the love of my life, Michael. I've never said that, have I?"

"You didn't have to."

"Yes, I did. Yesterday . . . I made a call, I—"

"You don't have to explain, or apologize, or anything."

"I know. I was only going to confess. But, of course, you knew."

Each was disciplined in the one discipline Las Vegas teaches: how to gauge and face odds.

They faced each other, aware of all the odds. That was all the good-bye they required.


Mike and Alvi were driving the Caddy east on Charleston.

"I wasn't good till I put this suit on," Alvi was saying, "and now I'm good, but in a bad way."

"You're good?"

"I'm better, okay? But in a lousy way. I feel like Pop."

Rose felt the weight of their father's gun against his chest. It hadn't been cleaned in thirty years, but it had been wrapped carefully in oiled paper. He wondered idly whether it would fire or explode. *Didn't even think of it with Mama's, and hers worked okay. We'll see. And who cares?*

"Well, you look great, Alvi. You look—"

"Like a man? I don't like men, Mikey. You're the only man I really like. You, and Pop, and Zig."

"What have you got against men?"

"I didn't take my medication tonight, Mikey."

"That's great. *Now* you tell me."

"You think Frank Sinatra would want me to take all those goddamn pills?"

"Aniello, you're a fuck."

Aniello was Alvi's given name. When Rose was very small, just learning to speak, he couldn't pronounce it. He'd called him Alvi, and the name had stuck. When Alvi was very depressed he would say, "Everyone calls me a baby name."

"Don't be mad, Mikey."

"Try to keep a hold on yourself tonight, Aniello."

"Why should I bother? This is the real thing, isn't it?"

"There isn't a real thing within five hundred miles of here."

"That's what I love about you, Mikey. You got a sense of proportion. And you got a gun. I ain't blind."

"Scared?"

"Not much. I didn't take my medication, remember?"

Alvi's eyes gleamed with mischief. Mike Rose laughed. Alvi did too.

"I guess I don't really give a shit anymore," Rose said.

*"That's* the style."

*So Joy slept with Sinatra. And Mama slept with Sinatra. And Joy slept with Kennedy, in those days when he was haunting Vegas with Sinatra's crowd. And Zig was approached to hit Kennedy. And Pop helped Zig whack some of the shooters who got Kennedy. And Joy slept with Giancana and Elvis back when she had two tits, and with God knows who else. I guess it's history, of a kind. "We're fucking with history," Pop told Zig, and it made him scared and got him killed. And the skinny lady said, "Human history has come here to die." I guess it's a good place for it. Mama, Pop, Zig, Alvi, me, Joy— we all saw those bombs go off. I wonder what that did to us. I don't give a fuck about the plutonium—everybody dies, who cares if it's plutonium? I mean, I wonder what that did to us. There's a kind of radiation they don't talk about, the radiation that comes off of people like us. The town's glowing with it. And everybody who comes here gets a little infected with it, a little sick with it. But it's why they come, though they don't know it. Look at that skinny lady. She's gone completely nuts with it. And the longer the town sits in this valley, radiating— it's like the whole country starts to glow. Till everything everywhere feels like it's made of neon. And everyone's judged by how they glow.*

"It's all about Zig, isn't it?"

"In a way."

"I'm *in* it now, Mikey, don't fake me."

" 'In a way' is the best I can do, Aniello."

"The best you *want* to do, you mean."

"In a way."

"Zig's dead, am I right? And don't say 'in a way.' "

They were crossing Decatur Boulevard, going east on Charleston. After a few blocks Alvi said, "Slow up, slow up."

They neared Cahlan Drive, and Rose pulled up on the corner. The house was the same color it had always been, a light, sickly green. There were cars in the driveway, Japanese models.

Alvi said, "I wonder who they are, what they're doing in there."

"Probably watching TV."

"*What* are they watching? *Roseanne? PBS? The 700 Club?* It used to look so much bigger, our house."

"Maybe because it was the only thing out here."

"Was this road paved when we were born?"

"Yes. No. How would I know, I was just born?"

"Mama used to talk about how it was a dirt road when they moved in, and I *remember* that, but I don't think it's a real memory, it was just her talking. And she said that if somebody was driving up the road, in those days, you knew they were driving to our house, 'cause there was nothing else around. And that when she moved in she wondered if there'd be milk deliveries out this far. Remember milk deliveries?"

*Bottles of milk left on the kitchen porch, and the clink of the bottles as the milkman set them next to each other in the early, early morning, while it was still dark, and how the clinks would wake me up. Why did I sleep so lightly? What was I scared of?*

"And," Alvi was saying, "how when we were kids we used to hunt quail and rabbits right out there, across this street— and one day I started crying about the hunting, and I never had before, and you got so mad at me for crying 'cause Pop got mad. Pop said, 'That's *it*, no more hunting if you're gonna cry about it.' And that *was* it, I stopped the hunting that way."

"So cry."

"I'm tired of it."

"Took you long enough."

"Anyway, I'm in love!"

"I don't think I've ever said this before: Alvi, you're crazy."

"I may be crazy but I am very well dressed."

Alvi was looking intently at the buildings across the street, where he remembered desert and rabbits and quail.

"I'm still living in *that* town, the way it was."

"Was it better?"

"It was ours. Now it's theirs."

"Let's go take it back."

Rose gunned the Caddy suddenly, rocking Alvi back in his seat, and Alvi laughed again, and then, rocking gently back and forth, he whispered for the next blocks, "Good-bye, g'bye, good-bye–good-bye–good-bye, bye-bye, good-bye . . ."

The faces coming toward them were livid. The bystanders looked anything but innocent. They glared over their steering wheels. Strapped in their seats, they sat glumly or sullenly, or fidgeted, tapping fingers on the dash, lighting cigarettes, crushing them out, putting their arms outside then inside their windows. Some who were alone spoke to themselves and those who weren't alone, some pointedly didn't speak, and some heatedly did, and in two cars children were crying, and in one truck a woman was crying, while some cars boomed rap bass lines. But in most the people just sat, with expressions of people so used to defeat that they didn't notice any longer—people whose whole lives seemed a detour, so one more detour didn't matter. But even their defeat was livid, and an anger they had long ago taken for granted stained the air like exhaust fumes.

Helicopters crisscrossed the air. Police were everywhere, in cars and on motorcycles. Some stood in the streets directing traffic with faces as set and glum as the drivers'. Where Charleston dipped under Interstate 15, Rose saw that the freeway had been closed. And the Strip blazed even brighter than usual with spotlights swinging their beams in arcs, like antiaircraft lights in old war movies. *That's what it feels like, like war's been declared, like everybody's evacuating.*

"What the fuck is going on?" Alvi said. "Is all this for Sinatra?"

"They're blowing the Dunes tonight, remember?"

"Whata they wanna do that for? Oh, yeah. Steve Wynn or something. I forgot."

Where Charleston crossed the Strip the sidewalks were packed with people walking south, shoulder to shoulder, all kinds of people, and they did not look happy, nor even expectant, for their faces were like the faces caught in the traffic jam, and their movement had the relentlessness of a mass evacuation, their faces the apprehension of an impending air raid. Rose could not clear his head of the impression. *But it's as though they're running toward the bomb, not away. They're heading straight for it. They want to explode.* He turned right and south into the thickness of traffic on the Strip, cars moving more slowly than the walkers, and it was as though the sound of the engines came as much from the people as the cars.

Slowly they passed the unfinished tower of Vegas World, and Alvi stuck his head out the window and twisted his neck to look straight up at the tower, which looked like a bare ruin, gray concrete bathed in light for its nearly one thousand feet of height. And Rose thought, *Someday maybe that's all that'll stand here, and nobody will know who we were in this desert, or why we came, or why we left—there'll be just this colorless, pointless concrete pillar as if to say, "Something urgent and perhaps terrible happened here."* And the traffic and the people pressed ahead to Sahara Avenue, and crossed it, and beyond Sahara the traffic and crowds thickened—which Rose would not have thought possible—nearing the spotlights that danced in the air, and there was the sound of sirens and helicopters, and the din of the people was dizzying, and Rose thought, *This is my home,* and he looked at his brother, and Alvi still rocked gently back and forth and he was smiling, and Alvi said, "Do you realize we're on our way to listen to *love songs?*"

Alvi laughed as they passed Circus Circus, and the enormous mechanical head of the clown at its driveway laughed back, and Rose did not get the joke. *When we were kids the neons were bigger than the buildings, and now the buildings have risen and risen and are sheathed in neon, and it seems there's no difference between the buildings and the neon, people sleep and gamble inside the neon, and bring their kids.* Across the street the Riviera's sign flashed with colors as harsh beside one another as discordant notes of music. *Something colorless is coming at us between the colors.*

"Love songs, Mikey," Alvi said again.

They gave the car to Valet Parking at the Desert Inn, and stood a moment watching what seemed like all of humanity passing relentlessly on foot and in machines. They lit cigarettes. They looked from the street to each other and back at the street again. In their fine dark suits, Aniello the white-haired and Michael the dark-haired, the Rossellini brothers, looked like what they had been raised to look like, and they stood with the satisfaction of looking that way, pausing and enjoying what they know might be their last free moments together—before the situation would intrude on them decisively. Alvi's mind, unchecked by chemicals for the first time in a long while, was a wordless swirl during these moments. He felt the answering tumult beneath Mike's surface and his excitement mounted, but it could only be seen in his eyes. Mike, for his part, felt breathless, though he breathed evenly. If he let himself think about it, he could feel every one of his aches with every breath. It was as though he was hovering a little above and behind his body, pushing it on, not caring what happened to it. The brothers were joined as they had always been, across the different stances they'd taken all their lives, by a shared recklessness. Neither was afraid. There was a sense in which this is what they'd each been waiting for. Mike smiled at his brother, who smiled back.

"Here," Mike said, taking out his billfold. "Pop's cards."

He peeled off five one-hundred-dollar bills and gave them to Alvi. Their father had always said that no one should go anywhere in Las Vegas without five one-hundred-dollar bills, and Mike Rose had made it his business to lead a life in which that was possible. "Those are the cards up your sleeve," their father used to say, so they always called them "Pop's cards."

"We're gonna have a time tonight, Mikey."

"Why not?"

Never before had Rose walked into a casino feeling that he'd entered a place quieter and more restful than the street. The D.I., the classiest of the casinos—the only casino left where people didn't look as though they were cruising a shopping mall. Men wore jackets and ties and the women good dresses, as people used to in Las Vegas casinos. The D.I.— where the round golden chandeliers brought out the reds and golds in the carpets and chairs, and where there was still a hint of the smell casinos used to have, a smell of leather and whiskey, rich carpet and thick smoke; where the table stakes were still high, a place for gamblers rather than tourists; where there were no children; quieter than the other casinos, where the women selling cigarettes still looked a bit like showgirls. On a usual night, one stepped from the street into a heightened world, a place where color and light and sound tensed one's body and quickened one's pace. But on this night the casino was a refuge from the chaos of the street, and seemed dapper and orderly compared to those grim-faced multitudes rushing toward nothing.

The Rossellini brothers, looking as they were meant to look and walking as they were meant to walk, breathed easier in the casino, felt at home, and moved with the authority of their kind. Aniello had only the slightest sensation of his feet touching the ground. For just these moments he let go the struggle of his life not to walk this walk, but it was as though his suit and shoes were walking and not he, and he enjoyed the giddy lightness of it. Michael walked with the first sense of relief he had known in a while, the release of a gambler who no longer had to win. *There is nothing I have to do now but be honest. I don't have to protect Alvi. I don't have to protect myself. I just have to be honest. I don't mind anything right now.*

They walked toward the bright sign that said, The Crystal Room. Men in fine suits and women in evening clothes were entering in a loose but orderly line. The "soldier" Rose thought of as Turquoise—though the young man now wore a metallic-red tie—stood by a gold-framed sign that read, VIPs. *He looks like a kid who has the comfort of following firm instructions.* Turquoise waited till the brothers stood in front of him.

"Mr. Rose."

"What's your name, kid?"

"Rizzo, Paulie Rizzo."

"Mr. Rizzo, this is my brother, Mr. Rossellini."

"Hello, Mr. Rossellini."

"Hello, kid." Aniello smiled, though even when he tried he could not smile like a killer, but rather like what he was at the moment: strangely, giddily free. His eyes unnerved young Rizzo slightly, and the younger man looked away, back at Rose.

"Mr. Lampedusa and Mr. Carlisi have reserved a table for you."

"That's very sweet of them," Rose said, smiling at his brother.

"*Very* sweet," his brother added.

"If you'll follow me," Rizzo said.

As they followed, Rose talked to his brother as though Rizzo wasn't there. "Twenty-four hours ago this kid was beating the shit out of me and calling me nasty names. Now he's acting like a butler. Maybe he's had a lobotomy."

"I'm learning," Rizzo said, "that things change every day, Mr. Rose."

"If you're *really* learning that, you'll go far. How's your car?"

Rizzo smiled sincerely. "That was pretty slick, that move you made at the Flamingo."

"I hope you're taking notes."

"I am."

Alvi didn't have to understand the details to understand what was in the air. He was proud of the respect the young man showed his brother.

Rose, for his part, felt the rush of a victory he'd stopped hoping for. *The kid's treating me with respect because he was ordered to. They mean to do business.*

Rizzo led them through the Crystal Room, down the tiers of tables, nearer and nearer to the stage, to a booth. On the table was an engraved Reserved card.

"After you've made yourself comfortable, Mr. Lampedusa would like to see you at his table." The young man pointed to a large booth where Gino the Gent, Sallie, and several determined-looking, well-dressed young men sat. Gino and Sallie nodded, and Rose nodded back.

"Thank you, Mr. Rizzo, for your solicitous attention."

"My what?"

Rizzo was grinning now. His mask was off.

"Look it up."

"I just might."

He left, the brothers sat down, and a waitress appeared as though on cue.

"Anything you want is paid for," she said.

"Did you hear that?" Rose said to his brother. "The price has been paid."

"I'll say it has."

"A club soda," Rose said to the woman.

"Scotch rocks," Alvi said.

Rose gave him a sharp look.

"Why not?" Alvi said. "The price has been paid. Scotch rocks."

"On its way," the lady said, and left.

"Are these the right clothes to hear love songs in, Mikey?"

"What's the difference, if it's love?"

"What do the 'boys' want?"

"Only what they always want: our souls on a plate. A shiny plate."

"We gonna give 'em to 'em?"

"Maybe. I haven't decided."

"Any special reason?"

"An experiment? We've tried everything else."

"I wonder what Zig would say."

"Zig's dead, Alvi."

"I know. 'In a way,' I know. I know."

The woman brought the drinks, and they downed them.

"Mikey, Zig's dead, really?"

"Really."

"Pop. Mama. Zig. There's nobody we can ask anymore."

"Ask what?"

"The stuff I used to wanna ask."

"It's time to pay our respects," Mike said.

"A telling phrase," Alvi said, smiling more strangely now.

When Lampedusa and Carlisi saw the brothers approaching, they signaled for the younger men to leave the booth. *I wish I was doing this part without Alvi. But then again, why? There isn't any winning now. Only different kinds of losing.*

"Mr. Lampedusa, Sallie, this is my brother, Aniello."

"Aniello?" Sallie said.

"That's my name, Sallie," Alvi said.

"Yeah, good for you."

"We want to thank you for . . . the amenities," Rose said.

"I'm glad you accepted so graciously," Gino the Gentleman

said. "Things are done by shorthand today—look at those people, with a cellular phone at the table. Terrible. It's good to be able . . . to do things the old way. The *conclusion* is the same. But arriving there . . . can be so much more . . . satisfying . . . when there's respect."

Since Rose was a boy he had not seen Lampedusa this close. The thin face had filled out and grown old, but the eyes, though watery, were just as vicious, with a sober and all-inclusive viciousness that measured anything in its path by the amount of force that would be needed to overcome it.

"Sit down, please," Lampedusa offered.

"Thank you," Rose said.

Mike gestured to Alvi to get in first, and assume next to Rose the place that Sallie assumed next to Lampedusa.

"Forgive me," Rose said, "but it's my understanding, sir, that a place like this loses its license if . . . a man like you . . . is seen here."

"There's no Mob in Vegas no more. Everybody knows that. Even—what was that magazine, Sal?"

"*Newsweek*."

"Even the *Newsweek* knows. Would *they* lie? In the *Newsweek* it says that Steve Wynn is the most powerful and *interesting* man in Las Vegas. It's all corporate now. No Mob no more. I don't exist. I'm invisible. Ask the *Newsweek*. I ain't here. Am I here, Rossellini, Rose, whatever your name is?"

"Maybe not. That must be why I see right through you."

"You think that displeases me? If you're telling the truth, then you understand me. If you understand me, we have no problems."

"A few days ago I had no problems. Now, no matter what happens, I got problems. Poor me."

"If you had no problems a few days ago, you know what that tells me? It tells me that a few days ago you were ignorant. Now, if you understand me, like you say, you're more intelligent."

"He's kinda got a point, Mikey." Alvi smiled the smile that made others most uncomfortable.

"Even your own brother agrees," Gino said. "You know, the Zig's disappeared. But you know, his car hasn't. We found it."

Rose felt his stomach twist.

"Well, you know, it was time. He was . . . an old man. Older than me. And that's *old*. Better this way than from, you know, a lingering disease. It's okay with us that it was you."

"Mikey? God*damn*it, Mikey. That's true, what this louse is saying?"

"I have to say something, Gino, about Mike Rose," Sallie said. "He doesn't lie. Nobody knows why. But he refuses."

"That's an interesting approach to life. Silly, but interesting. So answer your brother who called me a louse to my face, though I've never done him harm. Answer him."

*I respect you now, Gino Lampedusa. That was a pretty good move. You're practically a fucking guru. That's what the gurus do, the real ones, that's what Joy tells me they do, they make you face yourself and walk through your own fires and decide what to keep and what to leave behind, Joy says. I'm turning toward you to face you, Alvi. And your eyes are eating me alive. The thing that's been devouring you all these years is reaching out to feed on me.*

"You should apologize to Mr. Lampedusa, Aniello. He's told you the truth."

With eyes still fixed on his brother's, Alvi said, "I apologize, Mr. Lampedusa."

"I accept this apology."

"I'm never gonna talk about it, Alvi. Can you handle that?"

"Can you?"

They looked at each other from different cities of the mind, cities in different countries, that spoke different languages. Something in them would be more separate from this moment, and both knew it, and each greeted the other from their new and unbridgeable separateness.

"Never going to talk about it?" Lampedusa said.

"Never except to tell you, brother, God watched me in that moment."

"Sallie, you said it's the *brother* that's crazy. God watched him! But I don't care who's crazy, so long as it doesn't affect business. It's good what you've decided, Michael. Good for everybody. You with your goddamn 'insurance.'"

Rose pulled himself from Alvi's eyes and faced Lampedusa, but Alvi kept staring at the side of his head.

"That's right," Rose said to Lampedusa. "Let's not forget my goddamn insurance."

"You got talent, Rose. You could have been somebody. I knew that from the first dirty look you gave me, when you were a kid. I had my eye on you for a while. Then you went invisible, you went legit. Now . . ."

"Now?"

"I've got a suggestion," Lampedusa said. "I'll be very happy if you take this suggestion. Very unhappy if you don't."

Without releasing his stare, Alvi said, "You've got a suggestion for *my* brother? *My* brother doesn't listen to anybody, doesn't take *anybody's* suggestion."

"What's your suggestion, Mr. Lampedusa?"

"Compromise, Rose. Accept."

"I thought I have." *No. I just pretended to.*

Lampedusa said, "You got insurance? If something happens to you, then everything that you've promised now never to speak of, it all comes out? I respect that. But Zig talked—to you, he talked—this, I would bet a lot on. So *this* is what I suggest: We go into business, you and me. 'We make-a de biz-in-ess,' as my old man would say, rest in peace. My suggestion is this: that you and me . . . we have an . . . association. Nothing big. Even legit, if you insist. Just a little partnership. That way, I can trust you. We can keep an eye on each other. Respect each other. Otherwise . . . your family . . . you and your brother, I mean . . . well . . . you understand, I think. If you don't accept this, I'm just going to have to take my chances with your goddamn insurance. I am willing to live with your insurance, *if* you sign on."

*He might have to lose, but I can't be allowed to win.*

"Don't do it, Mikey. I don't give a shit about dying."

"I thought you were in love, Alvi," Rose said.

"She wouldn't want me to live that way."

"Then," Mr. Lampedusa said, "this 'she,' this woman . . . she must be a remarkable person. A fine addition to your family. May you have many sons."

"Mikey?" Alvi said.

"And, if I may say so, Michael," Lampedusa smiled, "*you* should find yourself a love. I mean . . . a woman your own age."

"For a change," Sallie said.

"Younger than you, even," Gino said. "Have children. A man without children is not really a man."

"Don't do it for me, Mikey, never think you're doing this for me. If you do this, you do it for you," Alvi said.

*Rosie Vee would have said, "Do it." Eddie Maybe, at the end—with all his "nervousness" about "fucking with history"—he wouldn't have been so sure, I think. He would have said, "Maybe." Father or mother? Which side do I go with?*

"I'll think about it. Give me a little time to think about it."

"You can't think and fuck at the same time," Lampedusa said.

"That's news to me." Rose smiled.

"Then I'm sorry for you."

"A *little* time he wants," Sallie said.

"A *little* time he gets," Lampedusa said.

*You guys are sure nervous of this insurance—or you'd never give me these outs. Why nervous? Seems like old news to me. Maybe it's not. Maybe someone's about to whack this president too. Or maybe they just have to keep the option open. So that this situation is just bad timing for them. But you know what I think now? I think maybe they don't even know what Zig was talking about, haven't got a clue about the details—I think that this situation has dragged them into something they don't even understand, and they're following some obscure orders handed down to them twenty or thirty years ago when all this might have still mattered, by people no longer alive, people they can't check with. But they gave their word to those people, and that was that, and they can't tell now whether it still matters or not, but if it matters it's too big for them to let pass. After all, Sam Giancana got whacked—by the CIA, the Outfit says; by the Outfit, the CIA says—just after he was subpoenaed to testify about this assassination shit.*

*They. Don't. Really. Know.*

*Ha. That's what makes the most sense. It explains their uncertainty too. Why they don't want to go too far—killing us, for instance, if they don't have to—with something they don't really understand. That's pretty funny. All this hoopla, blood, change, death, God coming out of the woodwork to watch, and no one in "the situation" really knows why, or even can know why. The situation itself is doing it. The situation has an intelligence all its own.*

"You understand," Lampedusa was saying, "that if you ever tell this brother of yours, Michael—whom I understand, forgive me, is not stable—"

"Compared to everybody else at this table, I, sir, am a paragon of health," Alvi said.

"If you tell him, then everybody dies. You, him, and, if he has a wife"—*so Joy even called him tonight, didn't she? Bitch*—"she dies. If you have a girl, even my old friend Joy, she dies. If you have a dog, the dog dies."

"I have a couple of plants. You could always kill the plants."

"Anything."

"I'm sorry, but that's not much of a threat . . . sir. Everybody's going to die anyway. You're going to die. Sallie's going to die. We're going to die. Joy. Even Sinatra's going to die. I don't care who dies when."

Alvi was smiling again.

Rose said, "Let me make that real clear. I. Do. Not. Care. Who. Dies. Or. When." He turned to face his brother. "If I take Mr. Lampedusa's suggestion, Aniello, it won't be because I'm afraid. Don't forget that."

"Good, Michael Francis. That, at least, is good."

"If not fear," Sallie said, "then what?"

"Call it an experiment," Rose said.

"An experiment?" Lampedusa said. His eyes had been so casually vicious that they'd seemed, for him, almost friendly. Now they focused tightly on Rose. "As long as you keep your word when you give it, I don't give a fuck what the reason is, you arrogant little shit."

Back at their booth Alvi said, "You're not really my brother anymore, Mikey. Not really."

"I know. And at the same time, I am."

"We'll see. And," Alvi said, "it's not about how maybe I'm gonna get killed on account-a your action. I don't give a fuck about that. Same as you. I really don't."

"I didn't think you did."

"And I'm proud of you for not caring about that. It's about fucking time."

"I know you are. And I know it is."

"'Cause that's how all those losers out there justify their losing. That they do what they do 'cause they're afraid of dying. Or afraid for their family. Assholes," Alvi said.

"I'm a *man*, Mikey. I'm not some lost little boy, like you think."

"I'm sorry, Alvi. 'Cause you're right, that's what I've thought, and I've treated you like . . . a lost little boy. It hasn't been fair. I'm sorry."

"I wish I could kick your ass, 'cause if I could I would."

"In the shape I'm in now, you probably could."

"In the shape you're in now, it wouldn't be any fun. It wouldn't count. Fuck, Mikey. This is not what I expected."

"No shit."

"This is not how I expected *us* to go down."

"You're surprisingly together for a crazy guy who isn't taking his medication."

"No, I'm not. And you can't even tell anymore how much I'm not. Shit. *Shit.* I hope Gino does kill us. I hope he fucking does. You deserve it."

"Probably."

"How little you think 'a little time' is?"

"Very little. This will all be over one way or another tomorrow sometime."

"You're a piece of work, you really are. You just sit there and tell me I could be dead this time tomorrow."

"I thought you didn't care."

"I don't."

"So?"

The house lights went down, the stage lights went up, there was relieved applause, and a very fat young man came out and started telling jokes about being a very fat young man. The audience laughed but the Rossellini brothers ignored him, except to speak more softly.

"I won't have much time to be a Mormon," Alvi said. "It would have been nice to save everybody. Even you. Especially you. Because now you're damned, you fucking killer, you know that?"

"Yes," Rose said quietly.

"Shit," Alvi said, "that Mormon shit seemed so important a couple of days ago, three days ago, whenever it was. And getting out of the hospital for the Dunes blow was big. That was what, two, three days ago, and I can hardly remember the feelings. I can hardly *remember!*"

They were sitting not far from the stage. The comic didn't flinch at the shout, but people near their booth did. The comic improvised some comment the brothers didn't catch, the audience laughed, and the comic went on.

"I wish I knew what it is," Alvi said softly, his eyes wet. "I don't know what it is."

*Mrs. Sherman would say, "It's this town." Where are you tonight, lady? Are you even still alive? Have you whacked your husband yet? Whacked for a situation controlled by a computer disk that doesn't even know what it's doing? Some detective I've been lately. I can't help it if there's nothing to detect. Nobody knows how this situation really started, nobody knows why it keeps going, except that it seems to have a mind of its own.*

Alvi said, "You're gonna keep that promise to that creep too, aren't you? You're not gonna tell me shit."

"I told you all I'm gonna tell you: God watched me when I killed Zig."

"What, God's got nothing better to do?"

A man stood at their table. They hadn't noticed him come up, they were too engrossed in each other's faces. The man was dressed well, was about their age, and looked like many another man who has paid too high a price for working hard all his life and playing by the rules.

"Excuse me?" the man said.

"*Is* there an excuse for you?" Rose said.

The man had the courage of his indignation.

"I have to ask you to keep your voices down. You're distracting us, and you're being rude to the performer. We paid good money—"

"Doesn't this cat know he's talkin' to a guy with silver toe-nails?" Alvi smiled.

"I'm just asking you to keep your mouths shut."

Rose said, "You don't want to talk that way to us."

Alvi enjoyed the menace in his brother's eyes, and enjoyed even more the surprised fear in the man as he registered the sudden, irrational implacability he had just been almost politely exposed to. No, Rose could never leave Vegas.

The man mustered the courage for a very dirty look and went back to his table. But the incident broke a barrier between the brothers, telling Alvi especially that they were brothers whether he liked it or not.

"God, eh, Mikey?"

"God."

"I'm scared, Mikey."

"Of dying?"

"I'm scared of you. Scared *for* you. You've left us. You've left everybody. You gotta find a way back, brother."

"What if I don't wanna come back?"

"I don't know. I guess maybe either way we all die. Is that what you want?"

Rose let that sink in.

"Maybe," he said. "Maybe that is what I want. I hadn't thought of it. I just can't remember what's such a big deal about all of us dying. I'm sorry, Alvi, but I really can't."

Alvi took his brother's hands in his.

"Come back to us, Mike. Michael Francis Rossellini, come on *back*, man."

And then suddenly Alvi let go of his brother's hands and disappeared under the table.

"Alvi? Aniello? What the fuck are you doing down there?"

In moments Alvi rose from under the table, grinning.

"I feel better now," he said.

"What was that all about?"

"I took off my shoes and socks."

And, though their distance hadn't really been bridged, the brothers laughed.

Everybody was laughing. The comic had said something unusually funny, apparently.

The jokes had been crude. Sinatra's shows always opened with a comic who did crudeness well, as though that was the best way to prepare for the sentimentality of the music. The Rossellini brothers took the opportunity to laugh too.

Alvi managed to say through his laughter, "What are we laughing at?"

"Life is a dare, Aniello. Most people don't take the dare. We have. And you know what's on the other side of that dare?"

"God?"

And the brothers laughed some more, and the audience joined in, though they seemed to be laughing at something else.

The comic was winding up. The brothers had said nothing for the last several jokes, though they hadn't paid much attention to the comic either. The fat young comic was preparing to introduce Frank Sinatra.

"Remember," Alvi said, "what Mama would say when she'd play Sinatra's records?"

" 'Listen to him pronounce—' "

" '—every word.' How he'd pronounce every word exactly, Mikey. She'd say, 'Listen to his s sounds. Most singers are scared of s sounds. They do them soft. He does them hard. He's not afraid of any sound.' "

"And she wouldn't play those records when Pop was in the house."

" ''Cause he'd break the furniture when she did," Alvi said.

"But he knew she kept the records, she bought every new record, he knew that, and he didn't break them."

"'Cause then *she'd* have broke the furniture." Alvi laughed. "But she didn't play Sinatra for a long time after Pop died."

"She thought Pop got interested in her at first because he thought Sinatra boffed her."

"Don't talk like that about Mama, Mikey. 'Boffed.' Why do you talk like that?"

"What do you want me to say? 'Had intercourse.' Who cares who came in her mouth?"

Alvi looked like he'd been slapped.

"I'm sorry, Alvi."

"No, you're not. You're not sorry you *said* it, you're just sorry you said it to *me*."

"That's not enough?"

"No, it's not."

The comic said the name of the man, and the words "Frank Sinatra" brought a roar from the audience.

"I'll go you one better, Mikey. We all bit on the same tit. Okay? You, me, Pop, Sinatra. Okay? I'll go you one *better*. That gives us some rights."

"It gives us nothing."

"He slept with my mother, that gives me some *rights* around here."

"It's your turn to come *back*, Alvi."

"Why should I, any more than you?"

"There he is."

As the old man walked out onto the stage a curtain came up behind him to reveal a large orchestra. Every musician wore a tuxedo. The conductor was a small round man sitting at a grand piano and wearing earphones. With a slash of the conductor's hand the rhythm and brass burst into a loud, up-tempo number and Sinatra flashed a smile that made him look uncannily young, a young smile in the old pasty face, and his eyes were the same as they'd always been, brighter in person than they ever registered on screen, and, like the smile, the eyes were young to the point of seeming unnatural. For though no makeup could conceal the sad ravages of the face, the eyes and the smile seemed untouched. As though to put his listeners at ease with these contradictions, Sinatra grabbed the microphone from the top of the black grand piano and sang about how they made him feel so young, these strangers in this room had that power, they made him feel so young and he would feel that way even when he was old and gray, the song itself was keeping him alive.

It was as though Sinatra's voice was living his entire life all over again, at different stages, throughout the song. The first bars were the voice of the old man, raspy, worn, unable to hold notes for longer than a beat, and only his mastery of rhythm kept the song alive and made each word surprising—surprising, though everyone in the room knew the lyrics by heart. Then on a high note the voice cracked, and for an instant the music soured, and the audience flinched as one person, but instead of retreating from that bad sound Sinatra leaned into it, Sinatra bent the note further, into a jazzlike harmony, and so he erased his mistake from memory by making it part of the performance—and then instead of softening after the mistake, as Rose expected, Sinatra held the new note longer and louder, as though diving into it, then took a quick breath and sang the next note louder still, and fuller, until seamlessly for several bars it was the voice of thirty or forty years ago, full and unfettered, resonant and suggestive, until again it began to crack and again he used the cracking to modulate back into the voice and style of the old man, on pitch but raw, one note per beat, sometimes right on the beat, sometimes just off it, keeping the performance tense until on the last note the young man's voice returned, as though saluting the old man who sang with it, and Sinatra let that note ride, and the audience cheered—Rose and Alvi with the rest. It was a breathless performance, like watching a trapeze artist work without a net.

With barely a pause he started singing of how the best was yet to come and wouldn't it be fine, an old man in some ageless space who could make them believe for the length of a song that the best indeed was yet to come, and the voice again going to and fro between strength and fragility, youth and age. Sinatra's foot tapped the beat with absolute certainty, while his posture was ever so slightly wobbly, as though his energy was too much for his body. And in his immaculate tuxedo, with the surety of his presence and the reckless confidence of his style, he seemed to be demonstrating his legend without trading on it, without needing to. If it were possible that someone in the room had never heard of him, they would have been just as fascinated, just as relentlessly pulled into the performance, as though watching not a human being but a changeling, a creature both created and possessed by the sounds that came from and surrounded him. The lyrics were trite, obvious, sentimental. Somehow he made them true. The music was simple to the point of childishness. Somehow he made it complex. They found themselves applauding and cheering at the song's end, not in homage but as the only way to release the energy it gave them. The man was dispensing something, a kind of vitality that surged from his darkness with bright light, and he was giving it away with generous abandon as though he had no fear that he would not have more to give in the next song, the next show, the next anything. In such an old man, where could this vitality come from?

*I lit my cigarettes like he did, I wore the kind of clothes he wore. I still do. I tried to stand as he stood, I tried to walk as he walked. I still do. Not because I was imitating him, not even because it was Sinatra whom Mama really loved, but because I was imitating all the people who gave and taught me life, and they took so many of their cues from him.* And where had he taken his cues from? From peasants who came to

America from an older, less sentimental world—peasants who came with the intention of becoming aristocrats, and who, almost as soon as they arrived, began to stand and walk like those aristocrats they'd watched so closely, yet from afar, for generations. European princes had taught them grace; American streets taught them flair. They didn't need to learn violence from anyone. That, they were born with. And Sinatra blended all this better than any, and sang as he did so—sang of love, and of pride, despairing of one and reveling in the other. And this was why Sicilians especially gave him respect, in the peculiar way Sicilians use that word, meaning homage, deference, consideration, and that invitation to betrayal, loyalty.

Rose and Alvi felt all this without articulating it, or needing to. They were watching the core of their heritage.

Now Sinatra sang about how they (whoever "they" were) couldn't take that (whatever "that" was) away from him—that somehow the way she held her hat and the way she sipped her tea was beyond the world's possibility to destroy or erode. *Is that why you left me the pictures, Mama? Because you wouldn't let them take your dark beauty from you?*

And thinking of those pictures he thought of others. A scrapbook his mother had kept. Since his father's death? From before? Rose had no way of knowing. He hadn't thought anything of it when he'd found it. It seemed to him no more than her one indulgence of sentimentality—Sinatra himself seemed, for her, that indulgence. But now he understood. They couldn't take that away from her. The pictures were all of Sinatra, but he was never alone: Sinatra with Lyndon Johnson, with Adlai Stevenson, with Eleanor Roosevelt (he was holding her hand and looking into her eyes), with Jack Kennedy, Bobby, Jackie, Nixon, Reagan, Nancy; and Sinatra with very different people, Sinatra with Johnny

Roselli, Paul Castellano, Carlo Gambino, Carlo's son Joey, Jimmy Fratianno, Sallie Spatola; and still another kind, Sinatra with Marilyn Monroe, Lauren Bacall, Humphrey Bogart, Marlon Brando, Louis Armstrong, Elvis Presley, Duke Ellington. *Mama was one body away from each of them. She'd taken the jism (what color had it felt like?) of the man shaking those hands, the man with his arms around those shoulders, the man looking into those eyes. She was one body away from Lyndon Johnson, she was one body away from Paul Castellano, she was one body away from Marlon Brando. She was one body away from Jackie Kennedy, who was one body away from Marilyn Monroe. And I was one body from Mama, and the rest had passed something to me, from flesh to flesh. She was one body away for she had taken that body on the stage into her, that body singing now about the summer wind and how like painted kites those days and nights went flying by. But they didn't fly away because that body on the stage, that old man, was where it all connected. Who else had held the hand of Eleanor Roosevelt and shaken the hand of Carlo Gambino both, and on equal terms? That body on the stage, that old man, was where it all connected. And why? Because he could sing love songs like no one else. History, of a kind. History transfixed by love songs. That's life, that's what all the people say, the body is singing now. Some people get their kicks from stomping on a dream but he don't let that get him down. And the Rosie Vee of the dirty pictures, the dancer at Bugsy's Flamingo, what a ride she must have given him, and how she must have kept the feel of his flesh in her memory as she collected the photographs of Sinatra with Jackie Kennedy and Sinatra with Salvatore Spatola. And now he's singing that we're much too mar-velous for words.*

Rose remembered hearing that Sinatra owned a company that made components for guided missiles. So he owned even something of those great explosions they'd seen long ago. And he'd heard that Dean Martin was afraid of elevators, and that Martin and Sinatra, those proud men, would only book rooms on the first floor because they feared to sleep higher. And that Sinatra's mother, when he was very small, often dressed him as a little girl.

The man, the body, was speaking now.

"I'm just waiting for a downbeat, not a bus. Where you working tomorrow?"

The musicians laughed. The conductor, that little round man, laughed.

"That's my son, the guy with the earphones. I had to promise his mother I'd give the bum a job."

More laughter.

"That's his *son*," Alvi whispered, staring wide-eyed at the little round man. Alvi bolted up but Rose pulled him back. "That's his *son*, Mikey, he slept with Mama and that's his *son*, that could be me, that's me."

"Mama *said* she slept with him, that's all we know."

But Alvi's eyes blazed. He sat not looking at the singer anymore, but at the round smiling man.

But something was wrong on the stage. The music was playing but Sinatra wasn't singing. He was looking around as though he'd forgotten where he was. He started a lyric, then stopped. It didn't fit the music. He looked frightened. A scared boy in the body of an old man. He turned toward his son, whose presence seemed to remind him of who he was, he was Frank Sinatra, he was there to sing love songs to history, and he wheeled around and began to beg, but in the proudest terms, that luck be a lady tonight, and that she keep the party polite, and that she not blow on some other guy's dice. But it had been an awful moment, to see that confidence suddenly abandoned, with nothing in the man to take its place.

He sang, more slowly now, that it seemed we'd stood and talked like this before, and he was right. That we'd looked at each other in the same way then, but there was no way to remember where or when. He sang in the young voice and the old, back and forth, where and when unknowable, and as the lyrics climbed to the final high note he became, in his voice, younger and younger, until he hit the last "when" roundly and fully, and held that note a long time, and when the note and the word were finally exhausted the loose muscles of his fatty face trembled, as though they'd been unaccountably left behind, and his eyes were frightened again. He had to know that it was very possible that this was the last time his voice would rise to such a height. And he looked like a man who had said an irreparable good-bye.

He took a few steps. Tried to recover. Slowly, he started to speak.

"I'm . . . what they call . . . a saloon singer."

For most of the performance he had been singing happily about love. Jauntily. Perhaps that was, in part, a function of age. It was easier, with that ravaged and undependable voice, to sing faster tempos that gave him the flexibility to go through many changes and use many approaches. Slow, sad songs required rounder tones and more control, could not be played with as easily, were far more dangerous.

*He's risking humiliation every moment. Say what you like, that's a very brave man.*

The song began. *He's telling us to drink up, all we happy people. Nobody here looks very happy, but he's admitting that we're happier than him. He says he's paying for the drinks and the laughs. He's paying for everything. Because a woman with angel eyes has gone. And she's really gone. What a tenderness he has for her. What a terrible, generous, all-encompassing tenderness. He's not bitter, he's not angry at her. Those angel eyes had every right to look elsewhere. He asks us to excuse him, because he must disappear. And his voice is disappearing with him. A scratchy whisper. Like an old wax record played on an old machine. Mrs. Sherman has disappeared. Joy has betrayed herself more than betrayed me, and so she has disappeared. Virginia disappeared before we ever met her. Mama's gone. None of them said " 'Scuse me," as he's saying. His Angel Eyes, she did not say excuse me. And Kennedy, Eleanor Roosevelt, Paul Castellano, Carlo Gambino, they have disappeared. Pop. Zig. None of them said excuse me. With unbearable politeness, with a tenderness close to death, the death of his voice, he is saying excuse me, I must disappear. There are no angel eyes left in the room, no reason to stay. No angel eyes except maybe Alvi's eyes, and now, the way Alvi stares, he too is disappearing. I am disappearing. Excuse me.*

The old man lit a cigarette, then picked up a drink from the piano and sat on a stool, and sang even more slowly. *In the city without clocks he knows it's a quarter to three, always a quarter to three, and that there's no one in the place, not really, but him and each of us. He is singing that though we might not know it, yet he is a poet, and he just wants to drink one for his baby and one more for the road. He sings with a terrible fatigue, the voice almost not there. He'd expected the road to end long before this. He's tired. He could not live unless he sang to us, but each time he sings he dares humiliation, lets us watch the dying relationship between him and his voice, him and his memory, him and that angelic one whom he could not hold, whom he was no man for, whom his tenderness could finally not sustain, whom his darkness drove away. Everything has ended, everything is over. He can't even say excuse me anymore. He thanks us. He's leaving us. He touched what we liked to think was our history and it has left him like this and now he is leaving us.*

Everyone cheered as he walked off the stage. *Do they know*

*what they're cheering? Do they know they're watching a man rehearse his death?*

"It's not bullshit, is it?" Alvi said. "He's really great, isn't he?"

"Yeah. You gonna put your shoes back on?"

"Fuck the shoes."

*I* gotta talk to the kid," Alvi said.

"What kid?"

"His *son*, I gotta talk to his *son*," and before Rose could register the remark Alvi had left the booth in his bare feet. The audience stood as one person, first to applaud and then to leave, and Rose watched his brother shove through the crowd. In those first moments he might still have stopped Alvi, but he lost that chance, so stunned was he to see his brother finally and terribly act on his own.

Rose wanted to run away, abandon his brother and the situation both, and hide in a bathroom or any place where he could have the situation all to himself again, but Alvi had catapulted them both forward and there was nothing to do but follow.

He did, keeping Alvi's white hair in sight through the crowd, pushing men, pushing women, and when one didn't give way with a push he hit, man or woman, he didn't care, a jab to the kidney or lower back, and left their shocked, pained protests behind him. Alvi had caught up with Gino, Sallie, young Rizzo, and their party. Alvi was just behind them and they hadn't seen him yet, they were at a side door at the foot of the stage, a door guarded by two large men in tuxedos, men who clearly had guns under their jackets. Rose elbowed, shoved, and jabbed his way, and at every contact it was as though he elbowed, shoved, and jabbed himself, for his bruised body registered every touch. He knew nothing now but that he had to reach his brother.

Gino and the others were so intent on where they were going, so enclosed in their dignity and in the purpose they felt when moving together, that they didn't notice Alvi fall in directly behind them. He walked with their air of authority. The tuxedoed guards, sheathed in the honor they felt when Gino the Gentleman nodded to them, didn't even look down at Alvi's bare feet.

Rose wanted to call out "Alvi!" but choked the word as it came to his mouth from an instinct that only the proper presence could get him past the guards. And in the next moment it was too late to call. Gino's party, with Alvi at the rear, passed through the door to the inner sanctum as Rose reached the large men.

*Be a pro. Pros do what? They think.*

*Think. Think right into their fucking heads.*

*You boys make way for darkness, so make way for me, 'cause my darkness is greater, richer, there's more in mine than yours, there's even light, and we've lived by the law that those with lesser darkness recede before those with more.*

And all this burned in Rose's eyes as he looked into the eyes of one of the guards, and they recognized his stance and walk as that of a man on a higher level of their world than they, and they didn't fail to notice the slight bulge of the gun under his jacket, and the guard he was looking at said, "You're with Gino an' them?"

Rose didn't trust himself to speak, just nodded the nod that gangsters had learned from princes to make their will known to inferiors. It was the right move. These soldiers respected anyone of their world who didn't think that they, the soldiers, were good enough to speak to.

"He's good," the other said, "he was sittin' with Gino, and then the guy he sat with later went in with Gino."

*That's very observant, very good. Just not good enough.*

But when Rose entered the inner sanctum he saw that he was too late, the commotion had started.

*I'm not good enough either.*

Sinatra and his son (who was hardly a kid, was Alvi's age at least) were at the far end of the corridor, among their protectors, about to enter a room—one of their protectors was holding the door open for them. Gino and his party were close, but did not look as though they intended or would be permitted to pass through the door with the Sinatras. For Lampedusa it was just a matter of paying respect, a handshake, a look, or simply being in the same corridor when no one else at the concert was allowed the privilege. And a dozen or so tuxedoed musicians were standing about, and a moment ago they had been drinking and talking. *I've never seen so many well-dressed men in so small a space. Robert Kennedy was killed in a corridor like this.* But whatever the decorum of a moment ago, now all were looking at the white-haired, dark-suited, barefoot man with bright, bright eyes shouting, "DON'T go through that door, DON'T go through that door! Remember Rosie Vee? You, kid, Junior, Pop ever tell you 'bout Rosie Vee? She looked a little like Ava but he met her FIRST. You and me, Junior, we got something to talk about, we're . . . we're not brothers, we're . . . MIKEY!" The protectors had moved on Alvi midspeech and as they grabbed him he'd seen his brother down the hall. "MIKEY! You, JUNIOR, we're not brothers, but we're, we're SOMETHING, I HAVE TO KNOW WHAT WE ARE, DON'T GO THROUGH THAT

DOOR. We got a common ANCESTRY! I know how to SAVE
US ALL! MIKEY!"

When he saw the protectors manhandling his brother Rose
snapped. He'd been living in car-crash time for days now, in
that elongated space between the skid and the impact that
seems to take so long and one notices so much and odd images
flash, so as Rose moved toward his brother and his hand
reached reflexively for his father's gun, he saw eyes,
everyone's eyes—Gino's full of hatred, Sallie's of menace,
Rizzo's, of amusement, the musicians' of fear and shock—and
it was as though he saw nothing but eyes, and had time to register each pair, and in Junior's he saw revulsed sympathy, and
in Sinatra's: *they're the real doorways to the inner sanctum,
those eyes, absolutely blue and unreadable, they could mean
anything, no wonder so many want to be looked upon by
them, I must be crazy as Alvi, crazier.* And he was close to Alvi
now, his gun was visible halfway out his jacket, and two were
holding Alvi and another was hitting Alvi in the gut and Alvi
was shouting, "KILL 'im, MIKEY, SHOOT HIM!" and Mike
knew that Alvi meant kill the guard who was hitting him, but
everyone else thought Alvi meant Sinatra, and there were lots
of guns now, the protectors pushed the singer and his son
through the door out of sight and Rose was close to Gino and
Sallie and had to choose between them and chose Sallie, press-
ing his father's gun into Sallie's throat and standing with his
back to the wall.

Somebody's gun went off.

It was very loud and near.

*Was it mine? Thank God, no. Sallie still has his head on.*

"OKAY. Okay. Stop. Everybody. Okay."

*Who's speaking? Me? Sallie. He has his hands up, palms
up, pumping his palms, gesturing, Slow down, slow down.
Sallie, you're a fucking genius at what you do, nothing ruffles
you.*

Rose's ears were ringing. *Must've shot at me, whoever it was. Bullet must've gone into the wall right behind me. Almost lost my head.*

He whispered into Sallie's ear, "Just let me get my brother out of here."

"You're dead, Mike. Both-a you."

"I know, but not here, not like this."

"What's the difference?"

"Jesus, Mikey," Alvi said. "I'm sorry. We're dead."

"That's what Sallie just told me. Let my brother go." *What a peculiar train of thought The Situation is expressing.* "Just let him go. See the door marked Exit just to the left of you, Aniello? Use it."

"Not without you, Mikey."

"It's my action now, kid, and you gotta just go with it."

"I love you, Mikey. You shouldn't a done Zig. And you *know* where I'm goin'." And Alvi went through the door.

"Gino," Mike said, "remember one word, say it to yourself slowly: *insurance*."

"I don't give a fuck," Lampedusa said.

"You don't know, in a few minutes you might. That's the difference between a pro and an amateur, right? Professionals *think*."

"I think you're dead. And not a good dead."

"Sallie, you got any suggestions on how I get out of here alive? 'Cause that's the only way you live."

*I know you're thinking, Sallie. You're the best, you always think.*

"You're the guy who doesn't care who dies or when, remember? Fucking prima donna. You were pretty convincing too."

"I care *how*. Not this way."

"Hypocrite," Gino hissed. His eyes glinted with contempt and hatred. It was mortifying for Gino, for this to happen in front of Sinatra on Gino's turf. *The guys'll talk about this, the guys'll laugh about this, Gino has lost respect bad, we're dead alright.*

"I die, you die, Sallie."

*Why is this all so fucking* awkward? *I'm* embarrassed. *I can't die embarrassed. Is that too fucking much to ask?*

*The Situation is* not *going to do this to me. Not this way.*

"Everybody take their time," Sallie said evenly, "we got plenty of time, these Rossellinis got nowhere to hide."

"It happens like this," Rose said. "Sallie and I are backing toward Alvi's door, and then I'm going out that door, and I'm gonna stand there a little while and kill whoever comes through next. Whether it's you, Gino, or some fucking janitor."

"How did you live this long?" Sallie said as they backed toward the door.

"I hid from my true nature."

The last thing Rose was aware of as he squeezed through the door behind the shield of Sallie's thick body and pulled it shut after him—eyes, the eyes of men stripped of all that really mattered to them: their fatal sense of style. Rose was more frightened of the nakedness of those stripped eyes than of anything ever in his life. *There's nothing there. Absolutely nothing.*


The door opened on the south side of the building, facing the parking lot. There were many more eyes, if he cared to look into them, eyes glazed with that determined yet dislocated look of evacuation or migration or whatever it was all these people with set faces thought they were doing.

There was no way to stand by the door and get Gino's boys one by one. Irresistibly Rose was taken by the crowd, and he strained to spot Alvi's white hair ahead. He holstered the gun and used his hands as he had in the Crystal Room, elbowing, jabbing, shoving, pushing through. These people weren't as docile as the well-dressed folk who had come to hear Sinatra, they would jab back or curse or turn and face him, *but something must be the matter with my eyes, nobody's facing me long. How many Situations are in play this night, exchanging their strange intelligences in the air, and it's like a labyrinth I can't find my way out of.*

At the corner of Spring Mountain Road police barricades closed the Strip to cars, and their revolving lights danced over the thousands of walkers who pressed past the barricades toward the Dunes. Searchlights roved the sky while helicopters flew low and their glaring spotlights swept over the heads of the masses.

"Hey, this guy's been shot!" a woman screeched.

She was pointing at Rose.

Others turned toward him as she screeched again.

He looked down and saw his white shirt soaked with blood. Frantically he felt his chest. And then he laughed. The shallow cuts that Mrs. Sherman had etched with her ring had opened with all the body contact and were bleeding through. He moved straight toward the woman as he was laughing and she scrambled to get out of his way, and he tried to button his jacket as he walked through the barricades with the crowd, and he was breathing heavy. Every few steps he looked behind him.

He was on the Sands side of the street. On the Treasure Island side, under the cartoonish leer of a pirate's head four stories high, was one of Steve Wynn's attractions: two huge, ornate pirate ships crawling with actors in costume—they battled every other hour for the children. Hundreds of flashbulbs popped as the mob waited for the moment this night when one of the ships would fire a cannon and, blocks away, the Dunes would blow. That was the conceit of the evening, *or the symbolism, or something, the New Vegas demolishing the Old, the victory of Disneyland over Bugsy Seigel and Meyer Lansky, as though it made a difference who pulled the strings, as though there were strings, because the gangsters hadn't built the town and Steve Wynn wasn't building the town, longing built this town, hunger and longing, and the people who think they control it are as much the servants of that longing as these people popping flashbulbs and playing slots. Longing and hunger and I'm going to die tonight.*

He was past Treasure Island now, passing the Mirage, *another Wynn idea of fun,* an artificial volcano that shot flames high into the air while the crowd oohed and cheered and hundreds more flashbulbs popped from their cardboard-box Kodaks. The "volcano" was three tiers of Disneyland concrete rock with constant waterfalls to reflect the lights and conceal the chintz, and thirty-foot-high flames belching from the top. That spectacle slowed the mass of humanity on the street and drew them toward the Mirage, making it slightly easier to move if he went straight forward. *What kind of man thinks of something like that and what kind of people flock to watch it? I'm afraid to look into their eyes, I don't ever want to see that Nothing again. But surely they have more than that, they have to endure so much, and endure it for so little, their endurance itself must give them more. It's said Wynn has an eye disease, the guy's practically blind, the Nothing's eating out his bulbs from the inside. And what's in Alvi's eyes and in mine on this night we're going to die? And what was in Zig's in those moments when they weren't even eyes anymore, what did I see that made me finally pull the trigger and pull it again and again and made all this unstoppable? Was he looking at God? I think he was. And the neon violet of Joy's eyes, and Virginia's, which turn from gray to green and back, and Mama's stone eyes full I know now of Nothing Nothing Nothing, a Nothing she'd come somehow to love. And where's Alvi and when will they catch us and kill us tonight?*

He steadied himself, and still couldn't see Alvi through the crowd, *gave him too much head start, took too long, talked too much, always do, some strong silent type I am,* and his feet hurt from all the people who'd stepped on them as he'd shoved through. *My feet were the only part of me that hadn't been bruised yet. Alvi's must be bloody by now.*

An old man with earphones on his head said happily to Rose, shouting to be heard, "One station says there's two hundred *thousand* of us out here, and another says two hundred *fifty* thousand!" And the old man went to tell others.

*Gotta find my brother. Gotta die with my brother.* The crowd was thicker, and Rose was vicious. He tried not to hit children, but he wasn't sure if he always stopped himself or not. When men turned to hit him back he held his jacket open and they stopped when they saw the bloody shirt and holstered gun. He was saturated with pain to the point where he almost didn't feel it, the way you almost don't taste water; he felt he no longer occupied his body, his eyes and his hands and his feet were all he cared about, all his will concentrated in those organs. *I coulda died with Alvi in that corridor, why didn't I let it happen? 'Cause they would have laughed, laughed that we were so easy to kill. It was just my pride. How fuckin' stupid. I still must want to win. What could there possibly be left to win?*

*And the Situation wasn't finished, I feel that, I know that, it wasn't ready to finish in that hallway.*

He swayed, thought he'd pass out, and grabbed a Coke from a woman and poured it over his head to wake himself up. The woman screamed curses at him but he made his way past her.

Rose was in front of the Flamingo now, its great pink-feather neon reflected in the faces of the crowd, and he could see the Dunes bathed in spotlights, the great, phallic five-story sign brilliant with red-gold, yellow and blue, the colors rising up the sign, glittering at the top as though bursting, ejaculating, and dropping down to the ground to rise again, and Rose's heart tore for the city he couldn't help but love—its neons that were, with the beauty of a few women, the only beauty he'd ever believed in, believed in helplessly, believed without wanting to, believed without believing, the way as a boy he'd believed in the grandeur of the bomb blasts. *They used to do their bombs in the desert. Now they're blowing up the town.*

Many around him wore the white face masks of body shops, to protect themselves from something, he didn't know what. Many carried videocams and disposable cameras. Spotlights tore the air, police lights strobed, and the ice-blue mass of Caesar's Palace backlit the crowd from where Ross stood, and a chant was rising—"BLOW the building! BLOW the building! BLOW the BUILDing! BLOW the BUILDing!" Thousands screamed it, and the sounds vibrated through the mob, Rose felt the words' tremors in his chest, in his thighs, and he wondered was Alvi chanting, Alvi who must be within two hundred yards of him but could not be seen, and the chant got stronger—BLOW the BUILD*ING*! BLOW the BUILD *ING*!—and Rose felt his mouth form the words and clamped his lips against them, *I am part of them after all, they are part of me*, and now he was seeing, seeing what? Joy would call it an aura, a kind of neon haze rising from the crowd like colored fumes, and booming from loudspeakers somewhere unseen was a voice, *it must be Wynn's*, "THIS IS THE BEGINNING OF A NEW ERA IN LAS VEGAS!" BLOW the BUILD *ING!* And Rose started to laugh, and his laughter hurt. BLOW THE BUILD ING! *Wynn believes in what he's doing because he can get two hundred thousand people in the street to watch him play,* BLOW THE BUILD ING, *all he can do is lead dorks around by the nose, that's power?* BLOW THE BUILD ING! *Poor fuck, he hasn't got a clue either, highest paid exec in the U.S., thirty-four mil a year,* BLOW THE BUILD ING, *wouldn't it be funny if he knew I was* *feeling sorry for him? 'Cause I can see where neon* comes from, *I see neon rising from these people like smoke, that's where neon comes from,* BLOW THE BUILD ING, *from our souls, Joy, I can SEE it, I—*

The neon of the Dunes sign flashed while a string of small blasts flared before the hotel's dark tower, then one explosion lit the far end, another the near, a great blazing ball of fire blew the bottom floor, which had been the casino, and at almost the same instant the sign was engulfed in blinding white, then floor by floor, from the bottom up, the windows blew with boom on boom on boom, the sign disintegrated and now the building hovered, sagged, seemed to stagger, a drunk on fire, then collapsed into itself with a metallic ripping screech Rose felt in his eyeballs.

*The Spectacle of Steve Wynn*

# THREE

# *Ancestors*

*Don't make work just a measly paycheck.*
*Make it life and death.*

—Sam "Moony" Giancana

•

*He made you feel happy to be at his mercy.*

—Chuck Giancana, Sam's kid brother

•

*You guys are sure good at walking backwards.*

—Meyer Lansky, to TV reporters

# THE DEATH

# OF FRANK SINATRA

*A*  thick cloud of smoke and ash blew toward the crowd, and the people closest to the explosion were lost in it. In panic they pushed against those behind them, who pushed against those behind them, and Rose thought surely people were being trampled, and there was the thump-thump-thumping of helicopters flying low above the wreckage to disperse the cloud, and people covered their mouths with their hands, with handkerchiefs, with their blouses and shirts, *that's why the smart ones wore masks.* He heard children crying, he heard laughter and curses and exclamations, amid hundreds coughing, and Rose just stood, jostled by all who were rushing to get inside the Barbary Coast, inside the Flamingo, inside the Imperial, away from the billows of dust and ash. His clothing was covered with the stuff, he rubbed it from his eyes, he coughed, the coughs hurt like everything else, and the air stank of explosives and burnt plastic and aviation fuel and smoldering rugs, and the roiling cloud was bright with the glow of Caesar's blue neon, Bally's lavender, the Flamingo's pink—the colors rose and twisted with the smoke, as though the neon aura fuming from the people had taken shape in the air for all to see.

He watched, coughing, until the cloud had thinned. There was almost no one left on the street. He knew it was dangerous for him to stand in the open, but he couldn't remember why it mattered. He'd hoped that as the crowd dispersed he would find Alvi.

*I don't believe this.* The yellow hair, the dark eyes, the purposeful, skinny walk—at first he could not see Mrs. Sherman for her parts. She wore a yellow dress to match her hair, smudged with ash now, and the same heels she'd worn the night before. Her mouth was mocking, and the closer she came the more her black eyes laughed.

"Lover! Wasn't that *great!* Look at you! What's wrong, my God. Oh. Ha ha ha ha ha ha." Gingerly, she touched his chest. "Did *I* do that, sweet? Of course I did. How'd you find me? And with such great timing?"

"I'm a detective," Rose said.

"You're a good one. But you've got to tell me *how*." Her eyes shifted away, shifted back. "But maybe it doesn't matter right now. We—I guess *we* is alright—we have work to do. I'll keep my bargain." Her eyes went back and forth again, quickly, twice. "Will I? I will. You'll get your twen'y grand. That's how you say it here, right, twen'y grand?"

"Twenty large. That's how we say it. Twen'y large."

"I love it. Twen'y large."

There was the ringing of a phone. At first Rose thought the ringing was in his head.

"Oops, just one sec." She pulled a cellular from the purse slung around her shoulder. "This is private, okay, hon?"

He turned away and walked a few yards. He was facing the Flamingo's neon, standing about twenty steps from the awning, looking up at the many-storied hotel. Wisps of smoke wafted past. The helicopters still hovered over the Dunes ruin, with their thumping sound, close enough to make small concussions in the air. There weren't many people about. It was uncanny, how crammed the street had been, and it had emptied so quickly.

Paulie Rizzo walked slowly toward him from the Flamingo's entrance. Rose waited to die.

Rizzo stared at his chest.

"Christ, someone's *already* shot you."

"No. You get the prize."

"That's a lotta brownie points now—in some circles."

"Congratulations."

But Rizzo didn't go for his gun. Rose didn't go for his either. *His eyes say he's not going to kill me now.* But Rose was puzzled. Rizzo was smiling.

"What's the matter, kid," Rose said, "this not a good spot?"

"It's *not* a good spot, but that's not the reason." The young man kept smiling. "The easiest thing would be to tell Lampedusa I couldn't find you in the crowd. That'll fly."

*The Situation is behaving very strangely.*

"Why are you being so nice to me, Rizzo?"

"Am I ever gonna know what the fuck this is all about?"

"Why should you be any different from the rest of us? And *why* are you being so nice to me?"

"'Cause I'm learning shit from you. You got those guys on the run. I didn't think anybody could—at least no solo flier like you. I don't know how you're goin' about it, and till I get the idea—"

"You wanna squeeze the last drop of education from the situation."

"Something like that. No guarantees, though. I'll probably kill you next time I see you."

"I'll look forward to it. There's a lot you're not telling me, but why should you?"

"Right. Why should I?"

"You're smarter than you look, kid. I don't mean that as an insult."

"Doesn't pay to look very smart at my level of . . . rank, I guess it is."

"I think I'm beginning to understand."

"Sallie always says you're smart. 'Watch out for 'im, 'cause he's smart.' That's what Sallie says."

"Sallie could be wrong."

"I hope not. 'Cause that would mean Sallie isn't smart. And that wouldn't be great for me."

"I *am* beginning to understand."

"You should, I'm throwin' ya enough softballs."

"Sallie's got plans, doesn't he? And I'm fitting right in, aren't I?"

"Mum's the word."

"This special dispensation you're giving me, Rizzo—it extend to my brother?"

"Can't promise."

"Sure you can. For yourself—for Sallie too, I think."

"Whata we get in return?"

"You'll think of something."

They smiled at each other, slight twisted smiles of amused understanding.

"Who's that toothpick broad lookin' at us, pretending she's still on the phone?"

"A client."

"You got time for clients tonight?"

"What else I got to do?"

"Can I ask a question?"

Rose said nothing.

"You can afford the suits, the whole nine yards, as a P.I.?"

"Thinking of a career change?"

Rizzo said nothing. It was a serious question.

"Mostly I charge a great deal of money," Rose said, "to find lost people. Or I did, until *I* got lost."

"Made some change when you sold the Garter too?"

"Big change. Big for me. And we still get a piece. You want my financial statement?"

"Maybe later."

"Thinking of charging for your dispensations?"

"Not yet."

"Good. I don't pay for my life. Remember that."

"See you, Rose—if you live."

"See you, Rizzo—if you and Sallie live. I'd say you're playing for dangerous stakes."

"Naw. We got approval."

*You talk too much, kid. Sallie won't like that.*

The young man's smile became a grin. He turned, and walked back toward the Flamingo. Then he stopped and called back, "By the way—the radio says Sinatra's dead."

Rose watched Rizzo walk away, and heard the sharp heels of Mrs. Sherman walking toward him from behind; for a moment he confused their steps and it seemed that Rizzo's shoes made that unforgiving sound on the pavement. *Sinatra dead? A stroke from the excitement in the corridor?* He was startled to feel her arm entwine in his.

"Sinatra's dead," he said.

"The guy who sat on my bar stool?"

"You know who he is."

"My parents' record collection. Easy listening."

"Soft, not easy."

"Who was that, your brother?"

"One of what you might call my 'extended family.' Are we going to kill your husband?"

Her eyes brightened and she smiled. *She's got those perfect shiny WASP teeth.*

"I told you last night," she said, "I wouldn't lie to *you*."

"Does that still go?"

"I don't know. Yes. Come on."

She increased the pressure on his arm and led him down the

driveway along the south end of the Flamingo, where they'd lost Rizzo and Lavender the night before.

"Where's it going down?" he asked.

"Straight ahead. That parking garage. Fifth floor."

"Guns echo like crazy in parking garages."

"*Shit.* I should have discussed this with you. *Shit.*"

"I don't strangle people. And I don't have a knife."

"He's too big for you to strangle. *Shit.*"

He stopped walking. She still clung to his arm. He put his free hand on her hip. She was trembling deep in her body. Her eyes met his, darted away, several times fast.

"Take it easy," he said.

"I want to *shoot* him." Her nails dug into his arm. "And *how* did you find me, *how* did you know? *He* got to you, didn't he? That's the *only* way you could have known."

Rose said, "Doesn't your body remember anything?"

Memories flitted across her eyes, but didn't stay long.

"Yes," she said uncertainly.

"I could have killed you last night, easily, and just taken the disk to him."

"That was last night, but people change, people *really* change."

"Tell it to the world. If it's true, then there's hope."

"Don't play with me."

"I haven't spoken to him. I'm on your side more than I'm on anybody's."

"Why?"

"I gave myself to you, you gave yourself to me. That doesn't happen every year."

"I'm taking myself back."

"Fine. I'm not."

"Why?"

*"Why" is a crooked letter, Mama used to say.*

"We haven't got time for this," Rose said. "This is the driveway to the parking garage. He might show up."

"I said, 'Why?' Nobody loves *me*." Tears came to her eyes, cried by whatever in her was still innocent.

"I didn't say I loved you. There isn't any 'why' for stuff like this. Get used to it, Mrs. Sherman."

Her eyes focused on his, and held. The paper-thin layer of flesh on her hip shivered less.

"Alright," she said very softly. "Alright."

They walked on, but her heels did not ring as sharply.

"I wish I knew what rules you're playing by," she said.

*Something . . . shifted somehow . . . because of you. So I'll back your play, whether you're right or wrong, good or bad. Tonight, those are the rules.*

The elevator in the Flamingo's parking garage was small, dirty, and slow. She stood across from him with her hand in her purse.

*Holding your pistol?*

She smiled a little shyly this time, as though embarrassed.

"What?" he said.

"All our blood last night . . ." She couldn't go on.

"It was drops, not buckets."

"More than drops. Have you had . . . an AIDS test?"

"Scared?"

"Nervous. You?"

"I spent my childhood watching A-bombs, lady."

"Well, I've had one. I'm okay."

"Sure you are."

They got out on the fifth level. She'd told him the meeting place was at the far end, catty-corner from the elevator. They still had to walk the equivalent of a block, down one passageway of parked cars, across another, down another. Her heels echoed on the cement.

"Stop," he said.

"What?"

"Take those damn heels off. If it's an ambush, let's not make it *that* easy."

"Sorry."

She took them off and put them in her purse. She took out her gun.

"You've got one too, I see," she said.

"It's that kind of evening."

They walked on, saying nothing.

*Alvi, I'm walking around with another barefoot person. Are you dead too, like Sinatra?*

*If you are, I'll whack myself. I'd owe you that. Though I think you're a little too possessed tonight for any luck you don't really want.*

"He's supposed to be around that corner, at the end of that ramp," she said.

Rose looked, carefully.

"He's not there yet."

"Then *we're* winning."

She laughed a bright adolescent laugh.

He said, "Were you ever a cheerleader?"

She hissed, "How did you *know?* You've been looking into my *background.*"

"In a way."

*Every two minutes you're clicking into a different person.*

Her lips bared back above her teeth and her eyes were a frightened animal's. She pointed her small gun at him and her hand trembled.

"It'll make a big noise, Claire. If they're close, it'll scare them away. What do you care if I know you were a cheerleader in another life?"

"I was another person."

"Exactly."

"What else do you know?"

"Not much."

"Nobody knows *me*," and her eyes teared.

"Why do you want that disk? And don't tell me money. You don't really care about money any more than I do. Why do you want it?"

"Because I *want* it."

"That's the best reason. Why do you want to kill your husband?"

"Because I *hate* him."

"Not as good, but it'll do."

"Why do you *care?*"

"Just a bad habit."

Her eyes clicked into the eyes of the woman he had first met.

"I didn't think people talked this much in these situations," she said.

"People do everything in these situations that they do in other situations."

He took her left hand and led her low against the far wall, behind the cover of the parked cars, up the ramp. *This killing will either tear her apart totally or bring her back together in a most unpleasant form. And if we stood up straight and looked over this ledge and down into the Flamingo pool, we'd see where Ben Siegel's suite used to be. They tore it down a few weeks or months ago for another expansion. And Virginia Hill tried to commit suicide four times in the years after Benny died, and she made it on the fifth. That little wrinkle wasn't in the movie.*

*Headlights. Here we go.*

They crouched behind a white Bronco.

Mr. Sherman pulled up in a rented BMW four-door. He was driving, the man who had threatened Rose in his office was beside him, the woman in the back seat.

*Christ, did she think she could kill them all with that little gun? Did she think he'd come alone? She doesn't look surprised.*

Rose motioned for Mrs. Sherman to show herself. She

walked toward the car, not pointing her gun but carrying it down at her side.

*It's the sure walk again. Good. Look at her, in nylon stockinged feet.*

"Hello, Mark," Mrs. Sherman said.

"Claire. You think this is funny?"

"I'm sorry. I'm smiling because . . . I don't know why."

When he opened the door he had a much larger pistol in his right hand, pointed at her. He kept it pointed at her when he got out.

"I feel . . . ridiculous," Mark Sherman said.

"You look splendid," Claire Sherman said.

"If you move the hand with the gun I *am* going to shoot."

*He's shaken. And he was so confident just days ago. Maybe it's that now he's wearing jogging clothes—top-dollar too— and then he was wearing a suit. No, he knows he's not in a movie now. He's given order after order to his people and they all got botched and came to nothing. Or maybe the poor sap just doesn't want to kill her.*

"I'm not going to let you extort me, Claire."

"Aw."

"I'm not giving you any money for something you didn't create."

"*Aw.*"

"I don't *understand,* California law would give you half the money *anyway.*"

And this time she stamped her bare foot with her "*Aw.*"

"So just give it to me," he said, "or I'm going to use this."

"I will not. And I have *help.*"

Rose was just about to stand and show himself, when she said to her husband, "Do *you* have help?"

In silhouette Rose saw the woman in the back seat holding a gun to the head of the man in the front seat.

*Ha ha ha. She's good. She's actually good.*

"Look behind you, Mark."

"Don't be silly."

"Mark," the man in the car said hoarsely.

"You don't have to turn around, hon. I'll tell you what's happening. Arlene has her gun stuck in Edward's ear."

*You could still get out of it, Mark. Your gun's pointed straight at her. You could just shoot her.*

"Ed?" Mark said.

"They're going to KILL us, Mark! Shoot her!"

*"He got what he wanted," she told me. "I made him crazy." But you didn't meet her craziness, did you, Mark? And she hates you for that, 'cause that's what love means to her. Maybe she's right.*

"Don't do this, Claire. Don't make me do this."

*Shoot her, you idiot.*

"Aw," she said.

Mark Sherman's eyes were still his eyes. He wasn't looking at death or God, only at his wife. And as she raised the gun, slowly, with utter confidence, every habitual expression disappeared from his ruddy, handsome, athlete's face. Superiority, ambition, earnest concern, even intelligence, left him. He was stupid now. Empty and defenseless. Rose thought he had never seen a worse face on anyone.

He died with that face, as the echoes of three bullets vibrated under Rose's feet and in his chest.

"Oh, please please please please," Edward was crying quietly.

Rose stood as Mrs. Sherman turned to him.

Her face was twitching in little places. The corners of the eyes and mouth, and here and there upon her cheeks. As though all her pasts were rushing around inside trying to get a look through her eyes at what had just happened.

Rose's gun was pointed too, but he knew he wouldn't shoot her. *Can't let her know that, though, or she'd kill me now. I don't wanna die in the same action as Mark. I'm very finicky about these things.*

"Don't forget your shoes," Rose said.

*The Death of Frank Sinatra*

"My . . . my shoes."

"Your shoes."

"Yes."

"Claire?" the other woman said.

"In a minute, Arlene."

"Please, oh God, please," the Edward person whimpered.

"Can you . . . get my shoes for me?"

"I think you'd better get them."

"Aw."

"If you say that again, I'll shoot you."

*That's what you wanted him to say, wasn't it?*

"Oh, alright," she said. And as she got the shoes she added, "You really didn't earn your twen'y large."

"I don't really want it," Rose said, "because, as you say, I didn't earn it."

Her face was coming back into place again. It was a lesser face than he'd seen on her.

"Anyway, the ring's worth more than twen'y." The ring was in the pocket of last night's jacket.

She put the shoes in her purse so that the heels were sticking out.

"What do you know about the law?" he said.

"Not much, apparently," she said.

"Just thought you'd like to know that legally I've committed this murder too. I'm an accessory before, during, and after the fact. What are you going to do now?"

"I . . . hadn't thought . . . except . . . getting his *disk*."

And quickly, with a slightly drunken step, she went to her husband's body and, stepping through his blood, went through his pockets.

"I *have* it. Ooooo." She touched the bottom of her foot with a fingertip. "It's warm."

She reached for her husband's gun, still in his hand.

"Don't touch that," Rose said. "Shit, look what you're tracking around."

There were several neat, long-toed, high-arched footprints of blood.

"Oh, dear," she said.

*Oh dear?*

"Put on your shoes. Smudge your tracks. *Not* with your hands. I'll do it."

He ripped his bloodied shirt and smudged her tracks.

"Now listen up, 'cause people might be coming soon and you still have work to do and you have to get out of here quickly. Listening?"

"Why are you helping me? You despise me."

"Why should other people have something to say about a beef between you and your husband, when you were both playing by the same rules and you happened to win? You had the stomach for it, he didn't, but he wanted to, and you won. Why should other people get involved in what happens to that Edward guy, in action he set himself up for? The guy was willing to do you if he could. What business is it of anybody else, especially the law? Consenting adults, right?"

"I really do like your mind."

"They find him dead with a gun in his hand, it's a whole different scene than finding him just plain dead. And the way cops think, they'll look for a man, and they'll figure it was a beef between them. But you better have an alibi, and a good one. You can say you and Arlene were in bed or something."

"Damn you," the other woman said.

"Doesn't have to be true. You're gonna have to do the other guy—"

"NO, please—"

"—an adult who consented to the wrong damn thing. Do him in the back of the head and the cops are going to assume it's Outfit action."

"Outfit?"

"Mafia, Cosa Nostra—the movies, remember?"

"The movies."

"And then get rid of your fucking guns. Wipe them clean, and, if they're registered to you, get rid of them where they won't be found. Drive out into the desert and bury them. Do that before you do anything else, as soon as you leave here. The cops will investigate you a little, but probably just a little—this scene just doesn't *look* like a husband-wife beef."

The man in the car was weeping softly.

"You don't have much time."

She turned toward the car.

"Wait a minute," Rose said. He went to the car, reached in and pulled the trunk release. He used his jacket to wipe the release handle. As he did this the Edward person watched him with tearful eyes. *He's not seeing death or God either. His eyes are a little boy's saying, "I didn't really mean it."*

"What are you doing?" Mrs. Sherman said.

Rose went to open the trunk.

"I thought so," he said.

"*What* are you doing?"

"I need a fresh shirt."

He opened a male-looking piece of luggage, went through it carefully, took out a folded white shirt, closed the valise, and wiped where he'd touched the luggage and the trunk with his sleeve.

"Okay. Tell him to pick up the gun. It'll look better if he's holding it."

*But Edward did mean it. Or he'd been trying to mean it. Willing to let his colleagues mean it for him. And those are the rules of the action, rules he was willing to play by as long as he won. You accept the rules of the action, that's the only law around here, and it's not a bad one as laws go.*

Mrs. Sherman had gotten into the back seat with Arlene.

Rose said, "Both of you, remember to wipe everything in the car you've touched. And try not to vomit. Vomit is great evidence. And hurry."

*God isn't looking. God doesn't give a flying fuck about this scene. I wonder how God decides.*

Mrs. Sherman, in the back seat, said, "Pick up your gun, Edward."

"Please," Edward whined.

*He's picking it up. Why the hell would he do that? But some people do, sometimes they help, and they must all have the same scared-little-kid look he's got. "See, I'm being a good boy, don't kill me."*

From inside the car the echoes weren't as bad. The two women fired at the same time, and the Edward person's head splattered upon the windshield.

Rose held down his vomit. It tasted of Hell.

The women got out of the car from separate doors, wiping what they'd touched behind them as they went.

After Rose swallowed his Hell down, he said, "You, Arlene. Check for any hairs you might have left in there. Though you could always alibi the hair—you were an employee, after all. Remember that. But check anyway."

"Too much sound," Arlene said softly, before she did what he told her.

"You never know, in Vegas. And with the Dunes carnival tonight, and most of the cops on overtime and going home by now, and a thin shift for the rest of the night—you've probably lucked out."

Mrs. Sherman was walking unsteadily, down the ramp, a strange and otherworldly smile on her face.

"Where are you going?" Rose said.

Halfway down the ramp she knelt and stuck her head under a car and vomited.

*Good thinking.*

She walked toward him with the same smile.

"That was fun."

Vomit rose in his mouth again. He swallowed it back down.

*It's their action. It's their fucking action.*

"You've earned your twen'y large after all."

"Don't want it, don't need it. In fact, I think it would make me sick."

"Hypocrite," she said gently. "Don't love me anymore?"

"You'd better get out of here."

"While there's one man left alive?"

They smiled at each other. Rose shifted position so he could watch Arlene too. *Nobody's holding a gun yet. They'd have to scramble for them. I could run, maybe. Naw. Don't wanna die running. And I'm not going to kill either one, not going to try. God wants me to live or die? What's Your experiment, Big Guy?*

"You're not scared," she said.

"Surprised?"

"You could testify. You're the only one."

"Why would I? I don't give a fuck who you kill."

"Ha ha ha ha ha ha. It's this town."

*That Arlene's eyes are glazed. She hasn't got the stomach for another kill. Not for about five minutes. It's up to you, baby.*

"I kill him, I kill him not, I kill him, I kill him not. I wonder why."

*God?*

"I HEARD that!"

"Heard what?"

"*'God'!* Ha ha ha ha ha ha ha ha ha ha." She lightly touched his bloody shirt. "I *like* you. I wish you could see yourself. Good-bye, Mike Rose."

# THE GHOSTS

# OF THE FLAMINGO

*T*hey left. Rose couldn't. He stood unsteadily, thought unsteadily, walked unsteadily a few steps in one direction, a few steps in another. He was two levels down in the Flamingo parking garage now, but not because he was going anywhere.

*She heard a word in my head.*

*I coulda stopped that mess. I helped it. I backed her play all the way. And I've been . . . allowed to live . . . anyway.*

*It wasn't my action. Consenting adults. I had no right. To stop it.*

*I hadda kill 'er ta stop it. Or turn 'er in an' rat. Or let her be stupid and get caught. I COULDN'T DO THAT.*

*Consenting adults.*
*Once your money's on the table, you're playing the game. Accept the rules of the action. The only law around here. Only law I respect.*

*Wish I'd known what the whole game was. Didn't. That's no excuse. Had t'accept the rules-a the action, like all the other consenting adults. Hell.*

Hell wrenched from him then as vomit, and it seemed it wouldn't stop, until nothing came but a thin clear fluid, and then nothing.

*God looks—IF you have a soul. If. It. Hasn't. Already. Flown. From. You. Sickened. By too much. Nothing. In. Your. Life.*

*God was looking at her. You don't get those eyes for Nothing.*

*I had a soul. Wonder. If. I. Still. Do.*

*Zig still did. And he killed lotsa people.*

*Nobody's come. Dead people up there. Nobody's come.*

*Not Nothing in my eyes. Please. Not that.*

*It has to do with . . . how you remember stuff . . . having a soul does. Zig?*

He knew where he was, and didn't. But he had the fresh shirt in his hand. He was down to Level Two now, but he didn't believe he could go to Level One.

"She's right. You're a hypocrite."

"Alvi?"

From between two vans his brother stepped toward him, hobbling, ghostlike with the Dune's dust on his suit and his face and in his white hair.

"I been following you all night."

"You followed good."

"You were easy. Even in the crowd, you didn't really care if the boys were following you."

"I still don't."

"I can see why."

"Your feet."

Alvi was walking like an old man. His bare feet were encrusted with dust and blood. Some toes were horribly swollen. Swellings rose in lumps to above his ankles.

"I hardly feel it anymore," Alvi said.

"I'll . . . I'll take you to . . . a hospital."

"No you won't."

There were only a few silver specks left on his toenails, where he still had toenails.

"You know that little tremor in my hands I told you 'bout? Other people can't see it, but I always feel it. Well, I didn't take my medication, so for the first time in years my hands feel like *hands*. The doctors always said it couldn't wear off that fast. Wrong again."

"You saw?"

"I saw."

"Zig. Pop. That's what they did for a living."

"Yeah. And that's what you did to Zig."

"Yeah."

"I've never seen one before, Mikey. I've been around people who did that all my life, never seen it before."

"Our heritage."

"Everybody's."

"What?"

"They call it history, Mikey. Mostly people fuckin' each other up. Big wars—or little wars like up on Level Five. We so special?"

"Yes. No. Useta be. Dunno. When you get so smart?"

"I'm so fucking smart I can't stand myself. Back in the corridor, remember? I shouted, 'Kill him, Mikey.' I been hearing myself say that all night. But you *are* a hypocrite. And look at you—you got a lotta people jumpin' aroun' in your face, brother. I see that a lot in the wards."

"So take *me* to the hospital."

"Naw. One of us gotta stay outside."

"Why?"

The Hell welled up in Rose again, almost exploding in his throat, but now it came out as tears—tears, tears, tears. His brother held him.

"Just watch your shoes, Mikey," Alvi almost laughed. "Don't step on my feet." And Alvi said softly, "I hate it, Mikey. I watched from behind the car where you puked. I hate all of it now. I hate you a little now."

They helped each other out of the parking garage, across the driveway, into a service entrance of the Flamingo, and into a washroom in one of the more unpopulated corridors on the east end of the building. Alvi sat on a toilet to rest his feet. Rose took off his bloodied shirt and T-shirt and unfolded the dead man's. *Must be Sherman's, it's pretty large.*

"You were really thinking like a pro up there, Mikey. I was impressed."

"I am a pro. From a long line of pros. What time is it, Aniello?"

"'In the unconscious there is no time.' That's a quote. Freud, I think. Some shrink made a big deal of it to me once. I told him he should write a book."

"The City Without Clocks. When we were kids the schools tried to make us proud of that line. It's nothing to be ashamed of, but what the fuck is it to be proud of? So what time—"

"Whata you care! Two, two-thirty, ninety-thirty, somethin' like that."

Rose looked at himself in the mirror. It looked like his face. Looked like his eyes. *I was different, that's what I thought. The soldiers killed, the businessmen killed, the gamblers killed, the hoods killed. Frustrated lovers, crazy people, politicians, religious nuts, true believers, they all killed. And a lot of nice people too, timid storekeepers and bored house-wives, who let others kill in their name for a profit or a cause, and cheered them on all the way. Even kids kill now. But I was different, 'cause even in the dirtiest town I didn't do the dirtiest thing.*

"What the fuck happened to your chest?" Alvi said. "And who *were* those fuckin' people? That skinny broad, she was a spook."

"I'll tell you that, and you tell me why you had to talk to Junior tonight. Changed our lives, that little impulse."

"And it *shoulda* changed our lives, it *deserved* to change our lives, it—Mikey, those guys—I had this all clear in my mind, I was gonna tell you, and then that *disgusting* shit you were into on *Level* fucking Five wiped it out—but—I'll get it back—I'll get it back."

*I pushed the fucking button, I've got another Alvi here now. I haven't got a brain in my fucking head.*

"It's okay, Alvi."

"Who says? But I'll get it back. Listen to that, they even got Sinatra on the speakers in the toilet at the fabulous Flamingo."

Sinatra was singing about going all the way, about how it's no good unless it's all the way.

"He's dead. Sinatra. They said it on the radio."

"What?" Alvi said.

"You okay with that?"

"I'm good. Yeah. He's dead. He's an old man. As old as Zig. Old as Pop woulda been. Old. Big deal."

"Yeah?"

"Yeah."

As Rose washed his face and arms he said, "They're probably playing him all over town. If the town hadn't already gone nuts tonight it would be goin' nuts over this. It will tomorrow. The traffic lights'll be playing Sinatra, or it'll seem that way. He's the last link. Last link to the people who started this town, who gave it its style—or what used to be its style—gave us *our* style. They were our people, Alvi."

"Right. Yeah."

"Watch, tomorrow night Sinatra imitators'll suddenly appear in half the shows, as 'tributes.' Bet they've already flown 'em in, bet they're rehearsing right now, no shit. And the honcho of every casino's pulling every string imaginable to get some stars or half-stars to come for tribute gigs, maybe every casino in town on the same night—Wynn would thinka something like that—and those guys'll be on the phone all night setting it up, it must be a long-distance satellite-hook-up circus."

He tried on the fresh shirt in the mirror. His shoulder holster was stained with blood too. He daubed it with a wet paper towel before putting it on, so it wouldn't stain the shirt. *Can't say this to you, brother, but I keep thinking maybe he had a stroke or something when he heard the shot in the corridor. If that's the deal, some fucking Situation, hey? Some fucking Situation you stirred up the other day over linguini. Linguini with red clam sauce. Or was yours white? You fucking killed him. How would that grab you, Alvi? You killed Frank Sinatra.*

But when Rose turned toward his brother, his brother wasn't there.

"Sonofabitch is a ghost tonight."

Rose looked for him. *How could he get far on those feet?* While he looked, Sinatra's voice followed him in the corridors, singing about how he got a kick out of someone, and about how everyone should fly away with him, fly, let's fly away.

*Alvi, sweet Alvi. You don't want to be found again. Probably in some janitor's closet, waiting for me to stop looking. If that's your action, okay, Alvi, I'll stop looking. You're not my 'kid brother' anymore, are you? You're my older brother at last, after all this time. 'Cause I've only just entered the territory where you've been for years. You gotta teach me how to live here, Alvi. 'Cause I have no fucking idea.*

*There's nothing for me to do now. There's no piece of information and nobody I can fight or kill that'll make any of this any better, or change a fucking thing.*

*Might as well get something to eat.*

•

He decided to go back to the Desert Inn and get his car. *That's the last place they'd expect me.* He walked down a long corridor near the new construction, into a functional corridor toward the Check-In lobby. There were dark shops and a few people. Some of them still had the dust of the Dunes explosion on their clothing. He took an escalator down to the cab stand. The escalator was in a hall of mirrors. To his left he could see himself closely, and he looked away. To his right he could see himself in the distance, as though he were riding the escalator on the opposite wall. Straight ahead, and a little closer, he could watch himself directly. He looked from Rose to Rose to Rose, *a Rose is a Rose is a Rose,* seeing what others saw, *but I left a good tie and an expensive tie pin in that bathroom, fuck it,* saw the certainty of the posture, reserved and somehow menacing, saw the tension of the line he cut in the air, the line of a graceful animal that might or might not strike if one came near. *Who says Sinatra's dead? Ha ha ha. Or Cagney or Bogart or any of them. Ha ha ha ha ha. What would I have looked like if I hadn't imitated the people I imitated? How would I have walked? What would I have worn?* The escalators sank beneath the level of the mirrors and the reflections disappeared. *Pop soldiered here. Mama danced. I am a reflection. Of a crime begun before I was born.*

As he got into the cab he looked down the driveway at the parking garage. *No cop strobes. I wonder how long it will go unreported. I'll bet the first twenty, thirty people who come across the scene will just back off and fade away. Which, technically, is itself a crime.*

The cab pulled too quickly onto the Strip for Rose to get more than a glance at the Dunes wreckage, bright with lights and workmen scurrying around it.

"The D.I. you said?"

"Right."

"I've been hoping to get a fare there. That's where Sinatra died. At least that's where one station says he died."

"Whata the other stations say?"

"Another says he's not dead at all. They'll know at the D.I. I mean, if that's where it went down."

"They don't even *know?*"

"Well, each station *sounds* like it knows, but they're all saying something a little different. But they always do, about *Vegas* stories. Stories out of state, they usually say the same stuff. Where you from?"

"Mars."

"Didja enjoy the trip?"


At the Desert Inn, Valet Parking was definite: Sinatra was alive. "But he's *real* mad. Someone fired a gun around him. Guards are getting fired. Managers are getting yelled at. You think it was Arabs?"

"Why would it be Arabs?"

"It's always Arabs."


Rose sat a few moments in his Caddy. *Might as well go to Zig's. And if someone is waiting to pop me . . . Survival is overrated.*


He turned right on Desert Inn Road. *It wasn't my action, I had no right. Consenting adults.* As those thoughts gripped again, he tried to push them away by turning on the radio. The metallic voice of a talk-show host attempted to sound sincere.

"Understand now, there are conflicting reports, yet I can't help but continue to feel the great grief, as of a personal loss, that struck my heart when the news first came to us. Frank Sinatra. The greatest star of the century. Of *any* century, as far as I'm concerned. A man whose name *means* Las Vegas.

Anyone earning a living within the sound of my voice owes his or her thanks to how Frank Sinatra, more than any other entertainer, helped give this city its reputation for great, classy entertainment." *I never thought of it that way. Gee, thanks, Frank. Funny thing is, the guy's not even wrong.* "But—and this will age me, ladies and gentlemen, in your eyes, or rather your ears—when I think 'Frank Sinatra' I think back to a bygone era not only of Las Vegas but of America, I think back to the Democratic Convention of 1960, in Los Angeles, and Sinatra's Rat Pack—and I use that term affectionately—sang, not 'One for My Baby,' but 'The Star-Spangled Banner'!" *With Dino holding a cigarette and a drink, I hope.* "And the Mississippi delegation walked OFF THE CONVENTION FLOOR in protest of Sammy Davis, Jr., being allowed onstage to sing with white men. Times have changed, ladies and gentlemen, and Frank Sinatra was a big part of that change. Frank Sinatra stood for freedom. Caller!"

"Hello, Biff?"

"Hello, what have you got to say about this great man tonight?"

"I enjoy your show."

"Thanks, and . . . ?"

"I'm a professor, I'd really rather not give my name—"

"Think you're too smart for us?"

"It's not that, it's—"

"Your Sinatra memory, sir? First time you did your wife was to his album *Nice 'n' Easy*? Were you nice and was she easy?"

"I wanted to point out that the word *Mafia* is the only word from Sicily now used in all the world's major languages."

*Now that makes me proud.*

"Sir, to besmirch a man on the night he may have died—you're not a listener I'm proud of, prof. No wonder you don't give your name. Scared of *omerta*, teach?"

"*Omerta* means, literally, 'the ability to act like a man.'"

"Well, try it sometime. Caller!"

"I'm an old woman now—"

"And we love you anyway—"

"But I was a cocktail waitress in the old days—"

"And your name, darling?"

"Mary Ann, and I'm a grandmother. And I want to say something that *all* us old-timers in this town *think* but nobody *says*, not in *public*."

"Grandma's gonna talk dirty, folks, plug your ears!"

"And that's that, when the Mob ran this town—"

"A criminal element in Las Vegas! Heaven forbid!"

"—it was a BETTER TOWN. The corporations *stink*. When the Mob ran things the *people* were better, everybody was *polite*, the *tips* were better, the managers were *nicer*, the *gamblers* were better, if I got sick the boss of the whole casino himself sent me flowers, people *cared* about you—"

"And what did you do for this boss, that he sent you flowers?"

"I served drinks."

"And did you serve the Rat Pack?"

"I did, and they were so nice, and—"

"And what did you do for *them?*"

"I served *drinks*."

"And what *else* did you serve, Grandma? Caller!"

Rose switched stations. There were reports that Los Angeles was on fire again, fires in the hills. *Vegas exploding, L.A. burning, and how many little wars on how many Level Fives?* He switched again, and Sinatra was singing that his heart was on fire.

The announcer broke into the song to say they had confirmation, earlier reports were false, Sinatra was alive, "thank God and this great country."

He'd been driving slowly south on Paradise. From far off he saw police strobes. He knew as soon as he saw them that they were at Zig's restaurant. His heart beat hard, reminding him of the pains that had faded into the background on Level Five. And the closer he got the harder his heart beat, he could hear it in his ears. He parked at the curb. They'd sealed off the parking lot with the yellow tape that warned over and over for all its length: Crime Scene. No Admittance. He knew now that he still had a soul, because it was his soul that screamed: A L V I ?

No one heard the scream, but it stripped the world for Rose.

He got out of the car, watched till he saw an officer he recognized, and walked slowly toward him.

"Hey, Tony."

"Hey, Mike."

"So?"

"The waitress? Dee? Assistant manager or something, wasn't she? Throat slit ear to ear. In the kitchen. Real neat job. You okay? You don't look good. You know her?"

"I knew her some."

"Yeah, this is one of your hangouts. Can you tell us anything about her? Enemies? Boyfriends?"

"She was a Mormon." *And she made phone calls.* "Nice person. I didn't know her people."

"I probably shouldn't tell you, 'cause you're his friend, but we're looking for Zig on this. No one seems to have seen him."

"Zig? An old man, Tony?"

"Old men have passions, Mike."

"Yeah. That's true."

"I don't expect anything from *you* about him, you're his friend, and . . . you got . . . principles, let's say."

"Let's."

"But do you know someone I could ask about him?"

"You just said I'm his friend."

"Well, it's not the same if you tell me someone *else* who could tell me."

"Oh."

"Gimme a break, Rose."

"Zig didn't do this. I'm certain of that."

"Well, you're his friend. I still gotta ask."

"Sure."

"He had a history, you know that. A history."

"Of a kind. Good night, Tony."

" 'Night, Rose."

Rose went back to his car, leaned against it, lit a cigarette, and stared longer at the police lights.

*It's funny, in a fucked kind of way. Zig's disappearance will probably go down as connected to Dee's death. The cooks and the other waitresses will say Zig didn't come in the day before, and that Dee was very upset about it, and blah blah blah, a lot of inconclusive stuff, and the cops will hear "Dee" and "upset" and think something was going down between them. They'll look for Zig, but as a criminal, not as a guy whose disappearance might itself be a murder. Which lets me off any hook I might have been on. Even if they find the car.*

*It's the kind of humor Zig would appreciate. He'd say something snotty about "answers."*

*Dee. "What's the score?" she'd always say. "Nothing, nothing," I'd say. She'd laugh and I'd smile. There's nobody left at the restaurant to remember anybody's tab. Lots of slates wiped clean.*

*Slit throat. Very bloody, a slit throat. Not a typical Mob hit. But sometimes. If they don't want it to look like a Mob hit.*

*Dee's death, far more than the others, calls out for something like revenge. And revenge is an impossibility. Nothing can fix this. Walk away. God killed her. God kills everyone. In self-defense, probably.*

# THE HINT

## OF THE PETERSON GUY

*M*ike Rose finished his cigarette, flicked it into the air, watched it burst in tiny sparks when it hit the street point first.

*So long, Dee. Maybe even you don't know who did it. Came up behind, grabbed, cut before you could scream. That would be a pro. A boyfriend would want you to know, would make a little drama out of it, and would be so excited he'd make a mess. Tony said it was neat. A pro.*

*But it could have been a rejected suitor who was a pro—she had contact with enough pros. Who the hell knows. Could be a whole other Situation, not part of the Situation I'm caught in.*

Rose got in the car, idled a few moments, did a U-turn, nodded at the cop who watched him do it, the cop nodded back, and Rose cruised slowly north. He made a turn and drove some blocks, made another, and another. The constant voice of his lonely mind was, for a short time, stilled, and he turned onto another street, and another, and rarely passed a moving car or a lit window. He wasn't tired. His pain seemed distant.

He lit cigarettes he forgot to smoke, they burned down to his fingers, the heat would remind him to take the last puff. He had nothing to do, and could imagine no action or thought that would help. It seemed that all his emotions had fled after his soul screamed his brother's name. He was driving like an echo of that scream, and he proceeded like an echo, bouncing this way and that, feeling something fade.

Rose didn't emerge from this waking but sleeplike state until he found himself driving the bleak streets where Las Vegas blacks live. Too poor to water their grass. The featureless government housing faced what were intended to be lawns but were now hard brown slabs of heat-cracked ground. The first words to enter his mind in forty minutes were "the Mississippi of the West"—that's what the people of these streets called Nevada. Blocks later he found himself passing the welfare office. It was about four in the morning, and already a ragtag line of men and women had formed at the door. Blacks, whites, browns, grim and with four hours still to wait for that door to open. Most sat on the sidewalk, with their backs to the wall. Some smoked. Rose vaguely wished he could see their eyes, vaguely wanted to compare them with the eyes he had noticed in these last hours, and to his own. The thought woke him enough to make him want to return to his own Situation— *it's the only place left for me to go, but right now I don't even know where to find it.*

"The Garter," he said aloud. An impulse he could not explain and did not question drew him to the last place of his past that remained in something like its original form.

*I'm nothing without the Situation. That's always been true, but I didn't know it. True for Alvi too, but he didn't know it either. We thought it was a style or a Mob or the town, but they're all just elements of the Situation.*

*Alvi's at the Garter, I know he is. There's nowhere else for him to go. This time tomorrow, it'll all be over—as over as any Situation gets. It'll go back to sleep for a while. He woke it up—the guy with the least power, except for the power to stir up the Situation. A power no one, least of all him, knew he had. I wish I could talk about this stuff to somebody, though I don't know why that would matter. Or is the wanting to talk, is that just another way the Situation has of flexing its muscle and reproducing itself?*

*Maybe I've just picked up where Pop left off, where he left off screaming, and then unable to scream, just begging, begging for it to be over for him, unable to beg finally with anything but his eyes. And maybe that's why Rosie left me those photographs, to goad me to pick up where they left off. What the hell other reason could she have had?"*

*I'm not trying to make sense of it all but I'm trying to make . . . something. This voice that I talk to myself with, that's all I have.*

He left his car with Valet Parking at the Plaza, where Fremont Street dead-ends into Main. It was about a half block west of the Golden Garter. There wasn't a soul on the street, no one but Vegas Vic, the five-story cowboy, waving his neon arm, and Sassy Sally, almost as high, sitting atop Glitter Gulch, a few doors down from the Garter, with her short neon skirt and her crossed neon legs. *I'm wearing a dead man's shirt, carrying a dead man's gun—a gun that once made others dead. Good morning, Las Vegas.*

He walked slowly down a street empty of everything but neon and himself. The street had existed, in one form or another, for almost ninety years, and Rose had been part of it for roughly half that time. The Strip that began with Bugsy's Falmingo was only four or five years older than he, and his people had been part of it from the start. Leaving the city had never seriously occurred to him. And at this moment he had the eerie sensation that he and the city were the same, and that everything about it was somehow recorded in him, and that Las Vegas knew his name. He felt no one would ever watch it again as he did, and for a few steps he realized that his hatred of the city was only an embittered love.

For one of the few times in his life he did not feel shame at how could love such a thing, such a place, such a crime. And he walked into the Garter feeling that every cheapness, every nakedness, every won and lost cent, every wheel and every pair of dice in every joint in town was a sign, a sign of something scarier and more thrilling yet, something he could not decipher but could not abandon.

He had never left home, but he had finally come home. His acceptance was complete. And for two steps God watched him again. Which is all he had been waiting for. And he felt like walking neon.

"What are you smiling at?"

The bouncer at the door was two heads taller than Rose and a hundred and fifty pounds heavier. Rosie Vee had wanted her bouncers to wear tuxedos—"When Benny opened the Flamingo, even the janitors wore tuxedos," was her only explanation—and the tradition had stuck.

"So you know too, huh, Marty?"

"The whole town knows who's lookin' for you guys. I don't know why they haven't picked up your brother yet. He's spent all his money but we're still serving him."

"How do they know he's here?"

The big man blushed.

"Well, Marty, you can make another phone call and let them know I'm here too."

"I'm sorry, Mike. *What* are you smiling at?"

"They haven't come for Alvi yet 'cause they're waiting for me. Make your call, Marty. Tell them they can take their time, there's nowhere for us to go."

"Hope I smile when it's my turn."

"It'll never be your turn. You don't play for the stakes we do."

There weren't many women working the Garter at this hour, and only two other men to watch them. One dancer on one runway. The strobes were the same, the colored lights flashing on the mirrored ceilings and walls, but in the midst of it all only one woman's body caught the beams and reflected in the glass—one body naked but for a G-string, a golden garter, and spike heels. Rose stood at one end of the central runway and watched her. When there were four and five women on each runway, and many men at the bar stools, and twenty or forty other women working the men at the bars and table dancing in the booths along the walls, then all that beautiful young flesh lost its beauty in a kaleidoscope of body parts, and it could seem that you were entering a factory where women were being assembled and disassembled. But one young woman on a runway was simply a pretty and lonely body, a little ridiculous with her gyrations and, as all bodies are, vulnerable. And all her lascivious posing, all her bumps and grinds, didn't seem a seduction or an offering but a way of hiding, lest you saw her for the desperate and fragile thing she was. It was a strange thing to see, and somehow fitting too, in the hour before you died.

She danced toward Rose, stood over him pumping her hips, swayed her breasts in his face, turned, brushed a buttock against his cheek, and her eyes tried very hard to gleam with nastiness but she wasn't a very good actress, and all those eyes registered was fatigue.

Rose gave her a hundred.

"Mister, I don't know what to say."

"It's okay, kid."

"You want . . . something special?"

"No, thanks."

"Are you laughing at me?"

"Just smiling. Dance. I like you."

It wasn't until then that Rose realized the dance music was, for this place, very unusual. *Sinatra! No wonder she's having a hard time doing her act.* Sinatra was singing about bells that go ring-a-ding-ding. It was music she must associate with her grandparents.

"How come Sinatra?"

"They've been playin' him since he died."

"But he's not dead."

"Well, I c'n still *dance* to him, can't I? He's *gonna* die, isn't he?"

He was singing now about how he wanted to wake up in a city that never sleeps.

Alvi was at the far end of the bar talking to someone. *The character he's talking to must have been here when Alvi got here, 'cause Marty sure isn't letting any other witnesses in. Alvi hasn't seen me, or hasn't let on? Look at him, so involved in talking to that guy. It's not like him to talk to strangers.*

Rose walked slowly toward them, the man Alvi was talking to noticed his approach but Alvi ignored it.

The man didn't look well. His eyes were puffy and his face was too full, as though slightly swollen. The eyes were probably blue but a trick of the light made them seem colorless. *They're a watcher's eyes. He's good at watching.* He was about Rose's age, and wore jeans and a white shirt. The jeans had a crease but the shirt had been slept in. His hair was long and full, and again the lighting made it hard to determine its color—very light, whatever it was. He was following Alvi's argument intensely, yet as though from a long way off, his face tightened in concentration as if trying to make what Alvi was saying fit with something else he was thinking of, something this man couldn't stop thinking of.

"Aniello," Rose said.

"And *this*," Alvi said, "is my brother, Michael Francis Rossellini. He calls himself Mike Rose. That's 'cause he hates his ancestors. He hates everybody. He hates you."

The man looked at Rose suspiciously. He looked like someone for whom a smile was a major event. He didn't say hello, but that didn't seem from rudeness. Rose couldn't shake the impression that this man was preoccupied with trying to make sense of something, and was not succeeding.

"My brother kills people. He didn't used to, but he does now. Don't worry, he won't kill you, he hasn't known you long enough. He only kills old friends. That's causa his ancestors. See his gun?"

Alvi pulled back Rose's jacket. The man was genuinely surprised and looked at the gun with hard interest, as though trying to memorize it.

"He called me 'Aniello,'" Alvi told the man. "That's my real name, my ancestor name. Aniello Hugo Rossellini. Got 'ancestor' written all over it. Now, some people call my brother 'Mikey,' and some call 'im 'Mike,' and some 'Michael,' and some just 'Rose.' Lotsa names. Depends on how my brother looks at 'em. What you gonna call 'im?"

"What's he want me to call him?"

"He won't tell you."

"Then I won't call him anything."

"That wiped the smile off his face," Alvi said. "He was smiling because it's all over, the last ancestor is gone, he can relax now."

"I'm sorry about your father," the man said to Rose, without much conviction.

"I'm sorry about him too," Rose said.

"This," Alvi said to Rose, "is Peter the Writer—"

"Kevin Peterson—"

"Peter the Writer's *Son*—everybody's a son here—an' he

thinks it's a little strange that I'd come to a place like this the night our father died, don't you, Peter?"

The man smiled slightly and just looked at them. He started to say something, but stopped himself.

"You're careful," Rose said.

"I'm drunk. Can I buy you a drink?"

"Buy *me* another one," Alvi said.

A tired waitress, wearing almost nothing but sitting within earshot—Rose could guess on whose instructions—came and took their order.

*I like this, I've decided. Talking to a stranger isn't a bad way to wait to die. Maybe it's a kind of practice, even. No one knows what anyone's going to say. And the Situation is like a circle we're in the middle of, and it's watching us.*

Alvi was sitting on a stool. His feet looked worse, more swollen. Rose didn't see how Alvi could walk on them at all.

"I'm worried about your brother's feet," the man said to Rose.

"Don't," Alvie said, "they're hereditary. It's a hereditary condition. I'm fine. They're like this every—what day is it now?—they're like this every day that this is, whatever it is."

Sinatra was singing that we should take it nice 'n' easy, something was going to be so easy.

"Ancestors . . ." Alvi started to say, then stopped. "What are your ancestors?"

"Swedish and Native American," the man said.

"We're Sicilians," Alvi said.

"You've mentioned that. More than once."

"You don't look like an Indian," Alvi said.

"That's bad for my career. I'd get better reviews if I looked like an Indian. Bad luck."

"You've mentioned *reviews* more than once."

"They don't really affect me. We're supposed to say that."

"Ancestors . . ." Alvi said again. "Mike's smiling again. Do you think that's healthy? You and I are not smiling."

"Maybe he has something to smile about," Peterson said.

"Believe me, he don't. Ancestors—"

"Tell us about ancestors, Aniello," Rose said. *This is actually a very pleasant way to wait to die. If I ever have to wait to die again I hope it's just this way. I wonder what's taking them so long. I wonder if they'll kill this man too. There are no innocent bystanders, not really. Even if there were, I don't think he's one of them.*

"Ancestors—I was going to save all our ancestors. Zig got mad at that, I don't know why. Upset, not mad. Haven't seen him since. Mike killed him. I was going to become a Mormon and convert all our ancestors to the Mormon church—they're dead, our ancestors, that's what makes them ancestors, but Mormons do that with dead people. They're dead anyway, they don't give a shit."

"But the whole point of ancestors," the man said, "if you believe in ancestors, is that they do give a shit."

"You think?"

"I'm afraid so."

"You think, Mikey?"

"He has a point, Aniello. A definite point."

"Well," Alvi said, "well, that changes everything. That changes *everything*. Mikey—Mike, Michael, whatever your fucking name is—our ancestors . . ."

The girl was dancing above their heads now, nice 'n' easy, as though in a dream. Peter the Writer's Son gave her a five. She frowned.

"I've spoiled her," Rose said. He gave her another hundred.

The writer, who seemed a hard man to surprise, was surprised.

"I think I'm in love," the girl laughed.

"Our ancestors—if they give a shit—you think they like me, Mikey?"

"They love you, Alvi."

"Well don't *cry*. Jesus. I guess we'll find out soon enough," Alvi laughed. "But *they* didn't love enough. Our ancestors didn't love enough. You can write that, Writer's Son. Michael's trying to be true to our ancestors. He's spent his whole life doing that. He's trying to reject them and be true to them at the same time."

"That—" the man said, as though gripped, "that may be th-th-th-the art of life."

Rose registered the stutter, Alvi registered the sentence. Alvi said, "The thing, the thing about ancestors—when they look at you, you better look back, look them straight in the eye. I just learned that. From you. Thank you. You're right. They give a shit."

"They must live . . ." The man's eyes were far off now, he had made the connection between what he was hearing and what he was trying to think about. "They must live in . . . the secret room. In a painting in the secret room. Or under it. The cellar of the secret room."

*You don't look drunk but you're very very drunk and you don't have a home to go to. That makes me feel better, in case you die with us. With just Alvi and I this wouldn't be an anteroom. With a stranger here, with you, this is an anteroom of death.*

"There are—th-th-three rooms. Everybody has them, that's where every person—it's what a friend of mine would call 'the structure of the psyche'—there's a public room, a private room, and a secret room. I used to think they were . . . separate . . . wrote about that . . . and that you had some control . . . over what went on in each room. You could open and close the doors. A public room, a private room, and a secret room. But now . . . I mean, what I think now . . . the public room has a secret trap door, the private room has a picture window, and the secret room is bugged. *That's* the structure of the psyche. But . . . once you *know* the secret room is bugged . . . then maybe you can get around that. 'Cause, if you manage to keep . . . one more secret . . . than everybody around you . . . and you *really* keep it . . . then you'll win. I don't know what you win, though." He smiled just a little. "That's a secret."

*Mama did just that. That's what the photos meant. How did this sonofabitch know?*

"That's good," Rose said. "That fits."

"Fits what?"

"The Situation."

*His Situation is talking to our Situation, and ours to his, and it seems like we're doing the talking, and we are, but only because the Situations are talking, passing notes to each other.*

Alvi's eyes had glazed over. *You're afraid of death, aren't you, Alvi? I'm sorry. What's taking them so long? Maybe they were asleep. It's okay with me. I'm having a good time, but Alvi's exploding with something he doesn't really know how to say. He's kind of dissolved. I'm so sorry, kid.*

Sinatra was singing about witchcraft. The dancer was trying to mime the words by making scary faces and holding her hands like claws.

*He's staring at the dancer now, this writer. Alvi's zoned out. This is the anteroom of death, and I like it here. He talks to himself like me, this writer, all the time, but he writes it down. I don't see the point but that's okay. I should tell him to leave, they might get suspicious, him sitting with us, kill him too. It's not fair, it's not his action, not his ancestors. He has not consented.*

"You oughta get out of here," Rose said.

"I . . . shouldn't be alone right now." His puffy face was frightened, and for a moment he had the air Alvi had sometimes, of being frightened of himself.

"I should have told you before," Rose said, "but I was having a good time. This is the anteroom of death. Colored lights, Frank Sinatra, a naked lady, and strangers talking. Write *that*. Really. Leave. There are some men coming. They're not *really* men, but that's a long story. They *are* coming."

"Are you going to use your gun?"

"No."

"Why?"

"Once was . . . more than enough." Rose pulled the gun. "I'd like you to have it."

"I don't want a gun. Especially not tonight."

"I know, but that's why it would be even more of a gift for you to take it. Think of it as gift from our ancestors."

"Give it to the waitress."

"I can't. I don't even know why I can't, but I can't. And I can't just throw it out."

"I don't want it."

"You can throw it out. As soon as you get outside. I don't . . . want to be tempted to use it. Just take it. Please."

"Alright."

Rose gave it to him.

"Now leave."

"They're going to kill you?"

"Maybe not. But probably."

"And him?"

"Probably."

"Then why don't you want the gun?"

"I'm learning the art of life."

*Without understanding, the stranger understands now.*

"Really, Peterson, you've got to leave. Now."

"The police—"

"Not with *our* ancestors. *Leave.* And for Christ's sake, don't call the police. You don't look like a square, don't go square on me now."

The man started to leave.

"Hey," Alvi said.

"What?" the man said.

"Your name isn't Peterson."

The man didn't know what to say.

"But why should it be?" Alvi said. "His name isn't Rose, my name isn't Alvi, that girl's name isn't whatever she says it is."

"He's gotta go, Alvi, no matter what his name is."

"The anteroom?" the man said.

"Yeah," Rose said, "you can add that to your other rooms."

"Thanks for the gun."

Rose watched the man leave. *We could talk to him. That's rare. He's the only one in all this who could walk into this Situation and walk out again—and barely know it. His own Situation must be strong, stronger than he thinks, for him to be able to do that. Or maybe he can just walk in and out of things. Maybe because he's a writer? I don't know. He's somebody maybe who can do that. We're not. We have to live in what we are.*

*Feels good not to be carrying the gun.*

Alvi had lain his head on his folded arms, on the bar rail, and then fallen asleep.

Sinatra was singing about Chicago—his friend Sam Giancana's town.

A new girl was on the runway to dance. She came right over to them. Her eyes were greedy. She'd heard about the hundreds. Rose put one in the instep of her high heel.

"Don't wake my brother up."


"Took you long enough."

"We were asleep."

It was Lavender, with two young men Rose didn't recognize. None of them had been in the corridor at the Desert Inn. They patted him down, checking for weapons.

"Come on, asshole, Gino's got something to show you—before we do you."

"Alvi," Rose said softly, close to his brother's ear.

"Just wake him the fuck up."

"Go slow, punk. 'Cause if I get mad enough you'll have to kill me here, and if those weren't Gino's orders Gino wouldn't like that, and he must be real sick of people botching his orders, and he might take that out on you."

"You tell 'im, Mikey."

"It's time, kid. Come on, I'll help you walk."

"I'm sorry I said that shit to you before—at the Flamingo."

"Let's not get into sorrys, brother. Sorry's a lousy way to go."

Sinatra was singing about the stardust of a song. Nobody was dancing. There were only two girls left in the place, and Marty the bouncer, and they all watched the brothers leave with their escort. *Defeated faces. Owned people. Nobody ever owned us, Alvi.*

"What you got to smile about, asshole?"

"I can't explain it."

"Keep smilin', Mikey," Alvi said sleepily. "I never saw you smile so much, you crazy bastard."

They were in the back seat of a Lincoln with dark tinted windows. Once they'd driven past Fremont Street's neon, it was too dark to see through the tint. They took a right—onto what street, Rose couldn't be sure.

When they got out of the car they were at a small low-rent apartment building on Koval. On the side of the building, in big block letters, it said "WEEKLY."

"Isn't this Zig's place, Mikey?"

"I don't know, I've never been here."

"Me neither, but I think it is."

"It's a dump, is what it is," Lavender said. "That guy was a legend. This ain't legendary."

"What do you know about legends?" Rose said to Lavender.

"That you ain't gonna be one." Lavender said to one of his helpers, "Give me the cellular." He dialed a number. "We're comin' up."

It was a small one-bedroom place, very cheap but kept very clean. Motel furniture. A place to sleep. To be alone. *A secret room.* It would have felt cramped for two people, but now it held the brothers, their escorts, Gino, Sallie, Rizzo, and another young hood. The apartment's other distinguishing feature, taped on one wall, were the twenty pornographic photographs of Rosie Vee.

Taped beside them was a note in the unsteady hand of their mother's last illness: "Take a good look, Zig."

Gino sat in a cheap, faded motel armchair.

"Now I know why you children are so sick. That *is* your mother?"

Rose looked around the room meeting Nothing in each pair of eyes. *No, in Rizzo's eyes there's a little Something. Watch your back, Sallie, this boy's on his way.*

It was different, seeing those photos in the presence of others. They were both more naked and more defiant. Her eyes did not quail before these eyes. He was surprised to find himself being proud of her. He had known many women who had sold themselves in one way or another, and, with the exception of Joy, almost all had ended dazed and crushed by having let themselves be used—that, or worse. But the woman in these pictures was out to prove something to herself, and was proving it. Even if you had seen a thousand pictures like these, hers would be shocking, not for the poses but for the challenge in her eyes. She was letting Nothing know where Nothing came from. No man in the room, with the sometimes exception of Rose himself, would dare sleep with such a woman, and Rose wondered, smiling, whether that was one of his good or bad qualities.

And his respect for his father grew.

"Look at this perverse bastard," Gino said, "he's smiling!"

When they'd come in, he'd sat Alvi down on a hardwood chair. When he looked now at his brother he stopped smiling.

"Sorry you had to see these, Alvi."

Some of the men snickered.

"When did you first see 'em, Mikey?"

"Not long after she died."

"I found these pictures twenty years ago, brother. She knew I did too."

Gently the brothers smiled at each other, two very old men now.

"They did me, Mikey. Convinced me."

Some of the men laughed.

Alvi went on, "Convinced me the wards were the best place to hide out in. Like you hid out in the world. I wasn't tough enough to hide out in the world, I needed to be harder to find. Ain't been with a woman since."

More laughter. But the brothers could have been in another room, another building, for all they seemed to notice.

"You two disgust me," Gino said. "You're not *men*, not grown-up men. That," nodding to the photos, "is no excuse."

"They ruined your surprise, though, Gino," Sallie said. "Gino thought it would be a big surprise."

"So," Gino said. "After I go, put on your silencers, push their faces against the pictures, and blow their heads off. Family reunion." And he added, "Tip the cops off tomorrow. Let them be found this way. Let it all come out in the papers."

*She left Zig these photos to drive him crazy, and they did, slowly, night after night they did. Revenge for killing her husband. Alvi's little conversation was the final drop. She won. Good for her.*

Gino stood up. "There's a little will or something here, a little deed or something, from Zig, giving you guys the restaurant. When we got the call I gave Zig an out, you know? He deserved that. I said he could prove he was still alright by whacking you two. He said, 'I won't do harm to Rosie's children.' And that was that."

*Gino's about fifteen years younger than Zig. Probably crewed with him sometimes. Maybe even hit Kennedy's shooters with him and Pop. Sure. That's it. Ha. And he's afraid Zig told me. Thinks Zig did, or he never would have gone after me. Ha. What a Situation.*

"And you, big hero, too proud to keep your Sicilian name, you whacked Zig 'cause he killed your father? Aw, lookit that. The cripple didn't know."

Rose was standing by Alvi, and Alvi was looking up at him with those eyes that were no longer eyes. *It's been done.*

"Yeah, he killed your father. I was there too. Oh yeah. A 'colleague,' as Zig would say. The cripple doesn't know what happened? We didn't just kill your father. We had to know something, whether he'd said something, so we—we *did* him. It was bad. Even now, I think back, I don't like to. Worst I ever saw."

Alvi was not going to give them tears. Rose was proud of him for that. And even Gino wouldn't linger on Alvi's eyes. He was concentrating on Rose. Of the hoods, only Sallie met Alvi's eyes. Alvi's eyes were formless and bottomless and burning. If you could go into them, you could go to the ends of space.

*You're the best, kid. You never hurt a living soul, and you never blocked a thought or feeling you ever had, and you painted your toenails, and you were everything but free. But free isn't everything.*

*Gino thinks he's hurting us but he's freeing us. Silly bastard.*

The purity of Alvi's pain was a force that spread like a pool from beneath his damaged feet, and Rose could almost see the others trying not to let it reach their shoes. It would destroy them—it was destroying them. They became smaller and smaller in the eyes of the brothers. Nothing must devour Something, that's the only way it can live, and here was a Something it could not devour, could hardly bear to look at.

"I was gonna give you such a deal"—Gino couldn't let it go—"you arrogant shit, you hypocrite."

"I used to be a hypocrite, but that was hours ago."

Alvi smiled, like an angel now.

*Thanks, Aniello.*

"You're not *anything* anymore, you fuck. I was gonna say, 'You got insurance, I want insurance. You write a confession. On Zig. You got something on me, I want something on you.' You'd say—"

"I'd say the confession's no good without a body. There's no dead person without a body."

"That's what you'd say, 'cause you're smart. And I was gonna say—I was looking forward to this, but you spoiled it— I was gonna say, 'Will Zig's head do? We been busy. Next time bury the head.'"

"Where you keeping it?"

"It's in the fridge here. Wanna see it?"

"It's okay with me."

"Well, I do *not* wanna see it again. I got *feelings*. And tonight *you hurt my feelings*. We were going to go into *business*. You get the restaurant, I get my piece of it, we got insurance on each other—*civilized business*. What are you two *laughing* at? At *me*? They're not human, *do them*, I wanna see, *do them now*."

Sallie said, "We got a little more business first, Gino."

"What are you talking about? I gave a *command*."

"I know, Gino, but . . . a little business."

"*What* business?"

"Gino, the walls are thin here."

A little fear passed through Gino's face. This was not how things were done—an underboss disagreeing in front of the crew. It could only mean one thing, but Gino wasn't admitting that yet.

"Sallie, is everything ass-backwards tonight?"

"Yeah, a little. It's a tough night. Blame it on Sinatra or Steve Wynn or these fucks, or that broad on the wall, but things are out of order. We got a little business. Please."

"Okay, okay. You said 'please.'"

*I'm not sure I like this. It's giving me hope again. I was so much happier without it.*

"You know, Gino, the restaurant plan—good plan. So in preparation of that, a thing was done. I jumped the gun, I admit, and I'm sorry, but—a thing was done. The waitress at Zig's place, I forget her name, she had an accident."

"I . . . I didn't give that order."

"She called *me*, Gino. She was the only outsider—'cause these guys aren't really outsiders—she was the only tie to *me*."

Gino sat back down in the chair. He knew now. He was trying to collect himself. *Like Zig. Wants it with a little dignity.* As he'd sat down, Rizzo pulled his gun. Rizzo said, "Vinnie, why don't you go sit by him. But give them your gun first."

Lavender, shaking and pale, handed his gun to the young man he'd come with, and sat on the arm of Gino's chair. "I don't see why me," he said softly.

"Think," Rizzo said, "and you'll see."

*The king goes, his most loyal boy goes with him. Anyway, you're not very good. Gino must have been slipping a long time to have you for a favorite.*

"Gino," Sallie was saying, "you're the last link . . . to whatever shit—let's just call it 'the old days'—whatever shit Zig knew, that he told Mighty-Like-a-Rose here. You're the last one who can really say anything. With you gone, it's just theory. I don't see why it's so fucking important anyway, after all these years, but you got nervous, Chicago got nervous, New York got nervous, New Orleans got nervous, *Providence, Rhode Island*, for fuck's sake, got nervous, the whole goddamn country. Nervous isn't good. I hate ever to be nervous. Here Mighty-Like-a-Rose—a zero, a nobody, and his brother less than a nobody—could make everybody nervous. With you gone, it's all hearsay. History. With you gone, everything's like before. Only a little different. I got approval, Gino. I was gonna move in a year or so anyway, if you didn't retire like the gentleman you say you are. This situation coming up again, that just pushed it all up a bit. You understand."

*Not bad, Sallie. And not bad, Gino—you're not copping a plea, you're not crying, you're not complaining, you're just staring. With Mama looking over your shoulder.*

"Paulie, boys, take Gino and Vinnie for a ride out into the desert. It'll be dawn soon, very beautiful. And take Zig's head, f'crissakes. Bury all three heads. And not together, Paulie."

"Don't worry . . . boss."

Vinne was weeping when they took him out, *how many people die like little children, and the meaner the littler,* but Gino walked with unsteady dignity, his eyes full of nothing but Nothing.

"So," Sallie said. "It's . . . messy . . . messy to kill people there's no more reason to kill. Messy is no good. Messy is unprofessional. So. Here's Zig's papers. You two can enjoy your restaurant. We get a piece, of course—we always did, we always will."

"This is too easy, Sallie."

"That's only because you don't understand. But you will, sooner or later."

*Alvi's eyes haven't changed. All this has made no difference. How could it, to him? It has nothing to do with us.*

"Rose," Sallie said, "you played this good. Elegant."

*I didn't do a fucking a thing, stupid. Except come up with that insurance bluff, buy us time. Except for that, all I did was trip over my own feet.*

"Thanks, Sallie. Coming from you, that's . . . something."

"I appreciate the respect."

*He's already becoming an asshole. Sallie, an hour ago, would never have said such an insipid thing.*

"But earlier tonight," Sallie said, "you threatened me."

"Sallie," *I probably shouldn't say this,* "you're already becoming an asshole."

Alvi laughed, but it was as though he laughed at something else.

"Well," Sallie said, smiling, "it's expected."

*Now, that's the Sallie we know and love.*

"Sallie, you can have a piece of the restaurant. You can have the *papers*, and take the whole fucking thing. I don't give a shit, Alvi don't give a shit."

"Whata I want with a restaurant? I got a city. It's not like in the old days, but still—all that *Newsweek* bullshit aside, there's still good business for us here. But you know . . . you *don't* give a shit, I see that. You thought we were gonna whack you, and you still didn't give a shit. How'd you do that?"

"Ask her."

All three looked up at Rosie Vee.

Forty of her eyes looked back at them.

## THE SOMETHING

## OR OTHER OF MIKE ROSE

*E*ven the dawns aren't innocent.

They're pretty, though.

The brothers drove through the pretty dawn toward the only place that Alvi would allow for the tending of his feet: The Church of Religious Discovery.

"But you hate Joy," Rose said.

"I don't hate anybody right now. You'd think I would, but everything's been blown away, even that. And she's . . . she's family, in a funny way. A cousin, like. She's not a stranger, anyway. I cannot spend this morning in an ER full of strangers—strangers talking to me, touching me, I'd lose . . . this thing. If I can stay in it longer, maybe I won't lose it at all."

"Alvi, Joy can clean it and put stuff on it, but you've got breaks, at least fractures, they'll need setting. Joy can't do that."

"You WANT me to . . . lose what I've found?"

"Aniello—"

"Then we'll call one of Gino's doctors—Sallie's doctors—

the Mob doctors are the only ones who make house calls any-more."

"Feet are complicated, Alvi, like hands. You'll need X rays. It's gotta be done in time or you may never walk right again."

"What's so great about walking? And it's only one foot that's *really* bad."

"But it's nice to have both."

"Stop acting like my big brother. That got blown away too, Mikey."

"Maybe we should go back to the condo and get your med-ication? I'm *worried* about your *fucking* feet."

"*You* can come to the fucking door naked with the shit beat out of you and I'm supposed to—"

"Okay, okay. Your action."

"My action."

"What else can we fight about?"

"I dunno but it felt good."

"You still in love?"

"With who?"

The brothers laughed tired laughs.

"I haven't thought about it," Alvi said.

"It's not supposed to be something you have to think about."

"How would you know?"

At the next stoplight Alvi softly said, "It's good my feet hurt so much. It sponges up some of the pain about Pop. Poor Pop. You gotta tell me, Mikey. All of it. You told Gino you wouldn't tell, but Gino's gone."

"After your feet."

"Now."

They had taken a cab from Zig's apartment to the Plaza, gotten the Caddy at Valet Parking, and were driving now slowly east on Stewart, up the long grade toward the moun-tains over which the sun was rising. Mike pulled the Caddy over to the curb of a big plot on which the bright wood of half-completed condos shone in the fresh light. Then Mike lit a cigarette for Alvi and one for himself, and told his brother everything. Alvi listened with his new eyes, what his eyes had become in Zig's apartment, and Rose met them as well as he could and wondered if his eyes were also new.

*It's as though a war is over. But wars are never over. They just sleep.*

As Rose spoke of one memory, another kept intruding, a memory he didn't speak of.

How thirty years ago—when they called Gino "The Touch" and he was thin and his eyes were merciless always and he gave the impression of being a walking knife, long before power and age had blunted his edge—how Gino had come to the house, how Eddie Maybe was nervous in Gino's presence, deferring, "Yeah, Gino," "Sure, Gino," and "It'll be done, absolutely," and Michael couldn't stand it and had to go outside and in defiance sat on the sun-hot metal of Gino's car, and how when Gino came out he recognized the gesture, and his eyes flashed not with malice but regard, a regard he had never shown Michael's father.

The boy had slid off the fender, and stood his ground when the man walked just a little too close to pass by him. The boy had purposely not watched the car drive off.

It was courage, for a boy, but it was the courage of a boy who knew that it would not have to be paid for. His father, standing in the kitchen door, had seen and understood. Eddie Maybe's face was troubled as he watched Gino back out of the driveway and into the street, but when he looked again at his son his expression softened.

"How ya doin', Mikey?"

"I'm okay, Pop."

"Anything wrong?"

"Nothin'."

"What you up to today?"

"Nothin'."

He motioned the boy to him and the boy came. He cupped the boy's face in his hard blunt-fingered hands and fruffed his hair. His eyes, a deep and rich brown like the boy's, tried to look fatherly. It was a way of asking for the return of his son's respect. But Eddie Maybe was frightened that afternoon, he'd been frightened all that day and night before, and with Gino's visit his fear had deepened. Wordlessly his son felt that fear. It may not be fair, but it is ancient: nothing is more unforgivable in a son's eyes than the sight of fear in his father.

"Ah, kiddo . . . come on . . . don' look at me like that. Give the old man a break."

The boy tried to soften his look, unsuccessfully.

"Where's your brother? I got a *little* time, maybe we can play some stickball, whataya say?"

"Alvi's with Mama, shopping."

"Well, maybe later then. Or tomorrow." The man stood and sighed. "You know, we ain't gonna be in this fuckin' Foreign Legion outpost forever. We'll get back to the real world someday. Subways. The *Daily News*. Knishes. Yankee Stadium." It was the litany Eddie Maybe always went through when he tried to comfort them.

Then Eddie Maybe went back inside, into the air conditioning, to be alone with what he was frightened of. And the boy wandered off in the desert heat, not knowing what to do with himself, afraid too and not knowing why and angry for being made afraid.

Now the man Mike Rose wanted to go back into the house with his father and stand with him against what was feared. And he wanted also, as a man, to wander off with that boy, and put a hand on his shoulder, and show him a man's eyes that were not hard but were not afraid. That boy had never seen such eyes in the men he'd been reared to respect.

Alvi's eyes would never be eyes again. At least it didn't seem so now. The world had been stripped before them to a skeletal essence that only he could see. *Not in terror, like Zig, but—I don't know—like an angel. That's what Alvi's like now. Not a sad angel, not a happy angel, just . . . not a person anymore.*

*You're like an angel and I'm like a ghost. Bye bye, world. Bye bye, Las Vegas.*

Rose looked down at the city in the valley. He would never leave it, but he had said good-bye. Good-bye to what? He wasn't sure. He was in a state no one had ever told him about, no one had ever hinted at. The city seemed small and toylike in the clear air, a complicated dangerous toy that grown-ups played with, naked people, stylish people, befuddled people, frightened people, dangerous people, people of every kind, never sure whether they were playing the game or the game was playing them. No one could be sure. For several moments Rose thought he could feel all the Situations in play at the same time, the way in a casino all the games and slots are being played at the same time, differently but in the same place, different stakes at each table, and people going from one table to another, and back again, and there were no clocks, and the place never closed.

*Scared money never wins.*

He stood in that thought a moment, then helped Alvi out of the car and up the steps and knocked.

Joy herself opened the door. She always wakened at dawn and sat alone with her tea at the eastern window of the large front room. She saw it right away, the changes in the brothers. It frightened her a little, but not as Rose's black aura had frightened her. This was a new fear, the fear of being left behind. They'd gone ahead somehow, these men.

She envied them.

*The phone calls she made aged her. She gave up some beauty to make those calls.*

"Alvi's feet," Mike said.

"My God. What happened?" Her face drained. "They didn't torture—"

"No, no. And it's all over."

"I know."

"Oh. You not only make calls, you *get* calls."

Alvi laughed.

She flinched. "I deserve that."

"Yeah," Rose said, "but I'm sorry anyway."

"Come in, I'll do what I can."

Alvi had said nothing when Rose passed on what Zig had told him, and Alvi had said nothing since. Joy cleaned and bandaged his feet as well as she could. He wouldn't accept pain pills. He was slowly agreeing that he needed a doctor and a hospital, but wasn't ready to go yet. She gave him antibiotics to fight infections, hoping it was the right thing to do.

There was a grief in her, and it passed to Rose. It was the grief of knowing that their bodies had closed to each other. That deep pleasure, with all its resonances, had been lost to the Situation.

Virginia drifted in and watched as Joy tended Alvi's feet. Alvi looked at her with his new eyes. She smiled, then let a veil drop from her expression. Behind the veil was pure terror—of everything. She raised the veil again and resumed the look she met the world with. Rose saw her do that and was impressed with the control that lay just beneath her seeming lack of control.

When Joy was done with Alvi she said to Rose, "A tub?"

"Thanks, no. Breakfast."

She made his breakfast herself—an omelette, juice, tea—and served it to him at the small table by the window in her quarters. From that window they could see the spearlike spires of the Mormon temple jab above the rooftops. The sun lit the mountains farther north and west, a rocky wilderness that had not changed in ten thousand years and probably would not for many thousands more. A-bombs hadn't fazed it. For that wilderness, Vegas was no more than a glow in one of many valleys.

"So," Rose said, "you work for Sallie Carlisi now."

"I'm afraid of him."

"I didn't think you were afraid of anybody."

"You were seeing yourself, not me. You were never *really* afraid of anybody. You didn't know it, but I think you do now."

"Seems like I've felt afraid now and again."

"Surfaces."

"Whatever."

"Gino . . . was a cookie cutter, like most of them. I mean just a slightly altered version of the same type. They mostly are. It seems to have been different in the old days, but I never met Meyer Lansky and those people, I wouldn't know. But Sallie—he's a pervert, a bad one. He takes a woman once a year. I think on his birthday. Fucks her, kills her. Then goes home to the wife and kids. And that's been going on for thirty years."

Rose let the information sink in. It churned the food in his stomach. He stopped eating.

"I know you don't supply *that*," he said.

"There are people I tell my girls never to go with. He's at the top of the list. Always has been. Gino was just a hood. Sallie's a monster. You'll see, now he has real power. He's going to change this town, or try—and change my little place. I'll probably have to give it up."

*The Something or Other of Mike Rose*

*Chalk up one more wrinkle for the Situation.*

Rose said, "He had approval for the move on Gino. The boys don't usually approve of monsters. They use them as . . ." He searched for a word, found it: "specialists. But they usually don't give them power."

"I don't think the Outfit knows. And it's not uncommon for girls in the Life to disappear. So I don't know how Gino found out, but I know Gino didn't let on to Sallie or anyone that he knew. He needed Sallie—there wasn't anybody else available to him who had Sallie's brains. I always thought Gino was saving this secret in case Sallie made a move on him. But Gino became too insulated, became too comfortable, didn't see it coming. If Sallie thought I knew, he'd kill me. He wanted me for the sacrifice one year, and I would have gone with him, I didn't know, but Gino warned me. So I owed Gino. I was the best Gino ever had, I guess he didn't want that wasted. That was when I was hooking. Solo—no pimp, no house. Dangerous in this town. Any town, really. I didn't call it hooking, I called it experimenting." Rose flinched at that. "It *was* experimenting too, all of it—showgirl, dancer, hooker. I learned . . . things of the spirit, Michael. It's a good way to learn, if you go about it right. I don't turn *every* girl, you know. Not even most, not many. That's why it was easy for you to pretend you didn't know. Only the ones I can teach."

"Teach what?"

"What I know. Many things. When you sleep with somebody you carry that person's vibe for the next six months. That's why hookers go nuts. Dancers too. It's almost the same, dancing like that for somebody. I teach . . . rituals, *you* know. I want to have a cadre of witch hookers." She laughed. "It's my plan to rule the world. Or at least Las Vegas. I'm kidding, Michael. But they say prostitution originated with the priestesses of the temple. Listen to me, I'm chattering. Because you're . . . you're not going to touch me and we're not going to talk again for a long time, I know, and I don't want you to leave. Chattering like a girl."

"How's my aura?"

"I can't see it. It's . . . beyond me." Tears came to her eyes. "You're not quite human today. You will be again, these states don't last, but they don't go away either. Beyond me. Maybe because, as you know, I've been on the phone a lot."

"As I know."

"Do you hate me?" she asked evenly.

"Survival is overrated. I thought you'd be the one to know that."

"Do you hate me?"

"I like your silver toenails. That's why Alvi thinks you're his cousin today."

"Michael—"

"It's not in me to hate you. I miss you. I'll miss you more."

"I miss you too."

"We'll have to get used to that."

"What did you have to grow up for? And in this . . . not-quite-human way."

"I didn't grow up. I grew . . . out. Something or other. It happened like you said it would: I went through it to the other side."

"God's surprise?"

"In a way. I don't know." *For two steps, two steps, I can feel them at the bottom of my feet right now, two steps as I was entering the place where I first saw you, Joy, and where I thought I would die, and where we sat in death's anteroom with a stranger. He was alright. He upped the ante. Hope we returned the favor. Hope he didn't shoot himself with Pop's gun. He seemed afraid he might. This is all gonna be harder when I really do realize that I'm not gonna die right away.*

"I'm afraid, Michael. I'm . . . alone."

"I can't help you with that."

*The Something or Other of Mike Rose*

"I know."

"And for the record," Rose said, "so am I: alone."

"Alvi?"

"He's gone."

"I'm sorry."

"Joy, you taught me . . . more than I knew you were teaching me, first to last. That's not going anywhere."

"Thank you. I *panicked*, Michael. I thought Gino would win and you'd lose no matter what, and—yes, it's overrated, survival is. I used to know that. You get old, I guess. Don't panic when you get old, Michael. It costs more. Remember that."

"I'll try."

"My last lesson. I'll stop chattering."

Rose wasn't tired, and his aches were finally easing. Alvi was asleep on Joy's bed. Rose sat on the bed by his brother. Virginia sat in a chair beside him.

Even in this short time her face had filled out a little with Joy's good food. Her long golden hair was shiny. *And her toenails shine silver. I guess they would, they were painted what, not twenty-four hours ago?*

She noticed him looking at her feet.

"I'm proud of my toes. They're the best thing that's happened. My toes are a kind of company now. I needed company. Did we save each other's lives?"

"Maybe. Probably. I'm not sure. No way of knowing, I guess."

"No way of knowing. I like that. No way of knowing, no way of knowing, no way of knowing."

They sat a while more, both watching Alvi's face, a face so much younger in sleep, the white hair even more incongruous.

"You don't want to marry me anymore," she said.

"Maybe he does."

"No. The storm has passed. Your storm. Not mine. Not mine."

"I know. I can see the lightning."

"Thank you. Hear the thunder?"

*She'll disappear again soon. She'd only stay if there was a storm to stay for, a Situation that could crash into her Situation and break the spell. We were almost it. She put a big chip down, but like most chips it just disappeared.*

*And that other skinny doomed blond, Mrs. Sherman—that's what happened, our Situations had a head-on.*

*I wonder if I'll ever see her again. I wonder which of those women made it out of the desert. It's a cinch one of them didn't.*

*So somewhere back there, a Situation started, and somewhere along the way a woman posed for pictures—a little blip in the Situation, it hardly noticed—and farther along the way, Kennedy gets shot. Big blip. And way down the way, I kill Zig, little blip, and Alvi's probably goin' to the funny farm again, little blip. But all the blips are flashing like lights on a slot machine while somebody sings a love song. And that writer, if he's still alive, is hoping to make some sense of it. And the president, if he's still alive, he's trying too. And me? I'm experimenting. Like Joy. But we're fresh outa test tubes.*

Several hours later Alvi woke. Rose was sitting in the chair Virginia had been sitting in. By now Rose was tired, but he hadn't wanted to let Alvi wake alone. Joy had mixed some painkillers with the antibiotics and they'd knocked Alvi out, but Rose could see the feet were feverish and that attention could no longer be postponed.

"It hurts, Mikey."

"We'll get it fixed. I'll get a couple of Joy's larger minions to help carry you out to the car."

"I don't wanna go back to that fuckin' condo, Mikey."

"I didn't think you would."

"Get rid of it, huh, before I get out again?"

"You goin' in?"

"I think I better. I think. I better. I can . . . absorb. Gotta . . . get away from you too. Sorry."

"It's okay."

"I'll . . . absorb. And lie to shrinks. That's the main form of entertainment in those joints. We can afford it, right? I don't wanna do a state hospital, I'm too old."

"We'll afford it. We're flush. And we got a restaurant."

"You really gonna run it?"

"I'll do *something* with it. Hire somebody to run it. Something."

"Keep the pictures behind the bar."

"If you want me to."

"I want you to. And when I get out I want to sit at the bar again, start over again, have linguini with clam sauce again."

"Red or white?"

"That's more decision than I can do right now. I didn't fail, did I, Mikey?"

"You did great, Alvi. Better than anybody."

"You're gonna keep finding lost people?"

"I don't know. I feel like a ghost. I don't know."

"I hate that Sallie gets a piece. Of the restaurant."

"That's another fight. I'm not ready for it. Maybe later. Right now, he gets a piece. He could have killed us and he didn't."

"Watch him, Mikey. He's lots smarter than Gino. He had more reason for not killing us than he said."

"Probably. That's something else I'm not ready for. The Situation's gone back to sleep. I can wait for it to wake up again. I can wait a long time. *I* sure the fuck ain't gonna wake it up. Not if I don't have to, and I won't. It'll wake up all on its own. That's the only thing I'm sure of. Till every card gets played, face up."

"Mikey, don't you know that *meaning* is against the law in

this state? You wanna get arrested for Attempted Meaning? Steve Wynn'll come and arrest you himself."

"Wanna go?"

"Yeah."

Rose said, "I tell you one thing I'm gonna do. I'm gonna rip those goddamn video poker games out of that beautiful bar. It's gonna look like it used to. It's gonna be the only bar in town that's a *bar*."

"Cut into the profits." Alvi smiled.

"I don't give a shit."

"Me neither."

*I think getting older is learning what not to give a shit about.*

And the old men who both brothers probably would never be smiled at each other through their changed and changing eyes.

Mike Rose drove slowly down the Stewart Avenue grade into the city. It was dusk, and the neons were coming on. From the Luxor's beam in the south to the glow of downtown straight west, they watched their city shine.

"I thought all this time you knew about Mama's . . . photographs," Alvi said. "I guess I thought if *I* found them you must've, and that you couldn't talk about 'em any more than I could. I wonder . . . Mikey . . . fuck, I can't talk about them."

"You mean you wonder who she was back then? Who took them? What that was all about? Why she kept them, why *really?* We ain't ever gonna know."

Rose remembered the old cameras, lights, and bedding in the building where Zig and their father died.

And Alvi said, "'Member how she was scared of snow?"